The Legend of Eve

dREAMWORDS Publishing, LLC
Publishers since 2018
New York 12207

dREAMWORDS is a registered trademark of DreamWords Publishing, LLC.

Library of Congress Cataloging in Publication Data
Anonymous.
The Legends of Eve: A Warrior's Past / Anonymous.—First edition.
ISBN (paperback): 978-1732788411.

Summary: "In a world where time is a repeating loop, a boy was created who had never lived before.
His actions now have the chance to change the course of Time and allow life to finally be lived after the Last Great War."—
Provided by publisher.

dREAMWORDS books may be purchased for business or promotional use. For information on bulk purchases, please contact the dREAMWORDS Publishing Premium Sales Department by email at FGB@DreamWordsPublishing.com.

First Edition—2018/ Cover design and illustrations by @RyKyArt

Printed in the United States of America and sold internationally

To the dreamers—
never stop dreaming
&
To the ones who are scared to dream—
believe in yourself, even if no one else does

Before you begin this journey, we encourage you to take the quiz (www.thelegendsofeve.com/quiz) to find out which element you were born to control. The quiz results give you the chance to have your own character be a part of the world of Gaia. Our first winner is pictured here! May the element provide you hope when you need it most.

THE ELEMENTIAL SCHOOLS

GROUNDSTONE the School of Earth

FUJITA the School of Wind and Wisdom

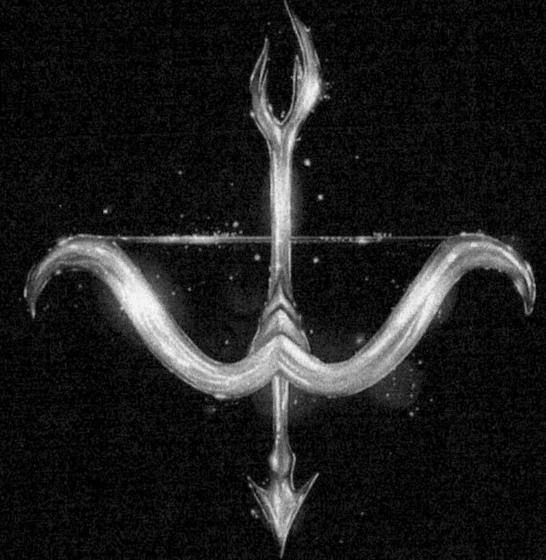

SERENI the School of Water

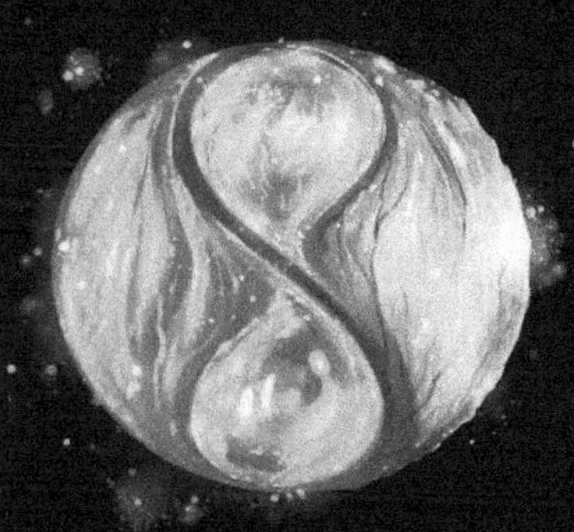

HARAHM'BE THE SCHOOL OF FIRE

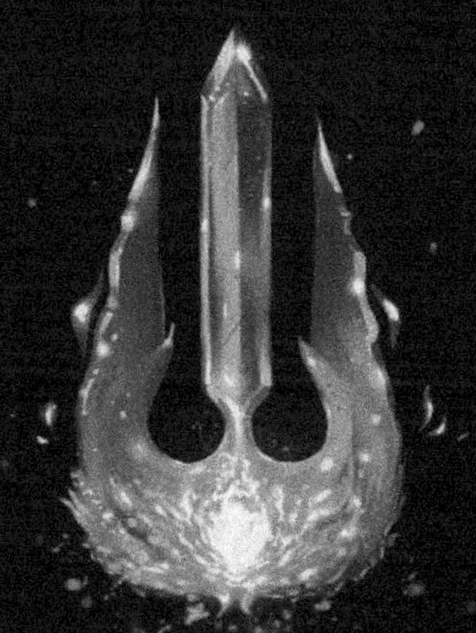

I LIVE FOREVER EVEN WHEN I DIE.

I have lived so many times there is not a number in any language that can count as high. I know. I have uttered every tongue. I have seen every person, dead or alive, and created a Shadow Army from their slaughtered souls . . . yet here you are . . . someone who, in the infinite times this moment has existed, I have never seen.

You must be who they called 'The Boy Who Never Lived.'

I know everything, yet I do not know how you were created. Tell me, Boy, what would you do to be given another chance to see your loved ones? To know you can live forever, even if it is the same life. That life does not end with your final breath. Your memories need not be only of the past but moments that you relive in the future.

I have found that secret. And you have the power to keep the Circle of Time going, but it requires a sacrifice. You have come all this way. Do not let it be for nothing. You are the first to ever survive this void of time and space. Most only last seconds, but you have remained for an eternity.

You may very well be the most powerful warrior Time will ever see. Its greatest secret.

I know now why you are here. You wish to save her. And you know what you must do.

I give you my sword. The Destroyer of Worlds. The Death. The Arm of Geddon.

Time can either be eternal or finite, where your story ends and you will be forgotten.

Choose. Me or her.

One must die.

The last known words of Geddon, the God of Darkness

This is his story.

THE BOY WHO NEVER LIVED

THE LADY IN WHITE APPEARED OUT OF NOWHERE, running through the vast, untouched snow. For a moment she stood still, her head turned back toward where she came from, barely noticing a tower made of ice. Behind it, lights blazed in the night sky. They moved like celestial rivers flowing through the atmosphere, bathing everything from the white hills to the black horizon in a red mist. Her body tensed, reacting to a gust of wind. A breeze scattered her dark hair across her bruised, pale face, sending a cloud of snow into the air. After a moment, she continued running ahead, despite having no idea where she was heading.

There was no plan, but the *where* wasn't as important as the *why* or the *who*. And she hadn't been able to put much thought into the *how*. There wasn't enough time to think, only run.

Though fully clothed, the snowy wind wrapped around her like cold fingers, sending chills down her spine. Her clothes were loose enough to flow, but tight enough to show that her belly was much too large for her petite frame. Her life wasn't the only one she was saving.

Reminding herself of the *why* and *who* was the only thing that kept her legs moving.

No matter which direction she chose, there was nothing but white—and the red reflection of the sky—as far as her eyes would allow her to see. Her eyes, swollen. Her body, bruised. Her arms, a shield blocking the snowflakes that pierced her skin like shards of glass. Running was indeed her only option. The Guardians weren't kind to runners; she couldn't turn back now.

After trudging through knee-high snow for an hour, she reached a wall of ice. If it had a top, it was hidden somewhere beyond the sky; vast and curved like a giant arc, it spanned the entire village. This was the *how*, her only way out. Freedom had never seemed so far away.

Now, for the first time, pain engulfed her mind more than freedom. Agony. She felt it. Everywhere. Her frostbitten toes. The pulsating headache. And now her ice cold fingers scraped the wall as she patted the icy barricade for something to grab.

Snow crunched beneath her feet when she lifted onto her toes and quickly wedged her fingers into a groove. Time wasn't in her favor. It wouldn't take long for them to find out she was gone, and tracking footprints in the untouched snow was easy pickings for experienced hunters.

Her breathing was heavier, her heart pounded faster. Despite having a crippling fear of heights that made her stomach twist, she climbed seven times her height.

Her belly made it difficult to hug the wall closely. And her hands trembled—too weak to hold herself up, too afraid to let go.

She was stuck, feeling a sense of dread creep up on her like darkness after sunset.

The silence was interrupted by the crunch of footsteps. The sounds of defeat. Of loss.

"No, please." She quivered, still hanging onto the wall. It was never about if they'd find her, only *when*.

"There's nowhere to go," said a booming voice from behind.

She couldn't breathe. Tears poured down her face, freezing against her skin.

Her body trembled. Slowly she turned her head around to spot a man.

He was three times the size of her, and his face was completely covered with white hair. He had a rounded nose and a long, white furry cloak, which somehow always reeked with sweat.

"You're the last one, and no different than the others. Shame."

"Stay . . . away," she whimpered, struggling to swallow her words as if being gagged.

"You're sick. You think you'd make it far even if you did climb the Wall?" He laughed.

She looked up at the Wall, then glanced at the man and away again, terrified to make eye contact.

"You do realize it's a death wish trying to scale the Wall. *All who wish to try are all who wish to die.* You should know this. Come down and I won't hurt you, or your child. I promise."

Her child. In an instant, she grasped the horror of the situation. "I refuse to let my child live this life," she gasped, her words hoarse with emotion.

"If only that was up to you."

She wished she could stay up there forever, but the truth was that, by the second, her fingers were losing grip and she slipped further down the Wall. She was exhausted, and her eyes began to freeze up. With the last of her energy, she leaned her head forward and whispered: "I'm sorry."

Her fingers slipped away, and she fell, crashing into the thick snow. The snow absorbed most of the impact, but the drop was

enough to cripple her.

She was too shocked to scream; a stabbing pain made her clutch her belly, and she gasped, feeling her baby kick inside her. A sharp thud against her lungs and heart.

"You should've waited." He threw his cloak on the ground. It was large enough to fit four of her. He bent over, and picked her up as if she was silk, and then placed her on the cloak.

His name had been Ko'Dral when he was a high-ranking official of the Crystal Soldiers, the elite group of fighters for the Kingdom. Now he was known only as the Guardian, forced to survey the Forest of Ness and report any abnormal sightings or Archons that may still be around. He lived in the past, boasting about how every inch of his body was once solid muscle, but after years trapped behind the Wall, he became rotund, renowned for his enormous bulk.

He dragged the cloak with the pregnant woman through the snow back to the Village.

Her legs were broken—but worse, her heart. Regret weighed her down, making every breath difficult. The scent in the air faded from a fresh winter breeze to urine the closer they came to the Village. Every time they hit a patch of uneven ground, she felt a stinging sensation in her spine that pushed her from side to side. Still, she kept her hands clutched around her middle.

She lay there, gazing at the moon and the red lights flowing around it. She couldn't help but question the purpose of life in this cold world. Could this be it: to freeze, and then die in this village blocked off from all life—from the Kingdom? On one end, there was the Wall, and to the east, there was a cliff that looked over the Forest. No one knew what existed inside that wooded area.

Rumor had it, that it was trees, darkness and misery—and Archons, the enemy to all living. None had seen one and lived to tell, but local myth told of beings that cast no shadow, for they were shadows themselves. The word had spread that they were extinct after the First Great War, hundreds of years ago, but the growls that echoed from within were enough to keep the most curious travelers away.

After an hour or so, they finally made it to the Village. Its fog carried the stench of feces.

There were dozens of small igloos, situated close together and circled around a crystallized tower that emerged in the distance, with a pathway leading straight to the Guardian's Tower.

They passed through the tower's massive ice doors that groaned open.

When she reached the maroon brown floor that marked the birth room, two men waited, as large as the Guardian. The Commanders each grabbed a side of the cloak and lifted it onto a block of ice. Though the Commanders were also Guardians, Ko'Dral liked to own the title.

The Guardian was composed as he grabbed a piece of rope and tied it around her body.

"Is such force necessary for a little one?" one of the Commanders asked.

She could tell by the shifting of his eyes that he didn't like the way she was being handled. He must be the only sliver of good left in the Village, she thought.

"It is, Commander Dres." The Guardian grabbed a cloth, which he handed to the other Commander. It was an off-white cloth that smelled of body odor. "The last time you went easy on them, she left with the child when we found out it was a girl, remember?"

"Yes." His tone was soft and calming.

"That could have cost you your life." The Guardian wiped his hands with another dirty rag. "What if she was the one they're looking for? If the Kingdom finds out, they'd make you find her. And we know what that really means."

Though her eyes were swollen, she caught a glimpse of Dres' hands trembling so much that he clenched them together. Something was holding him back as if he wanted to say more.

"Your silence says a lot." The Guardian pulled a chair closer. She winced at the scraping sound of the chair legs. "You don't want that to happen again, right?"

"No." Dres gulped, staring directly into her eyes. They told a story of a longing regret.

She heard the clangs of blades being sharpened, and so it began. Stripped from her own life and now forced to watch men take the only thing that she felt was truly hers. Three of them leaned forward, their hands holding large hunting knives, the sharp points digging into her flesh, along the pubic line, below her huge belly. She clenched her fists and screamed, her eyes rolling back, the pain unbearable. Their faces loomed over hers; they were cruel and heartless. That was to be expected. Just as they would be cruel and heartless to her child as he'd become another slave to the Kingdom. She knew she didn't have long left to live, as the intense agony combined with blood loss from the open wounds would surely kill her. It was the helplessness that made her scream louder, knowing that she wouldn't be there for her child just as her parents weren't there for her. And no matter how lonely her child would become, she wanted him to know that he was loved.

She felt a bitter taste in the back of her throat and a strange light-headedness. The pain fading as she began to slip into unconsciousness. The connection to her newborn son that she had felt for the past nine months heightened once his tiny body was removed from her womb—and she heard him wail with his first breath.

She shuddered, automatically reaching out her weak arms to hold him.

"Did that hurt?" The Guardian looked down at her, looking somewhat amused. "Pain is good—it means you're still alive, for now."

Her heart sank to her stomach as she heard a beautiful shriek resonate.

"Another boy!" The Guardian stomped his feet. The rolling thunder was drowned out by the crying. He placed the boy in the hands of Gronk, who wrapped the child in cloth.

Commander Gronk, as big as he was dumb, wiped his blood-stained hands on his own white cloak, painting red streaks across it. "Wot a waste of a good cloak," he grunted.

And while they fought over dirtying another cloak, the mother faded in and out of consciousness. She lay there. Her eyes swollen shut. In a haze, watching flashes from the past mix with the future. *Her* son. Death was greeting her, yet she smiled that her child wasn't a girl.

"Oh Divine!" The Guardian smiled devilishly. "Look! There's another!"

"Wot?" Gronk climbed over him, as another baby's head emerged.

"Another?" Dres said. "Never heard of two coming out at once."

Pressure swelled up behind her eyes; the possibility of a girl made her lips tremble and stomach sink. Horrific thoughts appeared, imagining her daughter going through what she had endured. She saw their greasy hands wrap around her body. Her heart tied into a knot.

When she blinked, a tear slipped out, freezing to her face. She curled her mouth shut to prevent it from forming into a sob. And screamed again as they pulled another child out of her womb.

This child seemed different—quiet, not wailing or shedding a single tear.

The Guardian held him in his hands, squinting his eyes curiously. "You're an odd boy. Never seen one so tiny and dark, and not a crier. Mer. Put them in one of the empty igloos."

The pressure was lifted. She felt weightless, as if her soul had already drifted off to a better place. With her remaining strength, she opened her eyes just enough to witness her *two* sons. "A miracle." She uttered.

Her cold body turned colder still, eyes closed gracefully. She had a serene, natural beauty with a locked smiled on her face. It was as if she had finally found her peace. And her freedom.

It was a miracle indeed. Though she felt as if her life was insignificant, the Gods would argue quite the opposite. It wasn't just any miracle. It was the miracle. The greatest Time had ever seen. For in that moment, she had given birth to Destrou, the boy who never lived.

He would mark the first change in the Circle of Time. This was destiny. And hope. Hope for a future beyond the last tick of time, before the Big Bang resets it. Maybe now it'd be different. Because maybe now . . . the Last Great War could finally be won.

FAR AWAY IN A VALLEY VOID OF LIGHT, two shadows emerged, darker than the night. Their presence alone drained the color from the moon, letting the world know once again that the end was soon.

"I felt *it* again."

"Déjà vu? And this one means?"

"That *he* didn't change the past enough to alter time. The end will still come."

"How do you plan to find her?"

"She's too weak to hide. Don't you see it in the trees? Look around. Nature is fading."

"But the Valley has been hidden for centuries. It is impossible to find."

"I have my ways. Remember the last time you foolishly questioned me? Gabrael and his prophecy of the 'boy who never lived' will fade to an oblivion. There is a purpose for the wait, just as there is a purpose for this war. Death will soak the land. It has already begun."

S'rae had waited years to get into GroundStone, the School of Earth and Rock. Once she took the quiz, the results would say Earth, and she and her brother would be taken away from their village. There she'd hone in her skills and move mountains with words. She knew her brother would get into the school too. He had to. He was amazing. Well, *was*. She could only hope he was better now.

But he taught her everything she knew. Except how to get a Sol. For some reason she could never spiritually link with an animal no matter how hard she tried. And oh boy, did she try.

GroundStone would change that. She could choose any specialty that she wanted. Sol Mastery was her top priority. For the first time, she'd finally have a Sol. She wondered which animal would be the one. An owl? A pup? Maybe a squirrel—weird, yes, but she liked how fun and quirky they were. Like her, she thought.

She daydreamed of linking with an animal telepathically—her favorite escape.

The beast's silver eyes stared into hers. She felt an internal stillness that was foreign. A weightlessness that felt like her soul drifted away. She was surrounded by light that flooded in through stringy leaves overhead. It looked like the one. Fur dark and shiny, ears wide and alert, mouth smiling, peaceful and beautiful like how all animals should be. But when she felt a presence enter her soul, the beast growled deeply. Its mouth widened to reveal fangs dripping with blood. It enlarged into a vein-bulging beast—far from cute— and lunged straight at S'rae's exposed neck.

S'rae opened her eyes. She had no Sol. She wasn't at Ground-Stone. Instead she attended Fujita, the School of Wind and Wisdom. Of course she had a bad vision today. It was only the most important day of her life, and she was in the classroom waiting for the moment she had dreaded for the past few months.

One more, that's it. One more and I'm done. Gone. No more pretending I'm not broken.

The professor, dressed in a white silk robe, floated into the air and said, "S'rae, your final grade rests on this performance. Everyone has done well. You must be perfect. No pressure."

She nodded, not trusting her voice. *No pressure. Yeah, right.* She lowered her gaze so he didn't see her doubt. That was the classic lie Professor Ki said before an important exam. She hated that about him. But he was funny and always picked her when she knew the answer—which was rare for a teacher—so he was the only professor whose class didn't make her anxious. Which meant no awkward squishes from her soaked socks as she walked the halls.

This part of the final exam was what graduates had warned her about since her first day. But she was ready. She had to be. There weren't enough hours in a day to prepare her more than she had already prepared. The hours cut into her sleep schedule so much she forgot what sleep was, she only napped. And she couldn't remember how her room looked, not the white walls nor the silk sheets connecting her bed posts, only how cold the marble floor in the library got at night.

I can't fail. I won't allow them to win. Not after everything they put me through.

The truth was she needed to pass this final exam to become the Fujiatorian, the top student at Fujita. It would allow her into the Elemental Program to become a Master of the Wind. Highly competitive was an understatement; only a dozen pupils were accepted each decade. If she failed at fifteen, that meant waiting until she was twenty-five to try again. Yuck, a whole quarter-century old. Might as well plan her retirement now.

She dug her nails into her silver robes. Its smooth silk always

calmed her down. Her palms were sweaty with anxiety, but she thrived when her back was against the wall. She imagined becoming an Elemental and changing the world of Gaia. She thought of breaking down air molecules to find cures for terminal diseases that couldn't survive in the atmosphere. She flew over clouds, manipulating wind patterns to create sustainable energy for poorer regions. There was so much she'd be able to do. This had been her dream since she first arrived.

Five years had passed since she left *them*. Since she'd last felt loved and normal. She'd grown used to falling asleep with the salty taste of tears on her lips each night. At times they poured, like she was drowning and no one cared enough to save her; they just watched.

"S'rae *perfect*?" A voice broke through the silence. "Perfect *loser* sounds about right."

The classroom erupted in laughter. She had heard that same annoying voice with the same unfunny comment too many times to not know it belonged to Fujak, the never-so-pleasant son of Headmaster Yosh'i. There was no respect in the groans she heard, no faith in her ability.

I'll show you who the loser is when you're under me on the podium. Hmm, maybe I'll let you smell one of Chung's farts. Hope you choke on it again. She giggled, remembering when she guided Chung's gas to Fujak's nostrils. *Jeez, who thinks of this stuff, honestly?* She rolled her shoulders back proudly and gave her hips a little shimmy. *Me, that's who!*

Then she heard gasps from the annoying girls who'd always swoon after hearing Fujak speak. Yes, girls would swarm after him as if they were starving and he was the last piece of meat in the galaxy; but she never understood why. No matter how pretty his eyes were, his spiteful personality made him uglier than the vomit she'd pretend to cough up when he'd walk by.

But though she tried to brush it off, Fujak's words still stung, no matter how numb she thought she was.

When she stepped on a smooth, almost slippery, white platform, dozens of different woodwind instruments circled around her, and they shone like ivory. Everything was white marble from the columns to the desks that semi circled overhead, like a theater. Swirls of wind carried a subtle scent of fresh soap, whistling through the gaps in the walls that caught the morning rays of sunlight. Tens of students filled the floating, cloud-like platforms, wearing silver robes that reflected a white glow. Hoods covered their eyes.

The instruments had been used for her previous exam, when she controlled wind to compose a symphony. Easy-peasy compared to what lay ahead. For years she had tried to create wind in the airless chamber. She anonymously crushed the school's record for most failed attempts. Needless to say, it wasn't her favorite accomplishment.

The professor twisted a lever at the top of the room. Suddenly a clear tube sealed around S'rae. She observed the glass and her faint reflection. The girl staring back at her was a stranger—windblown and weary—but she chalked that up to the sleepless nights spent studying.

A lot had changed since she made her decision to cut her hair short like the others. Her brunette locks were finally growing back. She saw olive skin, a narrow face, and round eyes, unlike the beautiful, angular ones like most of Fujita. She had permanent tribal face paint. A painted brown bar, like smeared clay, rested under each eye. It was the one thing that reminded her of the home she was taken from. Home. A word she used only when discussing her past.

Her mom said their mark meant more than being in a family. It

held beauty and history and love, it meant she was now one of the protectors of nature. But at Fujita her mark was gross. They said she wasn't beautiful, she was different. After hearing enough of it, she started to believe them. So she did what she felt she had to: conform. Cutting her hair had been tough, but she chickened out when it came to dyeing her hair black with silver streaks. She held onto a hope that one day Fujita would accept her for who she was. Hope was never enough.

Unlike most of the Fujitas, she wasn't born in the Wind region. She came from Opella, a small desert village in the Earth region hidden behind the Jabal and Nen'nex Mountains where the wind blazed like a phoenix's tail or a tundra's frostburn, depending on the time of day. Their location made her people outcasts; but their free spirits liberated them. While other regions followed strict rules, they created their own. S'rae was taught to question everything and not just accept. They hunted for their food, blessing its soul before eating. They never wasted any part of the animal. Bones to build, claws for tools, and skin for clothing.

At Fujita, food was served on a silver platter, and they worried too much about cleanliness to find use in what was left of the animals. Straight to the garbage. What a waste.

She never forgot where she came from. She was considered weird for treating her food with respect, as if they were still alive. To avoid fights, she worked quietly, never discussing her beliefs or why she acted the way that she did. Even in her dorm, where she was most herself, she avoided talking about how unfair some laws were to less fortunate regions. She didn't want any more reasons to put a bigger target on her back.

Yet here she was, one exam away from solidifying her rank at the top of the class.

Whoosh! She winced at a whistling sound that could only mean the draining of air. She felt her lungs spasm, and her back arched violently, her head struck the glass. Her heart thumped and hands clenched, curling so tightly they ached.

"You have a few seconds before brain damage occurs," she heard from a faraway voice.

She concentrated on her surroundings. Her dreams rested on this moment. She stopped thinking about the air being sucked out of her lungs and the feeling of knives poking at her chest. Instead, she thought of the wind.

Somehow it came. Her brunette strands shifted slightly. That was all that was needed to pass the test. It wasn't much, but it was enough.

"Congratulations, Fujiatorian S'rae," the professor said as the chamber wisped into dust.

Sighing through her nose, she unclenched her fingers, squinting before tears formed.

Air filled her lungs. Her heart pounded with excitement, but there was no celebration. If anything, a tension filled the room, and any chance of making a friend vanished like the glass that surrounded her.

She pulled her shoulders back and thrust her chest forward, straightening when she needed to bow. The students didn't deserve her respect. But Professor Ki did. She nodded to him as her feet lifted off the ground. These classrooms were designed to make flying easier.

The sea of shrouded faces parted as she drifted through the crowd, hearing their moans as they whispered together in jealousy. But she felt elated and no amount of verbal abuse could knock her down. She'd done it! Today, nothing was going to go wrong. This was her day!

The wind picked up, lifting her clothes, as she darted through Fujita. The rustling leaves and howling gusts drowned out her squeals of delight. She blew by the pink-touched Serry Blossom trees (which seemed to get brighter each year since she first arrived), the ivory-coated temples, and the marble-lined passageways. She leapt over the first-years' training pit as they guided arrows through hoops. They were Jiantou, specializing in archery.

Normally there would be dozens of Senshi creating twisters with their kicks and punches, but today they were most likely in the Mail Tower, waiting to see if they moved up a level.

Silver banners—in the shape of vertical Ws—had been flowing from countless poles and towers, at times with no assistance. Some students rumored they had minds of their own, seen flying throughout the campus and halls. Others, like S'rae, believed they were the spying eyes and ears for professors. A banner that once symbolized the Ws—Wind and Wisdom—was now something that she no longer valued or saluted. It had lost its meaning.

It no longer stood for doing good and creating laws to maintain balance—instead, Fujita only wanted to maintain their elite status and improve the lives of those who already had everything. She had dreamed to be among the brightest, not the darkest.

She slid to a stop, reaching a marble platform. Slowly she reached her palm out, feeling the cold, invisible wall. It was solid, not to be confused with glass. It was infinitely more transparent, but dissolved at her touch, like condensed air.

She stepped onto the platform. There was a light puff of wind at her feet that tousled her hair and caused a weightless sensation in her stomach. It was a feeling that at times caused dread, but nevertheless she felt herself smile. For a second she clenched her fists as the wind blew stronger.

Then she felt something squeeze her chest, as if she was flying. She was.

Wind lifted her through the sky toward the clouds. The sun peeked over the floating mountains, casting a white glow that reflected off the snow-tipped peaks and marble-topped towers and windmills. She saw floating sculptures change shapes depending on the wind's direction. She saw the Great Wall, stretching thousands of miles around the border of Fujita. Just like a metallic dragon, it wound up and down across grasslands to the west, deserts to the east, and plateaus to the south. It was for protection, they said, but considering war hasn't taken place in thousands of years, she knew this isolation was because of greed and power. Fujita's mountains possessed valuable minerals and resources that the other regions would kill for. When she leaned forward and twisted around, her eyes found the Mecha Monument—a one-hundred-foot tall statue made completely of white marble. This shell of an original Mecha was a gift to Fujita to celebrate the end of the war. The restoration of peace.

Mechas were humanized robots once manufactured to protect

the world. Now, no matter how powerful students became, if they saw a Mecha, they were told to flee. Run and never look back. Because there would be nothing left to look at. One could destroy a city, an army, the world.

At times, S'rae thought this Mecha was still alive or operational, at least. It hummed faint sounds that only she heard. Even now, its eyes appeared to be watching her, but it could have been in her head. That's what the professors told her. Why would a statue whisper random, extremely long numbers? She was almost certain they came from it, but was sure they weren't random. The number decreased each day, as if it was a countdown for something.

S'rae then slid her black goggles over her eyes as she tore through a cloud.

Poof! She landed on a crystal clear tiled surface, seeming like she was walking across a rippling sky. The air carried a freshness that burned her nostrils. A light breeze seemed to sing like wind chimes and flutes—the beautiful sounds of Fujita which at times she took for granted.

In front were gates leading into a marble castle with hovering towers circling around.

This was the moment she had been waiting for. Today she would be enroute to become an Elemential, a Master of the Wind. Today she would start her new life. Today all her sleepless nights would pay off.

And now she needed to claim her prize.

She pressed her palm onto a silver screen. A hologram of herself appeared then exploded.

"No new messages for Stupid Shallow S'rae. Check back when you have friends."

Being called stupid was obviously a terrible lie. Yes, she wasn't as bright as the other Fujitas who could memorize an entire book in minutes—that was why she studied harder. However, she never understood why they'd call her shallow. For students who supposedly knew a million words, it was an odd choice. Yes, she didn't have many hobbies, and was always alone in the library, but that wasn't her fault—they never included her. Not anymore at least.

The automated voice didn't bother her, she'd been hearing that for a few years, ever since she held the top spot; she knew it was Fujak's work. But what did bother her was how she hadn't received the invitation to the Elemental Program.

Fujita was never late. Something wasn't right. She felt it. *Can anything ever go my way?*

She ran inside, passing through double doors leading into spotless white chambers with forty-foot ceilings and drifting clouds that made chimes sing. One entrance always stood out from the rest. It was ornamented by detailed carvings and the doors were twelve feet high. She never asked what was inside, but now that she thought about it, she'd never once seen it open.

At once, she stopped running. With each step, she focused on the way her feet slid on the smooth marble floor. She respected its purity, and had never dared to break its sacred laws. In a city of wind and laws, this was the cleanest and strictest of all towers. The harshest of all punishments. The last thing she needed was to give the school another reason to hate her.

She slowed to a crawl, passing by a room of marble. A tall throne—made of long ivory feathers—was placed in the center. Rays of light peeked through, illuminating the domed ceiling.

This was *her* room. Never to be touched nor tainted by mortal hands. It was made for not just any God—Fujita, the Goddess of Wind, and Restorer of Hope. She was the most beautiful in all of Gaia, history claimed, but considering she was the only God vain enough to name a school after herself, S'rae did not put it passed

Fujita to alter the way history portrayed her.

Now, she was gone. Not dead. Gone. A God never truly died, they said. And understanding the afterlife of a God was beyond the teachings for students, even professors. Some things were better off unknown.

The professors promised to fail her if she kept questioning them on it. Her annoyance had always worked, but not for this. They must've genuinely not known the answer. *Oops!*

She reached another platform where wind lifted her through the sky into the Mail Tower.

Her lower half tingled as if the marble floor she sat on for hours was a bed of frozen needles. She tapped on the knees of her crossed feet to make sure she could still feel something, staring at the many holes that circled around her. *Feels like I'm stuck in a white honeycomb.* Her stomach growled. *Yupp, and now I'm hungry. Good job, S'rae.*

Each time she heard a message *whoosh* in, she danced around until she realized it wasn't for her. Student after student left the room, clapping excitedly with their friends, celebrating acceptances. She remained alone, keeping her attention fixed on the glazed, mirror-like floor.

She'd barely been able to look at the students as they soared away—flying proud, long staffs at their backs and messenger orbs in their hands. She resisted the urge to glance to where she knew her empty slot was, the one that should had been filled already. The thought of this being another unfunny prank momentarily drifted through her mind. It was that thought alone that kept her from screaming and pulling her hair in frustration. But were they capable of pulling off the prank of all pranks? Yes, Fujitas were crafty jerks—she knew there were no limits to how low they'd stoop—but this invitation was bigger than any of them. It was sent from a God.

Another hour and eleven invites passed. The next one had to be hers.

A swoosh of wind tickled her ears. It was coming. This was her moment. Her dream had finally come true. S'rae jumped to her feet and dashed to catch the orb.

A gust of wind punched her in the abdomen. She crashed into the wall then hunched over, wheezing as vomit climbed up her throat. For a moment she worried her stomach would burst.

"Too slow. This one's mine," she heard through the ringing in her ears.

She forced air into her lungs and looked up. A hooded figure held the orb, his chiseled jawline barely visible. It glowed into an ivory bird that said, "Congratulations, Fujak—"

"Impossible!" S'rae screamed. A rage filled her heart. She wanted to cry. "That's mine!"

"Yours?" Fujak said coldly. "Why do you think someone like you would ever get accepted before me? You're a pity case. I am a true Fujita."

As he finished his sentence, wind threw her onto the ground. In that instant, two shrouded figures crouched next to Fujak. The way one hand touched the ground and the other punched the air, S'rae knew they were Senshi, students specializing in fighting. S'rae was an Izado, one who studied the scientific components of air and wind. She took pride in creating new, different ways to use wind. But those who thought she wasn't a fighter had learned their lesson the hard way.

"You'll never be better than us. We can actually be Elementials, not peasants like you."

"There's a reason you weren't accepted. No one wants losers like you ruining our name. You don't even know Fujita's secret password."

"I do!" Nope, she had no idea what it was, but that didn't matter to her. All that mattered was the wind that spiraled around her feet and the arrows that formed at her fingertips, digging into her back. She wanted nothing more than to send one straight through their hearts, and that troubled her. Three flicks of her wrist. That was all that was needed to end the years of torture. Did they even know they were seconds away from their final breaths? Maybe not, and once they heard the swoosh it'd be too late for them. S'rae's release was too quick, and she never missed. Unlike the other times she considered it, this one felt real. This was the moment that haunted her dreams and kept her up when she was at her loneliest. *I don't care anymore.*

They pushed her too far, for too long. She felt the arrows sharpen into condensed air. Their points more lethal than the ivory spear strapped onto Fujak's back.

"What do you think you'll do to us?" Fujak said. "We're better than you. You'll never—"

"Actually," a deep voice boomed overhead. It belonged to Professor Ki, "you're wrong."

At once, she felt warm steam wrap around her fingers as the arrows dissolved. *What was I thinking?* The thought of shooting them made her chest tighten, but seeing Professor Ki finally reminded her to breathe. *Inhale. Exhale. Calm down.*

"What!" Fujak shrieked. "I'll tell my father on you!"

"Tell your father that you didn't get in?" Professor Ki chuckled. "I'm sure Yosh'i would love to hear that."

"I—I can't be the only Fuj who didn't get in," Fujak stammered. "I need to!"

"Neither of you are going." The professor floated down. The moment his feet touched the ground, wind knocked the hoods off their heads, revealing Chung and his younger sister, Aura'li. Like

Fujak, their silver, angular eyes sparkled like crystals. *Why do they have to be so beautiful? You're noticing his eyes, S'rae. Fujak's gross, stop staring! OMD, you're still looking. Stop now!*

"There's a greater plan ahead," said Professor Ki, "one that Headmaster Yosh'i has been very well aware of. As the myth states, today marks the three thousandth year since the Valley of Gaia vanished. And in this year, it was written by Gods before any of us were born, the three Elemential Schools must send their four most gifted pupils."

"Send us, to the Valley?" S'rae gasped. "Does this mean, we're meeting Eve?"

"Yes." His voice was tight from fear. "Some myths are fables, others are hidden truths."

S'rae shrieked as wind flurried through the room. She had wanted to meet her since the first story told, when she found out Eve was Mother Nature. Fujita considered her a fairy tale.

"When do we leave?" she said, watching Fujak pout and stomp his feet. She almost expected steam to hiss out from his ears. If not for his deep breathing, it very well might.

"Now. The airship's arriving. It will take you to Sereni then GroundStone before locating the Valley. It is unlike any other valley—it cannot be seen from the outside. You'll be its first visitors since the war." He paused, and his eyes held a long, worried gaze, as if he had more words to say but couldn't muster up the courage to say them. His voice cracked with the emotion of a final goodbye. "I do not know why you were invited. That secret is unknown to all outside of the Valley. What I do know is that it is home not only to Eve, but the most horrible stories in all of Gaia. I can only hope they are rumors. And if not, I pray our King of Gods has changed. For your sake. Be safe."

S'rae's excitement faded. Not because of the fear in Professor

Ki's eyes, his conspiracies, the missed Elemential opportunity, or because she was leaving Fujita—she had no friends. She ran away, finding a corner to hide in, and imagined visiting the GroundStone district for the first time since she had left. The vision saddened her. More than how ugly she thought she was. More than the lonely nights spent eavesdropping from afar—hearing the terrible rumors that made her gut churn. She thought about *him*. And cried until the airship came.

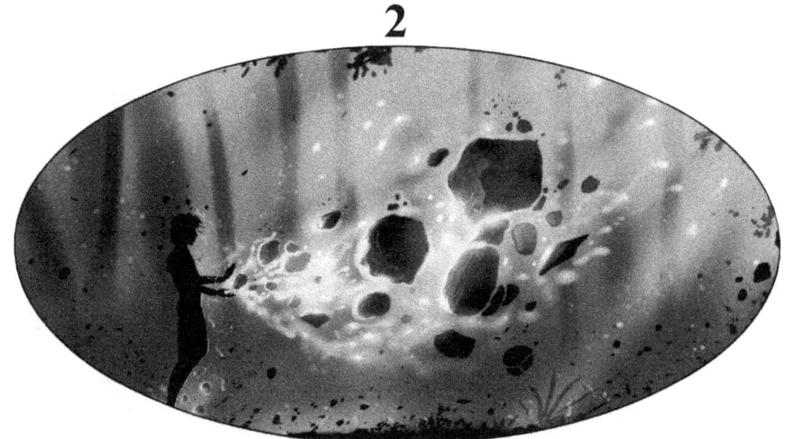

THEY SAID THIS NEW SETTING WILL HELP, but the screams only get louder. They also said that forgetting would help, but how can I forget when I promised him that I'll always remember?

They also said this airship would be fun. Well, they lied. Vayp tossed and turned, trying to get comfortable. It reeked of rust and metal and rotten fish. Even with his shirt pulled over his nose he couldn't mask it. The space was crowded and he could feel that the discomfort wasn't because of the bodies surrounding him. His temperature rose as if he was moments away from landing on the sun. He wanted to shove the bodies away, but GroundStone condemned that behavior. The Earthies, GroundStone pupils, were exceptional at being well-mannered and kind. He couldn't say the same for himself—a part of him still thought that the Quiz made a mistake in choosing him. Yes, he was a troubled kid who rubbed everyone the wrong way. He accepted that. He wasn't oblivious; he knew exactly why students didn't like him. Rage filled his heart whenever someone looked at him like he was different—even though he was.

He made no effort to be liked, to talk about his past, or the hor-

rific events that made him this way. Why make friends? It hurt less when they left . . . and they always will whether willingly or by the hands of time. He was miserable and would overreact, turning simple questions into physical contact. It felt like there were two people inside him. Himself and his enemy. One that appeared when he blacked out, doing everything without fear of consequences. And the other who would wake up from the trance, punished for the actions he never remembered doing. One shove got him a week's worth of boulder-tossing. He grew used to it; so the professors figured that it was more exhausting for Vayp to move them with his mind than his body.

They were right.

The minutes crawled by. The inside of the airship was so dark he felt like he had gone blind. His focus shifted to the crackling sounds underfoot that overwhelmed the hum of the turbines. Oddly enough, the exposed wires snapping at his fur moccasins weren't the source; instead, the black walls and floor resonated, dancing to the rhythm of the crackles like static.

And after a *pop* and a *sizzle*, the entirety of the airship became transparent, as if it had disappeared and they were twelve helpless students flying underneath floating mountains and waterfalls. The sun's light was blinding. And if it weren't for the way water dispersed in shimmering waves around their invisible barrier, this might have scared him. But it'd take a lot more than this to get a reaction—especially after what he had went through.

The other kids seemed unfazed. This was because they had the privilege of being dropped off by an airship when they first attended their schools. Vayp had no such luxury. He arrived by foot, bloodied, exhausted, a mess, and was sent straight to the Khas Section for special students. They sure didn't make him feel special; for the first few months they deemed him a mute with a difficulty in learning. That he was born different. That his refusal to speak meant the inability to. Little did they know he was born just like those they considered normal, but all it took was one day to drastically change the course of every single one after.

Vayp knew that this airship being transparent had nothing to do with wanting the students to experience the beautiful views the southern GroundStone region had to offer—not the golden pyramids from the Ramal sand tribes nor the lush forests from the Tierra earthen villages. Instead, the schools wanted to know exactly who was leaving and entering.

Safety over privacy was the Headmasters' motto, though he never really felt safe.

If anything, he felt punished for breathing.

The professors had tried many times to discipline him. They'd put him in front of the entire school to issue a public apology for his aggressions. He never caved, which would have been an easy way to get out of cleaning the Sol stables—their odors lingered for weeks. But he was much too stubborn. He had proven too many times that he'd rather wipe a Sol's butt than say sorry to an enemy any day of the week. Why should he apologize for being a trouble-maker when the true bullies should for bringing it out of him?

But soon GroundStone would no longer have control over his actions. The Nen'nex Mountains, named after the Headmaster of GroundStone, were almost behind him. Vayp watched the sea of golden peaks fade until a cloth wrapped around his eyes and tightened like a noose.

Darkness.

Silence.

His senses went numb, as if he'd become comatose. Worse, it wasn't the first time he had experienced this sensation. It reminded him of the time that he wished he could forget. Who could forget a

time like that? Death and horror and—He quickly closed the lid of his mind, blocking the memory from boiling to the surface. Tremors weren't his idea of a good first impression.

He was glad that he couldn't smell anymore. The terrible fish stench came from the chubby boy next to him. Vayp enjoyed the silence though. Maybe the shroud could help him finally sleep throughout the night. But the explosions and screams weren't actually sounds—they were memories that always dug their way back out no matter how deep he buried them.

The concept of time felt weird. He didn't know if he'd been flying for ten hours or days.

Anxiety crept in until warm leathery fingers pressed against his face.

The blindfold fell. And it felt like the world hit him with a stone hammer to the face.

After a minute or two of nausea, the spinning seemed to slow down and Vayp saw his reflection on the back of a metallic seat. He was bronze, medium height with short dark hair and a brown line painted under each eye. A gash stretched across his cheek. He quickly looked away. At times he forgot it was there. Mirrors were avoided for this very reason. He hated looking at it—not because it was ugly, which it was, but because of what was associated with it. He didn't see a scar, he saw a memory of what life was like before it existed.

He tried many different ways to cover up his scar, but they never made the pain go away.

Professor Leonna would always tell him, "You can look at a scar and see hurt, or you can look at a scar and see healing. This choice is yours." But she was a healer, what did she know about being hurt and living with scars? It felt like no one did.

Yuck! He was struck back into the moment by a scent of rotten eggs that made his eyes water. It came from the same smelly, short, round boy with dark hair, large nostrils and puffy, dimpled cheeks. He wore a white robe with the black cloth still wrapped around his eyes.

Since no GroundStone masters were here to reprimand Vayp, he didn't think twice before shoving chipmunk boy to the floor.

The airship shook.

Moments later, a frail man appeared and helped the boy up, untying the blindfold.

The man wore a black robe with a hood that covered his eyes—standard uniform for a professor. He was tall, thin, and very old, judging by the silver hairs that poked out from underneath his hood. One would never guess a man his age could be so lethal. But Vayp had heard many stories about him. He was Raaz'a, the Tsaro (Guardian) of Fire. Vayp was sure of it.

"Welcome to the Valley of Gaia," the man said in a soothing voice. "My name is Sir Raaz'a, and I will be your guide." It was him. Vayp could almost smell the blood of his enemies.

Vayp scrambled to his feet and jumped off the airship's ramp. Dust mushroomed into the air when he landed, but with a flick of his wrist, it settled onto the soil as if he had rewound time.

A wave of hot, musty air smacked him in the face, and he felt as if he might faint from it. Heat seeped into him, and sweat soaked his robe. Suddenly, he found himself on a mountaintop covered with dirt and rocks. In front was a stone wall so large it looked like a mountain stacked on top of another mountain. And when he peeked over the cliff, dark clouds swirled underfoot as if a thunderstorm was brewing.

Ahead, two boys stood on the ramp, shirtless. They were tall, pale and handsome, with the perfect combination of being lean and muscular. They had slicked black hair with silver streaks. Their sil-

ver pants flapped in the wind and, just below the black goggles resting on their foreheads, Vayp saw silver angular eyes. He hoped this new school would be different. At least, he hoped that he wouldn't get in trouble. But after seeing those twerps, he knew he was wrong.

They flipped and landed with a gust that swirled around them.

Vayp didn't have to know them to know he wouldn't like them. They were Fujitas. Fujita, the School of Wind and Wisdom, valued intelligence and nobility. But more than that, they always wanted to be the best, and made sure that everyone knew it. Fujita was filled with the brightest, and was known as the most difficult school to get into—besides Harahm'be, of course.

Harahm'be used to be the School of Fire, but now it was the Forbidden School, locked away inside the Valley of Gaia. No one had attended it in over three thousand years—until now. Rumors had spread throughout the capitals about why pupils were banned from entering. The stories had been picked apart so many times, and had been embellished in so many languages, that nobody knew what was the truth. But out of all of the rumors, one had survived the test of time: that Gabrael, the Headmaster of Harahm'be, the God of Fire, and King of Gods, was deranged, demented, and dangerous. He had a toxic school of thought that they didn't want influencing future generations.

Dangerous. Vayp faced forward without saying a word.

If Gabrael was as dangerous as history claimed, why would they be sent here?

It was that thought alone that made him briefly forget where he was.

His mind cleared up as three beautiful blonde girls, dressed in white robes, emerged from the airship. Their clothes flowed more like dresses that swept the ground, and sparkled blue when they walked, changing colors like tides breaking at the coast. Those colors belonged to Sereni, the School of Water. They valued loyalty, family, and, apparently, elegance. Their blonde hair fell perfectly straight over their jeweled headbands, crystal-blue eyes and pronounced cheekbones. Two of them appeared as their own reflections, and the third looked like a younger clone.

Vayp noticed the Fujita boys follow them with dropped jaws. He couldn't blame them.

"Waiddup!" The round boy waddled out of the airship, his brown hair plastered flat to his fat head. Dust trailed him as he dragged his feet. "Phew! Thanks for waidiating. Preciate it!"

Waidiating? Did he mean 'waiting'? Vayp shook his head. How someone so dumb could make it into a top four spot was beyond him. Maybe Sereni set the bar really low. And wasn't the School of Water all about beauty, anyway? There was absolutely nothing beautiful about him.

It seemed the girls felt no different than Vayp, nearly jogging away from the smelly boy.

Their song-like giggles as they sped away made Vayp's lips curl.

Though they sounded as enchanting as they looked, he hated seeing friends laughing. He wondered how his body could be filled with organs yet he always felt so empty.

He loathed happiness. More than his scar. Even more than his nightmares that kept him up at night. He hated what was taken from him. Wanting a normal life felt like day chasing the night—and rage overcame him when he saw others happier than he could ever be. They made it look too easy.

A sudden creak and moan shifted Vayp's focus to the airship. There were three beasts that strolled off the carrier. It shook as the animals clunked and clopped down the ramp.

One was a large animal with four stout legs, a body of stone,

hooves of granite, and three horns on its head. The other was a long cat. Its fur blended into the scenery, shining a bright gold. Its tail dragged along the dirt, invisible to the untrained eye. The last was a large bird that stood on two lanky legs holding up a fluffy body that sparkled like a rainbow. Its legs seemed too skinny to balance its body, but it glided across the ground with grace. Its feathers were like a phoenix's. When provoked, they'd give off enough fiery heat to melt stone.

They were Sols—animals spiritually linked to their owners.

"Okay, okay. Here!" Raaz'a said, guiding the animals to the front of the mountain where two statues rested. "Haven't seen a Sol in a few thousand years. My divine, such beauty!"

The Sols looked massive standing next to Raaz'a, but tiny when near the statues. The statues were about fifty feet high and a hundred feet apart. One was of a cloaked man with his hand out, and on its palm was a twenty-foot flame. The other was the same man wielding a sword. Its blade was a flame as long as his legs.

"Three Sols?" Raaz'a said. "Hmm . . . not desirable! Are we missing one?" His eyes wandered from side to side as he pointed his fingers, counting out loud.

"You, sir." Raaz'a pointed at Vayp.

Please don't come. Vayp turned away as the crunches in the gravel became louder.

"Excuse me." Raaz'a's black robes swished softly as he moved toward Vayp.

Vayp looked at the sky, clasping his callused hands together to stop them from shaking, hoping if he ignored Raaz'a he'd leave. But feeling invisible to the world was different than being hidden, an illusion he knew never to trust—no matter how often he tried to avoid people.

"Hello." The shrill voice from behind, and the taps on his shoulder, meant his plan failed. "'Scuse me, time is of the essence, Gabrael is awaiting us. I see you have brown robes on."

Vayp looked down. He wore a brown robe with a green vine as a belt. "Yep."

"GroundStone robes, I presume," Raaz'a said. "Where in the divine is the last Sol?"

He knew that was coming.

If there was one thing that Vayp hated more than happiness, nightmares, and ugly glares it was being reminded that he was the only one at GroundStone to be without a Sol.

His memories were like ghosts—haunting reminders of things he no longer had.

It brought him back to a vision of a small wolf pup, sitting on his knees, pressing its soft nose against his chin. He had a button-nose, different-color eyes—one white and one blue, and brown fur that felt like silk. Vayp named him Ah'nyx, claiming that he was going to grow up to be as strong as Ahnyxio, the strongest Sol to ever exist. Vayp had never experienced a love like this. As if at the tender age of eight, he had already developed several lifetimes' worth of memories with Ah'nyx. Having a Sol meant they had an eternal spiritual bond. They knew each other's emotions better than their own. He saw life through its eyes. Each day they played in the mountains until sunset. Ended their nights side by side. Fell asleep to the songs of their heartbeats. But one day, not wanting to place Ah'nyx in harm's way, Vayp trusted him in the hands of another. When Vayp arrived back from the hunt, he saw Ah'nyx lying in the center of the village as cold as ice. Motionless. Breathless.

In that one moment, Vayp's life had crumbled, and all that remained was its pieces trickling down into his frozen hands. That night he tried to fall asleep. He tried to listen to his favorite song, but the heart was silent. Ah'nyx's death remained a mystery, but he

had trusted her with Ah'nyx, and she had failed. On that night, she became dead to him also.

That was the beginning of the end of a normal life. And when he thought it couldn't get worse, somehow it did. Life was cruel like that. A concept that no fifteen-year-old should fully understand. But he did. Age couldn't lessen the pain. Or the trauma. The damage was done.

After pouring his heart out for weeks, he couldn't produce anymore tears. Ah'nyx wasn't just a pet—something the other schools would never understand. He was more than family. He was the other half that kept him whole.

Vayp's heart turned into a block of ice and had never thawed since.

His life became a shattered shield put together without glue, hardened and intact, but one wrong move and it would all crumble again.

"That's Vayp," a tan teen said, elevating out of the ground. Vayp didn't know if *he* was a boy or a girl, but she had a pretty face, short dark, spiky hair, like mountains, black lines painted under his eyes, and wore a brown robe with a grey belt that was rough and grainy like stone.

"Oh my, I was looking everywhere. Where in the divine are the others?" Raaz'a said.

"Here," a girl said, appearing from the ground in a similar fashion. She was small with dark features and the same garments and paint. Her sleeve was rolled up, showing a tattooed feline.

That was an earth mark, a tattoo that created itself and grew when the bond between Sol and the owner did. Vayp's mark had disappeared a long time ago. Yet another thing he hated.

"Me too," a deep voice appeared directly behind Vayp. "I was hoping to get a good look at Vayp trying to explain himself. It's a favorite of mine." He emerged from the ground. Mud dripped from his clothes before absorbing into them. He was Kaul, the tan, tall, long-haired jock who thought he was a King—the King of Messing-With-The-Wrong-Person, maybe. He hated Vayp. Even though it was years ago, Kaul never forgot the time when Vayp kissed his girlfriend. Vayp assured him how eleven-year-olds holding hands once a month wasn't what he'd consider a serious relationship. Get over it. But it was Tayna's first kiss; so Kaul never did let it go.

Kaul placed his hand on Vayp's shoulder. Vayp's body hairs prickled, and his lip curled with disgust. He felt his hand molding into stone, wanting to turn around and punch Kaul's teeth out. That was typical of Vayp, he was like a rabid beast who would strike without warning when approached. It wasn't his fault. Those moments would trigger horrific screeches in his ears, whistles from bombs raining down, and the *boom, boom, boom* as they eradicated everything around him. He'd black out and when he snapped back to reality a student would be unconscious. The professors scolded him, telling him that if he kept injuring students they wouldn't have enough healers to mend them. They would force him to stop his studies as a Dire and become a Shifa instead. Not a chance, he thought. Yuck, healing was for girls or weaklings not strong enough to fight. He was a protector. Not happening!

At the GroundStone district, tribes were differentiated by their face paint. It could tie back any family tree. These three jerks came from the same one: The Eazima Tribe.

One of the many problems that Vayp experienced at GroundStone was how his tribal mark was unknown, as if his people never existed. His life was an enigma to all, and he never spoke of it. He'd cry before a word came out.

He was eventually given his own room, not because he didn't get along with people, which was definitely the case, but because

his nightmares weren't just keeping him up throughout the night. Students had complained about Vayp screaming in his sleep. It was always the same word: 'Anything!' *Anything?* Whenever he tried to recollect his dream, it appeared distorted with images he didn't understand. But had he known screaming was the trick to get his own room, he would have added more flare to it—instead of apologizing—to expedite the process.

"Vayp doesn't have a Sol. Do you, loser?" Kaul laughed. "Pity peon gets peed on!"

"Shut up, Kaul," Vayp replied, shrugging the hand off his shoulder. He winced, remembering the time when Kaul and his gang of bullies dumped a bowl of Sol urine on him before an arena match. There was a time when Vayp tried to make friends out of his enemies, or at least pretend to not want to crush them with rocks, but that one moment ended all hope.

"I'm gonna tell you something harsh," Kaul said.

"Oh . . . now you're gonna?"

"How'd our worst student make it here? You're a Sol-less pity case," Kaul growled.

Vayp remained silent, his fists clenched so tight that his veins appeared like tubes underneath his skin. He wanted to lash out, and turn him into a statue, but he knew that Kaul was right. He wanted to believe that he was good enough, but that was a lie. He didn't really know how he became top four. Like the Quiz, GroundStone most likely made a mistake. He skipped more classes than he went to, and was on a first-name-basis with the disciplinary department. The last he remembered he was on the verge of failing out. Top four at getting expelled, maybe.

Vayp never forgot how eerie that day felt when he was declared top four. The professor's eyes were black like coal and his sockets were sunken. They were like staring into an empty well. The professor seemed more fatigued than the students, as if grading the exams was somehow more exhausting than taking them. Which Vayp couldn't fathom how that was possible. Lifting buildings with his mind, creating a stone clone with a jump, and shattering a boulder into a million pieces with his finger were much more draining. He bit the inside of his lip—maybe he really was the Sol-less pity case the jerks claimed him to be.

A moment later, his muscles relaxed as two girls exited the airship. They both wore silver robes. One was tall, pale, with beautiful, silver, angular eyes and short jet-black hair with silver streaks that framed her narrow face. The other was a short brunette with longer hair. His eyes narrowed.

They walked ahead, meeting up with the Fujita boys.

Vayp couldn't take his eyes off the brunette. He took one long sad look at her, as if she reminded him of Ah'nyx.

"Okay, okay. Looks like we have everyone," Raaz'a said. "Before we enter, I must go over some rules. Do not worry, not all rules are bad. These are simply things to be aware of."

"I heard so many wonderful stories about the Valley," one of the Sereni girls said.

"That it's the most beautiful place we'll ever see!"

"That it's the home of Eve, and all the prettiest colors, plants, and animals live inside!"

"Why, yes, those stories *were* true. But—"

"It's the safest place in the world!"

"Yes, that's definitely true."

"In case of storms are there any make up days?"

"You kiddin' me? I'm not wearin' make-up any day!"

Their words overlapped in a frenzy until Raaz'a clapped his hands. "Please let me finish." He straightened his robe before continuing. "Now, where in the divine was I?" He scratched his chin.

"I was about to—" He paused, looking up at the mountain. "Hmm . . . silly me, I forgot what I had to say. No worries, to not keep Headmaster Gabrael waiting, you pupils will be the first to enter the Valley of Gaia in over three thousand years! There is a great destiny ahead."

Raaz'a pressed his palm into the mountainside between the statues.

He pulled it back quickly, wincing as if it burned.

The ground shook as a fire appeared where his palm had been a moment ago. A flaming line cut into the stone. It shot hundreds of feet up the mountain, sounding like a shovel plowing through gravel. The fire burst into streams of light, free-falling like an exploded firework. It smelled like tar and burned charcoal. The glowing lines formed a perfect arch, landing next to the statues.

The mountain sizzled.

Vayp's face was lit up by reds and oranges, before a bright white light flashed.

He shielded his eyes with his forearm until they regained focus. In front of him were two enormous doors. They were stone with gold engravings.

Vayp could barely see the top of them.

The ground shook again as the gates rumbled open.

White smoke poured onto the field.

"Oh yes, I remember now!" Raaz'a said. "You will be free to wander as far as your heart pleases. You can venture off into all that the sun touches, but darkness is strictly prohibited. Although the Valley is the safest place in the world, we have our shadows like everywhere else. And evil finds home in the darkest of places." His voice then became high. "Welcome!"

As the smoke settled, the students' smiles faded, quickly turning to frowns.

The Valley looked like a wasteland with naked trees and a rocky terrain. In the center, stood the Spire as high as the sky with floating towers surrounding it. Bridges connected them to the Spire like strings on a kite. The sky was dark and gloomy. Light barely entered, and life seemed nonexistent. It was the exact opposite of what the students had expected.

Though heat bounced off the ground in waves, blurring the horizon, no one wanted to say it aloud, but none of them were happy with the visual. Vayp could read that in their faces. The look said that all the students agreed: the Valley of Gaia was terrifying.

The fear peeled their eyes open but not Vayp's. His eyes were flat. He felt nothing for he had seen much worse. He wished to explain, but talking about it would break him. It always did.

Time did not heal all wounds. He accepted it, and gave up trying to be normal.

3

S'RAE HAD EXPECTED TO SEE GREEN GRASS, red flowers, and pink trees in the Valley of Gaia. Instead she was surprised and felt a deep disappointment when she faced the ugly valley before her. It was nothing like the descriptions in the books. No flowers, vibrant colors, or grazing wildlife. Empty. The Valley was one of the few remaining parts of the world that hadn't been ruled over by the laws of the land and the feuds for borders. It was supposed to be the safest fortress in Gaia. But it didn't feel safe to S'rae. It felt like deception. She could feel the danger in the air as surely as a hunter felt the tightening of their bowstring before the arrow launched. She felt as though there were a target on her back, her muscles bunching involuntarily as if that unseen arrow was flying towards her.

Raaz'a guided the students into a cave, taking in the details of the sprawling opening inside one of the countless rifts. Unlike the disaster she had initially seen, it seemed as if this cave was meticulously built in honor of planet Gaia and its four Elemential

Kingdoms.

Her feet slid across the smooth marble that came from the mountains in the northeast Fujita Kingdom. Her hand grazed the walls, feeling the familiar roughness of stonebark with its rock-infused branches from the southern Groundstone plateaus. It reminded her of the missing piece of her heart that Fujita never filled: the feeling of home.

The alluring murals that hung overhead—flowing and changing frames—were the work of the magical Sereni watercolors from the western canals. Serenicea, the City of Water, was as beautifully designed as their world-renowned art. The paint flowed like water, creating the illusion that the ceiling was moving as she walked by. S'rae's head hurt trying to understand how that was possible. Some things were created to be appreciated, not understood. Fujita's students were trained to find logic in everything; Sereni, the School of Water, taught their students to appreciate life and its wonders—understanding how things worked took the magic out of it. Sereni was highly regarded for their casting and enchantments, after all.

S'rae continued to follow Raaz'a and the other students as they entered a tunnel. They were in a narrow dark passageway lit with flames suspended in air without assistance. The tunnel sloped steeply downward into a steam-filled area that made her feet sweat.

Raaz'a clapped and a long metallic pod appeared from the ground. They climbed in—and, after a few sizzles and cracks, they were off.

A flame boomed from the exhaust, catapulting them through the darkness like a missile through space. S'rae felt weightless, feeling her insides drift around in every direction. They blazed through twisting passages and steep nosedives, with no sign of slowing down.

She went to pull her goggles down to shield her eyes from the hot air—but before she grabbed them, she straightened up sudden-ly, looking over the railing. *What was that?*

They reached an open area passing over an underground pool of lava. A flash in the back of her eye had made S'rae feel like some-thing dangerous was watching her. Powerful and dangerous. But it was empty. Maybe it was the large bubble underfoot that burst into a sizzle.

She reached for her goggles again, but straightened up once more, her hand at her waist.

Something felt missing.

Her senses had never failed her. The shock that pulsed through her body made her feel like she was definitely being watched.

But what was there—at her hip—then disappeared?

Her eyes widened with fear.

Her safety belt—

Just as she realized she was no longer strapped into her seat, there was an earsplitting BANG. The pod jolted and scraped and screeched to a stop, and the next moment S'rae found herself thrown over the pod, falling into the lava below. And with a yell, she slid her goggles over her eyes.

She found no luck manipulating the wind that roared by—hot air was impossible to control compared to cold.

For a moment, she accepted the end of her life and wondered if this was accidental or not.

Professor Ki did warn her.

As she fell closer to her demise, the lava warmed her body in a way that made her consider—for a split second—how ridiculously hot the sun must have been.

Right before she swan dove into the lava, a puff of thick black smoke appeared at her side. An intense heat swept over her. The heat wasn't just on the surface. S'rae felt her insides roast. It passed through her as if grabbing her heart.

A cloaked figure appeared from the smoke. A hand reached out. It was more like bones with a thin, scarred layer of burned skin. Veins ran from its fingers, looking like rivers of blood. This felt like Death greeting her, a cold, evil presence, despite the scorching heat. It grabbed her.

Her entire body went ablaze, but it didn't hurt—it actually tickled.

And when she opened her eyes, she was sitting back in her seat.

Raaz'a brushed the ash off her clothes. "Make sure you are strapped in next time." He smiled. Smiled? Really? How could he remain so calm as if she wasn't peeing in her pants, screaming for her life? "Hmm . . . why did I get the feeling that this wasn't the first time I've saved you?" His eyes narrowed and blackened like the bottom of a well. "I've felt déjà vu many times, but this is . . . different." His eyes locked on S'rae's, making her stomach churn. After a few uncomfortable seconds, he shrugged then hummed a tune as he walked away. "Cannot keep Gabrael waiting. Carry on!"

In that instant—between almost dying and being saved—S'rae officially decided that she did not like him . . . in the nicest way possible.

They entered another dark tunnel, where a light appeared at the end.

Her head was forced back against the headrest.

Her arms fell to her sides.

She knew her body was awkwardly fighting gravity.

The pod had changed course, angling straight up, like a rocket. BANG!

S'rae felt her stomach sink into her spine. The wind fluttered her mouth. She zipped by streams of light until they flashed so bright that it took a few seconds for her to focus.

The pod disintegrated into ash. Smoke came billowing out from the ground. S'rae hunched forward to stop her knees from trembling. And as the smoke cleared, she gasped.

Somehow . . . she stood in front of the Spire in the middle of an open courtyard bordered by tall, bare trees. If it were not for the many windows scattered throughout its stone frame and pillars, she may had assumed the Spire was once a pointed volcano that had been sculpted by the hands of the Divine. Beyond it, she saw tall walls all around, as if they were inside a hollow mountain with its top cut off. The faint light that did shine through created an eerie glow that tainted everything in red.

She turned around with nothing to see but the dried-up shrubs, the wide red sky and the hovering towers overhead that revolved around the Spire with a low growl. When a tower slowly spun to the right and fell away behind the Spire, S'rae had a sudden, unexpected view of the whole valley. She could see giant statues of a goddess, undoubtedly Eve, nestled between steep hills, their long hair and dancing poses clearly visible. Across the Valley, set on the opposite hillside, was a large, half-destroyed colosseum surrounded by a wide expanse of charred grass.

A grey stone floor had swirls, rocks, and tiny cracks scattered underfoot; at least that's what the other students claimed. But from what S'rae had studied in her Creation of Matter class, she knew it as dried-up lava, or volcanic extrusive igneous rock, to be exact.

She stood upright with her hands to her sides. Fujita lived by the code: Display and maintain order. Order was their pride. It was rare to see a law that wasn't created by a Fujita.

To her side were Fujak, Chung, and Aura'li. They were the first to break away to explore the courtyard. It would have been unlike them to invite her; a new school didn't change old habits.

Her gaze drifted from the Fujitas to the Serenis across the courtyard. The three blonde girls were laughing and maybe singing while the plump boy talked to himself and kicked rocks. At the other end, GroundStone students were drawing spell scriptures on the floor, always looking for ways to manipulate their surroundings, while a lone boy sat a few feet away, underneath a statue of a sword, creating his own statuettes with a snap of his fingers.

She smiled, remembering the days when she'd make her own toy statues to play with. She made them move on their own and roleplayed stories with each one. Something to keep her entertained when she was alone—which was quite often. She then frowned, remembering when Opella's teachers had taken her toy family away. She pouted for weeks. She knew she was being stupid, knew that they were just little statues she created, but S'rae couldn't help it; she felt as if they had taken away her real family. A part of her.

Her village had wanted her to stop playing with toys and learn healing spells with the other girls instead. Boring! She was a fighter. She knew it. The girls definitely knew. And the boys found out one way or another whenever they tried to make fun of her. She made sure of it by doing things like turning them into statues of giggling girls. *Who's laughing now, boys,* was her favorite thing to say after. But girls were almost never invited to the hunts. Too dangerous, they said. Then why did they bring the boys who always lost to her?

S'rae pushed away her thoughts of the past and found herself standing underneath one of the many floating towers. It connected into the Spire by way of a bridge a few stories up. Her inquisitive mind raced around, thinking about the elemental physics used to make the towers float. *Most likely magnetic propulsion of opposites.*

She saw great statues that were broken and toppled over as if a war had taken place, stables (where the Sols were placed), a large crater which looked like a pond drained of water, and many cave

entrances sprawled throughout, looking like the exact areas Raaz'a warned them about.

Shadows were off limits, she reminded her curious self.

She wanted to ask why the Valley of Gaia was the worst place she had ever seen, but there was too much else to think about. *Why after three thousand years were we sent here?*

S'rae noticed that the schools were talking to one another now, except the loners. Her finger drew a circle in the air as if she were stirring a glass of water. She'd invented this trick to channel soundwaves, spying on students to find out the nasty rumors they'd spread about her. And there were many. Enough horrible, semi-untrue stories to fill a library. She had no idea why or how they came up with them. Their imagination for gossip and storytelling seemed endless.

She closed her eyes and listened. Her gut twisted, already expecting the worst.

"It looks like each one of our schools has at least one loser."

"Yeah, Sereni is supposed to be filled with all beauty and wealth, like us, but somehow smelly boy came from one of the ugly, peasant fishing tribes and made it to the top! Super ew!"

"There's always one pity case."

They laughed.

Sigh. S'rae was right.

Sounds funneled in quickly.

"We're called the Sereni Sisters for a reason. The best family the school has ever seen."

That's it! S'rae shuffled her feet and mustered up the courage to approach them. It was the first day of a new school, a fresh chance to finally make a friend.

With her best smile, not showing too much teeth, she skipped toward the crowd.

A few trailing whispers reached her ears.

"Speaking of super *ew*, that girl's coming."

"Quick, let's make a move now."

"I'm coming with you."

S'rae stopped. Her smile wavered.

She forced it wider, then awkwardly slid her feet backward. Her smile was her best disguise. She smiled all of the time so that no one knew how sad and lonely she really was.

"Phew, she's not coming! We're safe."

"Our first victory already! We win!"

She didn't need to steal whispers to hear the laughter that erupted shortly after.

"Laugh all you want," she mumbled.

Wind started to gather at her soles, but the voice in her head told her to not make enemies so soon. Maybe she still had a chance to make a friend if she was on her absolute best behavior. Or so she thought.

She looked at them and smiled with a nod. They returned with smiles of their own, the kind of smiles that came from shady back-stabbers. The ones she had witnessed too often right before a messenger orb—filled with every last bit of dust they could find—burst in her face. She felt foolish for ever expecting messages from a secret friend she had wished was real. She thought of those moments now as she watched the students frown, before their backs turned away.

Unfortunately, this was going just as she expected.

Minutes later, S'rae watched Fujak and Chung approach the lone chubby boy, who was still talking to himself and kicking rocks.

"Hey, what's up?" Fujak said.

The boy looked around cluelessly. "I'm the only one here. Did you mean to talk to me?"

"Umm . . . yeah?"

"Oh, okay, coolio. I'm used to bein' wrong when I think some-one's talkin' to me. That ever happened to you?"

The silence that followed was so awkward for the boy that even S'rae's skin tingled.

"Right. Course not. That stuff don't actually happen. Maybe to losers, you know, but not cool people like us. Your name's Fujak, right? I only know this because I was kinda listening to a little bit of the conversations you had, well, only the beginning, middle, and end. But, hey! I have an 'a' in my name, you have an 'a' in your name, I already think this friendship is off to a great start! So, how-dy? Hi? What's up, chicken butt?" He clicked his fingers into guns, then shook his head. S'rae saw that he pushed his palms along his legs like she did when she wiped off sweat.

Don't be nervous.

"Umm . . . they're right, you're very weird," Chung said. "And *very* stupid," he whispered to Fujak.

Fujak laughed. "But hey, that's okay, bro, we have a weird one in our school, too, she's over there." Fujak pointed at S'rae.

S'rae quickly turned around, trying to look cool by tossing her hair. She ended up looking like an old lady with a bad back.

"See, she's weird."

Sigh.

"We're used to it, no worries, bro," Fujak said. "But can you help us out?"

"Awesome! What's up?"

"You know those girls more than anyone here," Chung said, grabbing him by the neck and pointing at the Sereni Sisters. "What do they like?"

"Umm . . . this is me sayin' this as a friend, but—"

Fujak coughed. "Ahem, friend?"

"Okay, as a boy tryin' to help you out. Believes me, you don't want to talk to them."

"Why's that?" Chung puffed his chest. "You probably didn't hit the gym enough."

"First of all," the round boy puffed his chest and grabbed his belly, "I dunno who 'the Jim' is and what he ever did to you. Second, they only like each other."

"Listen, fatty, you must be dense." Chung pressed his finger onto the boy's chest. He used his other hand to cover his nostrils, as if the fat boy smelled terribly.

"Actually, I'm not him. I dunno who 'Dense' is either. My name's Han'sael."

"It doesn't matter what your name is!" Chung growled. "Just 'cause they don't like someone like you, doesn't mean they won't like someone like me. Look." He flexed the muscles in his arms.

"I dunno, I don't think they like boys skinnier than them," Han'sael snapped back.

S'rae chuckled.

"I'll show you how it's done."

S'rae watched Chung move confidently toward the Sereni Sisters. He slicked his hair back so a silver strand draped over his face.

"Why do such beautiful pretties look so mean?" he said smoothly.

"Because we thought that if we looked unapproachable—"

"You wouldn't *approach* us—"

"Yet here you are. Awkward!"

"Er . . . what are your names?" Chung rubbed his palms.

"Adalia," said the youngest one, stepping forward with a cheerful bounce.

"Alaricea," a girl said, grabbing Adalia's shoulders before kissing her on the cheek.

"And I am Aralinda, the oldest. We're twins," she said, grabbing Alaricea.

"But you can call us Ada, Ala, and Ara," Ala said, pointing at each one.

"You pretty girls should use Lia, Ricea, and Linda, easier to remember. Less confusing," Chung replied. He took a step forward then froze, noticing the girls' narrowed eyes at his feet.

"Yes." The girls each crossed their arms and grinned.

"It is."

"But we like them more. And they're our names."

"Not yours."

"So deal with it." Adalia flicked her wrist, as if to shoo him away.

They flipped their hair in unison, then snapped their fingers.

"Well, er . . . my name is Chung."

The sisters looked around at one another. Then at the sky. The ground. The Spire. They looked everywhere, even searched through Chung's clothes.

Then they backed up, with pursed lips, and observed him.

"Yeah." Ada sighed. "Couldn't find it."

"Find what?" Chung grinned.

"The care," the Sereni Sisters said together.

"We were looking to see if anything or anyone cared about your name, because we sure didn't."

"Nope. No one here cares. Bye, Bung."

"Bye, Drunk."

"The name's Chung," he growled through his teeth.

"You sure your name's not Skunk?" Adalia said, clamping her nostrils with her fingers. Her voice became nasally. "Whatever you say, Dung. Good . . . I mean, bad-bye, Chunk."

Chung's nostrils flared, and his lips curled.

S'rae fell to her knees, laughing. She had never seen girls insult Chung like that.

Chung stormed at Han'sael like a raging bull, with clenched fists.

"I tried to warn you." Han'sael chuckled.

"You're a nobody!"

"I am a nobody? Well, nobody is perfect. Guess I'm perfect then!"

"Shut up!" Chung shoved Han'sael to the ground. A burst of wind thrusted him several feet and he rolled like the sound of distant thunder. "You, fatty! Never disrespect a Fujita!"

Chung raised his fist in the air as wind spiraled around it, and immediately met resistance.

A boy dressed in brown clothes tightened his grip around Chung's wrist and the twister vanished. After letting go, Chung winced, shaking his hand, revealing bruises on his pale skin.

Fujak jumped in the way. "You made the wrong move, peasant."

"What move was that?" The boy stared Fujak in the eyes.

"Messing with a Fujita." Fujak was taller and made a weird noise in his throat, like growling.

"A Fuji-what?"

"Fujita, don't play dumb. But since your kind is at the bottom, maybe you aren't playing. Maybe you are as stupid as you look. GroundStone, how suiting for such low people," Fujak said with a squint. It was well known that Fujak was an elitist jerk, flaunting his status every chance that he got. It was his father's hope that he would one day become an Elemential, eventually taking the helm as Headmaster of Fujita. He was used to people who looked like this boy, with a caramel complexion, bowing down to him, not talking back.

"We'll see who's at the bottom when I'm looking down at you."

The boy grinned.

The ground trembled.

"Trying to be a tough guy. Do you know who I am?"

The wind escalated.

"I don't care."

"I'm Fujak."

Silence.

"Meaning of the name Fuj."

Nothing.

"Meaning a descendant from Fujita herself. I'm a direct heir and—"

"I don't give a damn which loser family you came from. We aren't in your district, so you better know who you are talking to."

The ground cracked open at their feet. S'rae noticed active lava forming around them.

All she could think about was how dangerous this could get, and went to stop it.

"I'm getting sick just looking at you," Fujak said, pounding his fists.

"Then stop looking at me. Simple. Aren't Fujitas supposed to be smart or something?"

"What garbage can of a home did you escape from where you think it's smart to talk to a Fuj like that? Of course I wouldn't expect you to know about my family's name with your years of poor GroundStone education. What are you going to do, throw some dirt at me like the dirty peasant that you are?"

The wind howled.

"I'll throw some dirt over the grave you just dug yourself in, softy."

"Heh, spoken like a true overly confident fool not staying in his own lane." Fujak grinned the same way he always did when he knew his next sentence would make his words sting. "You're that loser who doesn't have a Sol, right?"

And it must've stung, because the tremors that ripped through the Valley ceased at once.

Doesn't have a Sol? S'rae stopped, feeling a jolt surge through her body.

S'rae had spent many sleepless nights in Fujita's library searching for a specific answer. The library was home to thousands of books, though millions seemed more accurate, covering every topic ever learned. She must have read at least a hundred books about Sols, ranging from their origins to their detailed history. No matter how many books she read, she found no examples of a Sol dying on its own—they only died during or right after their human passed away. To her understanding, the connection between a Sol and human was one that could only be created by an Earthie. Since they possessed the closest link to nature, they were able to connect their mind, body, and soul with an animal; but, like choosing an element, the animal had to be a perfect fit or dangerous imbalances occurred. She read that no two Sols could ever look the same, even if they were identical twins from the same pack. The Sol would change shape, color, and, at times, even texture based on the personality and skills and passions of its owner. Sadly, it was hypothesized that the loss of a Sol would be the most painful emotional experience one could endure, like watching everyone you've ever loved pass away in a single moment. But S'rae needed an answer. She knew that a Sol could die before its human did. She'd not only seen it, but she was the one accused of killing it.

S'rae stood behind *him,* wanting to reach out and grab his shoulder, but her body froze in place. Her heart pounded against her chest as the hairs on the back of her hands stood up.

"Say one more thing and I swear . . ." the boy said, his voice

carrying more sorrow than rage.

The ground rumbled again.

S'rae saw students bracing themselves, holding onto one another.

Her hands were shaking so hard she had to clutch her robe to steady them.

"Vayp," she said softly. "I-is that y-you?"

4

S'RAE STEPPED IN BETWEEN FUJAK AND VAYP. Her breaths were long and deep. The familiar scent of wet sage made her nostrils flinch. *Is this a dream? It must be.* For she had dreamt this moment for years, since the day Fujita took her away. She had seen this very moment in her mind, giving her hope when she had none.

It was said to be impossible for a girl to stop two teenage boys from fighting, yet the tremors were gone. Dirt sealed over the cracks of lava like butter spreading over bread.

She clutched her robe tighter to brace herself as she looked up into Vayp's once blackened eyes, now as brown and wild as the sand that swirled around their village. They were so familiar that she could paint every detail of them in her sleep. In front of her stood a memory of the last time that she felt like herself. She could feel the muscles on her face relaxing.

Vayp shook his head, then looked into her eyes.

S'rae met his stare, his brown eyes sad and unblinking, his hair

swaying in the wind. It took everything for her to fight back the pressure that built up behind her eyes.

"S'rae?" Vayp said softly.

"You know this jerk?" Fujak said.

S'rae and Vayp wore identical brown markings underneath their eyes. She wondered how he'd gotten the long scar on his cheek.

She wanted to tell Fujak that Vayp was her brother—to her, he was—but he'd never once called her his sister. Never treated her as a real family member since she didn't even know who her parents were. She'd been taken in. Adopted.

S'rae hesitated. "He's like a brother."

"Like a brother?" Fujak laughed. "What does that even mean?"

"I was adopted," S'rae said in barely a whisper, but Fujak was too busy laughing to hear.

Vayp remained silent. She could see in his blank expression, and the way his eyebrows rested flat, that there was pain in his eyes.

"He disrespected my family name and can't even say anything to his like-a-sister?" S'rae didn't respond. "Hello? I know you're stupid, but is there a brain in there?"

Vayp took a deep breath. There was a watery glaze over his eyes.

She couldn't help it, she never wanted to cry in front of him. Never wanted him to think she was weak. But his glaze made her eyes pool up in response.

"This has to be the worst family ever." Fujak pressed his finger onto Vayp's chest.

Before Vayp could raise his fists, S'rae had already grabbed Fujak's wrist. A breeze whipped by her face as she watched her tears float in place. It was almost too quick to notice what happened. For being so swift, she had a gentle grasp.

S'rae turned around, and a burst of wind pushed Fujak back, his feet slid across the dirt.

"How dare you!" Fujak shouted.

"How dare I what?" she growled. This was the most emotion the students had ever seen from her. Her eyes faded to white. "There's a reason why you're second place."

The look the other students gave her was shocked and somewhat amused. She knew how she came off—prissy, cocky, like the classic Fujita she had always wanted to avoid becoming. She didn't like it, but she didn't like Fujak more. Besides, he messed with the wrong person. Not her, but Vayp. Talk all he wanted about her weirdness or how ugly she was, she could take it, but Vayp had gone through too much. More than Fujak's privileged, silver spoon-fed life could imagine.

"I don't know how someone low like you made it into Fujita, never mind to the top!" Fujak shouted. "I've always wondered how primitive brains like yours worked; but when my dad finds out about this, I'll have you expelled!"

"I'm warning you," S'rae snarled. Threats like his were made almost daily, but they never amounted to anything. Either he was too scared to cry to his daddy about what a mean, little girl said to him or he was ignored since he was the literal baby of the Fuj family. Most likely both.

"Never threaten a Fuj. You and your fake brother are bottom feeders. *Nothing!*"

S'rae vividly remembered when Fujak first became the devil. He wasn't always this mean. There was a time when he was the nicest person ever. She wished she was joking, but he was. She was the new girl and him being the son of the Headmaster, he welcomed her with open arms. Although she was still a wreck from leaving her home, family, and Vayp, Fujak did his best to make it a smooth transition. He even brought her to the floating terrace where only

elite members of the Fuj family were allowed. It was breathtaking, overlooking the entire sky.

She thought she made a friend. Maybe a best friend. Fujak even told her how she'd make a great Headmastress one day. She didn't know what it meant at the time. Years later, when she found out the truth of the word, she chuckled at being so oblivious. Even if she knew what she did now, she was unsure if she would take it as a compliment. She'd rather be the actual Headmistress, not the mastress. What was the point in being just the wife of one? Boring!

But all it took was just one word for their friendship to end. Who would had thought that a small word with only two letters would have enough power to ruin her life at Fujita.

No. That was it.

He wanted a kiss. She didn't want a disease.

Did he have any idea how many germs were carried in mouths? Yuck!

But because she didn't want to kiss him didn't mean they couldn't be friends.

She was wrong. More wrong than she had ever been.

This time there was no transition. Not a smooth one at least. There was no warning either. No 'Hey, I'm going to start hating you after tonight.' Nothing. It was like the flip of a switch.

In one moment, her only friend became her worst enemy. Her arch nemesis. The creator of almost every terrible rumor spread. And one of the reasons she never made a friend again. Maybe the main reason. Who knew?

It was as if they had never been friends. And maybe they never were. She barely remembered the times when he was the sweetest chubby little boy with a weird bowl-shaped haircut. This was long before he became Fujak, the heartthrob. Before the six pack and muscles and trendy hair atop his big-headed ego.

But that was then, the past. This was now. And now he needed to be reminded to never cross the line. A lesson she couldn't teach him at Fujita. But Fujita had no control here. How unfortunate—for him.

S'rae's eyes glowed white and her hands clenched tightly. She let out a whisper.

Raging gusts of winds came from all around, as if the group stood in the center of a tornado without warning. The wind pushed Chung back a few feet, and lifted him several inches in the air before he fell to the ground. Fujak stumbled as if a weight was pressed on his back.

Then the circling wind guided itself toward Fujak. It lifted his robe in the air with such force that it ripped, revealing embarrassingly thin underwear. Then the fabric wrapped around his arms, torso and head as he crashed to the ground like a half-naked mummy.

The wind vanished as quickly as it came. It couldn't have lasted more than a few seconds.

Fujak squirmed and flopped around like a caterpillar halfway into its cocoon.

Then came the eruption of laughter, overwhelming Fujak's muffled screams.

"Quiet, quiet. Enough!" Raaz'a entered the courtyard from the Spire. "Children. Students. Pupils. While there may be some debate on which word to use to describe you, there is no question in saying that each of you are exceptional. Each possesses a unique skill within your gift that awarded you the prestigious top four spots. You are all special in—"

"Are there any students here? Why are we here?" Aura'li interrupted. She was always the inquisitive type, wanting to know everything. S'rae looked at her, relieved. It was exactly what she'd been thinking herself.

"Well, there is one, Retro'ku, but he—" Raaz'a gasped. He stuttered for a bit, then continued as if no questions had been asked. "Contrary to the Fujita belief, there are indeed multiple ways to define intelligence." He giggled, glancing at Chung and Aura'li assisting Fujak to his feet. "It is not about how many books you can read, or how many words you know. True intelligence is understanding that you are your own God. Gabrael argues that the destiny you all possess is the greatest of them all. He has unlimited wisdom; keep your mind open and he shall show you life's deepest secrets."

"Why are we here?" Aura'li asked again, crossing her arms, as if this was the first time she'd ever been ignored.

Raaz'a pressed two fingers together, turned away, then whistled, the sound resonating in S'rae's chest. The light fixed at the entrance of the Spire flickered, hissing like it was leaking gas. And as the last few students entered the Spire, floating candles hurled themselves in front of them, some dropping onto the stone floor, revealing beautiful engravings, others clinging to the high-rise ceilings, showing the vast golden hallways glittering in the light. Some landed in long glass-like cylinders that torched twenty-foot flames, changing colors from blue to red to purple. They carried with them the scent of flowers in spring.

The students formed a single-file line as Raaz'a guided them through golden hallways. S'rae was at the tail end of it, and when she scanned ahead, she noticed Vayp was first in line.

Looking at Vayp made her feel warm inside. She couldn't believe that her brother was back in her life. It was as if the Divine One had heard her those many nights when she cried herself to sleep.

In next to no time, they came to an abrupt stop. Ahead there was a dead end.

Vayp stood in front of what looked like . . . S'rae blinked and looked closer. It looked like . . . a furnace?

"Step up," Raaz'a said, grabbing Vayp's hand. "Here."

Why is he putting Vayp into a furnace? S'rae felt something wiggling in her stomach.

Vayp stepped onto the platform, leaving deep imprints in the mounds of ash underfoot. His brown hair stuck to his face in sweaty waves. Raaz'a leaned in and whispered something. Vayp's fists clenched and his eyes squinted.

It looked like he was in pain . . . or was he concentrating hard or scared?

S'rae couldn't tell what was happening, but Professor Ki's words flashed through her mind. Her gut wrenched tighter, feeling like something terrible was about to happen.

"Wait," S'rae shrieked, pressing forward. "Vayp don't—"

All too soon, there was a crunch from his feet digging into the ash, a sizzle, then a hiss of steam and *poof!*

A flame sparked ahead, and Vayp was gone.

In horror, S'rae stormed toward the front, pushing students out of her way.

"Now where in the divine are your manners?" Raaz'a said, sticking his palm forward, halting her in place. "You must wait your turn."

"What happened?" S'rae shrieked. "I demand to know!" She had finally been reacquainted with her brother after five long years. The idea of him being gone again—

"You will have your chance, don't you worry." Raaz'a smiled, gently pushing S'rae to the side. "You're next." He grabbed Kaul's hand, pulling him onto the platform.

S'rae stood there, white-faced and furious, staring at Raaz'a and his ugly smile, hardly believing her eyes. Whatever was happening, she needed answers. Now!

After S'rae watched nearly a dozen students combust into a flame, Raaz'a grabbed her.

She was up next.

Raaz'a leaned in and whispered. She felt his hot breath seep into her pores, smelling like smoke.

"This will be painless, my dear. *Haz'tu ro'mah.* Think of those words and those words only. Don't think too hard. You do not want to end up like the others."

The others? Her mind was troubled by a million questions that appeared, like a stream of bubbles floating up to the surface. She needed to think of those words, but there was too much else on her mind.

"I pray you are ready." Raaz'a grinned in a way—showing his crooked teeth—that made her uncomfortable.

S'rae did not want to show it, but she was scared. Scared of the conspiracies. Of Raaz'a. Of the Valley. Of the furnace and the unknown that lay ahead.

She knew that something had been watching her. Something terrible was here, but she couldn't put her finger on it. She just felt it. And worse, if Gabrael was as dangerous as the rumors claimed, their lives weren't in danger . . . they were already dead.

Pop! S'rae's body tensed, expecting to burst into flames. Instead there was a ball of fire that crackled before her, morphing into a flaming bird. Its small wings moved too fast.

Raaz'a smiled. "To what do I owe this pleasure?" He flinched a little before his smile faded completely as if he was told someone close had passed away. "Gabrael will not be pleased!"

S'rae had to listen in. The bird spoke in a searing whisper: "The Mecha went missing. It left Fujita today and was last found heading straight toward . . . the Valley."

"WHAT!" Raaz'a said too loudly. He turned to S'rae, his eyes bulging. "Be gone! Now!"

Scared for her life, she squeezed her eyelids tightly. *Haz'tu ro'mah.*

BANG! Her eardrums rattled with a crack.

It happened too fast. Like really fast, all within seconds.

She felt a whooshing sensation, as if a hot wind were blowing against her. In that moment, blood rushed through her body, and sweat from her skin seemed to boil and sizzle. A roar surrounded her, and then . . .

Foot-long flames engulfed her, bursting out of every pore in her body, turning her into a wisp of ash. And gone she was.

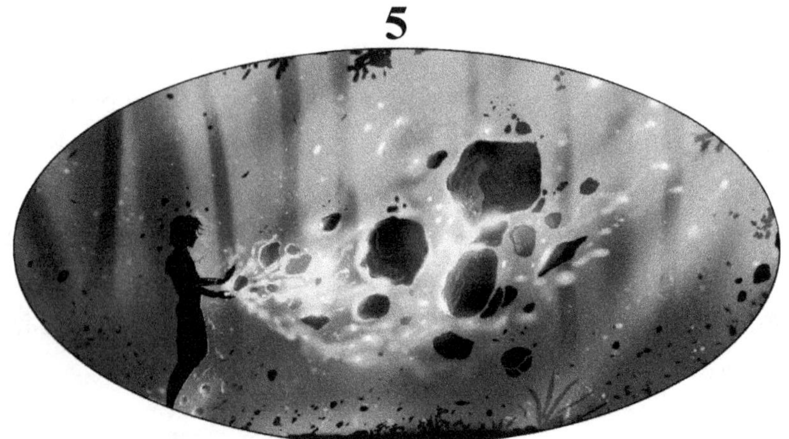

5

Your time will come!

Vayp woke up sweat soaked, trying to shake off the dizzying feeling of the dream. Nope. It still felt like a whirlwind ravaged in his head. But at least he was here. Alive.

He almost did it, not falling asleep, but this room was too dark and quiet and he hadn't slept in what felt like weeks. He heard the whispers of death, waiting for him in his nightmares.

But if never seeing or hearing them again meant giving up sleep, then he was fine with exhaustion.

He then looked at his bloodied palms, wondering how they'd gotten to this point. They only did this when he cast a powerful spell. But he had no such memory of doing so. Maybe he blacked out again—that'd explain why he couldn't quite remember the long walk into the room. He stared at his palms once more before hiding them in his pockets as footsteps sounded from behind. If only he could hide his memories just as easily.

For a moment he thought he was in a prison cell. The only window was high up and barred; faint noises came in through it, though mainly the sound of wind brushing up against the dark curtain. The room smelled like stale bread, and a thick layer of dust covered the floor, as if it had never been used.

Don't sit next to me, he thought, glaring at the students entering the room. They had a slow pace to their walk, seeming careful not to step on something. The room was dark and cold, despite being Harahm'be, the School of Fire. It was also smaller than he had expected, which made sense. There were only twelve students instead of the hundreds that normally packed inside a GroundStone colosseum.

This setup would make it more personal. The idea of that twisted his stomach into knots—he hated human interaction almost as much as his nightmares. That said a lot.

The seats were separated into four rows of four. They were stone, damp and uncomfortable. Vayp felt good about choosing one in the last row, furthest from the podium. If Harahm'be was anything like GroundStone, he preferred to be as far from the teacher as possible. It decreased his chances of being called on to answer. Or so he thought.

In front, there was a large podium made of granite and onyx. It had a black shiny material in some areas but a stone base. On top was the largest book he had ever seen. It was a foot wide and thick, looking more like a box. Before he sat down, he noticed that it had four empty circular sockets on each corner with a larger one in the center. It was covered in moss, which could explain the moldy smell of the room.

S'rae walked by and Vayp's muscles tensed.

He thought about their past, not seeing her in five years, and, for a moment, about maybe being nice.

"I was mean to her for the wrong reasons," he whispered. "It wasn't her fault."

S'rae, from her first-row seat, turned around. They made eye contact briefly before she turned away.

Vayp's eyes widened. "Did she hear me? No, that's impossible, she can't hear what I'm thinking. Wait, am I thinking out loud again?" He paused, hearing his own voice. "Dammit."

It came out louder than he meant it to.

He heard a faint, familiar chuckle. He thought that he was going crazy, but he wouldn't be surprised if she could hear him. There was one time when she wanted to know everything so badly that she stayed in a closet for a few days to listen in on everyone. She was punished by *the V-village*—Vayp felt his heartbeat escalate. *The screams*—he suppressed his memory before it became too vivid. He didn't want an episode in front of everyone, especially S'rae. She'd ask too many questions.

Asking questions was S'rae's gift and curse. She never ran out of things to ask—which got her into trouble. It didn't take long for her to be known as the annoying one. Villagers would run away before she started talking. Once she got going, she would drain hours out of their day without even trying.

Vayp never knew where she got her random questions from— and he was too afraid to ask. He valued his time too much.

Why did her eyes close when she sneezed? Why did hair grow from Vayp's nose but not his face? Was it true that Archons didn't eat clowns because they tasted funny? Why did the sun lighten her hair, but darken her skin?

S'rae had an infinite list of questions, but one always stood out from the rest—forever engraved in Vayp's mind.

How could he forget it, it was her only question that was never followed with a smile: Why wasn't she able to get a Sol?

Vayp vividly remembered her tears that poured—the only times he'd seen her cry.

It was the one question no one had an answer for.

Vayp helped her become the perfect Earthie. He trained her and she learned how to control the ground faster than anyone he had seen. But each time she thought she found her Sol, the animal ran away before the link finished. Weird, getting a Sol was usually the easy part of training. Vayp remembered how she'd often go a few days without taking a shower, but it wasn't as if she smelled too badly. That couldn't have been the reason the Sols ran away.

She was allergic to cleaning, she claimed.

Vayp recalled some close calls. Very close, as if the connections were clearly made. But the closer she was to getting one, the more it hurt to watch when she failed. Maybe that was why she went to Fujita. And why she . . . killed Ah'nyx—

Vayp tried to force the thought from his mind, but it was too late. Whispers sent chills through his body as if they were from Death himself. Blood surged through his veins. His fingers dug into his palms, tearing through his rough skin. His heart pumped faster. Breaths were heavy.

It was happening again.

Don't! Not now! Not here. Please . . .

He took slow, deep breaths. *Death will come to you. I will be waiting for you in your nightmares.* The cold voice sent chills down his spine.

I am fine. Breathe. I am fine . . . Brea—

Meditation was the only thing that helped.

His beating heart slowed down.

When his eyes regained focus, he noticed the classroom was

full.

As expected, S'rae and the Fujitas occupied the first row. The Sereni Sisters took up the next. And directly behind them was GroundStone, pushing each other around like idiots. Vayp would rather be alone than sit with those jerks. They kept practicing their musafa, a secret handshake from Earthie to Earthie that was always different. He never wanted a stupid musafa, anyway, he claimed. But the way his heart sank to his stomach, even he knew that was a lie.

Han'sael stormed in with an armful of food. Vayp didn't bother to ask how he managed to find it, though he was curious; that meant he'd actually have to talk to him—he had learned that lesson the hard way from living with S'rae.

"'Scuse me." Han'sael bumped into Vayp's elbow. A long, bright-blue fruit rolled off his belly and landed on the ground. Dust lifted into the air. "You can haves that one. You got like ten minutes or somethin' before it's bad. True fact that I just made up, trust me!"

Vayp shook his head, then watched the Sereni Sisters shoo him away.

The GroundStones shoved him away.

Vayp sighed as Han'sael waddled toward him. *Great, always left with the annoying ones.*

"Do you miyeeind if I sit here?" Han'sael nodded at the block near Vayp.

Miyeeind? Does this idiot really not know how to talk? It's 'mind.' Simple.

"Sorry, they're broken." Vayp winked. The stone stool crashed into a nearby one, crumbling into pieces.

Han'sael shrugged, which was somehow more irritating, then sat at the opposite corner.

Vayp could hear Han'sael's lips smacking as he ate. There was an odd, deep-breathing sound, as if it was impossible to eat with his mouth closed.

On top of his disgusting sounds, one conversation led to two, two led to three, and before Vayp knew it, silence had turned into an uproar.

Things were getting too loud when the door banged open.

The noise disappeared like a candle blown out by the wind.

Vayp felt footsteps rattle his insides.

The cold faded as if the room suddenly turned into a sauna.

The air became humid then dry all at once, feeling like a rough cloth was stuck in his throat. Sweat formed on his forehead, and his body felt a burning sensation as if he had sat too close to a fireplace.

As *he* walked by, the air normalized, though the scent of hot ash still lingered.

Vayp had never felt so much power from a single presence. *He* had to be Gabrael, Headmaster of Harahm'be, the God of Fire, and King of Gods.

He wore a dark cloak that swept the ground with a faint sizzle—there was no draft, but it flowed like it had a mind of its own. Though his hood covered his eyes, Vayp briefly saw the telltale sign of smile lines on the corner of Gabrael's eyes. There was nothing else that looked happy about him. He was tall with a chiseled jaw and the perfect amount of stubble. The candlelight painted his dark face gold. And he walked in a way that made him glide across the ground, as if he floated toward the podium. With each step, a flame was lit on a nearby candle, making the room smell like roses. The flames were faint, enough to create a dark, flickering auburn glow. The walls were bookshelves filled with cobwebs and books, most of them bound in aged brown or black leather. The way smoke bent around him, the way breaths were held in his presence, made Vayp imagine a Divine One who created the universe with his hands.

Gabrael stood at the podium, steam radiating from his hands, cutting through the silence like a sword through water. "Hello," he said in a chilling, deep voice. "Welcome to Harahm'be."

Vayp realized that he had forgotten to breathe; a part of him didn't know if it was allowed. There was something about Gabrael that required undivided attention with no interruptions.

Gabrael lifted his finger. A spark flickered and crackled at its tip before combusting into a flame. It drifted through the dark, shining down on the book.

"Do any of you know what this is?" Gabrael asked, placing his hands on the book.

Vayp swallowed his breath. Even if he wanted to say something, he was too frightened.

The question hung in the air for a moment. He saw S'rae raise her hand, then hesitate as if to touch the back of her head.

"You either know or know not, young one, but have conviction."

"I-I think—" S'rae paused. "No, t-that's only a myth."

"What is only a myth?"

"The Book of Eve, sir."

"Please . . . call me Gabrael." A flame floated down to S'rae, as if to get a better look at her. "You'd be surprised at how many truths rest in myths."

Vayp felt a tenseness, a subtle change in the texture of the air.

"It so happens that one man went on a quest for a myth, then came back with this boo—"

"So is that—" S'rae gasped.

"Go on."

"The Book of Eve?"

"It is," he replied. "Now, who knows of the Story of Time?"

Nothing was said, only the crackles from the candles were

heard.

"No need to be shy." The candlelight danced to each word that he spoke.

Vayp surveyed the students. Their wandering eyes said they were as clueless as he was.

"You," Gabrael said, "in the back. What is the Story of Time?"

A collective exhale echoed from the eleven other students who weren't chosen.

Vayp's face grew sour, and he swallowed the first words that came to his lips.

"I . . . don't know." He put his head down in defeat. The first to already be wrong.

"You don't . . . know?" Gabrael spoke in barely a breath, but they heard each word. He had the gift of making students hang on to every word that he spoke. "What do they teach you in schools these days if not the oldest, most sacred document ever found?"

Gabrael took a long, deep breath, and Vayp's face went hot. The smell of smoke lingered for a few seconds. Vayp watched the shroud covering Gabrael's face as two sparks of light, where his eyes would be, grew brighter.

Vayp's sweat bubbled up, absorbing into his clothes.

As the heat settled, Gabrael spoke once again. "Did they teach you nothing?"

The students shared the same expression, Vayp noticed as they twisted in their seats: puffed cheeks and pursed lips. He wanted to laugh, too, but couldn't give in.

"Do you know, at the very least, why the Quizzes came into existence?" Gabrael asked.

Vayp felt the temperature escalate as if the room turned into an oven.

The candlelight danced.

"The schools have failed." Gabrael turned around, shaking his head. "I was afraid of this. They are erasing our history. I am sure they did not mention the millions of innocent lives that were lost during the wars, on *both* sides. No hands, no matter how pure they seem, were clean."

The candles went still.

Gabrael stepped up to the podium and shared the story of the Elemental Quizzes. He told the history of the four Elemental Schools and their districts. He spoke of the wars, the ones between Good and Evil, and the even more dangerous ones between friends. He mentioned how some Elementials were unable to control their element and as a result they defected. When one studied an element that didn't align with their soul, dangerous imbalances occurred in nature. Instead of controlling Water, their hearts turned cold like Ice. For Earth, their bodies hardened like Metal. For Wind, their minds scattered like Lightning. And, most importantly, for Fire, their souls blackened like Shadow.

The corruption of the elements had started a deadly civil war amongst peers, led by another Shadow Army and the greatest evil to exist, Geddon. It was known as the Decades of Darkness. To stop a Shadow Army and a civil war from ever happening again, Fujita, the Goddess of Wind, designed a stricter Elemental Quiz to assign pupils to the school that best matched their values.

When a gifted child reached ten, they were forced to take the Quiz, and answer each question/situation truthfully, then sent to the correct school to control an element. The system had resistance, especially against the rule that stated they must leave their families to attend school. Some never saw their family again. Because of the resistance, with the help of Vy'ken, the God of Lightning, Fujita studied and recreated these giant robots, Mechas, to police the world and enforce order over all elements. Fujita was held at the highest esteem for restoring the balance of nature.

This was why peace had existed for thousands of years. And why Gabrael hadn't taught a pupil in just as long. But peace had become as fragile as glass. The Mechas were now controlled by an unknown evil. A dangerous force that could destroy Gaia ten times over, if left intact.

"Surely you studied about them when you learned of the Last Great War?" Gabrael asked.

S'rae raised her hand steadily. "What's the Last Great War?"

"WHAT?" The candles roared into large flames, scorching the ceiling.

Gabrael looked up, and for a second Vayp saw his eyes. He saw past the anger on the surface of them to the pain underneath, like a wound too deep for healing. He saw the same eyes that he had seen many times in the mirror.

The flames faded.

The candles sizzled to a flicker.

"They are succeeding," Gabrael said softly. "They are limiting what students should learn. Their idea had always been the less truth, the better." At the corner of the room a jar shattered. The smell of a campfire filled the air alongside the sound of ricocheting glass. "They have stripped you all of an open mind. Since when should students of the *elements* become puppets?"

Vayp noticed the candlelight briefly change to blue when Gabrael accentuated the word *elements*. He found himself thinking of a story he had heard, one of many his father had read to them before going to sleep. It had to do with time being a circle. Something about life re-creating itself over and over again. Because he had forced himself to forget most of his childhood memories, the words trickled in like snowflakes landing on his palm, disappearing before he could grab them. It was just a story though, he thought.

Suddenly, a series of words flashed through Vayp's mind. "The Arm of Geddon," he said.

Vayp winced as chairs screeched against the stone floor. *Stop thinking out loud, idiot!*

"What did you say?" Gabrael asked with a hint of excitement in his voice.

"N-nothing . . . just something from a story my father told us."

"Your father is a great man. He has restored my faith in the world."

Yes, he *was* a great man, Vayp thought grimly. A chill rushed through his body.

Gabrael walked around the podium and stood in front of S'rae. "You see, there is a truth that has been hidden. Like each of you, I too was taught that time is like a river. That you cannot touch the same moment twice, because the flow that has passed will never pass again. But how wrong they were. Time does not work in a line like a river . . . it exists in circles, a cycle like seasons. We all have lived life billions of times. And this is where the feeling of déjà vu comes from."

As Vayp recalled the stories that he'd heard about Gabrael and his dangerous yet crazy school of thought, he felt an odd sensation in his stomach.

"Some of you may be feeling it right now."

An eerie jolt tingled through Vayp's body. It shook with an un-explainable warmth that he had never felt, but, at the same time gave the feeling he remembered this exact moment.

He shook his head.

The reaction made his stomach weightless. He looked across the room to see if anyone else was experiencing it. If so, they hid it well.

But how?

"But how," Gabrael said, "is typically the next thought that comes to mind."

Vayp had the sudden urge to throw up. He grabbed his clothes to stop his hands from shaking. Though he heard his father tell this story before, it never felt as real as it did now.

"Thankfully, the poem is eternally engraved in my mind. Before I read you the Book of Eve, it is important to know the ancient, prophetic poem: 'The Story of Time.'"

He cleared his throat:

> Time is not a straight line, it is a circle and round.
> One cannot save Time unless the secret is found.
> We have lived this life many times, each ending the same way.
> The Last Great War triggers the Arm of Geddon, or the Big
> Bang we shall say.
> The Big Bang is not the end, but also the beginning.
> And it will continue this way if Evil keeps winning.
> Life gets recreated, the same circle, the same time.
> This is how déjà vu occurs, the same moment, the same mind.
> But the circle of Time had finally changed ever so slightly.
> Could new life finally be lived? There was never a dream so
> mighty.
> The secret is kept hidden, so one must look.
> To defeat the monster inside the darkness, you must open the
> book.
> There was a boy who never lived until he was finally given the
> chance.
> His father always took the same path, but this time a butterfly
> caught his glance.
> Instead of the road that always led him to the life of a peasant.
> He took the one never traveled, one that was unpleasant.
> He stumbled upon a new village that he had never seen.

And stumbled upon new friends, some nice and some mean.

He was no longer a slave; this time he trained for war.

He fought with conviction, for a love he never had before.

She gave him power, he made her a ring.

He gave her a flower, she made him a King.

He was no longer a slave, he ruled the land all under the sun.

He united the seven kingdoms, something that had never
been done.

For the first time it seemed that the war could be won.

The new King was close to victory, the last song ready to be
sung.

Until betrayal led to deceit, deceit led to defeat, and defeat led
to death.

Although this time was different than the others, he still
exhaled his last breath.

With the last tick of time, the Arm of Geddon was raised,
victory was his to claim.

But something was different this time, the King's death was
not in vain.

Before the Big Bang, he found a new village, a new path, a
new life.

He became stronger, found new friends, more importantly,
a wife.

He had never loved before, and it was love that he'd find and
he'd give.

For inside his wife's womb was the boy who had never lived.

Never once in the history of Time had this boy been born.

So when Time re-created itself, its constant circle was torn.

It was a miracle: Someone died who had never died before.

His soul was placed at the beginning of Time, his destiny
became much more.

This is the story of how the boy who never lived slayed the unkillable beast.

It contains the secret how it could be done again, the missing piece.

The boy thought little of himself, as if he was no one special, no one great.

But little did he know his existence alone was so grand, he could change Time's fate.

This is our first chance to do something that has never been done before.

To finally allow life to be lived after the Last Great War.

"And this, children, is when *this* story begins." Gabrael lifted the book.

"So what are we doing here?" Fujak said. "You just going to read us this bedtime story?"

"Your tone and arrogance ooze with Fujita," Gabrael said. "I sense within you that you carry the highest level of bigotry. You must be of the Fuj family, no?"

Fujak put his head down.

"Yes, children, when we are here, time will be dedicated solely to the Book of Eve. However, in your free time, you may explore all that light touches." He paused, then his voice became low and he gazed at Fujak. Even a God would have quivered under the look Gabrael gave him; when he spoke, every word burned with rage. "When here, I will read, and you *will* listen."

Vayp breathed a sigh of relief, thankful that Gabrael didn't stare at him like that. He thought of the terrible mess he'd make if he melted.

Gabrael opened the book. A soft breeze traveled around the room, smelling like a forest in fall. "I present to you, the Book of

Eve." Gabrael began reading.

Vayp wanted to pay attention but his focus was on the barred window. There was something about the air. . . something dangerously familiar.

He was about to turn away when the ground vibrated his toes. Only he felt it—a protective spell that warned him when danger had arrived. It helped him feel somewhat safe at night. But this was not good at all. There had only been one other time when the ground shook with this much force.

And in that single instant when he recalled that moment, Vayp felt all the hairs on his body tingle and a darkness creep into his soul. This wasn't danger he sensed . . . it was death.

Outside in the middle of the courtyard, there was a shadow that traveled slowly as if there was a dark cloud overhead. But the sky was clear, red—expected for the School of Fire—and empty. The shadow molded itself into shapes. A head. Then shoulders. Then torso and legs.

Two beings emerged from the darkness. The remaining shadow on the ground served as the taller figure's cloak, flowing as if weightless. They stood as beings void of all light, like they were made from the very matter that created space.

Shadows simmered from their bodies like black steam.

"Your plan worked," a cold voice boomed. "Your traitor guided us here perfectly. After three thousand years, it has finally been found."

"Of course the plan worked, it was mine." This voice even colder.

"Which student was it? Surely it wasn't the girl who escaped melting to death. If so, I would almost feel bad. The old man had to ruin my fun."

"I assure you, if she was, you would not be alive right now. Unlike you, I do not miss. But it is not your concern to know who the traitor is. I have my own agenda."

"Understood. As do I . . . So this is what the Valley of Gaia looks like."

"For now."

"Now?"

"Because there will be nothing left of it when the Mecha arrives. Finally, I am home. It is time." The figure fell silent, as if letting the victory of the moment settle over him. "Gabrael is the last believer of the secret. When he dies, it dies with him. Then nothing will stop us."

"We mustn't forget why we're here. The book. Eve. Then Gabrael. I must go home, too."

Spawning from the figure's arm, a dark blade slashed outward. The way it cut through air made matter bend around it, like a black hole. A dark substance, thicker than blood, dripped from it, splashing onto the ground like melted rubber, sticky and dry.

A long, scaled creature with no eyes emerged from the darkness. Four legs erected themselves out of its body, appearing as an opaque black panther with fangs, scales, and spikes that ran down its tail.

"It ends now."

The creature screeched as it ran into the Spire.

The poison that surged through its veins was potent enough to kill a God. The Valley was no longer safe, an unknown traitor made sure of it. Now death awaited all who had entered.

6

THE BOY WHO NEVER LIVED

DESTROU LOOKED THROUGH THE HOLE of an igloo, scanning a thin path covered with frost. From behind another igloo, he heard the pitter-patter of footsteps. Two figures appeared, making a gesture as if to alert others, then pointed in his direction.

Destrou quickly retracted his head, slowing his breath.

His body inched closer to the entrance, peeking around the corner. Cold waves chilled his cheek.

The igloo was empty. Nothing around but the familiar stench of urine.

The Village appeared deserted. Yet he knew that there were about fifty boys hidden, waiting to pounce on him. He felt many eyes were on him, but he had to remain calm, and wait.

There was silence but when he closed his eyes he heard the soft crunch made when feet slowly pressed into snow. They were creeping up on him. He knew it. When he concentrated harder, he heard their heartbeat—or was that his own?

If they found him, he was a goner. His location left him too vulnerable, like an injured calf surrounded by wolves.

Destrou's only task was to survive.

He wiped his sweaty palms on the side of his furry white cloak with brown streaks, it glowed against his dark skin. Other than his cloak, everything he wore was white and furry: his shoes, pants, even his shirt, which looked like a sweater quilted by a blind man. It had many patches, as if it had once belonged to a taller man who fought in many battles.

Brown eyes were visible between the cracks of his dark dreads. He brushed them to the side, pressing the back of his head against the cold ice. He clutched his waist, feeling the familiar bite of doubt in his stomach as the crunches became louder.

He didn't know why he was so nervous. Well, other than the whole one little mistake and everything would be ruined, it wasn't too bad. It wasn't like this would be the first time he failed—but it surely could be the last.

Destrou had seen what *they* were capable of and knew how dangerous it would be to get caught in the open. His main concern would be the Bruisers. It was not unknown for them to end a life with a well-placed blow. Speed was his greatest ally. He was fast, but too small, half the size of an average twelve-year-old.

The only thing that he liked about his size was his speed and ability to get in and out of tight spots. It helped him avoid many bad situations. Not all, but many.

Destrou's size was supposed to make his life easier—less of a target. But he had an unfair advantage, and that made him *the* target.

He was in over his head, but being given this job was *his* way of testing Destrou. There was always some kind of test. Since there was no bond, Destrou figured the tests were their closest connection—*his* odd way of showing that he still cared.

At night, when his loneliness was at its peak, Destrou often thought of the past as he tried to sleep. He wondered if the emptiness would ever end and if he would remember what it felt like to be liked, loved . . . he'd even settle for being noticed. The lack of words spoken didn't hurt him. The person who no longer said them did. It was then, during the darkest moments of the night, when he realized that the worst kind of sad was not being able to explain why. It may had been everything.

He felt like his life didn't matter. That he didn't belong. Just there, as if he was the extra piece of a complete puzzle that was unneeded. No one would notice him gone. Or care.

Destrou sat up, reacting to the crunch of a foot over a thin layer of ice. He placed his palms into the snow that rested between two chunks of ice, readying himself.

The sun had already peeked over the Wall, and Destrou knew that they would strike at any moment.

"We can finally eat something today," a voice said. It was so close that Destrou could smell him. An odor that he was too used to.

Destrou held his breath with puffed cheeks.

"Don't jinx us. We need to find him first."

"Good thing we have every path covered."

A gust of wind sent flurries of snow across the icy ground. Flakes landed on Destrou's head. He looked up, then smiled.

The voices appeared on both sides of him, slowly closing in. He was too focused to make out what they were saying. He needed a way out, and found it.

It was now or never.

His heart sank when he saw their shadows. They were here. As the boys turned the corner, Destrou leapt on top of the igloo, then sprinted across the Village, hopping from roof to roof. The igloos were close together and formed rings around the Guardian's Tower, which the boys named the NoGo.

He ran so fast that his hair and clothes trailed behind. The wind filled the gaps of his clothing, making him appear a hundred pounds heavier.

"There he is—" he heard a boy scream. The wind in Destrou's ears muffled the rest.

At once, an army of boys spawned out of the snow like ants.

"Why are we waiting?!" said a muscular boy wearing more layers than the others. Strapped onto his chiseled shoulders was large, white-furred armor. He had dark eyes and straight black hair pulled into a long tail, hanging over his shoulder. He was the Leader. That wasn't just his title, it was his name. Of all the boys in the Village, he was the worst. "Get him!"

The army of boys in white jumped on top of the igloos and chased after Destrou. Pouches filled with snowballs were tied around their waists, bouncing against their hips.

The Leader stayed behind. His eyes followed Destrou to the horizon. He was a bully, always looking for an excuse to show his power. This type of treatment had happened to Destrou for years now, but it hadn't always been this way—there was a time when they'd all gotten along.

Destrou remembered how the Leader's name used to be Eli'jah. Once upon a time he was a good person with a good heart, but the Village had a way of bringing out the worst in everyone. There was a saying that one cannot make friends during war; but when everyday was a war for food and survival, friends weren't made; alliances were. The Guardians were nonexistent, allowing the boys to set up their own rules as long as duties were met. They needed someone loyal, making sure order was kept. And on that day, Eli'jah died, and the Leader was born.

The boys only referred to him as such and followed his every command. He set an example early, getting rid of any who disobeyed him. Their names were forgotten, like they never existed—only their examples of what not to do remained.

The air was damp with moisture, Destrou felt his shirt stick to his back. He looked over his shoulder, feeling his heart pound in his chest.

He heard the constant pitter-patter of footsteps closing in on him from all around, like a fast drum roll.

The boys stampeded after Destrou, howling like savages. They were a few years apart, but that never mattered to Destrou—they were all the same to him: giant and ugly.

"Get him before he leaves!"

"Shoot!"

Instantly, the sky was filled with dozens of snowballs, raining down on him like hail.

Destrou placed his hands on a roof. The cold sent a chill through his body. Then he lunged through the air as balls exploded all around him into a flurry of snow.

His only job was to survive, and he did just that. If one touched him, it was over. He lost. And that meant waiting two more weeks for food. The way his stomach tightened, he knew that it would be too late.

"This is pathetic, you krillens!" the Leader screamed. No one wanted to be called a krillen, a term used to describe a worthless person who was good for nothing. "I can't count on boys to do a leader's job."

The Leader placed his knee down, gathering snow with his frostbitten hands. It was moist and dense, the type of snow that compacted into solid ice. With a devilish grin, he fixed his gaze on the boys on the horizon. Words need not be spoken—for the way that his brows arched, mouth curled, and nostrils flared, unveiled a malicious intent as solidly cold in heart as the ball of ice he created.

Destrou ran quickly. He leapt over boulders, slid on patches of ice, and dodged many cracks in the way. He ran with a smile on his face despite the boys closing in on him. He always smiled during these moments. In an odd way, being the focus of attention made him feel human, like his life suddenly mattered—even when they wanted to kill him.

As the pack grew nearer, snowballs were launched at Destrou's head. Turning around, Destrou saw exactly what he expected. He jerked his head to the side, feeling the force of ice burn past his nose.

They were cheating. He called them *poopmunchers*. It wasn't a real word, but it was the first thing that came to mind.

As he continued to dodge snowballs, the other boys weren't so lucky, one after another getting struck with some of the stray balls. Each hit caused them to give in to their exhaustion and stop the chase, pressing their palms to their knees and gasping for air. Destrou didn't let the close calls faze him; if anything, the smile on his face grew as the pursuit intensified.

Ahead was a small cliff that formed into a slope. Some of the other boys slowed to a stop, as if knowing the dangers ahead, but Destrou kept running. He jumped, twisted in the air, then slid down the ramp.

A brave boy jumped after him, and immediately lost traction. His body jerked backward, slamming his head onto the ice. Destrou heard a thud like a hammer hitting stone. Grunts and loud snaps, like the cracking of bones, echoed through the area.

One tumbling boy after the next; dozens soon regretted their leap of faith. The sounds of their bodies crashing onto the ice were drowned out by their screams. Destrou knew he should feel sorry for them, but then he reminded himself of the countless times they'd hung him from a spike by his underpants. It hurt just think-ing about it.

The boys sluggishly stood up, pressing their palms to their low-er backs.

"You gotta be kiddin' me—not again!" shouted a stumbling boy, pointing overhead.

"How does da stupid ones always win?"

They often talked about Destrou like this, as if he was the dumb-est thing on the planet—or, rather, as if his small body meant he had a smaller brain, like an insect ready to be squashed.

A long rope had been thrown down. Destrou pulled on it as he climbed.

A handsome boy stood heroically at the top, like an ancient statue. He had a tall frame, chiseled jaw, muscular body, with long, silvery hair tied into a bun and dangling strands that sparkled like white light. He looked young due to his pretty face; but his posture stated that he was a man. He was everything that Destrou wasn't: perfect.

Destrou tried many times to mimic him. Failure was an un-derstatement. His clothing was designed for a man, but unlike the other boys, there was no slack. He filled them in a way that con-toured around his muscles, like a glove. He had large hands that also seemed meant for a man, not a boy. In an odd way, he was a man trapped inside a twelve-year-old body. But, most important, Ranmau was Destrou's unfair advantage. His twin.

He hoisted Destrou up with ease, his muscles barely flexing.

Ranmau patted a pile of snow that looked more like a wall than a mound.

"Should be enough." Destrou chuckled.

"Good." Ranmau smirked. His voice had the rough texture of his calloused hands. But he wasn't as severe-looking as the other boys. He had small, light eyes that seemed welcoming yet cold and wore a white fur scarf that was probably an animal's tail. It was only when he turned to place both hands on the mound that Destrou saw dark bruises on the back of his pale neck. If he didn't fear ruining Ranmau's rare, contented mood, he would've asked how he'd gotten them.

Every night for over two years, Destrou had wanted to ask how he'd gotten his injuries. Every night he lacked the courage. He didn't want Ranmau to shut him out more than he already had. He was there physically, but not emotionally. There was no bond. The pain of losing Ranmau would hit him out of nowhere. *Why are you so distant?* He would cry out in his mind. *Are we still brothers? Do you still love me?* Of course, there was never an answer.

Though Ranmau was Destrou's protector, Destrou never wanted to see anything bad happen to *him*. The person who once carried him on his back for miles when he sprained an ankle, who made sure that Destrou was full before he took a bite out of any piece of meat. Sometimes Destrou would pretend that he was full just so Ranmau wouldn't starve himself to death. Yes, Ranmau was the strongest person he knew, but hunger would end him like it had ended countless others. So Destrou kept his pain a secret, no matter how tight his stomach churned.

Destrou quickly shifted his eyes away from the bruises. "Too easy," he said.

Ranmau shook his head, silently disappointed. That was his line, and much like the start of a slow-clap, precise timing was key. It only took two words to ruin the moment.

They lowered their shoulders, pressing their bodies against the mound. Destrou felt his body turn numb, and looked over at Ranmau who seemed normal. Destrou hid the aching feeling in his stomach by straightening out his face into a half-smile.

Though he was small, he never wanted to be confused for weak. He made the most out of his tiny pebble-like muscles.

"On three," Ranmau said.

Destrou grunted to make it sound like he was helping, but the mound collapsed over the cliff with almost no help of his own. Moments later, an avalanche tumbled down. Random limbs stuck out from the snow.

When the group of boys finally climbed and groaned their way out of the ditch, only one of them congratulated the twins.

He patted Destrou on the back, and whispered softly into his ear, "Great job again!"

Destrou smiled.

The boy's head was completely covered with a long white scarf, wrapped tightly around his mouth, nose, and forehead. So tight that Destrou saw he returned the smile with one of his own. His piercing blue eyes squinted with glee. Though obscured, Destrou swore that he remembered that face from somewhere. To him, all of the boys were the same, but a clouded memory appeared as smears of red whenever he tried to recognize him. Unfortunately, knowing his name was treasonous. Destrou wasn't allowed to speak to the other boys. The Leader would punish both of them if he found out.

But the Leader was nowhere in sight. Destrou could spot his big head from a mile away.

"What's your name?" Destrou smiled.

The boy glanced over his shoulder, then hunched in closer. Destrou could feel the warmth of his breath on his face. Unlike the other boys, he carried a fresh scent that smelled like citrus. It made Destrou's mouth water as if he could taste it.

In a world where resources were scarce and food was limited, the Village was the worst. Their supply from the Kingdom was almost nonexistent; whatever food they did retrieve, the Guardians kept most of it. Their massive frames put the *ton* in glut*ton*. They slept for days yet reaped all of the benefits. On occasion, the food they didn't eat would be shared amongst the Village. Rarely was the food split fairly. If it weren't for the challenges, Destrou and Ranmau would have died of starvation years ago.

The Guardians held a challenge every two weeks, giving the winner a prize. A different skill was tested each time: brawn, intelligence, speed, and agility. This one was for agility. It didn't matter which skill it was, the result was the same. Ranmau had won every challenge since he was ten years old, the age to compete. The Villagers despised that, and it affected everyday life. Because of that, Destrou had never made a friend. And it had only been about a year or two since he'd lost his only friend: the estranged Ranmau. They hardly spoke, rarely laughed, and never shared any affection. A lonely life was an understatement.

As the boy said his name, a loud roar trounced his soft voice.

"I win!" the Leader said, launching two balls at the distracted twins.

The ice blurred, whizzing through the air. Caught off guard, Destrou's muscles tightened and his eyes sealed shut, bracing for contact. He'd seen what ice was capable of at that speed: death.

After a few moments, he peeled an eye open, feeling the butterflies escape from his stomach. Like the hero that he was, Ranmau had both projectiles wedged inside his palms. It confused Destrou how someone could be perfect at everything, while he struggled for hours trying to simply pluck an eyelash out of his eye. Besides showing affection, was there anything Ranmau couldn't do?

Ranmau looked as if he had swallowed a pepper. Sweat soaked, he glared at the Leader, then crushed the balls with his bare hands. Shattered ice fell between his fingers, sounding like a rush of pebbles sprinkling onto the ground.

"Don't do it, Ranmau," Destrou said softly. He had seen those eyes before, the way his pupils dilated so his eyes blackened like ink. That meant danger.

Stepping back, the Leader tripped, falling onto his rear. His eyes widened with fear as Ranmau inched closer.

Ranmau stood at the feet of the crumpled leader. His eyes spoke a thousand words of fury, but his mouth said only two. "Too easy." He kicked snow onto the Leader's chest.

Destrou heard a collective sigh. All eyes were now on them: the twins.

This was the moment that Destrou had prepared for. He needed to do what no boy had done before: defeat Ranmau.

The boys watched with bated breath, waiting for the first move to be made.

The brothers—Ranmau, the handsome, well-built one, with silver hair, and Destrou, the small, brown-skinned one, with brown dreads—were contrasting brothers separated by only a few seconds at birth, though it seemed more like years.

Being the youngest in the Village, they pushed each other to become the best. Well, Ranmau was the best. The great. The untouchable. Destrou was the sidekick. It didn't matter how hard Destrou trained, Ranmau was always a few steps ahead. The sibling rivalry ultimately made it so that their only competition during the challenges was each other.

Their pouches were filled with balls as if this had been their plan all along—saving them for this moment. Though far apart, Destrou found himself looking up at Ranmau. How they both had come from the same womb was beyond him. But the Guardians told him that was what had happened, which was enough for him.

From the corner of his eye, Destrou could see a dark-haired boy jumping up and down. He and the blue-eyed boy grabbed each other's forearm with a firm shake, binding their words. Keeping their word was one of the most sacred laws of the Village. That usually meant that someone had placed a bet on who would win—most likely that Destrou would lose again. He never took offense; even he would have bet on Ranmau. He had no idea why anyone would be crazy enough to bet on him though. Food was too valuable to take risks.

But this challenge was different. There was more at stake than simply winning a prize. His relationship with Ranmau had deteriorated ever since he won his first challenge—and worsened after each one. He needed answers. Doubt seeped into his mind, making his empty stomach feel full of movement, but he didn't let it sway him. *If Ranmau can make the impossible seem possible, then so can I*, he thought.

He was the smallest in the Village, his body was bruised, emaciated; his hair was uncombed, unclean. His age was only twelve, and he was underdeveloped, so there wasn't an ounce of muscle on his body. Nothing had grown. Nothing was really there but potential and heart—two of the most underrated qualities that defined a true warrior.

Why are you so distant, Ranmau? In his head, he had the courage to ask the question. *Where did my brother go? Why do you leave me when I need you?*

Every night for nearly two years, he had wanted to ask. Every night, he had lacked the courage. Ranmau was all he had. He didn't want Ranmau to shut him out like he had everyone else.

But today was different. He knew it had something to do with the challenges and claiming the prize. He knew he needed to win. He had to.

Most boys cowered at the prospect of facing Ranmau, but today, he craved it. He had been practicing every night. *I'm ready*, he

thought as a fierce gust of wind howled through the valley, tossing his dreads across his sunken face.

It was now or never. *I know I can win.*

A gust of wind blew through the room, fluttering the book's pages.

Vayp saw S'rae rub her palms against her thighs. He assumed the wind was her fault. He remembered when she'd get nervous during the most random points in a story. If a cat entered a story, she'd freak out, hoping that nothing bad happened. The wind was most likely an outburst of emotion.

As Gabrael flipped through the pages, Vayp was alone in his silence, thinking about Destrou's world. It kept his mind off the feeling of danger as he connected the similarities between his own life and Destrou's torn relationship with Ranmau. He too was in complete isolation. For years, though he'd been surrounded by hundreds of earth-shaping pupils, he felt alone—out of place like a single charred grain found in a bowl of rice. He had nothing at GroundStone, at least nothing important. He had a bed, books, and the same dirty clothing that he'd been wearing since his first day. Something about seeing S'rae again made him feel like he had a chance to be normal again. He didn't know why. Perhaps that was a sign of how much he missed her, though he'd tried to forget that she existed.

He then thought about the greatest relationship he ever had. He dozed off into a lucid daydream, visualizing an Elder Shifa resurrecting Ah'nyx. He saw him in the clouds that stretched over Opella, growing into the grand Dire Wolf Vayp knew he'd become. That was his best friend, looking peaceful, powerful and perfect beyond words. His fur was rough, able to withstand any blow. His tails grew long and bristly, showing how powerful and agile he had become. Though Vayp knew it was only an image, a fabrication of his own imagination, he knew that was how Ah'nyx would look, if he was still alive. He did know him better than he knew himself, after all.

That was his best friend . . . and he missed him more than the savory smell from the meals that awaited him after a long hunt. More than the feeling he got when he mastered a new spell. Ah'nyx was the last thought on his mind before he went to sleep and the reason he was so excited to wake up. Why he was excited to live.

His thoughts brought him to a rare, happy place until a loud noise interrupted him.

Vayp looked to his side, wincing at the sound of mouth-breathing and Han'sael gnawing into a large green fruit.

"Shh!" Vayp hissed, pressing his finger to his lips, though he didn't mind the fresh citrus scent that lingered.

Han'sael stuck his tongue out at him, then bit into the fruit once more, this time louder.

"Can you stop that?" Vayp whispered.

"Are you kiddin' me?" Han'sael whispered back. "All that talk 'bout bein' hungry made me hungry!"

Vayp shook his head. "Is that all you think about?"

"I used to think about food all the time." His eyes rolled up,

muttering words to himself, bobbing his head side to side. "Still do, but I used to, too. Phew! Wonder why it got so hot here!"

Vayp's lip curled. *School of Fire? You really are as stupid as you look.*

Han'sael's teeth crunched into the fruit again and he winked at Vayp as its juices spilled onto his face. He wiggled in his seat, attempting to lick the liquid off the top of his cheek.

Vayp grimaced, thinking about how badly he wanted to absorb him into the ground, turning him into a big, fat boulder.

"If you're hungry, ask him when we're takin' a break." Han'sael smiled.

"This ain't about me, fatty." Vayp crossed his arms. He had moments like these a lot, when rage swelled up inside him, and the next thing he knew someone was stuck in the ground with their underwear on their head. The teachers had warned him about how he'd be a much better student if he wasn't always starting trouble. But it didn't feel like he started the problems; he ended them. It was as if no one ever noticed when he was provoked, only when he retaliated.

"You seem hangry. Hungry. Angry. Get it?" Han'sael snorted, spitting his food out.

Vayp's eyes narrowed.

The ground shook . . . accidentally.

He winced at the sound of stone scraping against stone. The chairs faced him.

He felt Gabrael's eyes burn into his skin like lasers. The smell of burned flesh hit his nostrils. Vayp refused to look him in the eyes, fearing that he'd go blind.

"Problem?" Gabrael's voice was so sharp that it felt like it cut through his body.

Vayp wanted to blame Han'sael, but when he glanced over, the tubby boy was sprawled over his chair, head cocked back, mouth wide open, with drool dripping over his lip. The fat faker—Vayp wanted to roll him down a hill. He swallowed his words, feeling them uncomfortably drift around in his stomach. The room became so hot that it was difficult to speak. He tugged at the collar of his robe. "Sorry . . . I'm hungry . . . wondering when we can take a break."

Vayp saw Han'sael open one eye just enough to wink.

"Is that all?" Gabrael flipped through the pages quickly before slamming his palm on the book. The boom rattled Vayp's eardrums and shook the room.

"Y-yes." Vayp gulped.

Gabrael pulled his sleeves up to his forearms and rubbed his hands together briskly, an idle smile playing over his lips. His hands tightened over a flame as rays of light striped out. When he opened his palm, a bird of fire hovered gracefully. Its chirp fluttered like a high-pitched gobble. Gabrael whispered words to it.

Before Vayp could blink, the bird appeared at his nose, nearly burning his face.

"Any requests?" Gabrael said. "If so, tell it. Softly. You do not want to find yourself without any eyebrows."

"No." Vayp turned away from the heat.

"Very well, then." Gabrael flicked his wrist. The bird twirled around the room; then vanished through the door behind Vayp, leaving a cloud of black smoke. "Lunch should be prepared soon. Follow the smoke trail. I expect all of you back here in an hour." His voice deepened. "Do not venture too far, and stay clear from the shadows, I am not responsible for negligence. But worse than any shadow is tardiness, you do *not* want to be late."

7

S'RAE WAITED IN HER SEAT for a few moments. A tear formed as she thought about Destrou's feeling of losing Ranmau. She related to the void of losing a brother even though he was still physically present; it was like playing with a favorite toy after its power died—it was never the same again. Like Destrou, she realized that at some point during her childhood, she and her brother went outside to play together for the last time, and neither of them knew it.

She had many questions, but would rather wait until everyone left before approaching Gabrael. Why were they sent here? And the message about the Mecha heading straight toward the Valley still troubled her.

The room cleared out. S'rae heard excited chatter erupt from the open door, then become quieter and quieter.

The idea of being alone with Gabrael made her palms sweat, but she also wanted to find out how he had become a King. His element wasn't everywhere. She could feel air, see water, and touch earth, but the way he created fire out of thin air shocked her. Maybe he knew how to materialize wind in an airless environment. He was the King, after all.

She opened her mouth, but before a word came out, Han'sael approached Gabrael. When she mumbled her question under her breath, Gabrael shot her a look and narrowed his eyes. At once, there was movement behind her eyes as if an insect was crawling its way out of her brain.

She shook her head then decided to scan the room. The bookshelves were filled with books—some she had read, others covering foreign topics.

Sol'adari Pact. The Legendary Flames. Elemental Fusion. Prophecies of Va'han. The Beast Within the Eve of Darkness—subjects that Fujita had never mentioned. Now that she thought about it, why were there no books about Gabrael either? There were no facts, only rumors, stories shared from parents to child. The schools must have really not wanted students to know about him. *Why?*

S'rae grabbed the book dealing with the Eve of Darkness, and immediately felt a burning sensation at her fingertips that still sizzled moments after pulling away.

"Ouch!" S'rae winced, blowing into her hands. Wind danced around in unnatural ways.

"Those books are not for pupils," Gabrael said from afar.

She sat in a chair and arched forward clumsily, still blowing into her hands. She didn't know if the pain was physical or mental. While her hands looked fine they pulsed as if a hundred bees had stung her. She remembered learning in her Psychology of Elements class about the illusion of pain and how an element could trick a person's mind to think—therefore feel—that they were on fire, like a pepper burning a tongue. Yup, that was definitely what happened.

For the first time, instead of hiding her favorite books in school

sections no student dared to be seen in—like Tutoring for Dum-
mies—she gladly considered shoving these into Fujak's face.

Sharing is caring, right?

She then busied herself with counting the freckles on her hands.
She loved the random marks on her body, calling them her personal, unique stamps, searching for any distraction to keep her from
spying on Han'sael. It was going well until she heard sniffles coming from somewhere.

It was her rule: Anytime someone mentioned her name, yelled,
or cried, she *had* to listen. She couldn't break her own law. Fujita
had taught her well: Justice and justification through just laws was
just fine.

"Do the bullyin' ever stop? Why does they do it?" Han'sael
asked in between his sobs. It seemed like Destrou's story struck a
chord deep within him. "What's the point? Why take innocent people and find a way to be mean to 'em? Why would people follow
someone who is so mean?"

"Because sometimes we are blinded by things beyond our
control, and we may never see who the true enemy is. Have you
heard of the story: The Forest and The Axe?" Gabrael asked. When
Han'sael rubbed his eyes and shook his head Gabrael continued.
"The forest was shrinking, but the trees kept supporting the axe
because its handle was made of wood and they thought it was one
of them. Fear is a powerful thing, when unquestioned it can control
a person, when unchallenged, the world."

"I honestly have no idea what that means, you lost me at 'axe.'
But do different people like me and Destrou ever make friends? I'm
so tired of being alone."

S'rae rubbed the sting in her eyes. She saw herself in his questions.

"The fear of being alone can make people isolated. It's like a disease. The more you see it, the more you believe and fear it. The more you fear it, the more you get paranoid about it, until it consumes you. That is how loneliness can be real. It is real in the same way that fear is."

"What do you do?"

"You embrace the fear. Accept it. Conquer it. And open your eyes to a world where you are the same as everyone else: a person trudging through life with fear. We all have fears."

"Do you live in fear?"

"We *all* live in fear. It just consumes some more than others. You have never been alone. They are out there. Friends. They will come in time. I promise."

"I don't need lots, just one is enough. I ran outta things to say to myself. "

"Loneliness is a terrible thing. If you don't know how to conquer it, it can eat you alive. *Haz'tu ro'mah*, it means have faith and faith will have you. The universe works in wondrous ways. Now, speaking of eating, go. Enjoy lunch."

As they finished, S'rae tried to wipe the tears away, but they wouldn't stop. She didn't need friends. She wanted to be liked, and that was entirely different. But in that instant, she decided to not talk to Gabrael. If she did, he'd notice her tears, then she'd have to explain what happened. If someone knew her secret, they'd never whisper around her again. Before Gabrael could open his mouth, S'rae ran out the door, flailing her arms.

She followed the trail of smoke. The hallways were composed of stout stone pillars and high ceilings—some had windows, others had candles for light. Smoke billowed from the gashes in the stone floor, giving the air an oaky smell. The rooms had doors like a prison, barred windows and no door handles. Occasionally an unlit candle or lamp would light up as she walked by. S'rae heard voices

as the smoke led her toward an open room.

She wove her way between the half-open doors. Overhead, the high ceiling was filled with black smoke and candles, appearing as a beautiful, starry night. A light atop a stove in the far corner shone like a flaming moon.

The room reminded her of the star-gazing nights with Vayp and Ah'nyx. S'rae and Vayp would lay on top of a cliff with their feet hanging off the edge while Ah'nyx cuddled in between them. She remembered thinking about how great their future would be. GroundStone would be their new playground. They'd excel. Master the books. Together there were no limits to what they could achieve. They made a good team. No, a great one. S'rae helped Vayp with reading, and Vayp helped with tracking and finding a Sol. Or tried to. But catching a Sol was something that couldn't be forced. It was left to fate. It was said that one found their Sol only when they least expected it. It would appear, stare into the owner's eyes, and they'd both know they belonged together. And that maybe life never truly began until after that moment. Solmate was what they called it, love at first sight.

Sol . . . She then frowned, not because her lack of one but because Vayp's loss of one. Everything changed after Ah'nyx died. Their dreams of a bright future instead became nightmares of a dark past. *If only I . . .*

S'rae took deep breaths to prevent the tears in her eyes from escalating to a downpour.

The room was warm and well lit by candles on the tables and a fire snapping in the oven. Four long stone tables were molded together, forming a square around a large stone island that radiated steam. Vayp sat alone, with his head lying on top of his crossed arms. The floor was covered with dust, but beneath the layer, in the spots where there were footprints, she saw beautiful paintings.

There was something oddly majestic about art depicting war on the dining hall floor but she couldn't put her finger on it.

Raaz'a stood in the center, wearing a long smock with blood-stains. In his hands, slung over his shoulder, was a giant leg of meat, probably from a cow.

Raaz'a noticed S'rae as she entered. "Food will be ready shortly, dear."

Before S'rae took another step, something collided into her back. She fell to her knees.

"Oh my Divine," Han'sael said, his nostrils flared, catching his breath. "You okay?"

Her hair hung over her eyes, blurring her vision. "Great. How do I look?"

"Terribgly." Han'sael smiled. "But don't worry, food makes everythin' better!"

Sigh. Terribgly? Did he mean terrible or ugly or both? Just what she wanted to hear.

S'rae looked for a place to sit. She didn't like the idea of sitting up front, probably for the same reason Vayp didn't: The thought of them staring at her while she ate made her stomach twist.

She hesitated, feeling sweat soak into her shoes. She glanced at Vayp, wondering if she should—

"You can sit with me," came Vayp's muffled voice.

Her eyes widened. "Really?"

The question hung in the air for a moment. Then Vayp shook his head and said, "Until I change my mi—"

In the time it took Vayp to finish his sentence, a cool breeze passed by, and S'rae was sitting next to him.

She flipped her hair to appear cool, not desperate. "Well, I guess I'll sit, then."

"Hi." His forehead was now planted on the table.

S'rae didn't mind his awkwardness. She liked the soft tone of his voice, the way it calmed her, making her feel like she was home again.

Tell him you miss him. Do it! Tell him you're the type of person who can be so hurt inside but can still look at him and smile. Tell him you thought about him every ni—

"Can you still move the earth?" he asked coolly.

She almost squealed, then laughed, pushing his shoulder, but didn't answer.

"So . . . can you?" Vayp asked again.

She couldn't help it. She became awkward whenever she was nervous. "Well, Fujita law states that no one can practice more than one element. It's strictly against the balance, and creates dangerous imbalances in nature." Her voice was robotic, as if she had read it.

Vayp lifted his head and raised an eyebrow. "That doesn't make any sense. Still got it?"

"Well, then . . . no, I don't. You?" She mouthed *You?* to herself, shaking her head at such a stupid question.

Of course Vayp didn't reply.

Well, aren't I amazing at making things uncomfortable.

After an awkward silence that felt like years, Vayp slid an amulet toward her. "Here."

"Wow, Vayp!" S'rae whispered, grabbing it. She loved surprises. It didn't need to be much—especially after a giftless five years. She'd be happy even if it were a random rock.

But it was neither a rock nor random. It was a circular medallion.

S'rae choked up as she held it closer to her face. It was heavy. Golden. Familiar.

Her fingers grazed across an imprint of a lotus.

Oddly familiar.

I've seen this . . . before.

Surely this wasn't the same amulet that Vayp had gotten her when he arrived back from Ah'nyx's last hunt. The one she dropped when Fujita hurried her into the airship before she left.

She left her home without a word. That hurt more than leaving. *No time for good-bye*, she remembered them yelling at her.

It wasn't her fault. They forced her, quickly. Fujitas were never late, was all they said—which was very true—but late for what? They had arrived hours earlier than the letter said they would and left immediately after. She remembered the bruises on her forearms when they yanked her into the airship. It was as if Fujita was in some kind of danger, but her village wouldn't even hurt an enemy. They were peaceful Earthies who mastered protection and tracking spells, not savages. Vayp's dad, Si'ard, the King of Opella, was said to be the greatest tracker ever. And he believed all fights could be avoided with reasoning. Fujita had nothing to fear.

S'rae felt the tiny hairs on the back of her neck and along her arms tingle as she twisted the amulet to its rear. She saw a rusted bronze case, with letters carved across it, reading: VAS.

It was . . . that amulet.

How?

"Vayp, Ah'nyx, and . . . S'rae," she whispered. She puffed her cheeks, stopping it from turning into a sob.

She choked up, anyway.

He kept it after all these years? She rolled her shoulders, bowing her head slightly, strands of her hair curling over her face as tears rolled down her cheek.

The amulet took her back, bringing her to the day when their lives changed. The day she tried to lock away in the deepest parts of her mind. The moment she relived in her nightmares.

My stomach twists when I hear his screams. They have been

going on for minutes, hours, now days.

"I'm sorry," I sob into my arms, choking on my tears each time he slams his fists into the wall. The thuds sound painful, but nothing compared to the pain I caused. I want to tell him what happened but what good will it do? Nothing good will come from the truth, the damage is done.

I walk into his room. He's lying on the floor. Fists are red with blood. Eyes black with rage. Body seems weighed down from sorrow. It's tough to fight my tears when I see his bare body with slashes, where his earthmark once was. The cuts rip across his chest. I did this!

I couldn't say anything, except watch and listen. Nothing can make him go to sleep, not even our mom's potion that works on Sols four times his size. The only thing that works is exhaustion from his body no longer being able to produce tears. I did this! "Forgive me!" I long to scream. But I know I don't deserve his forgiveness. And I'll understand if he never forgives me. This is it. This is the beginning of the end of us.

And she was right, it was the end. They never spoke again. She thought about breaking free from Fujita's grip before they took her away, to let him know how much it hurt to see them like this. But she couldn't fight off soldiers.

Not a second passed where she hadn't wished for a way to change the past.

In Opella, the lotus symbolized forgiveness and a new beginning. Was she finally forgiven? Or was she thinking too deeply into it? More than meeting Eve, she wanted this.

The ache in her chest expanded, and her eyes were suddenly hot.

Maybe time did heal his wound. Maybe choosing Fujita did work out for the better—

BANG! Raaz'a slammed the meat on top of the island. The impact sizzled, shaking the room. Vayp's head shot up, startling S'rae. His wide eyes darkened, staring straight ahead but not at anything in particular.

"Vayp," S'rae said, her hand shaking as she tried to reach for him, "everything okay?"

Raaz'a lifted a large glass bowl filled with something that looked like water. It had all of water's principles, the way it flowed and splashed around as it shook in his arms, but it roared like fire. It was liquid fire. Raaz'a poured it onto the meat. It dripped like water, but on its way down, the stream of blue rippled with red flames.

An explosion lit up the entire room. The meat sizzled and popped. Smoke filled the air.

S'rae felt her table vibrate. Vayp was trembling with fright. His legs and arms shook uncontrollably. His head jerked upright. Veins appeared on his neck, like snakes had slithered under his skin. Sweat formed into bubbles, dripping down his cheeks.

"Help!" S'rae screamed. "Something's wrong!"

The fear was sudden. Like a shivering toddler when the lights turned out.

Raaz'a was too distracted to respond, slicing into the fire with two swords in his palms. The blades moved so quickly—chopping the seared meat—that they looked like streaks of light.

The walls opened up, sucking out the smoke like a vacuum. After a few moments of screeching whistles, there were dozens of perfectly cut slabs of meat ready to be eaten.

"Lunch is ready." Raaz'a smiled.

S'rae looked back at Vayp and quickly pulled away as if she had seen an Archon. He seemed fine, like nothing had happened. His eyes faded back to a soft brown. His face no longer bubbled with sweat—rather, glistening like he had just taken a shower.

"You okay?" S'rae placed her hand on his shoulder.

"I'm fine." Vayp shrugged his shoulder so her hand fell.

"You can talk to me, you know." S'rae had never seen him like this. What'd they do to him at GroundStone? At once, she felt terrible for leaving him alone for five years. Especially after everything that happened. Maybe attending Fujita wasn't for the best. After all this time, maybe it was selfish.

"I said I'm fine!" He stood up with force, yanking the amulet from S'rae's hands. "I knew this was a mistake. I lost my appetite." He turned away and walked toward the entrance. Halfway there, his body shuddered and fists clenched. She heard a faint sigh. "It's not you," he said over his shoulder.

S'rae opened her mouth but no sound escaped. Just like that, Vayp was distant again, but she was grateful to him anyway, because for the first time since she left them, she felt less alone. She saw Raaz'a dart into a room with wooden plates in his arms. Han'sael quickly turned away; and the rest of the students were laughing, pointing their fingers at her.

S'rae ducked under the table to wipe the tears from forming. She felt embarrassed.

Thud! Something slammed the ground behind her. S'rae whirled around, ready for trouble. There stood Kaul, the tall boy from GroundStone, his dark eyes glaring into hers.

"Just when I thought Vayp might have a family," he said, grinning, "I look at you and realize you two can't be related. Hate to admit it, but he's too cute to be your brother."

S'rae narrowed her eyes. Through the opening of Kaul's robe, she saw a tattoo across his torso. It was of a rhino-looking Sol that she was almost positive had turned to growl at her.

"The Fujitas were right," Kaul sneered. "No one wants you, not even your fake brother. Why don't you tell him to stop with the lies and come forward? I may be able to get a real Earthie here, my bros. People who deserve to be here. He's the worst student to make it to the top four."

S'rae ground her teeth. She could stand insults to herself, but not to Vayp. "Vayp's better than me, and I'd crush you," she snapped back. "At least he made it here . . . unlike your bros."

"Funny. Why defend him? He never once mentioned your name. He doesn't care about you. No one does. That's why you kiss up to teachers." He puckered his lips, making kissing sounds. "I hate teacher's pets like you, asking stupid questions. No wonder you have no friends."

"Why are you being mean? What'd I do to you?"

She never understood why students were mean to her. She always had a smile on her face, treated people with respect, and was never knowingly rude. But it seemed like they wanted to be impolite for fun—where was the fun in that? There was a time when she'd confuse bullying with coincidences; when her writing utensils kept falling off her desk; when her papers flew out of her hands. And when the pages accidentally flipped whenever she read a chapter aloud. She wanted to believe these were coincidences, and that people were good, and no one would be jerks for no reason. But she was wrong. And if she found out Vayp went through the same thing at GroundStone, she was one wrong word away from making them regret every second of it.

"You're friends with loser Vayp. That's reason enough."

She stood up and wind swirled around her ankles. The rage crept in. *Give me one reason!*

"What are you gonna do? Don't be foolish, little girl," Kaul warned.

"Whatever. I'm not hungry, anyway. Enjoy your food." S'rae bowed. She kept her eyes on him the entire time. Her father told her

that she should never break eye contact with the enemy, especially during a bow. She then turned, and stared at the floor as she walked out.

"Hey!" Kaul said.

S'rae turned around, rolling her eyes. "Yes?" Her eyes landed on his tattoo, the rhino's eyes narrowed when their gaze met. It crouched, digging its hooves into Kaul's chest as if getting ready to—

BANG! At once the ground ruptured open and Kaul's Sol, the large stone rhino, lunged at Srae and chomped at her face, grazing her nose. She remained still, feeling its hot breath on her skin. She knew this was a scare test that she needed to pass. She had to show no fear or they'd think she was weak. It took everything to stop her from screaming.

"Does that actually scare people?" she yawned with a whisper. Inside she was horrified.

The Sol and Kaul fell to the floor, gasping, as if she'd sucked the air out of their lungs.

"Nothing against you, I'm sorry." She knelt, patting the Sol. Its gray fur felt rough. The Sol responded back with a smile? Weird. It was rare for a Sol to clash with the feelings of its owner. S'rae reached her palm forward to pet it once more.

Kaul stood up, breathing heavily. "Losers like you should really watch your step!"

The ground shook beneath her. She noticed the Fujitas from afar blow her a kiss, then wave. In a flash, a gust pushed her backwards as she tripped over a rock that appeared.

The back of her head crashed against the stone floor, rattling her brain. She winced as the throbbing sensation almost paralyzed her. It hurt so much that pressure welled up behind her eyes. Still, she stood up sluggishly, and forced a smile.

"Your element and words will never affect me." She bowed, her eyes locked onto Kaul's.

S'rae squinted as a gust of wind blew hair into her face.

She brushed the strands to the side, and saw the witch. Sorry, Aura'li.

"Oh, look, S'rae still can't make friends." Aura'li giggled, covering her mouth with her hand. Her fingers carried the smooth cleanliness of Fujitas who never spent a day working with their hands, no broken nails, or calluses, a privilege only for members of the elite. People who'd rather see a dozen suffer for the comfort of one of their own. "See, it wasn't just us. I think it's something about you. You'll never be liked."

"You think because you're pretty you can talk down to everyone?" S'rae lashed back. "You're arrogant. An elitist. A jerk. A—"

"Aw, thank you for noticing." Aura'li flipped her hair. "At least one of us gets noticed. Bye, peasant." Aura'li shooed S'rae away, like she was an annoying fly.

S'rae might not had been as cool or popular, but she refused to give them the satisfaction of letting them know their words got to her. She would earn their respect through grit, if nothing else.

As S'rae walked away with her head up, her fingers circled.

A frenzy of clapping, laughing, and low cursing whispers reached her ears. After several seconds of nasty comments, her eyebrows rose at one in particular: "Wow, she's amazing! I woulda curled up into a ball and rolled away."

S'rae turned around and saw Han'sael talking to himself.

He quickly hid under the table.

Her heart warmed. Despite being top of the class, that was her first compliment ever. Fujita was strict and Opella, her home, was humble. It was refreshing. She finally understood the healing power of kind words, the warmth that curled in her stomach.

She hoisted herself upright, correcting her posture. Her head still throbbed, making walking difficult. Thoughts of Vayp and the bullies slowed her down even more, but she was eager to find an empty room.

It was tougher than expected. None of the doors had handles.

She wandered aimlessly, climbing spiral staircases, and walking down dark hallways. The deeper she made it into the Spire, the darker it became. One hallway led straight into a large open space with high ceilings. It was so dark that she couldn't see where it ended. She looked up and saw a dim light shining down. Vines and moss grew up the sides of the walls, obscuring endless rows of statues and symbols carved into them.

She turned around to see if anyone was nearby, then took a long, deep breath, waving her arms in a circle. She used to think that she didn't make friends because the Fujitas were elitist jerks, but now it dawned on her: new school, different students, same problem. Maybe Aura'li was right—maybe she was the reason she had no friends. It was her fault . . . not theirs.

Immediately her body crashed, as if a heavy weight pressed onto her shoulders. She fell to her knees, and jerked her face into her palms, sobbing. Tears poured down her face, hands, and arms, soaking into her clothes. "Your words won't affect me! I won't let them!"

She cried for a few minutes and would have continued if not for the clank that she heard in the darkness. She rubbed her face with her sleeve, cleaning off the tears, and gazed down the hall.

"Hello?" She felt an uneasy discomfort in her stomach. Her nostrils were full of the smell of decay, ears alert for any sound of footsteps or voices from the hall. Her eyes scanned the darkness but she only saw a jumble of weapons cluttered against the walls, casting darker shadows.

Her eyes widened, suddenly grasping the horror of the situation. *Shadows were off limits*, she reminded herself. Fear sent a chill down her spine.

She stopped breathing and listened intently.

She knew something was watching her. She felt it shiver through her bones.

And as she put her guard up, it was too late.

Something pulled her by the shoulder. The air was sucked out of her lungs.

"Hey!" the voice shouted.

Her heart stopped beating for that moment, and she felt it sink down to her stomach.

"Whoa," Han'sael said, sweating from the heat or the walk, maybe both. "Sorry for scarin' you! I'm not a baddy, I promise. I'm not one of them. I'm not. I'm not. I just wanted—"

"Okay. Okay! I get it! What are you doing here?"

"I'm losin' my touch. You see, I got very thirsty after eatin' all that yummy food—really good by the way, you're totally missin' out—but he didn't give us any water! Can you believe it? None! I know what you're thinking. Rude, right? That's exactly what I thought, too! So, when I tracked water it led me straight here . . . Hi!"

"Oh." She paused. "No water here. Do you mind? I wanted privacy."

"No water here either? This is crazy! Madness! What are they tryna kill us of thirstivation? Hmm, is that right? Is that how you say it? Thirstiv—"

"It's just thirst. That's it."

"Really? Hmm." He stretched the *hmm* extra long. Way too long. "I always thought it was a lot longer than that. You sure?" He snorted, and she wanted to strangle him for it.

"Yes." S'rae was a few seconds away from blowing him up into a balloon, bursting him through the window overhead. She hated when her intelligence was questioned. "Privacy?"

"Right! Privatesee. I usually want some when I needa cr—wait! Were you—"

"No." Her eyebrows tugged together, and she bit the corner of her lip.

"You sure?" His eyes narrowed and his face leaned closer. She smelled meat and hot sauce from his lips. "Maybe that was the water that I sensed. Maybe I haven't lost my touch!"

"I—I just wanted to take a walk."

His eyes stayed on hers for a few moments, and then he nodded. "I'm a profreshenal crier. I know a cryin' face when I see one, and you were cryin'. It's okay, it helps your skin. I saw your face, cryin' can only help. I mean it's not too bad. Just not perfect and smooth like the Sereni Sisters, they must cry all the time!"

How, how, HOW did you make it into the top four!? "Can you leave . . . like, now?" She heard the annoyance in her voice.

"Sure, right!" It took about five minutes of searching around and a few dozen bumps before he finally remembered to leave.

"You aren't too good with people, huh?"

"I am very good with people because *I* am a person, and *I* get along with myself a lot! Hmmph!" He waddled away, taking the smell of fish and eggs with him. She then heard off-tempo steps, as if he was skipping.

S'rae rolled her eyes. Hard. And held the same blank expression, though she was happy to no longer be considered the weirdest person in school. She hoped so, at least.

With her free time, she channeled wind, searching for any interesting sounds.

After a few minutes of silence, she was about to give up, but was interrupted by a scratching noise. The sound stopped, then started up again, loud and insistent. S'rae frowned—probably a rat or something. She turned away and began to walk back to class. Before her first step, she heard a faint explosion.

She shivered. The next explosion sounded louder.

A terror-filled scream followed. S'rae could feel her pounding heartbeat in her ears. She heard more screaming—someone was in danger. She stood up, wanting to know where the sounds were coming from. Then came the loudest explosion yet. When she looked through the window, fire erupted from one of the towers. *Someone's in trouble!*

Before she could make her way to the window, she then heard a sharp, raspy sound, like a low-hissing growl. Unlike the previous sounds, this was so close she felt it graze her skin.

The hissing became louder, and she got goosebumps. Another noise sounded through the room, like something falling to the ground—a heavy object striking the floor with a thud. Her nostrils were filled with a stronger smell of decay. Her stomach twisted, as if she was being watched.

S'rae grabbed one of the swords that leaned against the wall, preparing for the worst. Unlike most of the Fujitas, she knew how to use it. Her village was filled with hunters; they fought for their food, not wait for it on a silver platter. She whipped the sword around her head before placing it in front of her.

"Han'sael?" *No, it's not him.* "I'm not afraid." Her voice trembled. "Show yourself!"

She observed a shadow that looked different. It moved in a way that rippled the air. A shriek ripped out of her throat. She staggered backwards, falling against the wall.

In that instant she looked away, she saw something out of the corner of her eye; panic made her turn and fear froze her in place.

Nothing there but complete darkness and a slow tapping sound.

Evil finds home in the darkest of places. S'rae hated herself for not listening to Raaz'a. But maybe this was all in her head. Her paranoia always did get the best of her.

I'm safe, she told herself. S'rae remembered reading something about how fear was one of the greatest weapons Fire used. Fear to intimidate. To control. Not her. She wouldn't let their scare tactics work.

And during that moment of fear, regret, then peace . . . that was when the shadowy panther emerged from the darkness.

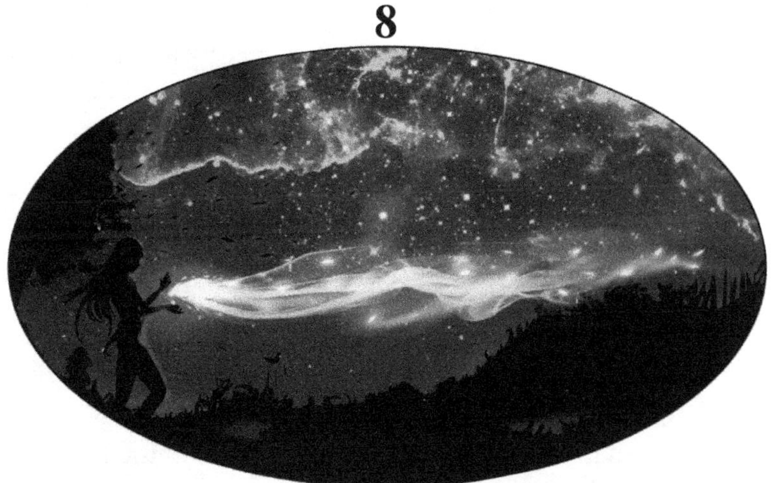

8

S'RAE RAISED HER GUARD as a shadowy panther struck at her sword. The force alone sent it crashing to the ground; she heard it clang against the stone floor before smashing into a nearby shelf. Her scream hung in the air along with the clamor of things being knocked over. Then a powerful blow from the panther's paw knocked the breath out of her. She fell backward onto a table, into swords and daggers that ripped through her skin.

S'rae looked down and saw holes in her robe, framed by circles of blood. Her adrenaline had kicked in, making her unaware of the pain that surged throughout her body.

"Help!" she screamed.

The panther vanished from her sight, fading into the shadows; but she felt its presence. Its rotten scent still lingered.

Heart pumping, she ran into the open where a bright light shone down on her. She saw stray weapons and broken wood scattered across the floor. She thought about running, but she didn't want to risk giving the beast her back. Even if she managed to get away,

then others would be in danger. What if Vayp got attacked next? It needed to end here and now.

Her hands clenched. A gust of wind howled through the room. She heard clangs from the sharp weapons spiraling around her, scraping against the walls and floor.

"Come get me, I dare you," she growled.

Then a heavy force threw her to the floor and she felt the beast's body absorb through hers. In that moment she felt weightless, like it had taken a piece of her soul.

She was pinned to the ground, but her hands were free to conjure up more wind. She closed her eyes and heard the sounds of the room, giving her vision in the darkness. She heard something slide across the ground, and then wind wrapping around the beast's body as it lunged straight at her.

Gusts twirled around her, picking up stray daggers. She placed her palms together.

The beast's mouth widened with a hiss.

"*Ka'ze.*" She then extended her arms upward, screaming so hard her throat hurt. "*HAA!*"

BANG! A burst of wind shot from her palms. Her back cratered into the floor and her hair and clothes danced.

Daggers torpedoed into the panther's body, blasting it toward the large window overhead. *That better be enough*, she hoped, trailing the panther's arc with her eyes.

BANG! Shattered glass sparkled its way down, roaring like a waterfall.

A breeze slid her out of the way then sent her into the air and through the window.

Her stomach lifted to her heart as she descended dozens of feet, the wind caressing her to the ground as softly as silk. And when she landed gently, the beast was nowhere to be seen, just bare spindly trees and broken, moss-covered statues. But still her nostrils twitched, catching its distinct odor.

She tried to pull her fists up, but she was weak and felt blood dripping down her legs. As she fainted to her knees, and saw bite marks on her arm, pain suddenly surged through her body like barbed wire in her veins. It was the poison. Yup, her time was up. She wished she was wrong, but she had studied this extensively for her Herbology classes. The way a cold finger of death drew a trail down her chest, she knew. She had only a few minutes—maybe less—until her blood hardened and strangled her heart. *Poison. Maybe this is what I deserve.*

Even if there was a cure within arm's reach, a part of her didn't know if she would take it anymore. She had almost completely accepted her fate. The hollowness that she felt in the pit of her stomach—the one that was afraid of the unknown—was no longer there. She couldn't explain it, but the closer she came to death, the more she felt connected to life, to nature, to the planet. It made her feel at home. Her body tingled, feeling the most complete she had ever felt.

S'rae wasn't superstitious. She did not believe in anything she could not see. Still, something told her that this wasn't the end. The end of her life right now, yes. But not her soul. As if there was something greater, like the circle of Time was as real as the circle of life. Maybe she'd come back as a vibrant red rose with thorns. Something beautiful but tough, she hoped.

Her head twitched, reacting to a snap in the wind. But when she tried to open her eyes, her vision was blurry and everything was red. If she could see her eyes, she'd know they were bloodshot. She rubbed them and grimaced at the streak of blood along the side of her hand. It was over. This was it.

She pinched the bridge of her nose as her head reeled from the

poison.

It was then when the panther re-emerged, she could smell it. It lunged at her, she could hear it. It aimed to kill, she could sense it.

She bowed her head and accepted her fate. It snuck up behind her, so close that she felt its hot breath; its fangs were an inch away from ripping through her body.

BANG! A powerful blow crashed into her side, hitting her so hard she tumbled like a boulder rolling down a cliff. By the time she managed to shake off the dizzying feeling, she looked up and noticed a massive blur rip a smaller blur in half.

She recognized the panther's squeal as a poof of black smoke materialized before drifting away like sand in the wind.

Was it dead? What killed it? *Is that a Sol?* She squinted, hoping to set her vision into focus, but all she saw was a fuzzy dot in the distance. It roared and just like that, it was gone.

Did one of the GroundStone students protect me? Or . . . was that . . . my . . . Sol? It only comes when you least expect it. Maybe that was the one. Figures . . . it would *come right before I die.*

Then, as if her mind was hallucinating, a bright light floated through the air, like a single snowflake. It called to her in ways she couldn't describe. At first she thought it was foolish to play into her mind's game. Then curiosity prevailed. What did she have to lose? She scrambled to her feet, as best as she could, and followed it with a limp.

She saw a narrow path straight ahead, that led her through waist-high lifeless grass, brown and dry, almost hidden by the shadows of protective naked trees. She crested the hill and saw the light land on a stone in front of a cave. It absorbed into a boulder surrounded by dirt.

A bright glow resonated inside.

She looked around to see if anyone was near. Her vision blurred for a moment, and she stumbled to regain balance. Her movements were sluggish. The wounds stung when they stuck to her robe, and the back of her head throbbed.

She considered opening the rock, but using another element was strictly against Fujita code. That was what she told Vayp. She looked around once more. *But I'm not at Fujita, am I?*

The ground shook as she clenched her fists. The stone rattled, slowly lifting off the ground. She pressed her fists together, then pulled them away.

BANG! The boulder split in half. A pearlescent orb dropped onto the soil. She picked it up. It was small enough to fit in her palm, but big enough that she couldn't completely close her hand around it.

She found it both beautiful and intimidating. And in that moment, it happened, she was dying. She was sure of it. Images rolled through her mind too quickly. Just as it was described in her Life Before and After Death class. She saw Ahy'nyx, Vayp, Opella. She saw Fujak, Gabrael, the Valley, and the panther. She then saw shadows, ones darker than the night. They whispered to her, telling her that the end was soon. That the Valley will fall. And a Shadow Army will be reborn along with *him. Him?*

Before she could think, a light flashed before her eyes. Lush trees and grass towered over her, violet and red petals crunched underfoot, meticulous stone monuments and spires rose from the ashes. Felines and phoenixes, large and small, leapt and flew by, their radiant colors made her jaw drop. Students in red robes, ran around laughing, shooting sparks and flames from their palms.

Though it was just a flash, the image of how beautiful the Valley once looked hurt when she finally noticed the gray rubble before her. *This is death. What happened to the Valley? It used to be so beautiful.*

As she tried to make sense of what happened, something more unexplainable happened. The rips in her robe stitched back together. The open wounds sealed up. Air entered her lungs in fresh waves. Her vision cleared. The poison . . . gone?

But how? She looked at her hands as if they were not her own.

What was happening? Was her mind playing tricks? Is this a sign or something? *Was I supposed to find this?* Maybe she was already dead.

Ow! She pinched herself. Guess not.

She'd never felt anything like this before, but there was nothing mentioned about a power like this in any of the books. She felt better than ever, more energized, more alive.

She spun around and noticed Vayp standing on top of the hill, smirking.

How long was he there? Did he see everything? To be safe, she hid the orb in her pocket. Something in her knew that this was too big of a secret to share. It felt like it was hers. A gift.

"Our hour is up." Before Vayp turned away, he smiled at S'rae. "I knew you still got it."

The sky cleared and a ray of light fell across them, illuminating Vayp's hands and the red lines on his palms.

"What's wrong? Your hands, they're bleeding!" S'rae gasped, pressing her hands to her mouth. She watched his hands, his long, scarred fingers. She almost forgot the damage physical labor caused on a body. At Fujita they wore no such marks, just the manicured hands of those who never had to fight for their food or build a fire. Vayp's hands had the power to crush stone but the precision to draw intricate tracking spells in the sand. Hands that she missed clinging to whenever a howl ripped through the darkness. Hands that made her feel safe. "Were you attacked by anything shadowy?"

"Heh," Vayp smirked. "Attacked? Me? You don't have to worry

about me. So don't."

And as they walked toward the Spire, S'rae was expecting to cringe at the sight of the broken window, but to her surprise, it was perfectly intact as if a battle had never transpired. "What the—the window?" S'rae whimpered. "It's not broken?"

Vayp looked mildly concerned. "That window was never broken. Are you okay?"

She was already suspicious about being here, now she was more worried and scared.

Be safe, she remembered Professor Ki's words—the fear in his eyes made her body tingle. *Be safe from what?*

So far, everything about the Valley seemed mysterious and dangerous, not safe. But more important, what was that thing that saved her life? For a second, she could almost understand the feeling of having a Sol. The idea of sharing life with another being that would watch over her and protect her at all times was amazing. That was what it felt like. Like something had been watching over her, ready to risk its life to save her. She wished she knew for sure, but now more than ever, she wished she had a Sol of her own.

"Do you know anything about shadow monsters? Talking ones?" S'rae asked Vayp.

His eyes darkened as he froze in place. S'rae could see his hands shaking from inside his pockets. And the way his face bubbled with sweat and how his eyes darted from side to side she couldn't tell if he was nervous or scared. "Why would you ask that? Raaz'a warned us about shadows."

"I know, but what if there's something they're not telling us?"

"You're right," sneered a cold voice from behind them. "We never told you what happened to students who are late."

As they turned, Raaz'a emerged from smoke, his blazing sword pointing directly at them.

9

DESTROU VERSUS RANMAU. The lowly versus the un-stoppable—the big moment that Destrou had spent sleepless nights preparing for.

While the crowd of boys surrounding them watched and waited, Destrou concentrated on his surroundings to calm his anxiety. The Wall, how could he not focus on it? It was the one thing that always stared back at him, letting him know how unattainable freedom was. It looked like it was carved from a bright white ice that held the sun's light even after it set. The sky was gray, as always, and he could see the slight shimmer of the Hanging Star, reflecting the sun. It was a type of orb placed on a pole, hundreds of feet high, and seen from anywhere in the Village. They never knew its purpose or how it got there—it was there before the Guardians came to oversee the Village a few decades ago. Once a week it glowed a bright white light like a star, and that was how the nickname became official. Destrou had never seen it up close, but Ranmau would stay up late, almost every night, just to see if it would glow again. Destrou knew Ranmau had never wanted anything as much in his whole life. But there was something calming about its presence that helped Destrou shut his eyes and prepare for battle. He inhaled deeply, feeling the fresh cold air bring life to his lungs.

Opening his eyes, Destrou reached his hands into his pouch and spun around, launching all but one of his dozen balls. They headed toward Ranmau, a tail of snow trailing behind, screeching through the air like a high-pitched whistle. They were well placed, covering a large circumference. Contact seemed unavoidable.

Ranmau remained frozen like a statue, despite the balls barreling in on him. His emotionless look, unchanged. His confidence, untouched. But right before contact was made, he lifted into the air, and performed an aerial flip, twisting and turning his body to avoid contact. Waves of cold air breezed by his body so close that Destrou noticed layers of frost appear on his clothes.

Destrou felt an odd sensation in his stomach, as if bugs were trying to crawl out. He took a deep breath, recovering from the shock, and lifted his head. When he stood up, he ran his fingers through the fur on his pants. His palms were sweaty, and the gesture helped him remain calm as he prepared for Ranmau's attack. Truthfully, he was as proud as he was defeated. He couldn't be jealous of Ranmau for his skills, because he admired him so much.

Destrou crouched, readying himself. Ranmau merely smirked.

Ranmau stretched his body. His arms hung over his head, his neck snapped into his shoulders, and he stood with his legs far apart, forming a triangle, just like he always did right before he won a challenge.

For a few moments, nothing happened. Then Ranmau grabbed a ball and somersaulted, catapulting it into the air. It created a high-pitched whistle, splitting through the wind. All eyes were on the spinning snowball. Destrou's shoulders locked; he realized Ranmau's strategy almost too late, dodging a projectile that boomed across his shoulders. Most didn't even see what happened. To the untrained eye, it looked like Destrou dodged air.

Then the real fight began. One after the other, compacted snow missiles blazed past Destrou. What was equally splendid was Destrou's ability to dodge what others saw as invisible streams of wind. He looked calm but his lungs wheezed for air.

Ranmau gripped the remaining balls with one hand and launched them simultaneously, spinning around twice. His back faced Destrou, as if he knew with certainty that the challenge was over.

Destrou wasn't to be taken lightly. He could make it, if he was careful, by focusing on the balls' patterns. It didn't matter where they were as much as where they were going. Ranmau had an interesting way to curve the wind, something that the boys considered cheating. Destrou saw the balls' twisting routes, and braced himself. He reached into his pouch, grabbing his last ball, then performed an aerial, evading each ball as it spiraled past the fabric in between his arms and legs. He felt the cold of the snow absorb into his clothes.

While spinning, he swung his arm as fast as he could. His shoulder burned from the sudden motion, releasing the ball with a roar. For that moment, the impossible suddenly seemed possible. His weeks of training had led to this.

"I did it!" Destrou shouted just as the ball reached Ranmau.

With a swift nod to the side, it missed, grazing past Ranmau's head. He didn't even blink as the force blew hair into his face, shimmering like liquid metal.

Destrou landed in disbelief, placing his hands to the ground, stopping his twisting momentum. Who won?

His body became tense. When he looked up, the snowball that Ranmau first launched had found its way back down, landing perfectly on his face, splashing over his snow-tipped dreads.

"Too easy," Ranmau said coldly over his shoulder. His words

sent a chill down Destrou's throat. Ranmau didn't turn around to witness his victory; somehow and some way, he knew he'd won.

There was no acknowledgment—not even a look in Destrou's direction. No celebration. Destrou noticed that Ranmau's seething eyes were cutting between the Wall and the Forest, as if he was deciding on which path to take. His mood suddenly altered as if there was a switch within him controlling his emotions. Destrou had seen that look before, a glimpse of hatred buried behind his brother's gray eyes. Ranmau shuddered for a moment, then he walked off toward the Village. He never once looked back. And just like that, Destrou lost his brother. Again.

It happened so fast. Their brotherly connection over. Now he had to wait two more weeks.

Why don't you love me anymore? You used to show me all the time. I miss it. I miss you.

Destrou remained unmoving as if the ball had sent a shock through his spine, freezing him in place.

After a few deep breaths, everyone was gone.

The area was empty.

Left in his solace, his gut feelings once again plagued his thoughts. This was what he feared the most. He never let fear get to him—at least tried not to. Before he went to sleep, he repeated the same words: *Ranmau won't leave me. I am still alive, not alone.* Those words helped him sleep better, but he wished they were true. He felt it in the darkest part of his mind that his time with Ranmau was slipping away. He needed to win but he had failed, again.

There weren't enough hours in the day to train, and it still wasn't enough. It could be too late. If Ranmau's mind had already wandered off, his body would soon follow—like the others.

The others were the boys who wanted freedom and tried to escape by climbing the Wall, only to be found a day later on the ice,

flattened like a puddle of skin and crushed bones.

Destrou looked over his shoulder at the Wall. Its top shrouded by thick gray clouds sweeping over the sky. If that was Ranmau's plan—to test his fate against the Wall—then no matter what, Destrou would be alone. Succeed and he was gone. And failure meant death.

Destrou wiped the icicles off his eyes and began his trek back to the Village. Directly behind it was the cliff looking down into the Forest. Its haunting presence terrified most boys but, to him, the closer the better. Because the Forest was his escape when he needed peace.

He saw its darkness just over the horizon, absorbing all light as if it was forbidden. For a moment he had a deep yearning for something . . . his brother, Ranmau, his comfort, letting him know that everything would be okay and that his thoughts of abandonment were untrue.

Why do you want to leave so badly? Why am I never good enough?

With a long walk ahead, he dove into his memories. Visualizing the past was his favorite way of escaping the present.

The Village delegated tasks to the boys based on their age, height, and strength. At only nine years old, Ranmau had a growth spurt, upgrading him to a more difficult task: hauling large blocks of ice for building. Although the Leader instructed him on his new role, he didn't want to leave Destrou alone, and refused to until they threatened to tell the Guardian. If word made it to the Guardian, the Village would have had one less mouth to feed.

Destrou's job was to dispose of leftover food from the NoGo. Most of the time it was only half eaten. Hunger was rampant in the Village yet still, no matter how hungry he was, he pried the meat off the bones and chucked them over the cliff or into the Maze. It was dangerous to feast on the job. Defying Guardians resulted in punishment far worse than death.

They had seen it done too many times. The nightmares still woke Destrou up at night.

Once in awhile, Ranmau finished his job quickly to help Destrou. One day, Destrou was minding his own business when a few teenagers hassled him. They pushed and shoved him around and pressed his back against a wall. He could smell urine in their breath as if they had drunk their own pee—most likely they had. There was no choice; he either had to prolong the beating or get it over with quickly. He neither resisted nor screamed for help, because if Ranmau came to help—and he would—they would've bullied him, too. He had seen what happened to the boys who tried to fight back. The pain, the welts from rope marks on their bodies and faces, the defeat in their eyes as they slouched their heads for days. The Village was cruel, turning boys into victims—if not from the Guardians, then from their peers. But not Ranmau. So Destrou remained silent as fists smashed into his face. He felt his jaw widen with the taste of blood—the same blood that stained the snow around him. If he cried, he'd risk more harm. He loved Ranmau too much to give in. He wanted to share everything with him, but pain wasn't one of those things.

The beating that had followed had been one of the worst ever.

Time ran out. His body couldn't numb the agony. It was shutting down.

The punches. The kicks. He kept telling himself that it was almost over but his eyes swelled up more and he choked on his own blood. The choking sounds did it. He didn't want to choke, but the whole Village could hear it.

Through the swelling of his bloody eyes, he saw a red hue of many distorted shapes and colors smear his vision.

He saw one of the boys, terrified.

That was *him*—the boy he couldn't recognize with the white scarf wrapped around his face. It all made sense why he looked familiar.

A few moments later, the boy ran off and came back, and Ranmau followed closely. Ranmau turned the corner in a sweaty craze. He saw Destrou curled into a fetal position.

The boys looked at him, then continued kicking as if he wasn't there. Ranmau had seen small acts of bullying but nothing like this. Before his growth spurt, he wouldn't act on it. But on that day, a new Ranmau was born. A protector revealed itself.

Ranmau's fists kept moving until he was the only one left standing. He lifted Destrou by his arm and said, "I won't let them hurt you anymore."

That was the closest they came to brotherly love. No more shared bed or laughs. They became strangers bound by blood but nothing more. Still, the only thing that Destrou feared more than death was losing his brother. He was all he had.

Destrou felt the muscles in his face tighten, remembering the past carried a bittersweet nostalgia.

The memory haunted him as he climbed the mounds of snow toward the cliff. A wall of tangled ice shards protected it from unwanted eyes.

Destrou snuck through unharmed.

A few krillens had tried, but the dried-up blood and ripped cloth stuck onto the spikes were reminders that they weren't welcome. Only small boys were allowed.

This used to be their place, but now it was just another reminder of a past they no longer shared.

When Destrou was done thinking about the pain, and being alone, and Ranmau leaving him, he looked up to notice that he had walked across the entire Village and stood at the cliff. "Wow . . . I'm here?" He scratched his head. He had forgotten walking the miles through the ice. At some point he had fallen, too, and lain in the snow, but he didn't really remember that either.

Crunch! He became wide awake at the sound of someone stepping in snow.

A boy sat in front of him, legs crossed, staring ahead at the Forest of Ness.

A boy. Alone. Miles away from Ranmau. From help.

This was no doubt a dangerous situation.

Destrou looked down at the footprints in the snow. The way they dragged, creating streaks, he couldn't tell if they were big or small. If they were big, he was in trouble; if they were small, he'd handle it.

I can do this!

"Hey." Destrou deepened his voice. "Who are you?"

The boy was about the same size as Destrou and had shoulder length blond hair that was pulled into a bun on top of his head. He grabbed a cloth that rested at his side, then wrapped it completely around his head.

Destrou's heart stopped as the boy pressed his palm into the snow.

The boy lifted to his feet. A sharp weapon—like a dagger— hung from his belt.

Destrou clenched his fist, preparing for the worst. He had nothing to shield himself.

Maybe if he defended the blow with his forearm, he'd be given one good strike. He had to make sure he aimed right at the jaw, just like Ranmau showed him. That was all he needed.

The boy started to turn around.

His back still faced Destrou.

This was the perfect time to strike—from behind. Destrou wanted to but knew he shouldn't. It was wrong. Something that Ranmau had said countless times. If he wasn't strong enough to beat a boy face-to-face, he had no business hitting him from behind. Still, even when Ranmau wasn't present, Destrou did not want to disappoint him.

Wait for it.

Destrou's heart raced.

The boy reached for his belt.

Now!

Instantly, the boy whipped around then grabbed Destrou's wrist and swung the weapon for his neck. Its blade—a whisker from his throat—felt deathly cold.

It happened too quickly. The grip was sudden and tight. He felt his hand go numb from the pressure.

Destrou gasped with terror—yet shocked to be alive—as he stared into the boy's blue eyes. He immediately recognized them. They belonged to *him.*

The blade slowly inched away.

Destrou waited for the boy to speak. This wasn't the best time to startle him.

"Sorry," the soft voice replied, "I wasn't expecting anyone here tonight." He pulled the blade away, twisting it back into his belt.

Destrou's muscles tensed and his eyes widened. He felt as if a chunk of ice slid down his chest into his stomach. He was nervous without really knowing why. The blade to his throat didn't scare him as much as talking did. Maybe it was because the only person he'd ever had a conversation with was Ranmau, and now the longest ones consisted of "hi" and "bye".

Destrou tried to open his mouth, but he mumbled incoherently.

"Excuse me?" the boy said. He leaned forward and made eye

contact.

Destrou scrunched his nose, and lifted his palms in the air. Anxiety had tied his tongue into knots.

"Oh, right, I get it now." The boy laughed. "That means 'I'm nervous' in mumble talk. It's okay, I don't bite, at least not anymore. My name is Elu'nex, but you can call me Elu. It's nice to finally introduce myself."

His smile made Destrou feel warm inside.

For the first time in Destrou's life a situation turned out better than he thought it would.

And in that instant, he realized that his life would never be the same again.

10

DESTROU FELT A WARM SENSATION tingle through his body. A name. This was the first time a Villager had introduced himself without it being followed by fists to the face. And it felt amazing.

Butterflies fluttered in his stomach. "Elu, that's a cool name. Mine is Destrou." He had a high-pitched squeal at the end, failing to hold back his excitement.

Destrou noticed how Elu's eyes sparkled a deep, sky blue when the light hit them a certain way. They were almost calming to look at. His fur scarf usually covered his mouth but today it pulled over his forehead and tucked under his chin. His mittens were torn, revealing scarred fingers with a layer of patchy, rough skin. With his eyes never showing anything less than squinted smile lines, it shocked Destrou to see that he was a victim of many painful frostbites. But then again, he too was a master at smiling off pain.

Elu laughed, patting his palms against his knees. "Of course, I know your name, silly."

"But I never talked to you before."

Elu raised his head, then lifted his hands in the air. There was something gentle about the gesture, something that would normally cause Destrou to raise his own hands in defense, but the way Elu did it seemed welcoming, like a hug. "You and Ranmau are the coolest people in the Village, how could I not know your name?"

"Really? You think I'm the coolest?" Destrou blushed.

"Duh!" Elu said, walking closer. There was a slight skip to his step. "Well, maybe not as cool as Ranmau, but what you two do every challenge is amazing. A whole village against two, and we can never win. What's not amazing about that?"

"I dunno. I guess I didn't think being hated is that amazing—it sure doesn't feel it."

Elu laughed, but when Destrou's face remained serious he said, "Oh, sorry, guess it's not that funny, my sense of humor isn't the greatest. I find the weirdest things funny."

Destrou sighed deeply. "It's okay, I used to love laughing."

"Yeah! Laughing is great, isn't it? Tough to have a bad day when you're laughing. But what do you mean 'used to'? When was the last time you laughed?"

Destrou's head started to ache as he sifted through his memories. "Oh yeah, I remember—" He giggled, as if reliving the moment. "It was about two years ago."

"Two years ago!" Elu's hands fell to his sides and his smile faded. "That was so long ago," he said softly.

"Yeah, we used to laugh and smile all of the time until, well, you know . . ."

"Yeah." Elu looked down, kicking his feet across the snow. "I'm sorry about all the bad stuff. I wish I could do something, but I'm too small to make a difference."

"I dunno, this is the best I've felt in a while. I think you're just the right size to make a difference. I can't wait to have laughs with

Ranmau again."

Elu's smile lines came back then faded away as quickly as they had appeared, his eyes seeming to lose their color. He looked uncomfortable, holding his steepled fingers in front of him. "But you don't have much time left with him, do you?"

Heart hammering in his chest, Destrou's eyebrows rose and his hands trembled. Negative thoughts of abandonment had already filled his head; that was the last thing he wanted to hear.

"You don't know?" Elu said, his eyes widened with shock.

Destrou was at loss for words, swallowing the first ones that came to mind. He couldn't tell if Elu knew something or was blatantly trying to scare him. "Is he okay? What's wrong?"

"You really don't know?" Elu walked up to Destrou so that they were face to face. They were almost the same height; Elu was half an inch taller, probably because of the scarf around his head. They stared directly into each other's eyes. Destrou's eyes told the story of a longing worry.

"You really don't," Elu said. "That means he's keeping it a secret—even from you. Follow me."

Together they walked the icy paths. The air grew colder over the next hour and a half—or was it the terrifying thought of Ranmau leaving that sent shivers through his body?

He didn't know.

Elu led the way to a high place in the northernmost corner of the Valley where they could look over the land. Behind them, the NoGo shone brightly. To the side, the Forest of Ness was void of light. And directly in front of them, the Wall, reflecting the last light of the setting sun. From this height, the igloos were small round specks no bigger than Destrou's fingernail. The land around them was white and snowy, where unsettled snow circled in the wind. The Maze of No Return was barely visible at the southernmost part of the Village. No one knew why its stone walls were designed like a maze, they just knew that boys went missing whenever curiosity overcame fear.

Far in the distance, to the southwest, he saw the dip that dropped a few hundred feet into the valley.

Destrou had never explored it; getting down was difficult, but climbing up seemed impossible. Beyond that was the Wall. The Wall was everywhere except to the east. The Forest of Ness claimed the east and most of the horror stories told.

Destrou heard a low rumble like distant thunder. It belonged to the tall, revolving pole grinding against the ice, like a drill through wood. When Destrou arched his neck back far enough, he could see the reflection of the Hanging Star.

Destrou pushed his fingers through his hair. "Why are we here?"

Elu's mouth twisted as Destrou turned to him. "Notice anything different?"

"No." Destrou walked up to the Wall. "I don't really like being anywhere near it. Why?"

Elu pressed his hand against the ice, rubbing his finger into a deep gash. "These markings started out low . . . but now"—he arched his head back—"I can't even see where they end."

Destrou staggered backwards. A bead of sweat frosted from his forehead to his nose. He wiped it off with his sleeve, then looked up at the Wall. *It's . . . true. You're leaving me—*

"He's getting closer each day. If anyone could climb it, I'd bet all my food on him."

As Elu had his focus turned away from him, Destrou walked across the untouched snow toward the cliff that overlooked the Forest. Elu kept talking but his voice trailed off—the sounds of Elu and the howling wind and the rumbling pole drowned out into a muffle. All Destrou could hear was his own heartbeat. It was racing, as fast as a drumroll. His breaths hitched in an occasional sob, which he suppressed. Destrou's toes poked over the edge. Chunks of ice broke off, falling into the darkness. *I can't survive without you. I won't hold you back.*

He stared down at the endless forest. He leaned forward and was about to jum—

"DESTROU? *DON'T DO IT!*" Elu turned toward Destrou. His eyes widened.

Hundreds of feet below, Destrou noticed a spiderweb of dark silhouettes, as if the Divine One had splattered black paint on top of a dark canvas. The branches looked sharp and mysterious and vast. The longer he stared at them, the more they turned into objects, as if they were different faces in the clouds. He turned his head at the sound of Elu's voice. It took a few moments for his eyes to focus. Destrou felt his heart sink. "I knew that it wasn't all in my head. When he leaves, I'm dead."

"Destrou!" Elu shouted. "Listen to me. You don't want to do anything crazy. It's not the end if he leaves."

"How do you know? You don't know what it's like to live in fear everyday, and the only one keeping you alive is the one who wants to leave."

"You're right, I don't know what your life is like, but I do know about mine. I know that I was right where you were, looking down over the cliff, wanting to end it all, too. I saw exactly what you're looking at right now. The branches that make an *X* and an *O*, and the ones right next to them that look like smiley faces." Elu took a step closer, slowly. "I wondered why those trees lived in darkness but still looked happier than me. And when you stand there long enough, the trees begin to stare back at you. Like they want you to join them. To jump. And I wanted to."

"You're just saying that," Destrou whimpered, his eyes streaming with tears.

"Am I?" Elu said softly. "Look for yourself."

Destrou looked down and saw exactly what Elu described. He felt a large lump in his throat, making it difficult to swallow. "Well, why didn't you?"

"I didn't for the same reason you won't."

"Why?" Destrou blinked, unable to focus now. Tears blurred his vision.

"Because, after all of the bad . . . maybe, there's something good waiting."

"There's nothing good about the Village."

"That's what I thought, but I was wrong, let me show you. I know secrets. A million of them! I can show you what you've been missing. I know there's more good here than what's down there. And now I'll have to go after you." Elu stretched his back, arms, and legs, as if getting ready to jump.

"You don't want to."

"You're right, I don't want to, but someone has to help you. And looks like I'm the only one here. I'm not even worried about the fall, it'll hurt, but I'm more worried about the beasts or . . . the Archons."

Destrou's eyebrows rose. The fear of what could happen sank in.

"What do you know about Archons?"

"I know that I'd never want to see them; that they can steal your soul and make you into one of them. My heart's too good for it to work on me, though." Elu winked. "I'd never want to become one, but you aren't giving me much of a choice now, are you?" He slowly stepped closer, like moving up on an injured wild animal. "Do you really want to?"

Destrou met Elu's eyes. "What else do you know?"

Elu smiled. "Enough to make me not shut up for a few weeks. We can start now."

"Promise?"

"I promise that by the time Ranmau leaves, you'd want to explore the world, too."

With slow movements, Destrou reached a hand toward Elu. Elu grasped it. He had soft hands despite the frostbite. Destrou's hands started to shake. His suppressed fear of heights finally came back.

"I'm not going to let you jump," Elu said. "You're not dying on me. Not now. Not ever."

A sudden joy shone through Destrou, breaking into a smile. "First secret: Do you know where we came from? Like . . . how?"

"Oh boy," Elu said. "That's a big question, save it for another day."

"Why?"

"Well, it's just awkward, you know?"

"How?"

"Well, if you really wanna know, it's about a girl and a boy and that's *all* I'm saying! It's nasty!"

"So there are boys here but no more girls. Why?"

"Girls . . . ummm . . . had it . . . rough," Elu said. "If you think your life is hard . . . imagine it a hundred times harder. They say that girls were used for one thing. And after they gave birth, some wouldn't survive. If a boy was born, he'd be taken away and kept in the Village, if a girl was born, she'd get taken away to the Kingdom. Except there was one—"

"A girl?"

"You didn't hear it from me, don't tell anyone!"

"Who'd I tell? You're my only friend . . ." Destrou hesitated, mad at himself for blurting it out. "I mean—"

"I'm your friend?" Elu said.

"I didn't mean it. I'm sorry." Destrou looked away.

"No, I like that!" Elu's eyes crinkled.

"Me too." Destrou turned back with a smile of his own.

Elu sighed for a brief moment before continuing the story.

"There was a rumor that a girl was born, but the mother didn't want her to live this type of life; so, she escaped with her. The last thing they saw was her footprints leading straight to the Forest. I guess death was better than life." Elu's blue eyes crystallized with a teary glow. "And the third Guardian. The good one. He was blamed for helping; so he was sent to the Forest."

Destrou remembered something about there once being a third Guardian. He was too young. The memory of him appeared as blurry images: a tall man dragging a large sword through the snow, toward the Edge. It was as if he was preparing for a battle he had already lost.

Destrou did not know his name. And he recalled a story about what the Guardian would do to anyone—including his brother—if he was betrayed.

Sad. The Guardian's own brother was sent to the Forest. In the dark. Alone. On a mission, they said, but the Village knew the real reason why the Kingdom banished him. No food. No way back. Maybe his screams were the ones Destrou heard at night.

The truth. The truth was that he—the missing Commander— defied the Kingdom. The truth was that the Kingdom was filled with bad men eliminating good people. Destrou understood the sorrow in Elu's voice. Proof why he never wanted Ranmau to leave. Life was cruel, unfair, and would turn the purest souls into nothing, a memory—or something evil, with enough time.

Destrou gently patted Elu, then heard the revolving pole rumble louder. "Why does the Hanging Star glow?" He pointed at it, hoping to lighten the mood.

Elu whipped his head around rapidly. He appeared confused. "That's *not* its name."

"That's what everyone calls it."

"Yes, *they* call it that, but *I* know its real name."

"How?"

"Because, I told you already, silly, I know secrets. And I'm the reason it glows."

"Really?"

"Yup! It glows whenever I say its name."

"What's its name, then? Show me!"

"I can't tell you!" Elu gasped, scrunching his chin to his neck.

"How about if I tell you one of my secrets, then you tell me this one?"

"Maybe."

"Well, my secret is . . . I haven't bathed in four months."

"Ew! That's not a secret, that's just gross."

"Yeah, but you didn't know that about me."

"Yeah, believe me I wish I didn't."

"But you promised to tell me secrets!"

Elu puffed through his nose. "Fine, but some *are* more important. Just promise not to tell anyone! Not even Ranmau!"

"Promise!" Destrou's eyes widened. He felt his stomach twist with excitement. For the first time, he felt important. No one had ever told him a secret before.

Elu leaned in to whisper, as if to make sure that not even the wind could hear. "It's called . . . the Eye . . . of . . . Eve."

At once, the Eye of Eve hummed and shone a bright white light.

S'rae's hairs stood up as a vibration on her leg startled her. She looked to her side and noticed that her pocket glowed a bright white light. Her eyes widened, hoping that she didn't get caught with it. Luckily, since she arrived late—a mistake she would never make again—her seat was taken and she had to sit in the back of the classroom. Raaz'a's threat was just a warning, but a scary one that involved writing scriptures on her body with a hot iron. She hated to admit it, but the scare tactic did work. She was never going to be late again.

She glanced around the room to see if anyone noticed the light. Han'sael was too busy trying to peel a layer of skin off a fruit. And Vayp was too busy glaring at Han'sael.

Phew, no one saw that. Can this thing be the Eye? A coincidence. It's just a story, right?

Curiosity consumed her mind and she had to ask. She cleared her throat. "Excuse me."

"Yes." Although Gabrael's eyes were covered, she could feel that his attention was on her, like two lasers sizzling her skin.

"I-I don't get it." S'rae paused. "Why are there no girls in the Village? Why is it all ice and snow? And what did Elu mean when he said they were looking for a girl?" At first she'd thought it was a useless exercise being read a story. She was fifteen years old, not months, but the story world intrigued her—so different from her own. Yet in some odd way . . . the same.

"Great questions. In fact, the same ones that I had. How I miss hearing questions, they are the one key to unlock knowledge that no law can take away."

His smile warmed her heart in a way that made her appreciate a professor—or anyone for that matter—who wasn't bothered by her barrage of questions. A light clicked on in her mind, and she suddenly understood where the saying a "warm smile" came from. It was the universal language of kindness, after all. Something that she had almost forgotten existed. At times, Fujita felt too cold and

competitive to be warm and kind.

"Throughout this story," he continued, "you will find yourself asking many questions, but I have found that with patience, answers appear even for questions you were afraid to ask."

As Gabrael was about to continue reading, S'rae rose her hand again.

"Yes," Gabrael said.

Heat pressed against her face, as if she dumped her head in a bowl of hot water.

"What exactly is the Eye?" S'rae asked, not wanting to repeat its name. She thought she knew everything there was to know about Eve, but despite the dozens of books she had read, they never once mentioned this. What else were the schools hiding from her . . . from them?

"The Eye of E—"

"Yes, that."

"Well, there are many stories about its importance. It originated from nature itself. And it is said to have healing powers, but can be very, very dangerous when in the wrong hands."

"Why's it in the Village?"

"Well, I imagine we shall find out when we keep reading."

S'rae felt anxiety build. She still had many questions to ask, but not enough time. She knew that Gabrael didn't have the big answers that she wanted though: Why her? Why was she attacked? Yes, evil lurked in shadows, but that didn't explain the screams that she heard? Was he being tortured? What led her to the Eye of Eve? If that was really it. And why were they really invited to the Valley after three thousand years?

She couldn't help it. She needed to ask one more question!

In the time it took Gabrael to finish the first word, S'rae interrupted him.

"But what about the girl they're looking for?" S'rae asked. She heard sighs, and knew the other students were already annoyed by her curiosity. "Oh, hush," she snapped.

"Out of all the girls you may have studied about, who could this one be?"

She placed her knuckles against her cheeks, then shuddered, throwing her hands in the air as if it was an obvious answer. "Eve."

He nodded.

Oops! Okay, one more question. Really, this will be the last one . . . for now.

"Speaking of Eve, when do we get to meet her?" S'rae's eyes widened in excitement. It was her life's goal since she'd first heard the story of Mother Nature. When she was a child, Eve was only a myth, a tale the adults told children who longed for epic stories. But now, now she felt more real than ever. Creating nature with a smile. Storms with a frown. And life with her presence. Yup, Eve was amazing. S'rae was her biggest fan—knowing almost all of her facts, stories, and myths—and would quickly challenge anyone to a game of trivia just to prove it.

Immediately, the candles dimmed blue with a sizzle. S'rae gasped as the heat around them snapped into a freezing cold. The chill chattered her teeth. She felt goosebumps surge across her body, and watched her breath dance in the air, as if all heat exited.

"One does not simply meet Eve as if she is some sort of an exhibit," Gabrael said in a cold, dark voice. "First, the book, then we will discuss Eve."

For a brief moment, S'rae noticed his eyes were gloomy, like the ones she remembered from Ah'nyx's funeral.

Gabrael finally continued reading . . .

11

DESTROU'S EYES FOCUSED on the residue of light that flickered away like snow thrown in the air. *The Eye of Eve?* The shock of the moment weighed down his face; there was a battle within him, struggling to come to grips with what was real or his imagination. For the first time in a while, he was unsure. He hoped that this friendship was real, not a dream.

Though he knew he had a tight schedule to fulfill—and would get in trouble if he was late by the next horn—Destrou wanted to take advantage of finally getting to know someone. Because at dusk, the horn would sound, and he would have to mentally prepare for the expected beatdown.

He never looked forward to that horn.

But the now—meeting Elu—was something that the Village could never take away. It happened. This moment.

In a world with little to offer, Destrou valued memories almost more than food. Good ones became so rare he forgot what they felt like.

Destrou's body trembled with joy. He couldn't contain himself.

"You okay?" A hand appeared on Destrou's shoulder. It was Elu's, soft as a breeze.

"I'm more than okay. I'm happy." Destrou sighed, that sadness he'd felt earlier wrenching his heart again. "I just don't want it to stop."

Elu smiled. "That's goo—"

The sound of a blaring horn interrupted him, letting them know that it was time to train—or as Destrou called it: bullying time.

That was the horn he was dreading.

He had forgotten about reality; the past few hours truly felt like a dream that he didn't want to wake up from.

"I enjoyed this," Elu said.

"You won't forget about me, will you?" Destrou said.

Elu tilted his head, cleared his throat, and spoke slowly. "Why would you say that?"

"When we go back, everything will just go back to normal. The Leader would probably kill you if he saw that we're frie—" Destrou stopped himself from finishing the word. He didn't want to get comfortable using it.

"It's okay, you can say it. We're friends now. And don't worry about Eli'jah, he won't do anything to me." Elu jumped up, grabbing Destrou by the wrists. "This'll be our secret, okay?"

Destrou felt warm inside. The idea of having a friend and a secret made his eyes water. "Never had one before."

"A secret?"

"A friend."

"Well, *friend*, we need to head back before we get in trouble. To be safe, let's not go together." Elu saw Destrou's shoulders drop. "Because you're my friend, I don't want to see you get hurt," he reassured Destrou.

Destrou turned toward the Forest, sniffling and wiping his eyes

with the back of his hand. "I don't want to go back yet . . . I know what's waiting for me." When he turned back around the cliff was empty, alone with only the wind keeping him company.

Just like that, Elu was gone without a sound, taking the citrus scent with him.

And Destrou began his hour long walk back to the Village.

He had a wrenching feeling in his stomach as he inched closer. While he grew tolerant of the daily torture, it always intensified into something more when Ranmau wasn't around. On days like today, he never knew what to expect. He knew that he needed to just get through the day, then everything would be fine: Ranmau would be back and the illusion of peace would be restored. He had to remain calm. Don't show any fear or weakness—that's what Ranmau had taught him. If only it was as easy as Ranmau made it seem.

Near the end of his journey, he turned off an icy path, which continued west. It led straight through shoulder-high ice that smelled like feces, and was nearly hidden by the shadow of the Wall. The pearlescent moon peeked over the Wall as the night bathed the Village in a darker hue. He crouched down, making sure to not be seen. No one expected a Villager to travel through such a terrible stench, but that was exactly why he did. The path ended abruptly, and he carried some of its odor with him.

Once he entered the Village, he heard drums, deafening screams interrupted by cheers and laughter. His heart pumped faster. His lungs struggled to inhale. On the outside he was calm, but inside, he was shriveling in fear.

He walked toward the noises, slowly so he didn't alert any of the boys. A scream like that only meant pain; just as he heard each time before entering the Crater. The type of scream that followed after broken bones.

He wasn't ready. His mind wanted to stop walking but his feet kept leaving imprints in the snow. He headed west until he reached the ice barrier surrounding the Crater and looked through its thin cracks at the boys below.

Destrou braced himself as he climbed over the barrier and fell into the Crater with a thud.

The Crater smelled like sweat and dirt and was completely enclosed.

The battle drums thundered as Destrou emerged from the crowd of boys. The dark blue sky deepened to violet, making it difficult to see what was in front of him. The night's shadows had blended together with the boy's bodies, making them appear like giants.

The Leader stood in the center, watching. Waiting. For Destrou most likely. His gaze remained unmoved despite the thuds and grunts and moans from the boys fighting around him.

Destrou scanned the crowd to see if he could find Ranmau.
No luck.

Instead his gaze met the Leader's. He stabbed at Destrou with his narrowed eyes. Destrou wanted to cower up into a ball, but the Leader had already made his way toward him.

With one lift of his hand, silence immediately swept through the Crater. Even the boys who were too far away to see had stopped fighting and turned their attention toward Destrou.

Destrou could hear his heart pound as sweat dripped down his neck.

The Leader pulled a staff out of the ground. One of the many that circled around tall, jagged spikes with deep gashes in them like battle scars. "You're up next." He pushed it into Destrou's chest.

Destrou forced a smile, pretending that it didn't hurt, but the throbbing proved otherwise.

His chest felt tight, and he hated himself for being such a coward without Ranmau.

It was too predictable. This moment. When the Leader wanted to make an example out of him. He knew it was coming.

The staff was too heavy. Destrou felt the muscles in his fingers cramp. "Can I get a lighter one?"

He already knew the answer. He knew that he could, and that there were plenty around to share. But what was possible was different than what the Leader wanted. Punishment.

"Sorry, the other ones are taken already." The Leader gestured to a few boys, then pointed at the stray staves. One by one, they grabbed the remaining ones, chuckling the entire time.

I'll never understand why they think this is funny. It's not. Never will be. The air around Destrou felt thicker. He bit back what he was about to say and stared at the staff in his hands.

He turned away from the Leader and saw movement from the corner of his eye. A muscular figure walked toward him. Judging by the aggressive way he walked, his feet stomping into the ground, Destrou knew that was his opponent. *Is this a joke,* he wanted to scream.

The opponent was simply too big for Destrou. He had long, bushy black hair that covered most of his face, hands the size of Destrou's torso, and his feet were so big that his frostbitten toes poked out of what was left of his furry shoes. He was even larger than the Leader; his arms and legs twice the size of his. Destrou looked tiny next to him. In his hands he held a staff that was almost as massive as he was.

A stab to the stomach would have been better. He didn't have to ask who his opponent was, he had feared this moment since the day Destrou saw him crush a boy's skull with his bare hands. This boy was called 'The Giant'.

Immediately, The Giant lunged forward, thrusting his staff toward Destrou, whipping his long, dark hair around with a twisting movement.

Destrou barely had time to react, bending backward farther than he thought was possible.

The Giant lost his balance, spinning around twice before crashing to the ground.

Destrou's heart pounded. He'd seen the damage a strike like that did. He remembered how long it took to clean up the mess.

The Giant stood up, and now there was a whip in his hand that shone like glass as he brought it down, curling around Destrou's neck.

Destrou hit the ground. His yell choked into a gasp.

The Giant put his knee onto Destrou's chest. Destrou could smell rotten meat, as if he bathed in it, and wondered if he would suffocate from the smell before they even did anything. In the back of his mind he hoped that would be the case.

"This is how we should always train, right?" the Leader laughed. He glared at the still crowd, and his voice became louder. "Right?" His laughter then became contagious. "Who wants first dibs? He's the one who takes food out of your mouths!"

The Leader paused after the moment of silence then stepped forward with a snarl. "I'm not the monster you think I am, Destrou." He bent his head to Destrou's ear, and Destrou cringed, his terror caught in his throat. "I'm much worse."

Destrou realized they could kill him. Considering what he had already witnessed at such a young age, death wasn't a crazy idea. He went wild, screaming for Ranmau, the Guardians, anyone. He almost screamed out for Elu, but he managed to bite back his words. That would've done more harm than good.

"Who's going to hear you? Stop wasting your breath. You'll need it for this." The Leader commanded the rest of the boys to have their fun. While some were hesitant at first, they succumbed,

knowing that could easily happen to them. Or worse. Fear kept order.

It began. A dozen boys raced toward him, eager to cause the first drop of blood. Destrou couldn't fight back if he tried. The Giant was too heavy and the boys stomped on every part of his body. Though this was the beatdown he was expecting, it somehow had a way to always feel like the first time. *Better me than Ranmau,* he thought as he coughed up blood.

The puddle of redness grew with each kick.

Destrou was suffocating, at times choking on his own blood. His face swelled up.

"Aren't you lucky that the challenges aren't based on one-on-one fighting—you'd go down each time." The Leader loomed his face so close to Destrou's that he practically stole the air that he struggled to inhale.

"Not as quickly as you'd go down." A voice traveled through the air, alerting the boys to turn around. Everyone looked blankly at one another, as if nobody knew what to do. "I'd advise you to let him go, if you know what's best." Ranmau entered the circle. He observed Destrou pinned to the ground. His eye twitched at the sight, then glared at the Leader, not breaking eye contact. "Again, you picked on the wrong person. I'm beginning to think that you really aren't good at making decisions. You'd think a leader wouldn't be such a krillen."

"How dare you talk to your Leader like that," Eli'jah said, appearing frustrated by the awe-filled reactions from the crowd.

"My leader? I know you're dumb, but you don't actually believe that, do you?" Ranmau took a step forward. The Leader tensed. "Everyone here knows you'll *never* be my leader. But, I'll give you credit . . . at least you're smart enough to know what would happen to you if you ever tried to prove me wrong." Ranmau cracked his large knuckles and his neck against his shoulders. "You'd have bigger problems than food and that ugly face of yours if you tried to do this to me." His mouth twitched when he glanced at Destrou. "Here's my advice: Whenever your poorly developed brain tells you what to do, just do the opposite. You're too stupid to know a good decision from a bad one."

A wave of gasps spread throughout the crowd.

Ranmau stood in front of the Leader, not even flinching at the fact he was outnumbered by boys seeking to destroy him and his brother. He had a similar build as the Leader, both tall and muscular. But due to their age difference, the Leader was only slightly more built; fortunately for Ranmau, size never mattered. The bigger they were, the faster they fell.

Destrou saw Ranmau's hands reach along the collar of his armor and find the silver clamp that secured it shut. He undid the hook and pulled his cloak off from around his shoulders. Beneath it, he wore an off-white sweater. It was tight, showing every groove in his muscles. He balled up his cloak and let it fall to the ground.

BANG! The ground shook, sounding like distant thunder. The cloak embedded itself deep into the ice, as if it was made of stone.

Another wave of gasps.

Ranmau slid his hands through his hair, untying the cloth wrapped around his head. His long silver hair fell with a metallic shimmer, draping over his shoulders. He let the headband fall to the ground. The way it sliced through the air, it looked more like a metal chain than fabric.

Destrou's coughing broke the silence. Ranmau's muscles clenched, as if every ounce of his body was tensed, wanting to make a move; but Destrou was in a delicate position. One wrong move and his neck could break in half.

"You'll respect me. You'd better," the Leader snarled. "You two are the babies. I have years of experience over you. You're not better than me, remember that."

"Comparing yourself to me is the most disrespectful thing I've ever heard." Ranmau tightened his fists. "I feel bad for you . . . it looks like your brain is another one of your weak muscles that you don't use enough."

The Leader breathed heavily, then gestured to The Giant, waving his hand down. The Giant pressed his knee deeper into Destrou's chest cavity. A faint sound occurred, like ice cracking. Destrou shrieked in horror as the pain intensified.

"Without us you wouldn't have survived," the Leader said, his nostrils flaring. "None of you would've. I've been doing this since before you were born. Who fed you? I did more for all of you than you ever would. If you keep this up, you may find yourself without something that means a lot to you . . . or should I say someone. We outnumber you—remember that the next time you steal food from us."

"There's only about sixty of you here . . . you're going to need a lot more than that to stop me."

"Your overconfidence will be the end of you." The Leader twisted a knife from his belt, pointing it at Ranmau.

Ranmau stepped into the tip of the knife so that it was pressed directly against his chest. "Not before it ends you first. One us will make it out . . . I'm sure we all know who that is."

"You're a fool if you think I don't want to kill you."

"I think you want to kill me. But you can't, your hand is shaking too much. And you know that if you miss . . . no . . . *when* you miss, you'd only have one second to regret the worst decision you've ever made."

The Leader's hands and legs had been shaking; now he went very still. Fear shook his every word. "E-even if you c-could survive . . . he can't." The Leader nodded his head at Destrou. "R-re-member that. Now bow to me, your leader, unless you want this to be how you remember Destrou, your dead weight. Admit it, you'd be glad to see me put him out of his misery. He holds you back."

Ranmau slanted his eyebrows, but said nothing.

The silence was interrupted by Destrou's sniffles. He tried his hardest not to cry in front of Ranmau. But the Leader's words tugged at his heart. He was right . . . *I'm just dead weight.*

"If you are a leader . . ."—Ranmau sounded calm. More calm than Destrou expected—"then I am a God." In an instant, his fist lunged towards the Leader's jaw. A burst of wind rushed over his hand and twisted around his elbow. At once, the knife fell.

BANG! The Leader flew backward over the Giant. Ranmau flipped forward, grabbing the Leader's disarmed staff with one hand, landing on his feet, and twisting into a batting motion. With one clear look at the Giant's big, fat, ugly head, he followed through with full force. The staff shattered across his face. The Giant's grip loosened immediately. His eyes rolled to the back of his head. His body stiffened, jolting his arms and legs upwards before locking in place.

Destrou gasped for air as The Giant's body crashed into the snow.

Ranmau loosened the whip from around Destrou's neck, lifting him to his feet. With the jagged staff clamped in his hand, he walked toward the Leader, who flopped around, screaming into his palms.

Another horn blared. This one had a softer tone that made Ranmau shudder. It hit a chord that curled his lip. He stopped, turned to Destrou, and then closed his eyes for a moment, pulling himself together. It was evident that this horn was for him. It was time for him to claim his prize. To enter the forbidden NoGo. To be alone with the nasty Guardians. Then to cry himself to sleep.

Ranmau's clenched fists tightened. He gazed at the Wall. His eyes were not targeting anything in particular, but rather his focus seemed to be locked onto a thought, an idea that had plagued him: "If only . . ." he whispered to himself, so soft that only Destrou could hear.

Ranmau returned his attention to the Leader.

Destrou saw, with some satisfaction, that the Leader looked vaguely panicky. He could see the sheen sweat on his pale face. Apparently Ranmau was the one thing he feared more than the Guardians and the Wall and the Forest.

"And if any of you *ever* threaten me or my brother again, re-member this. The next time will be much worse." Ranmau arched the staff over his shoulder. Destrou would not approve of him strik-ing someone when he's down, but the rage overcame Ranmau. He thrusted the staff downward, aiming for the Leader's head.

BANG! A loud rumble was followed by the sound of exploding ice. A snowy white cloud formed around them, one that could've been tainted with red mist.

"Too easy." Ranmau placed Destrou's arm over his shoulder, carrying him back to the Village. Destrou's face was battered, but beneath the blood, his lips peeled back into a smile.

They trampled over the Leader on their way back, as his body lay motionless on the ground. The staff was embedded a few inches into the ice, scraping his bloodied cheek—any closer and the Vil-lage would've been leaderless.

Ranmau had accomplished one thing: saving Destrou from a near-death experience. He proved the point that one cannot mess with Destrou while he was around, but deep in the back of De-strou's mind the thought of who would protect him when Ranmau was gone plagued him.

Destrou hadn't always been fortunate enough to have Ranmau

around. Those were the traumatic days that he forced himself to forget. To keep a smile on his face, he lived as if those terrible days never existed. There was something about this day that felt more horrifying though—it seemed like the bullying had worsened. It was hard to believe it could get any worse, but the seething look that the Leader gave Ranmau told Destrou the worst was yet to come.

Still, Destrou would go through a lifetime of torture and bullying if that meant keeping Ranmau around. There was no greater fear than loss. Not of his own life. His brother.

"I love you," Destrou's voice cracked.

Ranmau didn't respond. He remained silent when they reached their igloo, and even when he left for the NoGo.

Destrou leaned his head against the wall of their igloo and cried for the next hour. *Without you, I'm gonna be nothing.*

He cried because he lost his brother again. Because he knew Ranmau would come back even more disconnected, as if he left a piece of him back in the NoGo. And because he knew with all certainty that no matter how terrible yesterday felt or how horrifying today was . . . tomorrow would be worse.

Somehow it always was.

12

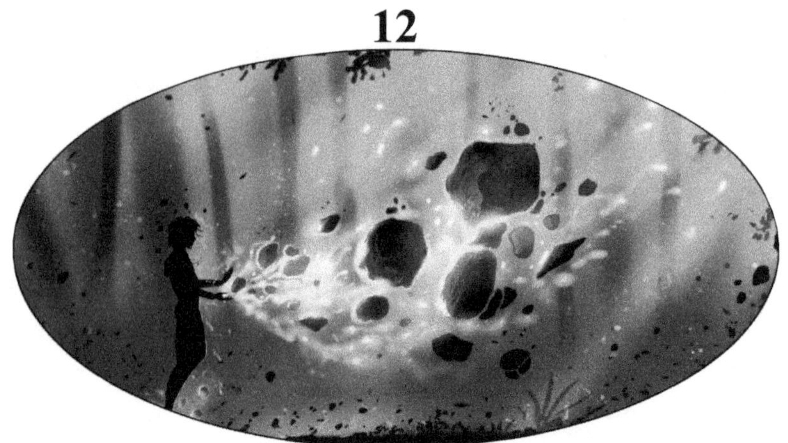

I *TRY NOT TO THINK ABOUT HIM . . . or them.*

But no matter how hard I try, it's impossible not to.

I see Ah'nyx, playing in the sand, always smelling like a hint of cinnamon.

I see my mom and dad, the way their smiles made me feel alive. I see them when they were alive. When their fingers would curl around their staffs as they waved them. I see the flowers and fruits bloom right before my eyes. They were so great at creating crops, something I could never do. The best Sahirs I knew. If only I learned from them while I still had the chance.

I hear the stories my dad told me at night. Ah'nyx barking as I arrive with fresh meat.

Then, the silence from his heart as I wrap my arms around his cold body.

The Sols and Villagers screaming as the whistles from the bombs make my ears bleed.

I think about their corpses giving life to the ground. To the planet. I think about the system that betrayed them. The culture they eradicated. The family trees that were burnt down.

I can never forget . . . no matter how hard I try.

Suddenly, a different voice appeared as a thought. *Your time will come, Vayp.* A shadow appeared in his mind, pointing a black sword directly at him. *Remember me in your nightmares.*

The shadow disappeared like a flash of smoke. Vayp's eyes widened, finally becoming aware of his surroundings. He gasped, hearing Gabrael's muffled voice.

Vayp dug his nails into his thighs and squeezed to keep from squirming. The motion was too sudden. He felt his face heat up as Gabrael stopped reading.

"Do we have a problem, Vayp?" Gabrael cleared his throat at the front of the room. A not-so-subtle reminder that he was annoyed.

Vayp had to think of something, fast.

"I need to use the bathroom," he said. *Bathroom? Really?*

"Bathroom?" Gabrael groaned. He snapped his finger and a stream of light blazed through the room, disappearing past the door. Vayp could hear the sizzles and cracks burst down the hall, leaving behind a trail of dark smoke. "It will lead you to the nearest bathroom." His voice deepened. "For anyone else who needs to go, I would advise you to go now. You do not want to be the next interruption. Trust me!"

Beads of sweat dripped down Vayp's back, but he couldn't tell if it was from the fire that scorched him or his heart hammering into his chest. He got up quickly and ran alongside the line of smoke. The last thing Vayp wanted to do was anger Gabrael any more than he had.

As he walked the halls, he heard many footsteps as if people were creeping up on him. But he knew they were just the echoes of his own. He hoped so, at least. That, on top of how dark it was, and

how he hadn't slept in a few days, did not help his paranoia.

He felt darkness seep into his brain. He couldn't sleep. Not now. Stay awake!

Nope! Not happening. The hallway was too dark. The echoes were too creepy. He felt his nightmares creeping in at any second. This was not the right time. His body was going to shut down, it always did. To avoid an episode, he ran back into the classroom and sat in his seat.

No one questioned why he arrived back so soon, they were too busy talking about something that may had been important if his mind wasn't preoccupied.

To clear his mind, he fixed on a different thought: S'rae. Vayp couldn't stop thinking about her and what he may had seen. He remembered standing on top of the hill, too far away to notice details, but he could've sworn that she seemed injured. *What was she doing there? And why would she randomly break open a rock?* He remembered feeling worried but trying to not show it; however, when she walked up to him, she was fine. There was no limp. Nothing. What he did know was that she still had her Earth abilities locked away. Being a natural like her, it would be impossible to forget; like learning how to walk, it was forever engraved in her memory.

She's keeping something from me, I know it! I guess, like Elu, we all have our secrets that are best kept hidden, even from ourselves.

He then fixed onto a different thought: Destrou. For the first time, he became deeply interested in the book—though he'd never show it. He felt involved in that world, wanting to know what would happen to Ranmau and poor Destrou and Elu, the one with a million secrets. Suddenly his life didn't feel as terrible. Yes, he couldn't go to sleep at night, but at least he had the comfort of knowing that tomorrow wouldn't always be worse than today. That would be a horrible life.

He related to Destrou. He knew that monsters didn't sleep under the bed. They were in his head. A part of him. He also found himself wanting to pick Elu's brain. Why was the Village blocked off and so cruel? How much stronger could Ranmau be—Vayp wondered if he'd beat him in a duel. And, finally, he wondered what type of Villager he'd be: a spectator, a bully, or the bullied? Sadly, he didn't know the answer.

"So," Gabrael asked coldly, "what is your answer?"

Vayp felt Gabrael's eyes burn into him. He was so busy sifting through his own thoughts that he had blocked out their entire discussion. When he looked up, he saw exactly what he dreaded: Gabrael staring directly at him. The top half of his face was shrouded, but like a cat prowling in darkness, though he couldn't see the eyes, he knew they were watching him. A chill shot down his spine, despite the heat that pressed against his face.

Vayp struggled for a moment, thinking about what to say. His experiences at GroundStone led him to the conclusion that saying yes was always safe. Anything was better than showing Gabrael he hadn't been paying attention.

"Yes." Vayp gulped.

"Yes?" Gabrael's lips barely moved. "So you agree that there is a bullying problem at Harahm'be and that you may be a part of it?"

Sigh.

"You see," Gabrael continued irritably, "the same students who talk ill of Destrou's treatments are indeed the ones who treat others like Destrou. Why? You see the wrong in it, yet you still choose to be a part of the problem. And by 'you' I mean as a class. You are not the only culprit, Vayp." He forced his voice down. "All of you should understand that each one of you is exceptional, and we shall prove it. You will be separated into four teams of three, and showcase your abilities in the arena. The winning team will be awarded

most prestigiously."

Vayp's eyes lit up. He loved winning prizes almost as much as the arena. It was the one place where he could show off his strengths and not get reprimanded for using excessive force. The objective was simple: use your elements to pin the opponent for five seconds. Victory came down to overpowering and outlasting. A blend between strength and endurance.

A smile appeared on Vayp's face as he thought about smothering Han'sael into the ground, and crushing Fujak with rocks. Then his priority shifted the moment his gaze met S'rae's. The thought of them being on the same team made his Earthie instincts take over. GroundStone valued protection and being one with nature over everything. Though S'rae was strong enough to handle fights on her own, his goal became protecting her. He was a true Earthie, subconsciously abiding by their rule: protect nature and defend those who help balance it.

Gabrael and Raaz'a led the students down a tunnel. The walls were made of some type of glass, as if they were walking through an aquarium, except instead of water, lava flowed overhead and to the sides in waves of reds and yellows. The ground was made of cobblestones with steam seeping through the cracks, and the path sloped, so it felt like they were descending deep into the core. The scent of burned charcoal hung in the air.

S'rae was directly in front of Vayp during the walk, her hair swinging from side to side. There was a cheerful bounce to her step, seeming like she hadn't lost her lust for competition either.

His mouth curled into a grin as a ball of dirt formed inside his palm. *Let's see what you got.*

He gave S'rae a few moments to move forward before throwing the ball at her head. For a moment, S'rae appeared oblivious—*I guess she's not as good as she used to be.* But as the dirt whistled near, she lifted her hand, and snapped her finger. All too quick, it shot back into Vayp's face, poofing into a cloud of dust.

Dirt shot into Vayp's nostrils, clogging up his throat. He wheezed for air, grabbing his knees as he hunched over.

"Now when did that ever work on me." Vayp heard through his coughs.

She smiled before turning around. And with another snap of her finger, Vayp felt a gust of air burp from his chest. It felt like he placed his mouth into a funnel that sucked the dirt right out of him.

"I still got it, remember?" Her voice trailed away as she skipped ahead.

Yupp, I definitely want you on my team.

They descended deeper. Sweat formed on Vayp's eyebrows as the air became hot and dry. The tunnel had some sections where the walls were made of stone. In the dark spaces, Vayp felt a cool drop in temperature, despite his heart racing and sweat pouring down his face. After what he had gone through, darkness was never the same. It was the reason he couldn't sleep at night.

He felt his body lose control. His fist was about to clench until a hand slid into it. The skin was smooth. The touch was soft as a mother's kiss. Even in the darkness, he knew it was S'rae's. In that moment he felt peace rush through his body like a wave.

The last time they held hands like this was when he saw Ah'nyx's frozen body, as he cried in the center of Opella. He needed to forgive her now, unlike what he did then.

Maybe being an Earthie wasn't the main reason why he wanted to protect S'rae.

The line of students stopped abruptly. Vayp felt a bump from behind as somebody bounced off him. From the way the stench of fish hit his nostrils, he knew it was Han'sael. Vayp stayed still, fighting the urge to turn around and shove him to the ground. *I'm*

better than the Leader. Don't do it, Vayp.

Gabrael and Raaz'a stood in a circle of light, at the edge of a cliff that overlooked a pitch-black void.

"This is where the battle will take place." Gabrael's voice echoed.

Gabrael snapped his fingers, creating a flame at the tip of his forefinger. His hands drifted through the floating fire, flicking the rest of his fingers open so his palms were spread. Dozens of embers split from the flame and circled around his wrists. He cupped them in his hands, as if he was holding water, then threw his arms in the air. The lights flew into the darkness like shooting stars through an empty night sky. Then a sound rumbled like distant thunder as Vayp felt his insides shake, giving him the weightless feeling of falling.

A flash of light erupted and before his eyes was a grand colosseum. He saw the top and bottom from where he stood, at the mid level. Fifty feet below there was a beautiful, oval-shaped battleground that looked like it was designed to be a heavenly oasis, not a warzone. Lush trees were sprawled about, streams of water splashed against the silvery rocks, hitting his ears like whispers, soft like the nights he spent lying by a pond with S'rae and Ah'nyx. And a gentle breeze created a harmonic whistle, carrying the fresh scent of a rainforest.

Overhead there were stone columns several stories high. Built into the sections around the oval design were long stone slabs serving as seats for spectators. It was grand enough to entertain thousands.

A circular dome formed the arena's roof, with the ceiling painted sky blue with white clouds—the way the short brushstrokes of bright colors represented the effect of light suggested it was done by the same artist who designed the floor in the dining hall. It made quite the *impression* on Vayp. In the center of the ceiling was a sun, a smaller, Gabrael-made one that blazed as bright as any ball of fire could. Its orange light stretched across the arena, bathing it in a reflection of sunlight.

The platform rumbled, then slowly brought them to the bottom level.

Once on the ground floor, Vayp saw that all along the walls there were cylinders of twenty-foot, color-changing flames, similar to the ones in the entrance of the Spire. Next to them was a string of mounted weapons, ranging from shields and staffs to swords and daggers. The sight of a shield made him smile. Shields were GroundStone's speciality, and few practiced them more than Vayp. He may not had been great at studying or reading, but he excelled at the art of shield blade fighting—the only thing at GroundStone that kept his attention.

The design of this colosseum was similar to the ones at Ground-Stone, except they were just variations of dirt, sand, rocks, and trees—nothing as elementally diverse as this one. This one seemed to be made for all schools to compete, not just one.

"Welcome to the Harahm'be Arena," Raaz'a said, clapping joyously. "Oh my, how I have missed watching all the great battles here. The greatest ones were during the times of war."

"This is true," Gabrael said softly, "but I have never looked forward to a battle more than this one—between the greatest pupils from the three schools. The destined ones."

Vayp felt a weightless sensation in his stomach, as if he had another déjà vu moment. *Have I been here before? That's impossible, no one has been here in over three thousand years.* His head whipped around, as if he heard something—but there was only silence. *Why does this place look so familiar?* His head twitched as a throbbing pain made his brain feel like it was ready to explode. Images burst like fireworks behind his lids when he closed his eyes.

He couldn't make out the details; they appeared in flashes, like trying to remember the contents of a room after the light went off. An image of a blazing dragoenix, a rare hybrid between a phoenix and dragon, soared through his mind. His eyes shot open. They narrowed the moment he noticed a familiar object in the distance. His heart pounded and his stomach squeezed into knots. Near the center, his eyes focused on a statue that had just appeared in his memory. *Is that . . . the dragoenix?*

Gabrael interrupted his thoughts. "Children, the team captains will be S'rae, Kaul, Aralinda, and Fujak." He turned to face each one. "Please step forward. S'rae, you will pick first."

"Why does she get to go first?" Fujak said. "Because she's a girl?"

"Well, yes, she *is* a girl, but she also happens to be a girl who scored the highest out of everyone. Maybe if you were a girl, you would have studied harder." Gabrael smiled. "But do not worry, the order cycles back, so she will be last to pick as well."

Laughing at the astonished look on Fujak's face, S'rae jumped up and down, twisting her hips while humming a tune. "Maybe you can learn some humility from me."

"Oh, but I'm humble." Fujak grinned. "I happen to be the most humble person I know. You'll never find a more humble person." He winked in a way that made Vayp want to throw up.

S'rae stuck her tongue out at him. "Well, my first pick obviously goes to the best one here." She paused. "Vayp!"

Vayp felt a heat pass through his body, turning his face red.

The rest of the order went as expected: GroundStone, Sereni, and Fujita picked their own, lining up behind one another.

Han'sael was the last remaining pupil.

"Oh, great," Vayp whispered to S'rae. "We would be stuck with him, this isn't fair."

"It can't be that bad," she replied. She scrunched her nose, placing her hand under her chin, as if putting thought into the decision. Han'sael stood alone, hopping with excitement, like an excited puppy trying to calm himself.

"Pick me! Me!" He shook his body. If he had a tail, it would be wagging uncontrollably.

"Okay! I pick you, Han'sael!"

"Yay!" he shrieked, running toward Vayp and S'rae with his arms wide open. "Thanks so much for pickin' me! I won't let you down, I promise!" He wrapped his arms around them. Vayp felt Han'sael's sweat drench his clothes. The stench of body odor caught his nostrils. "Sorry, I get very nervous when it comes to gettin' picked for things. I'm just gladiad I was picked this time!"

"Great," Vayp said blankly. "I'm *glad* you are. What are you even good at, anyway?"

Han'sael pulled away, rolling his eyes to the back of his head, as if searching for an answer. "Umm . . . great question! Let's see, nope . . . nope . . . mmm . . . mayb—nope. I dunno! But to be honest . . . at least I know I'm very good at nothing."

"This is gonna be fun," Vayp whispered to S'rae sarcastically.

"I'm already having fun. Like the good ol' days." S'rae smiled. "Remember, we were undefeated for a reason!"

Vayp returned the smile. Then his stomach clenched. *Those were the good ol' days.* The days when they were known as the two pupils who won every challenge thrown their way. The talk of their village, destined to be the two best Earthies to ever attend Ground-Stone. There was a rumor that even Nen'nex, GroundStone's Headmaster, was excited about the duo attending GroundStone after word reached the school.

I need to move on, but I hate that you left me for those elitist krillens.

Vayp almost didn't realize that he stared at S'rae with a face of disgust, curling his lip. His mouth quickly snapped into a smile the moment she turned to him.

"I have something to talk to you about after," S'rae whispered.

"What about?"

"Later. It's about finding out what's really going on here. Things aren't adding up."

"Come on!" Vayp threw his hands up in frustration. "You can't just say something like that and not tell me!"

But she can, and she did. S'rae scrunched her nose and didn't say a word. That was worse than saying something. The way her eyebrows tugged together, Vayp could almost see the crinkles spell out 'trouble'. S'rae could never keep her mouth shut; so when she was silent, she had a way of making you feel it. It wrenched your nerves. *She must know something.*

"So," Gabrael said loudly, his hand jerking up to silence the chatter. "The rules are standard for those who are familiar with the arena. For those who are not, this will be a last-team-standing match. A team is not eliminated until every member is counted out. Your body must be pinned for five seconds. The bladed weapons along the sides are off-limits, but everything else is fair game. Any questions? Perfect. You can start anywhere."

Vayp hid a smile. The GroundStone trio pretended to be tough but they'd never actually held a weapon. Mostly they sat around playing in the dirt, finding ways to manipulate it, then fought about whose sand-castle looked cooler or something stupid like that. He wondered if any of them had ever been in a real fight. Vayp had been in many. Far too many.

He knew that GroundStone's greatest strength was melee combat, like grappling. Though Fujita mastered an agile martial art, their ranged combat was legendary. It was said that they could guide an arrow through hoops no bigger than an eye. And Sereni were best known for their casting spells and enchantments. Vayp had never seen them in action; he laughed at the thought of water being dangerous.

He imagined it happening. What he'd do when it began. How he'd storm forward and tackle Kaul, smothering him into the ground, then make a run for the others. But those thoughts were for entertainment more than anything. He knew that the others wouldn't let something like that happen. Like before, he'd have to plan out every detail with S'rae to win.

"So what's the plan, team?" Han'sael jumped on Vayp's back.

Vayp shrugged him off. "Well, S'rae and I will finish this, you can just sit back and eat."

"We should take out *Soara Li* and *Flung* first," S'rae suggested. She explained how she'd had wind balance classes with them in her third year, and every time Aura'li and Chung would team up to blow her off the balancing beam—staying on the longest was the objective—S'rae saw that they put too much weight on one side, and she took advantage of it. She remembered the way that Chung flew through the air. And Aura'li fell so many times that she couldn't walk straight for a week. "I can handle the two of them."

As S'rae went into detail about the plan, Vayp kept glancing at her, wondering what else was going on in her head. He wanted to tell her that time did heal their wound, that he wanted to be that old Vayp and the brother that she longed for, but the young Vayp was just a memory of who he used to be, no longer who he was now. He wanted her to know that he longed to be normal, but it felt as forced and unnatural as seeing a stupid S'rae or a fun Fujita.

"Great." Vayp scratched his head. "And what are we gonna do about the other krillens?"

"Hah, krillens! I knew you'd like that word!" S'rae snorted, then shrugged her shoulders. "I have absolutely no idea. Hopefully they take one another out, then we can play it safe."

"I got an idea!" Han'sael raised his hand.

"That's great, tell us about it after this is over. We'll finish the job once you fail." Vayp ignored him, then hunched in closer to S'rae. They huddled up, reaching their arms over one another, making sure that they planned in secrecy. Han'sael hopped around for an opening.

"Five!" Gabrael's voice boomed from above.

"It's already starting?" Vayp shouted, yelling over the echo.

"Four!"

"What's the plan again?" Han'sael shouted.

"Three!"

"Why are they all looking at me?" S'rae screamed.

"Two!"

"I think they're all goin' after you!" Han'sael pointed at S'rae.

"One!"

Vayp looked at the others. They circled around S'rae as if she was an injured calf and they were predators disguised as students. He could almost see their hunger drool through their pursed lips. "I'll protect you, don't worry," he screamed. He felt only the slightest bit of surprise when GroundStone teamed up against him. He would've been more shocked if they'd allied.

"Try not to hurt his pretty face," Kaul said, clapping his hands together before placing his palms on the ground.

The arena rumbled.

"Vayp's not even half as pretty as her," the GroundStone girl said, winking at S'rae. She then blew her a kiss with her hand before clenching it. "Don't you dare touch her, she's mine."

"You guys always get first picks. Not fair," the GroundStone boy or girl said. *He* kicked his leg out, placing his hand on his hip. "I guess I can have some fun with roundy over there. Nothing wrong with a little extra meat. But don't forget the Eazima way, sharing is caring."

Can they just shut up! And jeez, this is the longest second ever, making it all extra dramatic.

Though Vayp made sure not to blurt out his thoughts again, he saw S'rae's brows furrow as she tilted her head, as if she read his mind. But before they went to separate schools they did spend every second of every day with one another; maybe she could hear what he was thinking.

Frustration warmed his face, but when S'rae placed her hand on his shoulder, he felt a cool chill pass through his body.

"It's okay," S'rae said softly. "We got this!"

"*BEGIN!*" Gabrael's roar resonated inside Vayp's chest.

She's right, we got this! You all are going to need a lot more than that to stop us. The Vay'rae duo is back!

13

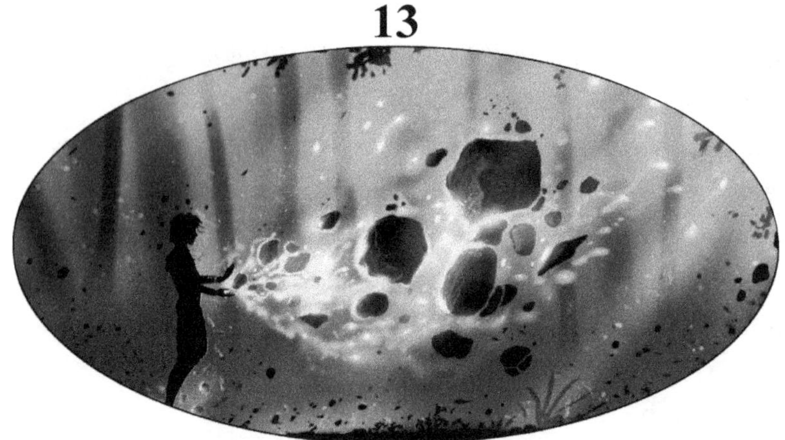

VAYP'S BRAIN RATTLED as the floor tore open. He saw the GroundStone trio stomp their feet and thrust their palms forward as large boulders launched from the ground. The Fujitas then created a wind channel that accelerated the rocks, ripping through the air with a high-pitched screech.

S'rae was their target.

Vayp dove to her, slamming his palms together. Instantly, the walls shook and a shield dislodged and launched toward Vayp.

As he caught it midair a hardened shell domed around them. The flying stones splattered off the shield like splashing waterdrops. The barrier crumbled, forming a mound of dirt around S'rae. She tugged at Vayp's robe; he saw fear in her eyes.

"Why are they all going after me? Why do they hate me?" Her eyes welled up.

Only then did he realize he had never seen S'rae in this state. At times he'd thought she was a robot incapable of showing emotion. He looked around wildly. They were surrounded. His stomach clenched as he realized that he needed to be the rock now, letting her know that everything was okay. He helped her up with shaking hands.

"It's not because of hate—it's because you're great. They're only targeting you because you're the best one here." Vayp noticed that his words made the worry in her eyes fade away. "I don't blame them, it's what I'd do." Vayp smiled. "You should be flattered that you're the best."

S'rae smiled back at him—there was a fire in her eyes. She performed a flip, landing on her foot, then twirled around, waving her arms like a ballerina. A gust of wind appeared at her feet. In a few seconds, it turned into a raging tornado, uprooting trees and draining the streams.

Vayp's eyes widened.

She pushed her palms forward, sending the tornado at her opponents.

Fujak, Aura'li and Chung took a step back, then exhaled a deep breath. The tornado faded to a breeze—its roaring winds silenced to a chirp.

"Well, that didn't go as I expected." Vayp's shoulders slouched.

"Yeah, I definitely thought it was going to be a lot cooler." S'rae giggled.

"It's okay, we can do this." Vayp squatted down as the ground shook.

"I don't know. That was my best and it wasn't enough. They outnumber us three to one."

"That makes it an even fight—" A rock smashed into his jaw. He winced at the taste.

When he looked up, he saw Kaul snap his finger as dozens of floating rocks launched straight at him.

Vayp's shield materialized again, rippling like mud before hardening into stone.

Before he fully shielded himself, the rocks had exploded into dust. When he turned to S'rae, she held a silver bow in her hand that swirled in waves as if it was made of wind.

"That's it!" S'rae stomped. She held out her palm as lightning crackled from her fingers. When she clenched her fist, gusts spiraled through the cracks, straightening the bow into a long stick. It appeared majestically solid. She slammed it down onto the packed dirt. Wind howled, pushing Vayp backwards with such force that his chest tightened.

She dashed toward the Fujitas, her feet barely touching the ground as she charged, twirling the weapon overhead. Rushing forward, wind howling, S'rae struck the trio.

The moment her staff made contact with Aura'li, she rocketed into the wall, spinning like a windmill.

Vayp's eyes widened. His ears flinched as if he heard a spell being channeled, though he could not possibly have done so over the thundering roars of the wind. Vayp turned to Kaul. Kaul nodded at the female GroundStone student. Her body slowly descended into the soil before disappearing completely. Vayp thumped his chest, showing that he was not afraid of them and was ready for whatever they had planned. *Bring it on! I'll show why I made it into the top four!*

Kaul puffed his chest and lifted a shield, waving it, and across the arena the GroundStone girl emerged from the ground, waving her shield. Vayp turned toward a door, hearing the clangs of shackles behind it. He gripped his shield tighter as dirt traveled up his body absorbing into the shield, doubling its size.

The metal gears groaned and churned and the stone door began to rise, but before it had opened fully, a Sol the size of a rhino surged forward. Its hackles rose at the sight of Vayp, and it barreled straight for him as if it had been launched from a cannon, its growl audible even over the roar of the students.

"*Vayp!*" S'rae screamed, but he didn't need her help. Vayp held his ground, stepping aside at the last moment and bringing the huge shield around as if it weighed nothing at all. A boulder shot from his shield, hitting the Sol's side, and it roared in pain. With the corner of his eye, Vayp saw Kaul fall to his knees.

"What?" Han'sael screamed. "How is this fair! They get to use their Sols?"

"Shut it!" Vayp growled. "They're linked so their powers are split in half. If you help me separate them from their Sols, I could take out these peasants in no time! Let's do this!"

When Vayp turned to Han'sael, he was curled up into a quivering ball. *Useless!*

A whistle reached Vayp's ears. He heard that sound before and became more alert of his surroundings. That was a stealth command. Something was creeping up on him, he felt it.

Before he could react to the hiss of a feline pouncing on its prey, a stone hand appeared out of the ground, smacking the wind. Vayp's village mastered protection spells. This one made the earth have a mind of its own, protecting him before he knew there was an attack. But was it the wind that it struck? Whatever it was, it flattened the grass as if a great weight was on top. *The invisible Sol? Not good. At least we don't have to worry about Sereni. What's water gonna do?*

He thought too soon. He spun around in response to a roar that made his chest shake. The Sereni Sisters had placed their hands together, and a rush of water revolved around them in spurts. The droplets condensed into a solid matter and shot at Vayp. He lifted his shield just in time.

BANG! The blast shattered the barrier into rubble, propelling him into the wall.

Vayp tried to yell at Han'sael, but water splattered into his face, making it difficult to breathe. He threw his hands in front of his face, gurgling for air.

His clothes were drenched. His hair hung over his head in waves, sticking to his face. He heard the roar of a rushing waterfall behind him as pressure swelled up in his ears. The water was so dense it resembled a blue laser that ripped through the terrain like a bulldozer.

"We should have traded you for one of the girls, piggy *Ham*'sael!" Vayp shouted. A rage burned within him.

"We shoulda traded you for one of the GroundStones with a Sol," Han'sael mumbled, and somehow, despite the roars from the water, despite the shrieking of the wind, Vayp heard him.

"What!" Vayp pouted his lips. He couldn't even be mad at Han'sael because that was actually a very good comeback. He was impressed by Han'sael's ability to not let words affect him and fight fire with fire. *Maybe he's not a pushover. Hmm . . . I kinda like him now—*

Speaking of girls, Vayp thought, not wanting to get sidetracked. *I need to protect S'rae.*

He saw her flipping through the air, kicking and striking at lightning-fast speeds. Vayp wasn't surprised that she was fighting the other three Fujitas, but it shocked him to see that she was actually winning. S'rae managed to block and counter a number of their thrusts, but was thrown off by a well-placed strike—only for it to rip through her as she dissolved into smoke.

Fear immediately flooded Vayp's body.

Moments later, she appeared overhead, striking all three Fujita with one swift kick.

Wow! Maybe she doesn't need my help.

S'rae jumped and twisted. Her staff materialized back into a bow, shooting arrows of wind that exploded into cyclones. The Fujitas were blasted into the air.

Vayp watched Kaul stomp into a crouching position before slamming his palms on his knees. "Watch out!" Vayp screamed as a boulder, followed by a mountain range of spikes, rocketed toward S'rae.

She turned around and pushed her palms forward. The boulder slowed, barely touching her hands, then, with a *BANG*, launched back to where it came from. Like a wrecking ball, it obliterated the wave of spikes as the GroundStones dove out of the way. She shot arrows of condensed air into the Sereni Sisters' wave, but it was ineffective. She then flipped to the side, avoiding a stream of rocks shooting at her like bullets.

Wait . . . is she the one protecting me?

There was too much going on, too quickly. One mistake and the match was over.

As S'rae avoided the rocks and wind, and Vayp avoided the waves, Han'sael cowered up into a ball, squeezing his eyes and ears shut with his arms.

"I told you he'd be useless," Vayp yelled over the waves.

"We need to think of something *fast*," S'rae yelled back. "I'm running out of energy!"

A high-pitched screech forced Vayp and S'rae to cover their ears. As his eyes searched for the source, a large bird with lanky legs stormed by them as fast as lightning. Its rainbow feathers grazed his skin. He looked at his arm as a dozen red lines appeared. *His fur is too sharp.*

"Don't let that ugly thing touch you!" Vayp shouted.

As if understanding what Vayp said, the Sol's colorful feathers enlarged, creating a fiery mane that glowed like magma.

"Why'd you do that?" S'rae said. "Now look what you did!"

"What? That one is so cool! Why can't you do anything cool like that, Vayp!" Vayp heard from behind.

He turned and grimaced at Han'sael. "Can you not talk and actually do something for once in your life other than eating . . . and breathing!"

"You mean do something like—" Han'sael cleared his throat. "—getting a Sol?"

"Wh—" Vayp growled. "I swear . . . if you weren't on my team right now!"

Vayp heard a sizzle. Before he could turn, dirt and sand pillared around him like tentacles, swatting away feathers that melted stone upon impact. Vayp took a step back, in awe of the Sol's abilities. His lip then curled, frustrated even more by the sight of them. He wished he could have grown with Ah'nyx, watching how great he knew he'd become. Maybe Ah'nyx would take out all three of them by himself.

The other students roared as they channeled spells. Water circled them in waves. Wind howled. Boulders lifted from the ground. They were surrounded, outnumbered, and out-classed. "There's no hope," Vayp thought to himself . . . or was that him whispering again?

"All is not lost," S'rae said. "Together we've never lost, and it's *not* happening now." Cold air wrapped around her body like a cloak as a bow formed in her hand. She soared dozens of feet, twisting like a gymnast, evading a shooting range of rocks, before finally getting struck.

Vayp watched her fall like a phoenix that lost its wings. Thirty feet beneath her were dislodged swords and daggers.

As he moved his arms in a circle, his limbs went stiff before finishing, as if he had just been paralyzed. He lost all control of his body. His veins bulged, trying with all of his might to connect his hands together. There was a trembling resistance, like people pulling his arms from behind. His eyes surveyed the area, noticing a sapphire aura glowing around the Sereni Sisters.

Are they controlling my blood? Everything slowed down for him. He saw the Sereni Sisters channeling their spell, the Ground-Stones laughing, and the Fujitas boasting—all while S'rae was falling to her death.

Not on his watch!

Vayp blinked his eyes. Boulders lifted underfoot, ejecting the sisters like rockets.

He regained control and his heart pounded faster. The fear of loss surged up inside him. He tightened his fists. *I can't lose you. You're all I have.* Jumping over a wave, he pushed his palm in the air. "*Hijr'yd!*" A giant stone hand formed from the ground, catching S'rae.

This wasn't a friendly game.

S'rae lay unconscious as a line of fire burned around her, creating a separate slab that lifted her to a safe area.

"It's just the two of us, are you gonna do something?" Vayp screamed at Han'sael.

The sound of ground shattering echoed ahead of him and a voice yelled, "*Mawja'ko!*"

Years of hearing that at GroundStone left Vayp no doubt what spell was cast. He responded immediately.

"*Mawja'ko!*" Vayp slammed his fists deep into the soil. The ground curved underneath him like the wave during a cannonball into water. Instead of splashing outward, it retracted, creating a barrier around him. In that moment, a wave of rock and dirt and stone crashed over him, flowing like water.

Vayp was covered in knee-high mud, and the only thing that stopped him from drowning in it was a shield that withered away

with each wave.

"I don't know why you thought you stood a chance," he heard Fujak's laugh over the roars. "When will you peasants learn? People like you never have what it takes to be good. Stick to slave labor and cleaning up after me. That's where you belong, with my garbage."

Their laughter disappeared as their chants grew louder, their killer instincts emerged.

"*HAN'SAEL—HELP!*" Vayp's eyes widened as a tidal wave of rock eclipsed the light.

It was then, when all hope seemed lost, a high-pitched shriek like an amplified infant's scream froze everyone in place. The water all around, from the streams to the sisters' wave, rippled in unnatural waves, moving forward, then stopping for a moment before receding, as if time had rewound. It continued until the water froze in place. And bubbles floated into the sky.

When Vayp looked at Han'sael, his eyes were as white as the moon. His hair and clothes floated upwards, as if submerged in water. Instantly, the arena became filled with droplets of water, like a still picture of rainfall. And when Han'sael belted another shriek, the water burst into mist, swirling around the arena.

Han'sael's mouth continued to move but everything was silent, except for a droning, ringing noise. He became thin. Almost too thin, as if he drained all of the water from his body, looking like a skeleton dressed in baggy clothes.

Vayp's eyes widened. Maybe Han'sael really wasn't as dumb as he looked or sounded. Maybe he stored all of that extra fat and water weight for a reason, an unfair advantage. Maybe Vayp was giving Han'sael too much credit, but for that one moment, he looked at Han'sael as if he was a genius, far from an idiot. All doubt that he had of Han'sael being good enough for the top four was destroyed.

And for the first time, looking at Han'sael didn't remind Vayp of himself, another pity case undeserving of the top four spots.

Vayp saw the person who belonged.

He saw the heart that was overlooked by peers, but revered by professors.

And now he saw they actually have a chance.

14

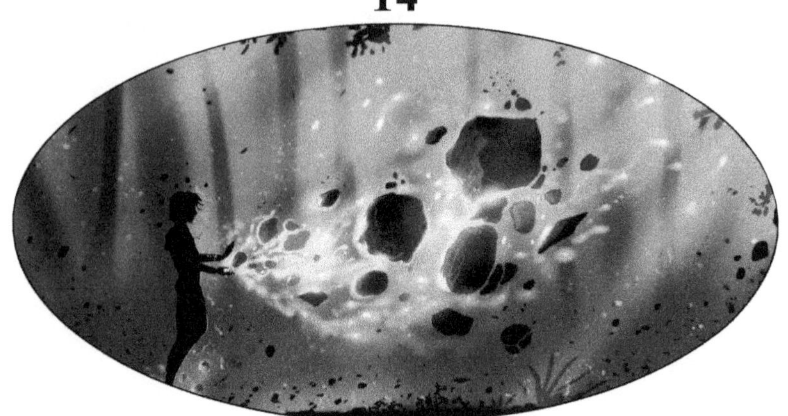

VAYP HAD SEEN POWER BEFORE but nothing like this. Although Hansael's power caught almost everyone by surprise, the smirk that Vayp saw from Gabrael told him that he had known all along. This was no secret. And what happened next finally proved why Han'sael was good enough to be here.

The mist that spiraled around the arena condensed into an orb in Han'sael's palms. The way that space bent around it, it seemed like a white, crystallized black hole. When Han'sael pressed his palm into the orb, the arena shook as if the planet had stopped spinning.

BANG! The universe exploded between Han'sael's palms with so much force that the students were knocked into the air. Vayp screamed, but his shout froze in his throat just as he froze in the air. It seemed as if time had stopped. The water, the students, the sounds, everything remained as they were, yet time couldn't have stopped, because Vayp was still able to think and formulate sentences in his mind. *How is this possible? What's happening?* The blues and whites of a wave breaking along the coast twirled around the orb in Han'sael's hands. Vayp's heart seized at the beautiful sight.

The flickering stars between Han'sael's palms swirled and danced with one another.

Before Vayp could appreciate it for a second longer, a channel of mist shot from it, soaking him, and lifting him further off the ground. His torso floated parallel to the ground, his clothes, arms, and legs feeling weightless.

Vayp's heart raced so fast that it no longer felt like it was beating—it vibrated like a jackhammer. His body shook with an energy that he had never felt. He saw particles in the elements that he had never seen—Earth molecules were all around him, appearing in bright colors he never knew existed. The element of Earth was everywhere—in the air, water, and fire. It felt like he possessed the power to create a planet with the snap of his finger. *Is this the power of a God?*

His body expanded, doubling his size.

"This. Is. Amazing!" Vayp's voice was deep and muffled, like screaming underwater.

Though it was happening to him, even he couldn't believe what he was seeing. Han'sael chanted with a dampened scream, Vayp heard inflections that he'd only heard once before. The same ones that resonated in his chest when a God spoke their tongue.

Vayp gazed down at the students. Their frightened looks suddenly made him smile.

He raised his hand and the ground beneath them dematerialized into particles smaller than grains of salt. The particles engulfed the students like a sandstorm in a desert—then spiraled, taking the shape of a twister. He clenched his fists as the twister tightened around the students. Vayp's eyes blackened. He squeezed his hand tighter as muffled screams erupted from inside the storm. His eyes turned bloodshot with rage. He felt blood surge through his veins, like the opening of floodgates. The screams became louder and more horrific.

"You *all* deserve this," he said. He sounded so relaxed that it troubled him. He felt their bones about to break. One Sol screeched so loud that he heard it over the roars of the arena. It wasn't fair how they had Sols and he didn't. He wanted to change that. He wanted them to go through the pain he went through. And he was almost sorry for feeling no guilt. Almost.

"*ENOUGH!*" Gabrael boomed. "Team S'rae wins!"

The storm stopped at once. The particles trickled down from the cylinder like sand in an hourglass. After a few moments, bodies poured down like clumps in soured milk.

Shaking off his sense of revenge, Vayp floated to the ground, not noticing the crimson drops that dripped from his nose and hands. He felt tears in his eyes. *What was I doing?* He looked at his palms with regret. *Why did I do this? I didn't want to stop. Was I going to kill a Sol? What's wrong with me!* He squatted, his hands deep in his pockets, trying to stop them from shaking. When he looked up, he found the students stumbling out of the mounds. They were covered in mud; it was tough to differentiate them, they looked like half-melted statues.

There's something evil in me, I feel it.

"You did it." S'rae rubbed her forehead. She was staggering.

"We did it." Vayp walked over to S'rae, the rocks and gravel crunching beneath his feet. He looked down and felt a mixture of exasperation and joy. Then he looked at Han'sael who was shivering in a fetal position, sucking his thumb, rocking himself side to side. Somehow he had turned back into his usual round self.

Before Vayp said another word, someone slapped the back of his head; a sting so hard that he felt welts instantly take the shape of five fingers. *Ow!*

"You did nothing!" Adalia screamed, her blueish eyes glazed. "You not only almost killed us, look what you did!" She pointed across the arena.

His heart stopped. *No . . .*

Before his eyes, the feline Sol was motionless in the pit of mud. He immediately thought of Ah'nyx and felt empathy. How could he do such a thing?

"I'm sorry . . ."

"No you are not!" she screamed. "You are a terrible person. This was just a game and you went too far! *Too far!*"

It was difficult. Not the accepting the blame part, but trying to take someone who looked absolutely beautiful seriously—especially when she looked even cuter when she was angry. Her light eyes were hypnotizing and her skin was flawless. She couldn't look ugly if she tried.

Even the way she stomped her feet as she marched toward the feline was adorable.

When she crouched next to the body of the Sol, she placed her

hands on its chest and whispered words.

The silence of the crowd immediately turned into an uproar as the Sol started breathing again.

"I messed things up badly, didn't I?" Vayp said to S'rae, his eyes still on the group of students walking away together, holding hands. Though they were defeated, they still had one another. They seemed like they were real friends. Something Vayp would never understand.

S'rae may not have heard him. Her eyes remained locked on the Sol as if it was her own.

Vayp pushed his hands into his furry pockets to calm his nerves. He couldn't let everyone else know how frightened he truly was. It'd only make it look worse, as if he didn't want them to know that he felt guilty. But his fingers started to shake, he didn't know if it was from the adrenaline or his terror. *How did that happen? When did I become so evil?* "Was I that bad?"

S'rae said nothing. But that said more than enough. She was disappointed, not mad.

Vayp then noticed her pointing at each of the Sols, scrunching her nose and resting her finger on the side of her cheek.

"Which one could it have been?" S'rae whispered.

"Which one could what have been?" Vayp replied.

"Oh nothing." She fluffed her hair.

Vayp's eyes narrowed. "Where's Han'sael?"

"He's still there," S'rae said softly, pointing at the ball rolling around. "He's saying that he ruined his only chance to finally make friends."

"How do you know?"

There was no reply.

Vayp looked at her curiously. *Everything is still so secretive about you.* He turned around and met Han'sael's eyes. Vayp was sure in that instant that they were both wondering the same thing: *What happens now?* Then Vayp walked on and Han'sael continued rolling around. He felt different, like he needed to stop being such a jerk. Why did he feel like he was the bad guy? As if he was the Leader in everyone's story without ever knowing.

"We didn't do it." Vayp looked down at Han'sael. "You did it." He hoisted him to his feet. "You know what, piggy ham?" Vayp's eyes narrowed.

"What?" Han'sael sniffed, wiping his nose.

"You're officially the coolest person here!" Vayp bearhugged Han'sael. "That was so freaking awesome! The best, coolest thing ever!"

And then S'rae appeared at Vayp's side, jabbing him in the ribs. "Ahem! Oh, just standing here. You know, just here . . . *not* being the best, coolest thing ever."

Vayp sighed, then smiled. "Silly me. You're the best thing ever, too."

"Yay!" S'rae twisted her hips and shuffled her hands. "You aren't too bad yourself."

"You really, really think so?" Han'sael's eyes sobered up. His glazed eyes met Vayp's.

"Of course! We made a great team . . . we could practically finish each other's—"

"Lunches?" His eyes widened. "'Cause I'd share my food with my frien—I mean . . ."

An awkward silence hung in the air. Vayp shook his head. "Yes, lunches. Exactly what I was thinking." He paused. "But, I like the sound of us being friends. You're not so bad."

Vayp plugged his ears as Han'sael screamed, then ran around the arena faster than anyone could've imagined. He slid to a stop, looked up at Gabrael, who stood atop of the platform, and shouted:

"Me and Destrou *can* make friends! You were right! We can! We can!"

"Congratulations, Team S'rae." Gabrael cleared his throat. "And a special one to you, Han'sael. You have proven yourself to be quite the pupil. As for the prize, the three of you can now . . . ahem   . . . sit together in the first row. The most prestigious of honors."

"What?" A vein in Vayp's forehead pulsed. "You mean to tell me we went through all of that for nothing?"

"I get my seat back!" S'rae smiled, patting Vayp's back. "Ya-hoo! Whoop, whoop! Let's go! Let's go!" She danced around, pushing her hip into his, almost knocking him over.

"Best. Gift. Ever!" Han'sael jumped, though his feet barely left the ground. "Guess who ain't sittin' alonely no mo'?" Han'sael made drum sounds with his mouth while jiggling his belly. S'rae danced to his rhythm, flailing her arms from side to side and twisting her hips.

"Whoop! Whoop!" She belted with a smile, looking as if this may have been her best day ever. She twirled around and around until she collapsed to her knees, looking up at Gabrael.

"I hope we all learned a valuable lesson today," Gabrael said. "The greatest warriors never need to talk the loudest to stand out, their true power exists in the heart, not the mouth. For what you have witnessed goes beyond greatness, it is in the realm of legendary. A power where you could live for centuries and never once witness it. Han'sael, you are truly special indeed. However, I sense fear. Too much of it. A power like yours must be mastered before used again. For you are altering a power that is even beyond the reach of Gods: Time." Gabrael's breath turned more ragged with every word. His voice cracked in a way that made Vayp lift his head. Something was wrong. What was he hiding beneath his words? Vayp was too familiar with how words sounded when pain was attached to them. "I will meet you all in class. Do not be late."

Can a God feel sorrow?

Vayp was quiet as Han'sael and S'rae broke into laughter. He looked at them with a teary gaze. This was the happiest he had seen her in . . . well, forever. But his tears weren't just of joy, something troubled him, eating away at his heart. Something within him knew that there couldn't have been a worse time to form a friendship. It wasn't because of the dread he heard in Gabrael's voice. There was something else. An evil lurking in the shadows. He felt it.

As the students exited the war-torn arena, it slowly molded itself back to its original state. The trees, streams, and lights appeared, untouched. Everything was the same except for a large shadow that appeared in the center. Two shadowy figures emerged again from the darkness.

"Oh, how grand life works. On a quest for Eve, but we find ourselves a myth."

"The fat one has an extraordinary gift, indeed. He reminds me of a certain someone I used to know." He paused for a moment, and when there was no response, he continued. "What about the rest?"

"Let *them* deal with the others. Eve has fled. Plans have changed . . . slightly."

"Is it time?"

"Yes. Call them in."

"One is already on the way. How many do you want?"

"*All*. The King of Gods won't fall until his heart stops beating—and even then, I still wouldn't underestimate him. The secret rests on his life alone; he will not go down easily."

He pressed his palm into the ground, forming a puddle that looked like ink. A crow made of liquid darkness spawned from the

shadow, small enough to fit in the palm of his hand, its wings dripping like melted rubber. It whizzed around his head, landing on his shoulder, and screeched as he petted it.

The taller figure leaned in and whispered to it coldly. "Tell the Mechas that it is time. Tell them that destruction will finally rain down upon the Valley of Gaia, dousing its fire once and for all. The Shadow Army will be resurrected."

"You truly enjoy watching others suffer."

"There is nothing wrong with vengeance. If the world knew what suffering truly was, they'd understand I'm doing them a favor. The good can slaughter all they want and it is justified, but once they get slaughtered in return, we are considered evil. There are no clean hands in war . . . at least I accept that mine are being covered by the blood of my enemies. But the good has no such courage. They lie while their hands are drenched in the blood of their own."

The bird jumped onto his outstretched hand, showing no details. Just pure darkness.

The shadow lifted his arm. "Go, Ndege. It ends tonight!"

Flying into the air, the crow screeched excitedly, then vanished into a shadow with a ripple.

15

DESROU LAY ON A BLOCK OF ICE covered by a large skin of white fur. His palms were pressed against his cheeks as he rested in a fetal position, recovering from the attacks. The beating didn't bother him as much as how long it was taking Ranmau to return.

While Destrou waited, he gazed out of the igloo window at the night sky and the pearlescent wall reflecting the moonlight. He cocked his head toward it. Through the thin walls, he heard the wind's whistle, and there was someone laughing, and someone else screaming, along with the droning clunks from metal hitting ice. Familiar sounds. Sounds of the Village.

This had happened every other week for the past two years. The waiting. The worrying. The wondering what happened when Ranmau entered the NoGo to claim his prize. The reward process was unknown to nearly all. Only one other boy knew what happened inside: Eli'jah.

At times, the award was clothing and fur, which was useful during their coldest times of the year; other times, they received

their most cherished luxury: food. Nothing was more rare and valuable to the ever-starving boys than food.

Destrou valued moments the most. He tried his hardest not to forget the good ones. The ones with Ranmau. The ones that had been outnumbered by the bad, making them difficult to remember. But they were there, somewhere, hanging on for dear life. Not many remained. The ones about their friendly relationship, with the sounds of laughter, had long gone. At times his head hurt trying to recollect them. They found a way to blend in with his most lucid dreams. He'd wake up frustrated that their great day was just his imagination. At times he wished he never had them. It was like waiting for a gift that never came; he hated getting his hopes up.

Destrou then heard something else. The blood drained from his face, and dread flashed in his eyes. It was that soft type of gasp used to suppress a sob. "Ranmau?" he said.

In that moment, the fur skin covering the igloo's entrance was pulled to the side. Destrou stood up as Ranmau walked in with a blank gaze and cold eyes, a defeated version of himself. Destrou's heart ached at the sight of him. At least a few hours had passed since he'd gone away, but Ranmau showed no emotions. No celebration for winning. Nothing. In his hand, Ranmau held his prize: a slab of meat. He hobbled to his bed, as if his legs were made of wood.

Destrou knew to not ask any questions. He remembered the promise to himself that he wouldn't anymore. The way Ranmau's eyes welled up after trying to answer the questions haunted Destrou for weeks.

The brothers exchanged no words, and Ranmau did not even glance in Destrou's direction. He sluggishly positioned himself to roll onto his bed. Destrou knew he was in pain but was too proud to say so.

"Here." Ranmau sounded calm. Calmer than Destrou felt. He ripped the slab of meat in half and threw it at Destrou.

Destrou struggled to smile back. It pained him—more than the bruises and beatings ever could—seeing Ranmau like this. He felt like a ton of ice had dropped on top of him.

The meat was ripped into a semicircle wedged between two ivory-colored bones. He pinched it between his fingers, unsure what to make of it. It had a foul odor that stank of rotting corpses, and there was a good chance that it would make his butt explode the next day. He wrapped the meat in a piece of cloth, and tied it around his chest—the heat would finish thawing it. Not all of his ideas were terrible.

Ranmau turned away from Destrou and peered into the darkness, unblinking and unmoving, like a housecat wondering what life was like beyond captivity.

The sky was cloudy. It always had some overcast, but it was never as cloudy as it used to be. The Guardians said that there had been a time when dark clouds trapped all light from entering for decades—maybe centuries. Something bad had happened; that was all they were told. It was only a story, though. Just like the stories about the Archons and how it took armies to battle only a few of them. If that was the case, how could they lose the war? Stories. He loved them—the way they took him away from reality and pain— fascinated by how they painted the picture of a world so different from his own, yet the same. It was a time when all races lived in their kingdoms then united for peace. But there couldn't be peace without war, they said. There was a rumor that Archons couldn't die; that they were never defeated, only banished to the Forest. Just a rumor. Destrou believed the words—he needed to so he could sleep at night.

Destrou watched as Ranmau's gaze remained locked on the

Wall until his eyelids finally gave way to gravity.

Then he was out, and Destrou was alone. His legs shook like leaves in the wind, his hands like frozen ice. *I can't stand to see you like this. I will win for you!*

The sounds of Ranmau's whimpers were enough to keep Destrou wide awake. They always did.

He couldn't allow whatever it was ripping them apart to win. The crumbling of their relationship was far beyond his understanding, but he knew that it involved the challenges.

Whatever happened in the NoGo, Destrou would rather experience it. They were brothers. They were supposed to look out for another, right? Ranmau would do the same—

Wait . . . was that why Ranmau always won, Destrou thought. To . . . protect him? From accepting the prize. The Guardians. The NoGo. Maybe Ranmau wasn't the cocky competitor the Village claimed him to be. Maybe there was more to him that even Destrou didn't know. As if he didn't want what was tearing him apart to do the same to Destrou. As if he cared. *Maybe. . .*

But one thing he did know was that Ranmau's fire died long ago. Destrou no longer saw it in his eyes. The way they'd sparkle at the thought of a challenge. When he'd smile and they'd laugh and play and train. Instead, the stars faded from his eyes, leaving an empty night's sky. Destrou wanted them back. He missed the stars.

That thought alone made Destrou more driven to train. To win.

While everyone was sleeping, Destrou spent the night pushing boulders and punching and kicking slabs of ice. The other boys were two to three times his size but if he increased his training, then maybe he could overcome the disadvantage. With bruised knuckles, he embedded deep imprints into the solid ice. With calloused palms, he moved boulders twice his size.

After his mind sparked with another crazy idea, he went back into his igloo with a plan. He always had inklings for a new invention. His imagination was vivid and at times evolved into an odd plan or two or ten.

One time, he was tired of getting picked on for being the small krillen, so he thought it was a good idea to tie bones together and place them under his feet to appear taller. It sounded better in his head than it looked in person. Another time, he tried to fly. Yes, fly. He observed how discs stayed in the air longer than balls, so he tied bones and fur onto his arms and jumped off the edge of a ditch. He swan-dived into a belly flop, leaving a five-foot deep imprint of an angel in the snow. His inventions always failed, but that never stopped him from pursuing more. He didn't believe in giving up— just because one didn't work didn't mean they all wouldn't.

Destrou silently tiptoed toward his bed and extracted the sharp claws from the fur skin. He used rope that he had found lying around and tied the claws around his fists.

The claws embedded into the ice. His eyes widened as if he had uncovered the greatest mystery. *The marks on the Wall?* He thought about it for a moment. *Does Ranmau use this to climb?* He gasped. *Maybe if I get the Eye of Eve, that'd keep him around. He always wanted it!*

Destrou started his hour long trek to the northernmost corner of the Village. From there, he got a good look at it. The Eye of Eve. He squinted his eye, placing his thumb in the air. It was only the size of his thumbnail—at least from where he stood. It seemed impossible to get—not even Ranmau could; he'd tried more times than he'd like to admit.

The separate layers of the pole shifted in different directions at random, making it tough to hold a grip. The boys had always tried for it until one day someone climbed higher than anyone had ever

seen. The fall ended his life.

Destrou couldn't remember his name but he was one of the almost-good ones. By almost-good he meant indifferent—someone who wasn't okay with bullying but let it happen anyway. They weren't completely good. Because to Destrou, watching and letting something bad happen was just as bad doing it. That was why he liked Elu—he was the only hope that good people existed in the world and weren't myths like Archons. Since that accident, the boys figured that life was more important than a random beacon of light—no matter how cool it looked. Destrou had other plans. He knew how much Ranmau loved it and maybe that could get him to stay. Maybe.

The claws dug into the pole. It began rotating, slinging him around until he had the urge to vomit.

He crashed to the ground, pressing his palms to his face and wiping snow from his brows. His stomach twisted and his head felt dizzy.

This was going to be much harder than he thought.

He must have fallen over a hundred times throughout the night. But each time he failed, he knew that he was that much closer to succeeding.

S'rae observed Gabrael as he stopped reading and pressed his fingers to his lips. The candelights along the walls softened to a burnt orange.

"You see, children," Gabrael said. His words normally soft, were now crisp. "There are two types of greatness in this world. One who is born with it. Who lives, eats, and sleeps greatness. One who is born with the strength of a thousand men and the intelligence of a thousand minds. And the other who isn't—isn't born blessed with the natural abilities, superior genetics, or the brightest of minds, but excels because he believes. Do you know the difference between the two?"

"Nothing?" S'rae said, relating more with the latter. She felt like she was the only one at Fujita who wasn't blessed. She had worked thrice as hard as any other Fujita. But she was smart; before class started, she'd hidden the Eye of Eve underneath a cobblestone. She didn't want to risk its name being mentioned again.

"Precisely. You see, they believe so diligently that they can achieve greatness that they apply all their effort to become exceptional. It is then . . . when they realize that they are capable of something more."

"More than great?" Fujak scoffed. "How'll Destrou become better than Ranmau if no matter how hard he trains, Ranmau is always better?"

You would be the one to bring that up, you big-headed elitist, S'rae thought.

"Destrou may never be Ranmau's equal, but sometimes if you reach for the stars, you will fall onto the clouds. Even if you fail, you're still higher than you ever thought possible."

After falling from the pole yet again, Destrou turned around, reacting to a crunch in the wind. He squinted his eyes to focus, noticing a dark silhouette walking toward him. "Who's there?" he said in his not-so-deep voice.

"You know that voice won't ever work, right?" a familiar voice said. "And it'd be *much* easier if you wrapped a rope around it and used your feet to climb."

"Elu!" Destrou felt a warmth in his chest. "Yeah, it was dumb to think it'd work."

"Well, it wasn't *that* bad of an idea. Maybe I can learn some things from you."

"Learn from me?" Destrou said almost to himself, hoping he wasn't going mad. Because the truth was, and he knew it well, that he had terrible inventions. If it weren't for his strong bones, he would've been paralyzed a long time ago.

"What's that?" He noticed a sharp object in Elu's hands. "Is that an ice pick?"

"Oh, this?" Elu gave it a quick juggle. "Why, yes it is."

"The Guardian's ice pick?"

"Maybe." Elu smiled.

"Aren't you quite the thief," Destrou joked.

"No, it's not like that at all . . . I borrowed it."

"Without them knowing?"

"Those are little details. I'll bring it back to them."

"How you gonna do that? Isn't it always inside the NoGo?"

"How do you think I find out everything? Oh, I'm sooo sorry, this is sooo rude of me. Hello, Sir I Don't Know A Million Secrets, I don't think we've met." With a straight face, Elu stuck his hand out toward Destrou. "My name is Elu, the person with a million secrets. Nice to meet you!"

Destrou shook Elu's hand, then burst into laughter. Elu's seriousness wavered before giving in completely. Destrou's laugh was contagious—Elu joined in with a snort of his own.

"Speaking of secrets . . ." Elu hesitated, then slammed the pick in the snow. "Lemme show you some fun ones!" He looked at Destrou, then up at the Eye of Eve. "You might as well stop now, you'll never get it that way. *Trust me!*"

Destrou's eyebrows rose as if he wanted to argue, but he accepted that Elu was right.

"Follow me!" Elu grabbed the pick, humming a pleasant tune. The way he held a harmony with trills and whistles sent pleasant chills through Destrou.

Elu spent the next hour or so showing Destrou different pranks to pull on the Village before curfew. He showed Destrou a hidden spot, wedged between two glaciers, where he could throw snowballs and not get caught. They hit The Giant who then turned around and blamed it on a nearby boy. Destrou and Elu laughed as The Giant shoved the boy's face in the snow. He showed Destrou a place in the courtyard, south of the Village, where his voice magnified to sound like a bassoon. They scared everyone who walked by. But Destrou's favorite was when Elu came back with a piece of rope. Each time they pulled on it, boys would trip and face plant.

"You have a great laugh!" Elu giggled as they slid behind an igloo.

"Do I?" Destrou snorted, catching his breath in between bursts of laughter.

"Yeah, I can't believe its been two years! Did you see the look on their faces? One of them looked like a snowman." Elu puffed his cheeks, hobbling stiffly from side to side as if he was frozen solid. "And another like this." He jumped up, falling face first into the snow.

Destrou laughed. "No, like this!" He mimicked Elu, but instead landed in a soft patch, falling a few feet deep.

"Hello?" Elu shouted. "Maybe if you laid off the food, you wouldn't have sunk so far!" He laughed. "I can help and borrow some of your food."

"Sure. Just like you borrowed the pick!" Destrou chuckled, climbing out of the hole.

"Exactly!" Elu drew himself up proudly.

"Here, have some." Destrou unwrapped the meat from around

his chest.

"Huh? You'd really give that to me?" Their eyes met with a piercing gaze.

"Why not? That's what friends do, I think. I dunno, I'm new to this." His stomach growled as if disagreeing with him.

Elu laughed, punching Destrou's shoulder. "Put that away, you earned it!"

"Maybe next time."

"Yeah, maybe." There it was. The piercing gaze again. "You know what?"

"What?"

"I want to show you the biggest secret of them all!"

"How big?"

"The biggest! It's the secret place that has like a million stories!"

"Whoa, a million? I wanna hear 'em all!" Destrou's eyes widened with excitement. He shuffled his feet, so happy he felt his empty stomach swell up.

"Okay, but be ready to be amazed! And don't tell *anyone* about this or I'll personally throw you into the Forest myself." He smiled so wide that it seemed like he was joking yet serious at the same time.

Destrou was alarmed but he was drawn to it. He looked straight ahead, following Elu as he sprinted passed igloos.

Elu had a gift for running without making a noise—Destrou not so much.

Destrou wanted to focus on the back of Elu's head, the way the cloth flowed in the wind, but the terrain became unfamiliar to him, and the path was rocky, needing all of his attention. He passed by a boulder with many carvings on it. If his memory served him correctly, that was where bodies were buried.

They reached a plateau that was south of the Eye of Eve.

Elu slammed the pick into the ground. "Follow me!"

Destrou looked puzzled as they passed the same spot more times than he'd like to count. He didn't want to be rude, but he had to say something. "Do you have any idea where you're going?" He pointed at the pick. "We passed this like a million times already."

"It's a lot quicker with two people instead of one, covering my tracks. You don't understand." Elu grabbed Destrou's collar, bringing him close. "Absolutely no one can know about this." He let go, brushed Destrou's shoulders off, then smiled.

Elu knelt down, then shuffled his hands in the snow. A tunnel appeared. A warmth surged through Destrou as he gazed into it. Maybe there was more to the Village than just starvation and pain.

The cold air wrapped around them as they slid down a slope descending toward the Forest.

Destrou was thrilled not only because he had finally made a friend, but also because Elu opened his mind in a way that he had never thought possible. Something in him started to appreciate the Village for more than it was. And what he saw next changed everything.

"Oh . . . my . . . Divine!" Destrou's jaw dropped.

16

WHEN DESTROU CRAWLED THROUGH THE HOLE and landed on solid ground, little specks of light shimmered through thin ice. He rubbed his eyes, unsure what to make of what he saw. He rubbed and rubbed, again and again. It didn't make sense. How could this place be real? He marveled as they entered a cave decorated like an art gallery of murals in ice. It was so wonderful that he could hardly speak. His mind was only familiar with scenes of disorder, but in here, everything was flawless. Each groove was made with perfection in mind.

Destrou couldn't believe the images that were sent to his brain: it looked like a lush, frozen underground forest. Even the air carried the freshness of an underground forest, burning his nostrils with a damp, earthy scent. He spun around to take in everything all at once.

There was an eerie juxtaposition of opposites, the sense of being underground with lights streaming in and snow crunching at his feet. An intimacy of being in a cave, yet the columns were sometimes forty feet high.

Destrou's hands grazed along the walls as they traveled deeper through a series of tunnels lined with icy leaves, roots, and vines along the walls, accompanied by the rhythmic tapping of Elu's ice pick on the ground. Finally, they reached a room. It expanded into a circle with many tunnels leading into it. In the center stood a large crystallized tree. It looked rough but was smooth when Destrou touched it.

Sprawling branches of ice arched into doorways to the other rooms. A spiraling staircase led them deeper. Icy flowers now sprouted from the walls. There were none anywhere in the Village, but in here floral designs were everywhere. Odd.

Destrou's stomach twisted as Elu guided him throughout the cave. He had many questions but wonderment took over his ability to speak.

Destrou froze, shocked by how small he felt. "W-where are we?"

"This place is called the Tree of Eve, but I call it the Tree," Elu said.

"Is this a real tree?" Destrou eyes widened. He felt an unexplainable warmth within him. This place looked more glorious than the best image he created for a heaven.

"No, silly, everything here is ice."

"Did you do this?"

"Hah! I wish. Well, some of it . . . I wanted to finish what they started."

Destrou's eyes widened. "Who started?"

"I don't know, but I think it was our mothers' escape—a place where they could feel free." Elu looked up through the ceiling. A light bathed his body in a tinted blue.

"Our mothers?"

"Yeah. Part of me thinks this was how life used to look."

"How come no one else knows about this?" Destrou pulled his face closer to a series of designs that molded into a flower. The lines were smooth. Perfect.

"It's for people looking for a peaceful escape. Not everyone knows about this place because they shouldn't. That's what makes it great; it's a place that's meant to be hidden—keeps the feeling of purity—which can't be destroyed. I won't allow it!"

"Wow." Destrou absorbed the moment. "It's amazing." He saw an object on the ground and picked it up. It was an ice pick with dull edges and its bone handle creased like an hourglass. "Did you borrow this one, too?"

"I don't know what you're talking about." Elu smiled. "I was going to give this one back. My word! I kinda needed to finish more work, and that one is too old. Plus, they're fat slobs who won't use it, anyway."

They exchanged a moment of laughter. There was a beautiful echo that made their laughter extend even after the moment ended.

"Why do you do it?" Destrou looked at Elu with a glowing respect.

"When I add to their work, there's a moment when I feel like I'm a part of something greater. Whenever I'm here, I think about how simple and good life could be. And the stories, oh my Divine, the stories take me away!"

"I want to know them!"

"I'll show you them, I promise! Like Eve, she's just sooo amazing and sounds too good to be true. You must be amazing to have a tree and a star named after you, you know?"

Destrou's eyes narrowed. "Who's Eve?"

"Oh, my poor, little, tiny Destrou, you really don't know anything, do you?" Elu sighed, patting him on the shoulder. "An Eve story is in one of these rooms, I'll read it to you; but before I do that, I'll show you one more thing!"

Elu walked up to a hole in the wall. It was barely bigger than his torso. He climbed up into it, crawling into the darkness. After a few moments passed, Destrou followed. It was so tight of a fit that Destrou felt the cold seep into his clothes. The tight space made his heart pump faster. His fear of closed spaces started to kick in. His feet and palms frosted over with sweat.

He held back every urge to scream for help.

The end of the tunnel looked at first like a black wall. As they crawled closer, it opened up more, allowing light to enter. Relief flooded Destrou, no longer feeling trapped.

When they reached the end, it was a different view of the Forest; the closest that Destrou had ever been. Everything was different. The trees were stark and bare of leaves but with a new perspective—he could see texture. They were jagged and ripped.

Elu sat down. His feet dangled over the edge. He motioned for Destrou to sit nearby.

Destrou's fear of heights made him hesitate at first.

Fighting his fear, he perched his hands down through the thin layer of snow, stabilizing himself as his butt slowly made contact. His heavy breathing calmed, and he enjoyed the salty, unfamiliar scent. His nose tingled with a freshness that was raw. Destrou understood why Elu loved this. The Forest wasn't so scary. Not anymore. Not at all. It was actually quite the opposite.

"Isn't it amazing?" Elu said. "Don't you get the feeling that there might be something good inside there—something they aren't telling us?" Elu had a fire in his eyes, as if he was waiting for some deep, thought-provoking comment to keep the conversation going.

"I can't feel my butt, can you?"

Elu's fire vanished. He ignored Destrou's question and turned his gaze toward the Forest.

Far ahead, Destrou recognized carvings on the tips of the trees that resembled the ones he previously saw on the stones.

"Did things used to live on top of the trees?" Destrou asked.

"I don't know," Elu said excitedly. That rejuvenated him. "But I'm glad you asked the same question I did when I first came here!"

Destrou was shocked to find out Elu didn't have an answer. But something bothered him that he needed to get off his chest. "If everything is so great and your life seems so perfect" —he paused, feeling ice slide down his throat—"why jump?"

"Oh," Elu said, his cheeks flushed with red. "I don't want you think of me that way. I'm not crazy. Really, I'm fine."

"I don't think you're crazy, I just want to know what could bring such a happy person down to that point. What happened?"

"You're very special, Destrou."

"Huh? That was random. Why?"

"You see past the cloth, you see me as a person. As me."

"What do you see when you look at me?"

Again, there was a piercing gaze when their eyes met. "I see someone . . ." Elu paused. "I see someone who'll do great things with his life. And who wouldn't have jumped, either. "

Although Destrou understood that Elu didn't mean harm with his comment, a rage burned within him. "What do you mean? Don't act like you know what it's like to live my life."

Elu was taken aback. "I didn't mean it like—"

"Like what?" Destrou interrupted, forcing his fingers through his dreads. His head stung as if it was punctured by a thousand needles. "Your life is great compared to mine. I actually had a reason to jump, not you!"

"That's not true!" Elu screamed, tears swelling up in his eyes. Then he dropped his voice. "I may not understand what it's like to be you, but I do understand what it's like to wake up every morning feeling trapped in a world where I don't belong. I wake up every morning in fear. Every morning knowing that I'll never be accepted for who I am. Do you know what it feels like to live a lie, just to survive? I thought about jumping because at least in the Forest or dead I could be myself. I could be accepted. I could die knowing that for the first time in my life I was free."

"Well, tell me." Destrou hesitated, feeling a mass grow in his throat. He felt ashamed for lashing out. "What can be so bad?"

Elu's voice was calm and quiet in his reply. "Believe me, there are some secrets that I wish I could tell you."

"You promised!"

"This secret is different though!"

"Why?"

"The other ones are the Village's. This one's mine. This could kill me . . . or worse."

"I promise to keep it a secret. My word!" He looked at Elu with the best sad face that he could manage. His lips curled downwards, and his eyes drooped.

"There's only one other person who knows this, and that's because he's my brother. This means I trust you more than I ever thought I could trust a person."

"I'll protect it with my life."

Elu turned around, asking for help with his scarf. Destrou placed his hand on it, pulling it toward him as the bottom part unraveled over Elu's mouth. Some strands of blond hair dropped down, landing on Destrou's bare skin, making his skin tingle. His mind buzzed with questions, wondering when would be a good time to ask them. Elu's voice became soft—almost too soft. When the scarf fell to the ground, beautiful, blond hair flowed down onto his shoulders. His shoulders? What was going on?

When Elu turned to thank him. Standing before him was the

most lovely person he'd ever seen. The hesitation in her lips showed that she wanted to say something, but was too afraid of breaking the moment to ask any of them. Her hair was wavy and voluminous, her eyes were beautiful, the light leaching the blue out of them. Her skin was creamy and smooth; her breathing was soft.

Destrou didn't know what to say. Shock froze him in place. He couldn't explain what he felt or saw. *Is Elu a . . . girl?*

Before today, everything about his world was ugly; from the slush and the grime to the awful everyday stench. But in a moment everything had changed. The beauty of this cave was easily the most appealing thing he had ever laid eyes on. But of all the incredible things he had seen tonight, Elu was the most rapturous. Her high cheekbones and Cupid's bow lips; she was too pretty to pass as a boy—no wonder she always had her hair covered. His eyes wandered down to her figure for further clues that he may have missed. Her clothes were ripped, stained, and above all loose, not revealing any indication of her shape—yet now he looked more closely he could see the faint curve of her breasts and hips. She pulled a lock of blond hair behind her ear, and a sprinkling of freckles were revealed. He had never seen someone so perfect. She was—

"Perfectly beautiful." His thought escaped as a whisper. He was too shocked to say anything else. This was a real girl in front of him. The world was so ugly that he appreciated having someone in his life that brought him as much joy as she did mystery, as much adventure as beauty.

Their eyes met. Again, they exchanged a piercing gaze. Elu's hair flowed between them as a gust whistled by.

Elu gulped a difficult breath before speaking softly, "I'm   . . . a girl."

A powerful gust of wind blasted through the room. Gabrael wrapped his hands over his hood as the book's pages fluttered about, sounding like an airship was landing.

"Oh. My. Divine!" S'rae screeched, squeezing her palms together as her hair danced in the wind. "I knew that I loved Elu a lot, but now I really love her!" She squealed, shaking Han'sael back and forth. She loved many things about Elu. How she saw herself in her by the way she wrapped the scarf around her head and face, just as she would do when they trekked through the blinding sandstorms in the Ramal Easifa flats. The way her smile would shine bright during the darkest times, and how her eyes shone with kindness. Beauty was within her. It was in her mannerisms and personality.

Han'sael puffed his cheeks, as if he was ready to vomit.

Gabrael couldn't help but smile at her excitement.

"OMD! I'm so like Elu, right? Don't you see it?" She turned to Vayp, shaking him harder. "I am, right?"

Vayp shook his head.

"Come on, she's so awesome and smart, it's practically me, right? You know, I can be cool, right?" She turned to the side, tossing her hair, and grinning. The way her face scrunched and her mouth curled open, she looked like a troll. She knew that she failed to impress him, but she didn't care.

"Umm . . . if only you could see how cool you look right now," Vayp coughed, then smiled. "But, isn't she smart?"

"Ha, ha. You're so funny." She rolled her eyes. "Ahem, not to brag, but I'm in Fujita, remember? And who do you think got top of the class?" She smiled, pointing her finger at every part of her body while dancing in her chair, "Me, me, me, S'raelu."

"So about that humility you were talking about earlier?" Fujak said.

"Oh hush, number two!" S'rae scrunched her nose at Fujak. She felt happy beyond words. It shocked her, especially after the horror

she had just gone through. But she felt connected. The characters in the book were much more than words on a page. They were real. She saw herself in them. In Elu. "Let me have my moment!" She turned back to Vayp. "So?"

"I guess."

"Come on! Just say it even if you don't mean it!" She smiled.

"Oh, yes, you're just like Elu," he said unenthusiastically.

"OMD! Like, thank you so much! I had a feeling I wasn't the only one who thought so." She shuffled her shoulders excitedly, humming a tune. "Okay, sorry about that, I got a little too excited, you can keep reading now!"

"Oh, I can, can I?" Gabrael smiled. "Well, since I have your permission, then I suppose I shall continue on . . ."

17

ESTROU SAT, PEERING OVER AN EDGE inside a tunnel he had never been to before. For a moment, he wondered how the stars aligned to make this possible—how he'd befriended someone who was kind and wonderful and mysterious, and, most surprising, a girl. And a beautiful girl, too. For once he didn't stumble upon a new, random scene because he was lost, but because he had found a friend. Exhaustion crept in, urging his body to sleep but his mind was awake, mesmerized by the effect of this new found companionship. He was so used to being alone and never being able to explore the questions that rushed through his brain that he never wanted to stop asking them. If only the moment with Elu would never end.

"So what else would you like to know?" Elu asked. She sat on the ground, and raised her knees to her chest, clenching her palms over them, and resting her chin. Her hair hung down either side of her heart shaped face like golden silk. She gazed at him, seeming to have the same hunger in her eyes as Destrou, as if they'd both been deprived of affection and loving communication. Together it was like they were learning a new language. A language of understanding, of comfort and ease.

"I want to know everything about you," Destrou replied, leaning forward—"can we talk about your life as a girl? How you came to the Village? Who your brother is? Why you pretended to be a boy? Wait . . . are you the girl that you were talking about? The one that got away?" He stood there awkwardly, shuffling about, his cheeks flushed red.

"I'm sorry," Elu said softly. "I'm not ready to talk about that. Anything else, but that. I promise I'll tell you when I'm ready."

Destrou swallowed his words. He saw her look of anguish, and understood the pain in her eyes—the way she looked away. Like a fresh wound, he knew very well that some things were too sensitive to touch when opened.

"Why me?" Destrou asked. "Why did you want to become friends with me? Bad things could happen."

"Of course it's dangerous." She hesitated, "but there was something about you that was different. I saw it the moment I laid eyes on you." Their gaze met for a few seconds until Elu looked away. "Everyone around here is so angry and full of hate, but you, you get picked on, beaten up, bullied everyday and you're never angry. You always have a smile and a glow in your eyes. I guess I wanted to know more. What made you like that?"

"I could say the same thing about you . . . you don't seem angry either. Why's that?"

"Hey, I asked you first, silly. That's not how this works." She laughed, pushing Destrou.

"Okay, okay. Sorry. I guess . . . I think that instead of being mad about the past—be happy that there's a now and a chance for a better future."

"I like that . . . a lot." Elu smiled.

"I mean, I do have Ranmau. If he wasn't around, things would be much worse. I don't think I'd still be alive," Destrou said, rubbing the sting behind his eyes.

"Yeah," Elu replied, "you're lucky to have him, but you underestimate yourself . . . I think you'd still survive and be happy. You seem like me—to make the best out of any situation."

"I guess, but I have it pretty bad—" Destrou was interrupted by a faint sound coming from the Forest. His instincts took over then. He stood up and gazed into the darkness. "What was that? You hear that?"

"Yeah, just sounds of the Forest; that happens from time to time." Elu stood up, cupping her hand around her ear.

"Huh? And they don't scare you?"

"Why would that scare me? It's just a noise."

"Yeah, but you don't know what's making the noise."

"Why should I be afraid of the dark when the things that I see in the light are scarier?"

Destrou's mouth opened but words failed to come. He paused for a moment, digesting Elu's words. "True, but that means it could be an Archon—do you believe in them?" Destrou glared in the direction that the sound came from.

The fire in her eyes blazed again. "I've read some stories—I don't know how true they are, but if an Archon was in there, why would it scare me?" Elu joined Destrou at the cliff. "People have told terrible stories about you and Ranmau. I could have believed them, but I didn't. Once I got to know you, I knew the stories weren't true. The same can happen to an Archon."

"I never thought about it like that."

"Yeah, like, let's say this . . . I know me and my brother can fight about something, but then we find out it was for the wrong reason. So maybe we fought the Archons for the wrong reason and

never got to talk to them about it, you know?"

"What you're saying kinda makes sense . . ." Destrou's voice wavered a bit. What Elu said challenged everything that he had ever heard or thought about the Archons. It intrigued him—he was more curious about why she felt that way toward Archons than he was about discovering who her brother was.

Elu stood up, shooting her hands in the air, yelling random words with a high-pitched squeal. Destrou backed up, leaning against the wall, wondering if Elu had gone mad.

"You said that I made sense!" she shouted. "So I'm not crazy . . . well, maybe a little but at least not a lot." Elu's voice was a higher pitch. She couldn't contain her excitement. She danced around, humming a melody, flailing her hands and legs in every direction.

Destrou didn't know whether to run away or keep watching. The song put him at ease and made him more curious than frightened.

Elu danced until she collapsed to the ground, pressing her palms through the thin snow.

Destrou pressed his fingers over his mouth, holding back a chuckle. It couldn't be contained. His mouth widened. A jolt of laughter escaped. Something came over him, unable to explain why he was laughing. He enjoyed the moment no matter how wacky it seemed.

The laughter was contagious. When one laughed, the other laughed harder. They were laughing so loud that they rolled around, clutching their sides, until the two of them lay on the ground, gasping for air.

Elu sat up, leaning against the side of the tunnel, hanging her leg over the rim.

"That means the world to me," Elu said. "You have no idea how great it is to hear that I'm not crazy. That's all that everyone says when I talk about how life really could have been like."

"Really?" Destrou was taken aback. "I think you're the smartest person in the Village. What do those krillens know, anyway?"

Elu smiled.

"But . . . why aren't you afraid of them?" Destrou asked. "I mean, they were the most evil things, killing everything and everyone."

"I thought you'd never ask."

Destrou mimicked Elu and sat down, leaning against the tunnel, hanging his leg over the edge. Painted with a white light, Destrou and Elu sat on the cliff, shoulder to shoulder. It was a magical moment. Destrou observed Elu's eyes looking into the distance, as if collecting her thoughts.

"I've never been the type to listen to only one side of the story," she said, gazing into the Forest. A few moments passed before she continued. "What if the Archons aren't bad and the Kingdom uses them as a way to keep us trapped? And if the Archons were real and alive, don't you think that the Kingdom would start preparing for a war or something? They'd recruit everyone—even little Villagers like us. And if Archons are real, and the Kingdom wanted us to fight against them, why would I fight them when I don't know the truth?

"Just because the Kingdom says we need to fight them because they're our enemy, we fight them? I would tell them: 'No, they're *your* enemy. And you're *my* enemy. They aren't the ones keeping me starving, trapped behind this stupid wall. They aren't the ones forcing me to hide who I am.' Just like you and Ranmau aren't the ones keeping me starving.

"You and Ranmau keep winning but that's not a reason to hate you. People who don't ask questions will always believe the first thing that people tell them. We aren't the problem. We live in a problem—and no one's searching for the answer because we don't

even know that there's a problem. That's why I like you . . . you ask questions." She took a deep breath. "Phew, sorry, I told you that I wouldn't be able to shut up!"

"Wow!" Destrou scratched his head, absorbing all of the information. "That was . . . a lot . . . and amazing. I don't know what to say."

"Say whatever's on your mind. You're free here."

"What if there was a war . . . would you fight in it?"

Elu smacked her lips. "Of course!"

"But you don't seem like the angry type to fight."

"Speak for yourself, little boy!" She laughed. "I'd train everyday if I had to. I'd start right now."

"Why wou—" Destrou started, but Elu didn't wait for him to finish.

"'Cause I'd rather be a warrior in the Village than a Villager in a war."

For a moment he couldn't breathe. Fear paralyzed every inch of his being. The concept of war terrified him. It simmered beneath his skin, prickling sharp and hot. But when he lifted his gaze and caught Elu's eyes . . . something unexplainable happened. The fear that made his lips shake vanished. A smirk revealed itself. "Well, which side would you fight on?"

"I'd fight for whatever side Eve is on!" Elu smiled.

"Eve? Oh yeah . . . tell me about her!"

"I will, but first—" Elu raised her fist, then bonked Destrou square on the forehead with her palm.

"Ow!" Destrou rubbed his head. The way it throbbed, he knew that her little hand packed quite the power. "What was that for?"

"That's for not knowing who she is! I had to, I'm sorry." Elu shrugged. "Don't worry . . . I forgive you! But now, it's storytime. Follow me!"

Elu grabbed Destrou's wrist and pulled him toward the entrance.

The first thing Destrou saw when he entered this new room was a carving on the wall, a large circle with gashes all around it, like a clock. The whiteness of it stood out from the aqua-colored walls of the room. Light seeped in through thin patches of ice overhead, bathing the room in light blue. The room was a perfect circle at least fifty feet wide, and at his feet there was a tree carved into the ice.

"What's this?" Destrou pressed his fingers to the wall, touching the smooth circle. Two gashes stood out from the rest—creating an oval shape. "What do these mean?"

"It took me some time to understand what it means, and I know it may sound crazy, but I think it's a way to measure time."

"Time?"

"Yeah, you see this one?" Elu pointed to the top. "That's, I think, the beginning of time. And these" —she grazed her finger around the circle—"are different moments in time. Don't ask me how, I'm still learning. But these different ones"—her fingers touched the two oval shapes—"tell us when the story took place and when it was written."

Destrou wanted to think that she was crazy, but something within him warmed up with trust and curiosity. "What story? I don't see anything." Destrou looked around. And then it hit him. He was so focused on the clock that he missed the drawings carved into the walls. There were dozens of those circles scattered around, each slightly different.

"These are the stories." Elu pointed at pictures that looked like a collection of lines and shapes carved into the walls. "They are called Dream Words, and I guess they were created by a prophet

named Va'han."

"Dream Words? How do you know? Can you read them?"

"Well, there's a really cool trick that shows you the story in your mind, like a dream, but it's really hard to do. You're not cool enough for that secret yet." Elu smiled at Destrou's frown before punching him on the shoulder. "I'm kidding . . . maybe I'll show you how to do it later. But I didn't want to just see the stories in my mind, though. I wanted to teach myself how to read the symbols also, it took a few years. I'm still learning, so I may mess up a little."

"Which story does this one tell?" Destrou pointed at the circle where an oval shape was above the circle, at the very top.

"That story takes place at the beginning of time. It's about . . . Eve." Elu cleared her throat. Then, with her piercing gaze, she looked mournfully into Destrou's eyes.

Destrou sat down, pressing his butt onto the ice. He took a deep breath, understanding her look—they were the eyes of someone who was ready to relay something sad.

There was a moment of silence. Then Elu opened her mouth and began.

THOUSANDS OF YEARS AGO, there was a time when the world was filled with life and love. There was peace in all corners of the land. Imagine a place much larger than the Village, and all around, as far as your eyes could see, were trees with beautiful colors of every kind. Each of the four corners was controlled by an element. And each of the elements had its own God and people. The Gods all worked together like family—because they were. Of all the Gods, there was one who didn't control a corner, or an element, and that was because her power was harnessed in nature and life. She went by the name of Eve.

Her power being nature, she was considered nature's mother and had the ability to make rain fall with her tears, or flowers bloom with her smile. Her presence alone made civilizations flourish. And with such power came a fatal flaw. The place where she remained the longest would blossom more than the others. That civilization would have more wildlife to hunt and more crops to farm—there was also less destruction, diseases, droughts, and disasters—but this created jealousy amongst the Gods and their people.

Eve was once loved by all, until she fell in love with a God. They spent all of their time together, she was filled with life and joy and his kingdom thrived because of her. While they lived in happiness, the other Gods plotted to take Eve away from him. To avoid war, he agreed to their terms: They would create a forest in the middle of the planet where Eve must live alone, allowing all corners to flourish equally. Her home was called the Tree of Life, located inside of the Great Forest.

Peace was restored, but Eve was forced to live without love—a great sacrifice to keep the balance of nature.

After many years, her love's closest friend, Den, fell terminally ill. The only person he loved more than Den was Eve herself. Den's heart was so pure and good that the God called for Eve to heal him. She longed to be with him again, so in secrecy, she spread her wings and flew the night, arriving the next day. Eve possessed the powers to heal, but reviving the dead was a different magic—a dark one. A door that was to remain closed. It seemed there was nothing that could be done for him. He was destined to die. However, after the God pleaded his love for Eve, she finally performed the ritual, resurrecting his friend. But nature always needed balance. With death came life, but with life for the dead, came death to the living. Once she ruined the balance, danger weighed over the horizon.

Den was reborn, but was different. He starved, but food couldn't

cure his hunger. His skin became blacker than the night. His eyes became red like blood. After trying to keep him a secret, it was finally revealed and the other Gods once again came together. They issued a command for the capture of the Man of Shadows. The God refused to watch his friend get murdered—refusal meant war. And that night, when Eve, her lover, and his friend came together to discuss their defense, she found the God's heart no longer beating. What dark magic was capable of killing a God? And the question of who soon followed. There was a mystery, and in a fury, Den's eyes blackened into a blind rage. That night Den massacred an entire civilization, turning its people into shadowy, soulless beasts. And in just one night, he had amassed the Shadow Army. The Man of Shadows became their God. His past became a forgotten myth—a story about how evil can corrupt the purest souls. He was no longer remembered as the God, Den—he became Geddon, the God of Darkness.

Eve's heart turned black. In a shrieking roar, a veil darker than night eclipsed over the land. For that split second, they were stuck in a realm where time and all senses were removed, as if all who were touched by its darkness temporarily died. The dark God, Geddon had barely survived that void, an eternity inside there was only a blink of an eye to mere mortals. When the darkness faded, Geddon had witnessed the hidden secret of Time, one only the Divine One should know. And that was the first ever glimpse of the destroyer of Time known as the Eve of Darkness. Geddon stopped at nothing to attain her—he thirsted for that power to create a world of darkness. And so the First Great War began. It was a war for Eve— not to protect her, but to possess her.

The Gods united to fight off the Shadow Army. Their combined forces were barely enough to defeat the powerful army. If not for the death of the God and the volcanic winter that frosted the land ten times over, they might not have won. Ice swept the land, and the Ice Kingdom rose from the ashes, becoming the most powerful kingdom. With the help of its Crystal Soldiers, they overcame the Shadow Army, pushing the Evil deep into the Great Forest—where they were bound away for an eternity, to rot and decay.

There wasn't much victory to celebrate. Nature began to fade away. Trees withered. Animals became extinct. Mother Nature's heart was broken, and nature suffered because of it. Eve sensed how important *he* really was to her, because when he died, months later, her heart stopped beating as well. And with her last heartbeat, and the loss of the element, cold and death swept through the planet, encapsulating it in an eternal winter called the Ice Age.

However, as the cycle of life exists in nature through the changing seasons, Mother Nature, Eve, was no different. As the leaves perish throughout the fall and winter, and become green with new life again in the spring and summer; so too does Eve. It was said that after thousands of years, winter will end, and nature will spring forth with its new mother; then humans will repeat the same mistakes in their search for power. Civilizations will fight for her again, and wars will occur, and destruction and extinction will follow, until humanity starts over again. This cycle continues endlessly until the circle of Time ultimately resets.

It wasn't until Elu stopped speaking that Destrou noticed how lost in the story he had become. He tilted his head and observed Elu's movements as she walked over to the circle.

"This is the Circle of Time." Elu touched the wall. "And I think these gashes show each time a new Eve and humanity was created. These are . . . the Legends of Eve."

18

THE ROOM LAPSED INTO SILENCE. The story. Elu's words. They had clouded Destrou's mind. He almost didn't catch what Elu had said.

"Do you believe that story?" Destrou felt a sudden surge of uneasiness. "Because if that's true, then wouldn't this mean the next Eve's coming?" The full force of his words snapped him out of his fog.

"I don't know, but it's one of my favorite stories." Elu looked away, rubbing her eyes. "I just love her so much. All she wanted was to be happy and in love. And they wouldn't let her. They just wanted to control her."

"You ever wonder why girls aren't in the Village?"

"It's because bad things happen to us."

"But . . . maybe the reason they take girls away is because they're . . . searching for Eve?"

Elu glanced around suggestively as if that thought had never crossed her mind.

"What if . . ." Destrou felt energized, realizing he made some sense. ". . . Eve is almost here? And they're looking for her . . . and—" continued Destrou as he looked into Elu's eyes.

"And?"

"And what if . . . you're Eve?"

Elu laughed so hard that Destrou thought he felt the ground shake. "Oh my, aren't you one silly dilly." She gasped for air in between her laughs.

Destrou's shoulders slouched. "Was it that stupid?"

"I'm sorry." Elu's faced turned serious. "I thought you were joking. I didn't mean it like that—it's just that Eve is a Goddess, the real mother nature, the most beautiful, compassionate, amazing person to ever live."

"And?" Destrou said. "So are you."

She gazed piercingly into his eyes. "You're so silly. . . well, there was one story about how nature could also create a new Eve from the ground, and the girl wouldn't even know she was Eve."

"Exactly! Just like you don't know you're Eve."

"You're such a krillen butt! Stop!" Elu smiled. Her pale face flushed red. "I didn't come from the ground! But I like that nickname. Hi, I'm Evelu!" Suddenly, Elu jumped up and down, clapping her hands, as if something had just appeared in her mind. "I have one more thing to show you!"

She pointed at one of the clocks. There was an oval shape above it, just left of the center.

"Out of all of the stories here, this is the only one that tells a story about the future."

"The future? How's that possible?"

"I know, it sounds crazy, but it's interesting that it's the only one, you know? It's not just in the future . . . it's at the very end of the circle."

"What's it about?" Destrou's eyes widened.

"You know what?" Elu placed her fist under her chin and smirked, as if noticing the stars in his eyes. "I won't tell you   .. . I'll show you instead. Or try to."

"You mean show me how to see the Dream Words?" Normally this idea would be considered crazy, but since it came from Elu, he learned to no longer question the impossible.

"Mmmhmm." Elu smiled. "It takes forever to master, but at least we can start tonight!"

"You really think I'm ready?" Destrou rubbed his hands together with excitement.

"Oh, you? Ready? For this? *Ha!*" Elu burst out in a quick, sudden laugh. "Oh no, no, noo, my poor little Destrou! You're not even close! You're at least this"—Elu spread her arms out as wide as possible—"far away. If it took me years to master, I don't even want to know how long it'd take you. No offense, I just don't want you to get your hopes up! But, hey, everyone starts somewhere! And this one's an awesome one to start on!"

"Thanks for your faith in me." Destrou rubbed the top of his head. "So, what do I do?"

"Press your hand here." Elu gently pulled Destrou's wrist toward the circle on the wall. "Close your eyes."

Destrou did as instructed.

"Good. Now whisper '*tra'um ais'ling son'he paro'la*' exactly how I said it."

When Destrou asked Elu to repeat the words again, he tried his best to mimic her. She made it seem too easy, the way her tongue rolled effortlessly to create foreign sounds. Destrou didn't even know how those guttural noises could come from such a tiny mouth. Then suddenly there was a flash in his mind. He couldn't describe what he saw. He thought he saw trees with some type of random green stuff on top of them. Then there was a sudden *BANG* followed by an explosion that obliterated all the stars and moons. The blackness of space illuminated into bright light.

"I think I saw something!" Destrou's eyes shot open. "It only lasted a second though, but I think I actually did it! What's this story supposed to be about anyway?"

"Oh my divine! Maybe you'll learn quicker than I thought!" Destrou saw stars in her eyes as their gaze met. "I'm impressed!" She puckered her lips, nodding her head several times. "Well, this story is a short one, and incomplete, but it's about three countries sending their four best warriors to the forbidden country—something like that. But anyway, if we think that our life is bad, apparently what happens to them is much worse."

"How can anything be worse than this?"

"Because one of them is a traitor who tells these scary, evil things where they are and they don't even know that something very bad is going to kill them all. It's the end of—" A gust of wind roared through the tunnels, tossing their hair across their faces. "Let's get out of here!" Elu screamed over the sound of rolling thunder.

She grabbed Destrou's hand and ran toward the entrance.

A gust of wind blew through the room and interrupted Gabrael's reading. S'rae tried to calm herself down, but anxiety surged through her like a wave. She clenched her hands together to stop them from shaking and glanced around to see if any of the other students felt the same. Han'sael was once again picking at his food. Vayp was nervously gazing at the window, preoccupied with other thoughts. The Fujitas looked bored. The Serenis looked at one another, probably admiring their beauty. And the GroundStones were too far away to notice.

How is no one else freaking out about this? S'rae wondered. *Is Elu warning us? Is Eve? There are too many coincidences with this book, why are we really reading it? I don't think this is just a story. Gabrael wouldn't waste our time reading a regular story. But why this one? Why us?*

By the time Elu and Destrou made it out of the cave, the wind had died down to a soft breeze. Destrou collided into Elu, pushing her to the ground as they slid across the ice.

"Whee!" Elu shouted, gliding on her back. "That was fun, let's do it again!"

They spent at least a half hour playing in snow and sliding on ice. Destrou felt a warm sensation erupt inside him despite the chilly air. Amidst the fun, Destrou's food was lost. On any other day, that would be crushing news, but not today. Food was less important than the moment. This had been his best day ever.

He now only cared about what was officially his favorite game ever: the staring contest.

To Destrou, it wasn't about winning or losing, because he lost every time. It was about gazing into Elu's eyes and seeing much more than the beautiful blues and whites that reflected off them. In her eyes he saw swirls of sapphire like the sky when it was not heavy with clouds. He saw the light of a morning a thousand days in the future. And felt a sense of completeness inside, a fullness that went beyond what it might feel like to eat enough food. He saw a moment that he never wanted to end. He didn't blink, not because he wanted to win, but because he wished he could stare into her eyes forever. Elu may had thought Destrou kept challenging her because he was competitive and wanted to win. But that was far from the truth. Because Destrou felt like he was winning even when he lost.

And as Destrou and Elu rolled around, playing in the snow, they finally stopped as Elu sat on Destrou's stomach, pinning his shoulders down with her palms.

"I win!" Elu shouted for what felt like the hundredth time.

"I didn't know this was a challenge." He chuckled.

"It wasn't, but I win again!" She laughed.

They shared their laughter for a few moments, then Elu stopped abruptly, gazing into Destrou's eyes.

A beautiful silence hung in the air, as the reality of the moment settled over them.

"Destrou . . ." She paused. It felt like time froze. "I—"

As Elu spoke, the ground shook as if there was an earthquake. They both felt weightless, like the ice was a rug that had been swept from underneath them. Their eyes widened. Then their eardrums popped as an explosion erupted from deep within the Forest of Ness.

BANG! A white light, resembling a spiraling beam, traveled rapidly, rippling through the clouds like a propeller through water. It reached past the sky, vanishing as quickly as it had appeared. Shortly after, they heard a roar that sounded like waves crashing against walls. Then a blast of energy crashed through the ice and snow, knocking Elu and Destrou away from the Forest.

Destrou felt the wind get knocked out of him. A ringing noise overcame his senses as he stumbled to stand upright. He had been hit many times, but had never felt power like that.

Elu glared at Destrou. Through the ringing, he heard a sizzle overhead. The Eye of Eve flickered for a few moments before brightening up the sky.

Destrou's eyes narrowed then he cringed. *It has been a long time since the First Great War . . . but I don't think the Forest is so empty anymore . . .*

"This isn't good," Elu said in between her deep breaths.

"What happened?" Destrou felt his stomach sink.

"It's glowing now. It never glows," Elu said, in an almost-calm voice, but Destrou had seen her pupils contract with sudden fear.

"What happened in the Forest?"

"It never glows." This time fear heightened her voice.

"Elu? Do you know what that could've been?"

Elu's gaze remained fixated on the Eye of Eve.

"The Eye?" Destrou said. "But it always glows. You made it, remember?"

Elu whipped her head around at the sound of his voice. She frowned, looking confused, and then shook her head. Her voice was softer. "Yes." She turned toward the light. "But it never glowed like this."

"What do you think this means?"

"I have no idea, but—"

A loud horn with a deep bass echoed throughout the Valley, reverberating through every tree, igloo, and building. That type of horn meant something was coming from the Kingdom, usually a message.

Why would the Kingdom send something when everyone's sleeping? Destrou thought. They hadn't received anything in months but it was still too early for the next ration. And much too late to receive a message. They only came in the morning, never at night.

"What do you think this horn is for?" Destrou looked at Elu who appeared confused for the second time.

She mumbled to herself while counting her fingers. "This isn't right. Not at all."

"What's not right?"

She ignored him, bobbing her head side to side while moving her lips. "The Kingdom works in numbers. Even when they send a package early, it'll be on a specific day, and time. They never break from routine."

"Do you think this has to do with the light we saw?"

"Let's hope not. This will be very bad if it has anything to do with the Eye of Eve or that explosion." Her eyes widened.

"Why?" Destrou said. Elu's look of fear made his heart sink.

"Do you remember what I talked about tonight?"

"Of course. I'll never forget it."

Elu's frightened face revealed a smile for a brief second. "Well . . . I think it's happening."

"What? What's happening?"

Immediately the sky tore open, spreading the clouds with a ripple. Moonlight cascaded down from the opening as a glow resonated brightly. Blue dust swirled, blown by a soft wind that gravitated toward the center.

BANG! A stream of light zapped through the sky, striking the NoGo.

Elu stared at the NoGo, then looked behind her, where Destrou stood, and said, "It's war."

"What does it mean when the Eye of Eve glows like that?" S'rae asked. "Is that bad?"

"Ah, when it glows." Gabrael's words were so sharp that she felt them pierce through her body. "That is a very good question. It is said to glow when the yielder is in trouble and danger is nearby."

"What if no one's holding it? Then what?"

"What do you think?" His voice was soft and deep.

"I guess . . . it means . . . that the entire Village is in danger."

Her eyes scanned the room for a moment, confused at the thoughts that burned through her brain. *What does all of this mean? Is Eve in trouble? Are we in danger?*

She paused for a few moments. *That's it—I'm finding out why we're really here!*

19

ESTROU RAN AS FAST AS HE COULD through thick snow, reluctant to pass Elu. He leapt, then a sudden thought entered his mind . . . *Where exactly is she taking me?* Confused, he ran faster to catch up with her. She was smiling. He didn't know how to express it into words, but he admired how nothing held Elu down for long. A few minutes earlier she was scared at the sight of the Kingdom's message after the white light tore through the sky. Now, she was filled with energy, as though the light shocked life into her. Destrou tried to say something but couldn't speak.

"We made it!" Elu said, sliding to a stop. "That was the quickest I've ever been." She pressed her palms to her knees, heaving giant breaths. "Phew, I must be getting old. That took a lot out of me."

Destrou held back a chuckle. "What are we doing here, anyway?"

He noticed they were in a small clearing that was empty save a few chunks of ice and a mound of snow. The wind made his teeth chatter. And there was a low trembling growl that came from his empty stomach.

Elu slammed her pick into the ice. "I'm a girl of many secrets. Here's one more! I'd say this is the best secret of them all."

"What does this have to do with the message from the Kingdom?"

"Oh my poor, little Destrou, you have sooo much to learn!" Elu's voice trailed off.

Destrou blinked once and Elu was gone. *How does she always do that?* Without anything better to do, he sat against a chunk of ice and watched the snow falling. Minutes turned into what must have been an hour, but Elu still did not return. *I hope nothing's wrong.*

As the waiting dragged on, Destrou grew bored and started to explore his surroundings. He made snowballs and threw them to see how far they'd go. When he became tired, he sat back down and noticed the mound take a different shape, as if it was alive. His imagination went loose, turning the snow into a snake-like monster.

Destrou stared at it and thought about Elu. *Maybe something is wrong.* He breathed deeply and closed his eyes. In his mind he formed a picture of a different monster—the one that lived in his head—trying to make it as lifelike as possible. A massive, wide body, with a black sword, its blade dancing as if made of flowing shadows. Visualizing it was more difficult than usual. During his darkest moments, when he was alone and sad, it was effortless. It'd appear on its own. Unwanted. But now, it seemed impossible. As if it only preyed on him when he was weak. Depressed. Which was often until Elu came into his life.

Is the monster gone? Destrou smiled at the thought of no longer having nightmares, when the monster would slaughter everything in its way. The way its weapon sliced through bodies like a knife through wind. It was horrific . . . but now it was gone. He hoped.

Crunch. Destrou's eyes widened, staring at the mound that seemed to be wiggling. *Is something inside there?* Then a bubble formed on its surface. Destrou crawled toward it slowly. "Hello? Anyone there?" His hand inched closer to it.

His heart raced. Maybe something bad happened to Elu. Maybe—

SNAP! Something grabbed his wrist, yanking him deep into the snow. His heart jumped. He tried to scream but his voice choked into a gasp as snow filled his mouth. His body went rigid with shock. He needed help . . . but he didn't call for Ranmau. Instead he shouted for Elu.

He didn't know how to feel. Was Ranmau already a thing of the past? As if life was moving on fast. Too fast. And their lives as brothers came to an abrupt end. It scared him to think that there will be a time when they will no longer be brothers. By blood, yes, but the bond would never feel the same. No more laughs. Dreams. Memories. That was their old life, and now there was a new one with—

"Elu!" Destrou gasped as he landed on solid ground. He gave himself a few seconds to recuperate, then hugged her. His fear faded. Elu's face eased his nerves. "Where are we?"

He heard his echo back.

"Where are we?"

"Where are we?"

"Whereee areee weee . . ."

"What was that?" Destrou said, shocked to hear his voice magnified ten times over. His voice echoed once more.

"Shh!" Elu whispered, pressing her finger on Destrou's lips. "This place is called the Chamber of Echoes. Do not say anything."

"Okay." Destrou whispered. "Why are we here?" Their surroundings were pure white, but Destrou could see moist snow, like slush, underfoot.

Elu wandered the area, then returned to Destrou with ice in her hands.

She muttered some words, then placed the ice on the ground.

When Destrou finally took his gaze off of Elu's almond shaped eyes, he noticed that the surface of the ground became completely flat, frozen by an invisible force. He could see his reflection. It would ripple with the slightest shuffle of his feet.

Elu knelt down, eyes glittering, palms open.

"What's going on? I don't get it," Destrou whispered.

"I need to hear what the message is about," Elu whispered. "I don't have much time, they could have already read it by now."

"Umm . . ." Destrou looked around aimlessly. "We aren't anywhere near the NoGo."

"You're like a baby," Elu said while her eyes closed. "I'll teach you everything, don't worry." She hummed a melody before speaking. "*Ge'hirn klin'gen.*"

At once, the liquid ice rippled as if an invisible stone dropped into it.

"Hey!" Han'sael shouted. "I've heard about that spell before. I know I have, I know I have! That's one of ours. It was in my Mindiend, Body, and Soul class! But . . . how does she know it?"

"Interesting," Gabrael said softly. "Are you sure you heard it correctly?"

"Yessuh!" Han'sael replied. "But I could be wrong, it can't be the same one."

"And why's that?" Gabrael said.

"Because, that's a seriously hard spell! Just like the Dream Words one! I knew it sounded familiar! That's something only an Elemental could know how to do! And she ain't no Ele!"

"Maybe you are right. Maybe she is not. For maybe . . . she is something much more."

Beads of liquid ice floated into the air, spiraling around Elu and Destrou. Destrou's jaw dropped open with shock. The droplets then crystallized into a mirror underfoot.

"Elu . . ." Destrou was at a loss for words. "You sure you aren't Eve? There is absolutely nothing normal about any of this."

"Destrou!" Elu laughed. Her cheeks turned red. "Stop it! It's really not that special, I promise. It's just something I learned from one of the stories. Anyone can do it. Watch, I'll show you!" Elu grabbed Destrou's wrist. "Okay, close your eyes and think about a person."

Destrou knelt beside her and shut his eyes. The first person who came to mind was Elu.

"Okay, now I want you to picture him in your mind."

Him? It occurred to Destrou that Elu had no idea that she was always on his mind. She probably assumed he was thinking about Ranmau. So, he thought about Ranmau instead. He envisioned him standing proud like the champion he was.

"Now whisper these words then open your eyes," Elu said softly. "*Lato'*mas."

"Latomas."

"No." Elu braced herself, placing her hand on Destrou's shoulder and inching her lips so close he felt her breath tickle his ear. "*Lato'*mas," she whispered.

Between the warmth from her hand that sent chills through his body and the sound of her soft voice that made his heart race, he almost forgot where he was and what he was supposed to say. To bring himself back to the moment, he drummed his fingers on the side of his leg, trying his hardest to focus on her words. How they sounded, not how they felt. The "hiss" sound on the end of the phrase sounded like a strained squeal when pronounced correctly. Destrou took a deep breath before whispering, "*Lato*'mas," as he gazed at his reflection.

His reflection disappeared and everything became clear. On it shimmered an image of Ranmau. There were no surroundings. And instead of him standing proud, he was curled into a ball, screaming in his sleep.

"No . . . no . . ." the vision of Ranmau shouted. "I can't let you win. I can't let this happen to you . . ."

"Soo," Elu said with widened eyes. "Awesome isn't it? What'd you see?"

Elu's words hadn't registered yet. He was too busy trying to understand not only what he saw . . . but how.

"Okay," Elu said. "It's my turn! There's not much time."

"Wait, I don't think I did it right." Destrou lied. "Please, let me try one more time."

"Make it quick." Elu said worriedly. Destrou could see the anxiety in her eyes. She really wanted to know what was in that message. But Destrou had something else that piqued his interest. The monster. The one that lived in his head and haunted his dreams.

What happens if I try to think about something that isn't real?

It was too great of an opportunity to pass by. He knelt by the liquid ice once again.

After fixing the nightmare in his mind, he spoke the words and watched his reflection. He waited, but nothing happened. He was about to stand up when a shadow swirled across the room, bathing the room in black. A vision of a monster appeared amidst the darkness, emerging as a color darker than black. The monster from his dream had his back facing Destrou, dragging a sword as massive as its body. At once, it lifted its head and slowly turned it around. Its red eyes stared directly at Destrou. He froze, the force of its gaze sent chills through his spine. Then the monster roared with a fury Destrou had never seen before.

The room shook. Destrou fell to his back, gasping.

The roar's echo trembled the ground like an earthquake.

"What was that?" Elu screamed, holding Destrou. "This has never happened before! What did you do?"

"I don't know!" Destrou's voice trembled. *It can't be real! It's just a monster in my head. How did it know I was looking at it? What did I do?* Destrou shook his head, wondering if his nightmares were something more. It didn't make sense, but nothing did anymore.

"It's *definitely* my turn now!" Elu pushed Destrou aside. "You really are like a baby, it's just two words and somehow you almost killed us! Jeez! It's okay, I'll forgive you."

"I'm so sorry." Destrou stumbled, taken aback by the cruelty of her words. Elu had never yelled at him like this. He'd never seen such anger in her eyes. "I didn't mean to do anything wron—"

"I know, I know, but shhh!" She rose her hand, silencing Destrou. "I need to listen."

Destrou was stunned. He said nothing because he knew she was disappointed.

Elu whispered the words and her eyes widened, staring into her reflection. She watched intently, as if it was the most fascinating thing ever. But to Destrou, he only saw his reflection. Far from exciting.

"Really?" Elu shrieked.

"Really what?" Hesitantly, Destrou made his way to Elu and asked again. He waved his hands in front of her, but her eyes remained unblinking.

"Oh. My. Divine!" As if Elu's eyes couldn't get wider, somehow they did. "The Kingdom is really going to go into the Forest?"

"Why would the Kingdom do that!?"

"The Kingdom finally found what they've been looking for . . . She is alive."

"Who is alive?" Destrou waited for her to answer, but she didn't respond. Her face glowed with each passing second—she was seeing more, something he couldn't.

A blue light pulsated inside the room. Watching Elu, his curiosity built. How did she know about any of this? The thought of this chamber still made his heart race, part of him wished he brought Ranmau here to experience it with him. The image of Ranmau crying in his sleep began to fill his mind until he heard Elu's nails squish into the slush.

Astonishment widened Elu's eyes. The widest Destrou had ever seen. She placed her hand in her mouth, biting down hard. Her eyes glazed over as if she was ready to cry. Her body shook with excitement. Words tumbled out of Destrou's mouth as he quickly tried to get answers.

"She is alive . . ." Elu said once more, her lips trembling. "Eve is alive."

20

THE CRISP WINTER AIR WHIPPED through Destrou's open window, waking him up instantly. In his bed, he rubbed his eyes gently as he tried to clear his thoughts. He only had an hour or two of sleep. His long night with Elu had left him feeling weary but he had to get up before the Village started the day without him. The image of Elu's widened eyes remained locked in his mind. *Eve is alive?*

The day after the challenge was called Liquid Ice Day. And after what happened last night, he could never look at it the same now.

The boys lined up in front of the NoGo to take showers. Just like the other jobs, the roles circulated between the boys until they found who was best for each task. Destrou had spent his whole life waiting to have a role, but today was his first attempt as the melter.

The Leader barked orders at the boys. Destrou watched him carefully as the boys hooted and hollered by and climbed up the NoGo. Chunks of ice dangled from the ropes tied to their torsos, like a pendulum on a clock. They weren't rough, but smooth like polished glass, and glowed in the light.

The creation of liquid ice was founded by a visionary from the Kingdom and then adapted in the Village. The tower was approximately one hundred feet tall with three large bowls stacked on top of one another. Each one required someone inside to complete a task: chopping, melting, and stirring. Widely accepted as the greatest invention of their time, it was never expected to be replicated by lowly Villagers. Yet here it was. And once the giant shower was created, the Guardian prized it as his favorite object despite the myth of him never bathing.

When Destrou thought back to his last shower, a vision appeared in his mind—so vivid it felt like he was there. He didn't really know much about liquid ice, except that everyone loved it even though they were allowed only two baths a month. But since Ranmau was happy to take a bath, then Destrou was happy. He remembered the smile on Ranmau's face when the liquid drenched him, but he had no way in knowing that was the last day he'd see Ranmau smile. Never again since then.

Destrou was jerked back into the moment by the throbbing of his heart. It raced. He was nervous, and it didn't help that the Melter's gloves wouldn't fit. They were white and furry and used to melt the ice quicker. And they were oddly large. Maybe designed for a Guardian, but definitely not a boy.

His body tightened as fingers clamped around his shoulder.

"You'll do fine," Elu said, her voice muffled by the cloth wrapped around her face. Her eyes were the only features not covered.

"Thank you." Destrou smiled, hiding his hands. "Sure you're okay with talking to me?"

"Of course!" She laughed. "I'm not afraid of these little boys. Don't disrespect me."

The gloves kept slipping off Destrou's hands. "Yeah, but what

about the Lead—"

"Oh hush!" Elu grinned, drawing herself up proudly. "Don't worry about little Eli'jah either. Remember, we have a big secret that we need to keep between us only!" Elu then leaned in closer to Destrou's ear. Her floral scent calmed his nerves almost instantly. "I mean . . . Eve is alive. So, yeah, absolutely nothing can make this a bad day!"

It shocked Destrou to see how normal yet excited Elu was, as if nothing had happened the night before. As if an explosion didn't erupt from deep within the Forest. He didn't know how to bring it up. "Have you done my job before?"

"Melter? No. But this is the second time I'll be a Stirrer. I guess they liked how I did last time." She jumped excitedly. "We get to work together to give the best showers ever!"

"Sounds great to me." Destrou smiled anxiously, still struggling to put the gloves on.

"We're waiting—let's go, already," the Leader shouted from the top of the NoGo, waving the Crystal Sword. A light sparked off it. The blade as clear as crystal, as sharp as the bitter cold on wet skin, the handle was set with light-blue gems. Made from an unbreakable type of ice, nature had never created a blade as powerful as this one. It was said to be the same weapon that the Guardian used when he had been a member of the Crystal Soldiers. The Leader bragged about being the only one allowed to yield it. As if his ego couldn't get any bigger. "I'm starting this with or without you krillens."

Destrou felt a small quiver in his belly as he climbed the ladder, equal parts nerves and anticipation. The gloves posed another problem. The closer he got to his bowl, the more sweaty his palms became, and the more the gloves seemed to slip from his hands. And before he grabbed the last rung, the gloves finally slipped off, tumbling to the ground, leaving his hands to freeze, making it nearly impossible to melt the ice now.

Destrou didn't have a clear idea of how he managed to climb as high as he did. The boys below looked like little snow caps. All he knew was that he couldn't think about the climb, and what he was supposed to do, because his head was still pounding from the memory of last night. He remembered it all too well. He still felt the bump of his head hitting the ground when Elu pinned him down, her smile when she was looking down at him; and how quickly it faded when that explosion happened. *What was that?* Then the message. The chamber. Eve. And . . . the monster. *Was that just in my head or is it real?* He couldn't believe that happened only last night—it felt like an intense dream he'd had years ago.

He wasn't given much time to react. The first batch of ice shavings had already tumbled down the chute, landing in his bowl. He hated to admit it, but the Leader was great at chopping the ice.

The loud grunts, moans, and slashing noises from above sounded like an epic sword fight, making it difficult for Destrou to concentrate. He focused on his surroundings to calm himself down. His bowl was created from a special kind of dense ice with patches of brown skin—probably from an animal or person—that had a slithery texture and a rotten scent. At his feet there was a hole no bigger than his fist, surrounded by ankle-high ice shavings that increased by the second.

"Rub your hands together really fast," Elu shouted to Destrou through the hole. "You can do this!"

The Leader had no intention of stopping; he'd already continued onto the next block, going against protocol. Destrou closed his eyes, bringing his palms together. His anxiety calmed as he took deep breaths in a rhythmic trance, moving his palms in a circular motion. The motion gained in speed as the shavings around him gained in size. Something took over him; he was no longer in con-

trol of his actions.

"You need to be faster," Elu shouted.

Destrou opened his eyes to the sound of Elu's voice. His lungs burned; his next breath rumbled on the way in as he prepared himself. *I can do this.*

When he stared up at the shavings falling down onto him, his body felt different. There was a warm sensation that pulsed through him, traveling from his head to toes then back up through his body. He had never experienced this feeling; for the first time he didn't feel cold. He'd never realized how freezing he was until he wasn't anymore. His heart pumped faster. *I will do this.*

His hands pressed into the ice shavings. They were thin and delicate and liquefied upon impact. Within moments his bowl was filled with liquid ice.

"Destrou," came a soft voice from below. He was in a trance and hadn't realized that his foot was clogging the hole. And when he moved, gallons of liquid ice poured down, overflowing Elu's section.

The boys below jumped around in laughter as a fountain of liquid ice spilled over.

Ranmau took no part in it. He stood below, waiting in line for a bath. Normally, he looked forward to this, but now his brows arched with worry as his lips pressed against his teeth.

The shavings weren't the only thing melting; the whole support appeared to be weakening. Countless showers were created but nothing of this magnitude had occurred before.

At first Ranmau stared at Destrou in silence. Destrou stared back, expecting a pleased look on his brother's face. Seconds passed and Destrou began to worry. His heart pumped faster. Destrou had seen Ranmau worried before, but this was very different. The look on his face was fear.

"Get out!" Ranmau shouted.

Everything stopped, and so did the laughter. In the silence Destrou then heard the creaking of ice and looked down as it created a spiderweb of cracks. Through the hole he saw Elu biting her fingernails.

"Help!" Elu shouted, looking suddenly horrified, as if she knew it was about to collapse.

Destrou gripped the layer of dead skin in his palms and pulled it off in one yank. He tied it around his hand and lunged all of his power into the hole. He stepped back and threw his fist into it again, once, twice, three times, four times. He hit the hole until his fist ached and felt broken. With one final, screaming attempt, he lunged his fist downward, bursting through. He fell into Elu's section, grabbing her with his bruised hand and Elu's stirring staff with the other. The rumbling sounds of collapsing ice interrupted Destrou's train of thought for an escape.

The Leader's platform burst as he jumped off and landed on the NoGo. His widened eyes met Destrou's, and it was in that split second when Destrou realized he no longer saw a terrorizing bully, but he saw someone who cared. It was the same worry he had seen many times in Ranmau's eyes when Destrou was in danger. He saw a leader actually worthy of the title, as if he was ready to sacrifice himself to stop the bowl from crushing the both of them.

"We're goners!" Elu shouted, wiping her eyes free. Soaked strands of her normally blonde hair now stuck to her face in brown waves.

Massive chunks crashed down, obliterating the platform at each point of contact.

"I won't let you die on me. Not now. Not ever." Destrou pulled Elu out of the way as ice crashed down only inches from where she had stood. "Hold on."

"What are you going to do?" Elu hesitated.

Judging by the battle marks on the staff, Destrou had faith that if it was good enough for the Crystal Soldiers, then it should be stout enough for his daring move. He sat down and scooted toward the shattered end of the bowl. Without thinking, he unwound the cloth around his hands, pulled Elu closer and wrapped it around their waists.

"Make sure it's tight," Destrou shouted. His palms became sweaty when he saw Elu's scarf falling off her head. Her drenched hair poked through, looking like weeds growing through cracks.

What little color there was in Elu's face left instantly.

Elu finished tightening the knot as Destrou grabbed the staff. He wished he hadn't seen her fear-filled eyes. The sight of them almost made him stop dead. It would have been impossible to say which eyes showed more fear.

He pulled himself together. "Ready?" He jerked his head behind him at Elu.

Her frostbitten hands clamped around his hips as she pressed her cheek against his cloak. Her headscarf was nearly unraveled. Destrou's heart sank, thinking about her secret being revealed and refused to let that happen. *She'll be taken away . . . or worse.*

"I can't get caught like this." Elu pushed her hair to the side, freeing her eyes.

"I won't let anything happen to you." Destrou grabbed her wrist as if to comfort her. "I promise."

He looked up at the sound of rolling thunder. With no room for error, Destrou pushed off the ledge.

The gasps from below let Destrou know what they were thinking—it was exactly what was first on his mind. That they were dead. Goners. Another sad story of two villagers who would be forgotten in a few days like the others.

Destrou had other plans.

One small mistake and they were both done for. Normally during these situations it felt as if his body received an electric shock, but now he felt calm. It was different. It wasn't for him. Not Ranmau. Not the challenge. Or food. This was for a greater prize. For someone else. In that moment, he realized just how important Elu was to him. She was his world. His light. His laughter . . . His . . . love?

Yes, he didn't know what love was, but he knew that he would his risk his life to save her and not think twice about it. Maybe he was too young to love. Maybe he was a fool. Maybe it was a fleeting thought before death. But when his life flashed before his eyes, he saw her. He saw Elu. And if that wasn't love, he wished he knew a stronger word to describe how he felt.

Destrou wrapped the staff around the spiraling column, tightening his grip, bracing for the momentum to shift. Their legs kicked out, twisting parallel to the ground. Every muscle in his body tensed as he fought the grip from loosening. The boys watched in awe, observing Destrou and Elu spiraling down the column with an avalanche trailing behind. While everyone ran away from the chaos, Ranmau rushed toward it.

Destrou's body twisted and turned as air spouted up, wrapping around his torso and legs. He attempted to open his eyes, but the force was too great. Peeking through, he saw that the ground was getting closer. Adrenaline rushed through his body as he picked up speed. Destrou contained his horror with inaudible screams, in stark contrast to Elu shouting the entire time. It was unclear whether Elu was horrified or ecstatic; each shriek was followed by a high-pitched laugh.

Their bodies smashed to the ground, shoulders first, embedding deep into the slush. They strove to free themselves but that

proved to be impossible; their arms were immobilized, surrounded by dense, moist snow.

They heard something tremble above them, like an earthquake in the air. They looked up and saw three massive bowls flipping around, making fluttering sounds, bearing down on them. Elu's bowl came within a moment of crushing them before Ranmau lunged over the crater of snow, kicking it. A *BANG* shook the ground as it crashed into the NoGo.

With Ranmau still airborne, there was nothing to stop the second bowl from falling onto them. They pressed their palms to their faces, crouching into a fetal position. Destrou then hunched over Elu to shield her and felt his warmth drain into her body. She was as cold as the ice about to crush her.

The crackling sound of scraping ice alerted Destrou. He lifted his head. The Leader, with the Crystal Sword clenched in his hands, leapt toward the bowl and threw all of his weight into a sweeping strike.

With ease, it sliced through the bowl, cleanly separating it in half.

Destrou's eyes were wide with energy and curiosity. Immediately there was a symphony of yells, so loud they made him cower: "Nooo!"

The final bowl came crashing down.

BANG! The ground shook with a force that could crush a God, lifting snow tens of feet in the air.

Of all the terrible sights the Village had witnessed, this may had been the worst.

21

RANMAU AND THE LEADER stood opposite one another, and for the first time they had a common goal. Ranmau broke the silence by charging into the cloud of snow, his legs trembling with fright. The Leader followed moments later.

When Ranmau arrived at the site, the snow cloud had begun to subside. He pushed ahead with his hands until he made contact. The cold of the bowl sent a chill through his body. His bare hands dug deep into the snow, his eyes wincing with each shoveling gesture. The thought of Destrou being crushed had made the air around him heavier. When Destrou was out of harm's way, it was easier for him to pretend that he didn't care. Today he couldn't pretend—not this moment.

Through the cloud, he heard squishes, deep breaths, and a grunt followed by a shriek from unsheathing a sword. Ranmau knew who those sounds belonged to, he barely had time to question the Leader's motives. If he wanted them dead, why would he help?

The snowy fog finally cleared away. The bowl had landed upside down, with the opening on the ground. That gave Ranmau

hope.

The Leader arrived wielding the Crystal Sword, nostrils flaring.

Without hesitation, Ranmau pulled the sword from his hands. Had anyone else done that, their bodies would have been buried the next day; however, the Leader took one long gaze into Ranmau's blazing eyes—he had seen that look before and knew to not get in his way.

Ranmau sprang into the air with an acrobat's somersault and landed on top of the bowl. The blade effortlessly sliced through it with a piercing shriek. His face turned white. He embedded the sword and put all his weight into separating the sides. Ranmau turned the sword in his hands, his fingers pressing over the hilt. Fear rampaged inside of him, in his chest and in his hands. He threw the sword away and punched his hands through the opening. Every muscle in his body bulged and his fingers bled as he pulled the two halves apart.

The ice began to break. The Village was in awe of Ranmau's strength as the ice broke in half.

He stared inside the hole, stunned. It was unclear if he was furious, horrified, or relieved.

A few moments later, a hand reached up. Ranmau clenched it as the Leader ran in to assist him. The two of them pulled out Destrou and Elu.

The Divine One must have heard Ranmau's prayers. It was a miracle. They were alive.

"Wait, stop!" Destrou screamed, fearing that Elu's headscarf was undone.

Before he could finish, the Leader had already pounced, grabbing Elu by the collar of her white coat and lifted her away.

Destrou had never seen the Leader act with such haste, worry, or care for another person.

"What'd you do up there?" Ranmau asked angrily, his vein pulsed in his forehead.

Caught off guard, Destrou smiled. "I don't know, the ice melted quicker than I thought."

"You shouldn't be smiling." Ranmau's eyes narrowed in a way that was unfamiliar to Destrou. "This isn't good. I don't think you realize how bad this is."

An image of a screaming boy being thrown into the Box flashed in Destrou's mind. He turned around and looked out to the Wall, forcing the picture from his mind.

"This isn't good at all," Ranmau growled. Destrou felt a familiar twinge of disappointment as his eyes met Ranmau's. "Not even I can save you from what's going to happen next. The Guardian will—"

"It's just liquid ice." Destrou smiled nervously.

"*Just* liquid ice?" Ranmau grabbed Destrou's wrist, cutting circulation like a vise grip.

Destrou winced. He knew that Ranmau didn't mean to hurt him, but sometimes he didn't know how strong he was.

They lived in a world where work was valued more than life. And Ranmau knew this.

Ranmau reminded Destrou of the story about the forgotten boy. He was the one everyone tried to forget because of the way the Guardian had publicly executed him. It was horrific. The reason? He damaged a piece of rope. Repairable fibers of skin and tissue. Not even the Guardian's most prized invention. The worst was expected now.

"Destrou . . . I can't save you."

The urgency in Ranmau's eyes gave Destrou some comfort knowing that he cared enough to be concerned. The comfort faded

the moment he realized the danger he'd be in when the Guardians found out. They always did—nothing got past them.

"Nothing bad will happen to Destrou, right?" Vayp said, raising his hand.

"What do you mean?" Gabrael said, lifting his head.

"Well, he's not actually going to die, right? This story is about him. What's the worst that can happen?"

"Judging by your eyes"—Vayp felt a sensation that burned his brain, as if Gabrael searched his thoughts—"and the pain I see in them, you of all people should know that there are much graver things in life than your death. Your death is final. The pain ends. But living through death's aftermath can be a torture greater than any end. The pain doesn't fade. It lives on."

Vayp glanced over at S'rae, wondering if she knew how much he cared for her. Even Han'sael grew on him with each joke they shared. His weirdness became more funny than annoying. It was tough for Vayp to be open, but that didn't mean he didn't care. Emotions were what destroyed him—he needed to shut them off to survive. To live. But there was something so good and pure about Han'sael and S'rae, the way they could love unconditionally, that he never wanted to see fade away. Their smiles made his heart warm—though he'd never show it.

Vayp heaved a sigh and sat up, as if things started to make sense. More than his own death, he feared losing this friendship that finally made him feel sane again. His loss of Ah'nyx still weighed his thoughts down, wanting nothing more than to find a way to resurrect him, but he began to appreciate the present as a gift.

If only it wasn't too late.

A dark shadow loomed overhead.

The end was coming. He felt it. And somehow . . . he knew it.

S'RAE'S HEAD SHOT UP, reacting to the roar of distant thunder.

Gabrael turned away from her, gazing out the window. His movements were normally slow and calculated, but this was the quickest she had seen him move. His fists clenched. S'rae saw his heartbeat throb in his veins, like balloons swelling inside him.

As if trying to ease his nerves, Gabrael rubbed his fingers together in slow circles. Then, distant thunder boomed and lightning crackled like amplified static.

S'rae winced as Vayp and Han'sael sandwiched her tightly with their arms, crunching her insides. Their shaking made her nauseous. She felt the temperature in the room rise—her hair uncomfortably stuck to her head, feeling it frizz up.

"It's just lightning. Relax," S'rae said, wiggling her arms free.

"Nothin' like this before though." Han'sael squeezed his eyelids together.

"I guess after having classes in the clouds, I'm used to this,"

S'rae said.

Though she told them to not be afraid of some noise, still, she wished that Vayp would never let go. She remembered the last time anyone had hugged her like this. Her body shuddered, thinking about poor Ah'nyx.

"Aww, look at the little babies up front," Fujak mocked. "Scared of a little thunder?"

BANG! A rolling thunder ripped through the room, rattling S'rae's eardrums.

"Ahhhh!" Fujak shrieked, falling off his chair.

"Who's the baby now?" S'rae laughed.

Though Gabrael's eyes were barely visible, S'rae noticed him glance down at the Book of Eve, seeming almost disturbed. He reached for it, but then reconsidered, angling up at the class instead. "Have any of you heard of the story *The Traitor and the King*?"

The room went silent, only the hisses from the candles were heard. Gabrael turned his gaze again to the barred window, flashes of white lights shining on his face as the sky crackled.

"Do you know what's so special about Elu?" he said.

"Because she's—" Fujak started.

"Not because she's a girl." He glared at Fujak, who at once went silent, as if Gabrael squeezed his windpipe with his eyes. "It is because she saved him. She saved him in ways that even I wish I could thank her for. Because if he were to have jumped, his great destiny would have ended along with it." Gabrael turned his attention to the Book of Eve nestled on top of the podium. "It is easy to think that during your lowest points your life is worthless—meaningless; but you could also be one step away from beginning it. A new life where fear no longer controls your decisions, but hope does. It allows you to see the light despite being surrounded by darkness."

He placed his hands to his sides as sparks sizzled from them, fizzling to the ground, like embers from a high-snapping fire.

"Let me tell you the story about the Traitor and the King," he said in a strained whisper. Floating embers, crackling above his shoulders, combusted into two flaming orbs that spiraled around his head so the students could get a clear look at him.

"By the guidance of the elder, two brothers traveled away from their dying village in hopes of finding the missing link to a better life. They stumbled upon a cave and in it there was the boo—" He hesitated. "The most priceless jewel ever created. The elder brother said this was the place they had been searching for and they needed to dig deeper to find the   . . . gem. The younger brother suggested that they should keep searching elsewhere, but after words were exchanged, the elder finally convinced his pessimistic brother to join him.

"So they dug and dug until days turned into weeks, and weeks turned to months, then years. The elder brother, who originally suggested the idea lost faith, no longer believing in their dreams—and the secret to a better life. He apologized to his brother for wasting their time. However, the younger, pessimistic brother became the optimist, telling him that they couldn't give up now. Convincing him to stay, they spent the night sleeping in the depths of the cave.

"When the younger brother woke up, he was alone. The elder had left him and gone on to live his own life—no longer believing in the secret. While sitting there in his lonesomeness, like Destrou, he too began to question his own worth. Wondering if there was a point to this madness. Fear had settled on him, crushing his ambition.

"Wanting to do one last strike before he gave up, he lunged his pick into the stone, breaking through the wall, finally revealing the gem that money could never buy. His elder brother ended up living

in the mountains, becoming a servant for evil. An evil they thought had died away long ago . . ." He paused and gazed at nothing in particular. "You see, there are some evils in the universe that are simply just that . . . One does not need to understand them, or seek to change them."

"Okay . . ." Fujak looked around awkwardly. "So, what about the other brother?"

"The other one? Well, he became the King."

"Like how you're the King?" Han'sael asked.

Gabrael paused for a moment, soaking in the question. One of the flaming orbs vanished, leaving a trail of spiraling smoke.

His eyes darted from side to side—the same eye movements that S'rae had whenever she searched through her thoughts. He shook his head, as if forgetting that a question had been asked, then turned to Han'sael.

"Yes," he said coldly, "but the message is to never give up on your dreams—no matter how impossible they seem—because you never know how close you are to succeeding."

I've heard that story before. S'rae remembered learning about a similar story in her Myths and Legends class. *Wasn't this about Vy'ken, the God of Lightning?*

S'rae stared at Gabrael, then whispered, "Vy'ken?"

At once, the candles all around roared into tall flames, fading to a dark blue. He whipped around with a glare that turned her body into stone.

S'rae shut her mouth and closed her eyes, her thoughts a swirling tempest of fear and regret. *Stupid S'rae.* She felt Gabrael taking dead aim at her head with his eyes.

The fires sizzled, and S'rae felt a searing heat burn into her. She wanted to shrink into the shadows.

"What did you say?" he asked loudly over the thunder. The candlelight danced around.

BANG! Another lightning strike brightened the room. The ground beneath them shook so terribly that they feared the Spire was crumbling. The students jumped, clutching one another. The strike was so close that its force blew out the candles. S'rae's senses tingled when the wave of fresh air, smelling like rain on a cold morning, hit her. She saw that it affected the other students the same way by their startled expressions.

The wave blew Gabrael's hood back enough to show his dark eyes trailing off toward the earth-shattering sounds of rolling thunder. He squinted at the lights, stopping tears from falling. He muttered a few words—which S'rae wasn't quick enough to hear—and took a deep breath before looking back at her.

The glow from the lightning faded away, leaving the room in darkness. Dimly lit candlelight crackled on, like the flip of a switch. Gabrael again turned his attention to the window, this time his brows creased with worry. There had been no more lightning strikes—only silence. A tear rolled down his cheek, landing on the floor with a sizzle, like water on a hot stove.

"Class is adjourned," he said in a chilling voice. "We shall meet back in an hour."

Gabrael and S'rae's eyes locked and never broke contact until he vanished beyond the door.

"What was that about?" Vayp said, leaning closer.

"Yeah." Han'sael leaned in much closer. His nose practically touched her lips. "I woulda peed in my pantsies if he looked at me like that." He hesitated and looked down. "Actually, I think I might have."

The glazed look in her eyes showed that she wasn't paying attention. "Elu," she said to herself, almost in a whisper.

"What about her?" Vayp said.

"Elu . . . you said I was like Elu."

"Well, technically—"

"Shh," Han'sael shushed Vayp.

"Elu knows everything about what's going on," S'rae said. "I need to find out, too."

"How you plan to do that?" Han'sael asked.

"The same way she did . . ."

"And?" Han'sael and Vayp asked.

"Spying on them."

"You're crazy!" Vayp shouted.

"Yeah, you gonna get in so much trouble if they find out."

"Who says they're going to find out? Like Elu, I have my ways. Trust me. He's probably going to talk to Raaz'a about something right now and I need to find out. Why'd the thunder bother him so much? Maybe it has something to do with the screams I heard."

"Screams?" Han'sael pulled away. His eyes widened.

"I'll tell you more about it when it makes more sense to me. Here's the plan." With the confident tone of a girl on a mission, S'rae explained what was to be done. Halfway through, Han'sael belted out a laugh. The sound made her chest swell. Her lips peeled into a smile. She had always wanted to be the funny one, but her jokes were never really funny, she was the only one who laughed at them really. It felt amazing to be appreciated until Han'sael opened his mouth again.

"Sorry, did you say something?" Han'sael rubbed his forearm across his mouth, holding back the last remaining chuckles. "I wasn't listenin', was thinkin' about deflating Chung's muscles."

"Have you been listening to the plan now?" S'rae said to Han'sael as they ran through the halls. He had a glazed look as if he was a shell without a soul.

"Have I been listening?" Han'sael shook his head. "That's a very weird way to start a conversation." His focus was on a torch they passed by that flashed from red to blue.

S'rae sighed, breathing in the scent of a damp forest.

"He was too busy listening to the voices in his head." Vayp laughed.

"Listen, Vayp, there's nothing wrong with having voices in your head. It's perfectly normal. That's what my therapist told me. Arguin' with them is common, too. It's when you start to lose the arguments, that's when you know you got issues."

"You're right, Vayp," S'rae laughed. "Han'sael lives in his own world."

"Yes, I do, but it's okay, everyone knows me there."

"Maybe that's why you never had friends before us." Vayp smiled, patting Han'sael.

"Not true! I had plenty of friends, until my therapist told me I shouldn't talk to them anymore."

When S'rae ran down the halls, her skin tingled with excitement. "Shhh, boys! I finally found Gabrael's voice!" she clapped. *One hour,* she told herself, happy that it was more than enough time to get the answers she sought.

"Found his voice?" Vayp questioned.

"Stay here," she told Han'sael, sliding to a stop, ignoring Vayp's question. They appeared in front of a thick stone double door with blazing torches on either side, casting a yellow light in the otherwise dark hall. "Remember, let us know when someone's coming."

"Kay, I'll make this noise: *cluck cluck coo!*" Han'sael sounded like a dying rooster.

"Um, please *never* do that again." Vayp patted Han'sael on the back.

S'rae pressed her shoulder against the door. Her body warmed

up as if it was a furnace.

"Wait, you not goin' in there, are you?" Han'sael squealed.

"I need to. I found his voice, but I can't understand what he's saying."

"You can hear him?" Vayp shouted. "I knew it! I knew I wasn't crazy!"

"Shh!" She pressed her finger on Vayp's lips. "We can't get caught." She grabbed Vayp's wrist. "Come with me, watch my back in case anything pops out of the shadows."

"What will pop out?" Vayp's eyes widened. He made a sudden motion with his arm as if to grab S'rae's shoulder, but stopped. There was a moment's silence, then—

"Nothing." She hesitated. Her voice had held a momentary inflection, like the squeak of a mouse. "Just expect the unexpected." She looked away to avoid eye contact.

Vayp raised an eyebrow, suspecting a truth hidden behind that lie. "Don't worry, I have your back. Plus, smart one, doesn't expecting the unexpected make the unexpected expected?"

"Oh hush!" S'rae thought it was better if he didn't know about the panther.

But Vayp's promise seemed unlikely. He was always the forgetful type, at times leaving S'rae to fend for herself as he chased down a pretty girl. She remembered the time they played hide and seek and he forgot that he locked her in a closet with a protective spell. She hadn't learned how to break open boulders yet, so she was stuck in there for a few days until he finally remembered where he hid her. Luckily, she knew how to harvest crops out of nothing. If it weren't for her food, she didn't know how she'd make it. To not put the blame on Vayp—or see him get punished—she told the village it was her plan all along to eavesdrop on everyone.

She was punished instead. Wasn't the first or last time she sacrificed for Vayp without him knowing. Better if he didn't know. She didn't want him to feel like he owed her something.

S'rae cracked the door open and moved forward as silently as she could, and with every step she took her mind felt more and more numb, but she forced herself to think about the person trapped in the tower—someone needed help. She needed answers—the Valley was nothing like what she had expected. It was a mystery that needed to be unraveled.

Moving through the dark hallways was terrifying: A spider the size of her hand scurried by her feet and she jolted back. The small candles that lined the floor lit up as they passed, and she felt sure that Gabrael could sense when someone was nearby.

It became more terrifying when they reached a bridge of floating rocks fifty feet above a pool of boiling lava.

As her feet passed over the warm stone, she stared at Vayp, still unable to believe that they were back together after all this time. This felt like the good old days when they'd sneak out at night and allow curiosity to dictate their adventure. She wondered how their parents would—

"I'm not going there!" Vayp grabbed S'rae's wrist as if he suddenly realized the pool of lava. "This is crazy, you'll get us killed!"

"I need to know what's going on!" S'rae pulled her wrist to her chest. "Trust me. There are things here that need to be explained. Don't you want to know why we're really here?"

Their eyes met. Silence hung in the air for a few moments.

"Please"—S'rae gently grabbed Vayp's shoulder—"just trust me."

"Fine," he puffed. "Jeezsh, you really are like Elu."

She smiled and curtsied, then stared down the bridge. It seemed far away now, but they weren't even a tenth of the way across. Above her hung long spikes like icicles made of stone.

A gust of air pressed against her right side, throwing her body weight to the left. She panted, and clung to the closest thing: Vayp. His warm hands clamped around her waist. The wind was momentarily sucked out of her as he squeezed.

"Good thing you came." S'rae chuckled. She may have appeared calm on the outside, but inside she was a wreck.

"I've never seen you this shaken before." Vayp smirked. "I guess you aren't perfect."

"There are *plenty* of things I'm not that I wish I was . . ."

Vayp looked at her curiously, as if trying to understand what she really meant.

They finally made it across the bridge. They stepped onto a stone island that had spiraling stairs leading downward. She circled her fingers and picked up sounds of muffled voices.

She closed her eyes to listen.

"Something else troubles me, Raaz'a."

"What?"

"I no longer feel Vy'ken's presence. As if his element never existed."

"Do you think he's gone?"

"Dead? I am not sure. I fear there would be a much larger storm if he was."

"Do you forgive him?"

"I hope that I can, Raaz'a. But he may have been protecting us."

"Oh my! From what?"

"That is what I do not understand. But it must be a force great enough to kill a God."

"To kill a God! Do you think this has to do with the shadows we found?"

Huh? Why aren't you telling Gabrael about the Mecha the bird warned you about?

"Yes. I think he has finally come back home, and darkness has indeed consumed him. I wish I did not push him. He is no longer the same. He is here to kill."

"Oh my! One of the students must have given away our location then. There is a traitor amongst us; it's the only way he could've found the Valley."

"Sadly, this is true, Raaz'a."

"Do you know who could be so evil?"

"I am not sure, but I have my suspicions about the Fujitas. It has always been in their best interest to stop this from happening."

"Fujita . . . yes. You could be right, Master."

But you know about the Mecha that escaped from Fujita! Why aren't you telling him?

"It seems like Fujita's plans have failed. They sealed up our walls . . . without realizing that Fire is the one element *they* are most afraid of. Now Fire Elementials are as rare as life in the Valley."

"Oh my!"

"We must only worry if he is able to create another Shadow Army. Which he cannot."

"But what if—what if they somehow find the Eye of Eve?"

"They cannot take it, it can only be given to them. But if that were to happen, Gaia would be in grave danger. We would need to find more students of Fire . . . I know they must be out there."

"I'm afraid you were right, Master. As you always are."

"About?"

"Him. You said, 'A child who is not embraced by Fire will burn the world down to feel its warmth.' He was not ready, but do you think Retro'ku is?"

"I do not know. He needs to be. He has fire in his eyes, unlike him."

"And if Retro'ku is not ready, will his sacrifice be worth it?"

S'rae could hear footsteps as if someone was pacing up and down the room.

"He and the students must be ready, Raaz'a."

"Will their sacrifices be worth it? We must leave!"

"Leave the Valley? *Never!*"

S'rae felt her soles tingle as if she stood over a fire.

"Please, Master, remain calm. You must stay focused. But your instincts have never been wrong. If it is danger that you feel, it is danger that will come."

"Then let it! And let that decision be their last! They will regret ever stepping foot here."

S'rae's feet bubbled with sweat. The floor was getting too hot to stand on. She tried to quiet the unease rolling through her, and patted her thighs while Vayp hunched closer. Their ears nearly touched as if he was hoping to catch some of the sounds.

"Your pride will be the death of all of us, Master. And what of Eve? Without her, the Valley is no longer the safest place. The wall is fading—it will fall. The Valley will fall."

"Leave Eve to me. This place will become a battlefield soon. Leave if you wish. But as long as I am here, this valley, and for what it really is, will *always* be the safest place. "

S'rae stopped breathing. She went into a trance as she tried to absorb all of the information. Were they here to get sacrificed?

Her body tensed as something gripped her shoulder.

"What happened?" Vayp said.

She took a moment to answer. "I . . . think . . . ." She sounded shaken. "I think we're all in trouble." Her eyes widened with fear. "I think we're here to get sacrificed." With a shudder, she fell silent. Suddenly Professor Ki's words made sense. Gabrael was dangerous, after all.

Vayp looked at her, concerned. "You sure you heard that right?"

"There's a traitor who told evil shadow people how to find the Valley—"

S'rae felt Vayp's grip tighten around her shoulder, then stammered, "P-probably that j-jerk Fujak!"

"And now . . . bad things are coming to kill us." The life went out of her eyes. "Just like Elu warned us about!" She shrieked, then cupped her mouth. But how could she possibly know? *What is the connection that we have to Destrou's story? And why do I feel like I'm a part of it?*

Vayp released his grip. "We need to go—*now!*"

"Why?" She appeared shocked.

Vayp closed his eyes. "I feel movement . . . They're coming!"

A whisper then reached her ears. "Go find out, at once! We cannot have any students knowing about this. It will ruin everything."

Horror-struck, S'rae waved madly at Vayp to follow her as quickly as possible; they ran silently behind the door, away from Raaz'a's voice. Vayp's robes whipped around the corner when they heard Raaz'a's heavy breathing at the other end.

"Someone is up here," Raaz'a growled. "I can sense you. You've made Gabrael mad. Big mistake. You don't want to see what happens when he's angry. Never felt real fear until you do."

All your fault! Vayp mouthed to S'rae, and they sank deeper into the shadows, pressing their backs against the stone wall.

It was a dead end.

They could hear Raaz'a getting nearer. S'rae let out a frightened squeak, and as Raaz'a turned around the corner, S'rae felt her stomach collide into her lungs. She felt weightless as Vayp pulled her into the stone wall, like a fish through water.

It was an eerie sensation of free-falling, one she wasn't used to. Normally, there was air resistance, but instead it felt soft like she fell through a mountain of feathers.

Thud! They collapsed onto solid ground, drenched in mud from head to toe.

"Wow!" S'rae screamed excitedly, jumping on top of Vayp. "That was so awesome! You saved us. You actually did it!"

"Hey! What's that supposed to mean?" he scoffed. "You're not the only gifted one here. I was top four as well!" He then pulled goggles from his pocket and smirked. "You forgot these."

"Where'd you get them?" S'rae sounded shocked, patting down her robe and searching its pockets. Empty. "How?" S'rae then noticed smudges of blood on the lens. "Umm—"

"I borrowed them." He mimicked a girl's voice, quickly hiding his hands in his pockets. "My hands sometimes get like that when I cast a powerful spell. It's nothing to worry about so don't look at me like that." Vayp then went on a long monologue about his accomplishments at GroundStone—which S'rae half paid attention to—ranging from using the ground to pickpocket students to tracking spells to breaking down earth's principles into water.

"That's it!" The last one caught S'rae's attention. "You're a genius!"

"I know. I know. 'Course I am." Vayp brushed his shoulders, then hesitated. "Wait, why am I a genius?"

"Particles into water, why didn't I think of that?" she said. "I'll test that one out later."

Vayp looked concerned. He then shuddered as if the reality of the moment finally settled in. "Wait . . . where are we?"

The way their voices traveled made it seem like they were in a large, dark space. A slow river whispered at their feet. The scent of fresh flowers catching her nose. Then dropping from the ceiling were floating lights like the one that had led S'rae to the Eye of Eve. They spiraled around, illuminating a sweeping forest that appeared before their eyes. S'rae and Vayp stared with widen eyes and open mouths as trees over a hundred feet tall, and others no more than ten, emerged from the darkness. While they varied in height and width and leaves and bark, they remained consistent in beauty. This underground forest was so colorful that she saw vibrant colors she didn't know existed. There must've been hundreds of different shades of pinks and blues and purples in the leaves that hung overhead. This was easily the most spectacular spectacle she had ever seen, even better than how she pictured the Valley of Gaia would look.

Water flowed from a statue of a goddess' head like luminous sapphire hair, accompanied by the rhythmic splashes of waves crashing against rocks. The luminescent water shimmered in the darkness with their bright blues, making the ground sparkle like stars in the sky.

"What's this?" Vayp had to pick up his jaw.

"This is"—S'rae remembered her Life Before and After Death class—"a burial garden?"

"Burial . . . garden?"

"Yeah, I think so. Instead of burying loved ones in the ground with a gravestone, some ancient cultures planted the dead. They'd be sown into the ground as a tree from their region, giving them a life with nature after death." Her eyes widened. "The words didn't do this justice. They said it was beautiful . . . but this . . . this is perfectly beautiful."

"Are you sure that they buried plants from their region?" Vayp said the last word so quietly that S'rae almost didn't hear it, and his tense, worried look returned.

"What's wrong?" S'rae asked before the silence got too long.

"These trees are from . . . GroundStone." He pointed at twisting trees with stringy leaves.

"You're right. And these"—S'rae analyzed a large white-barked tree with bright pink, blue, and green petals—"these are Serry Blossoms from Fujita." She paused. "Why are there plants from all over the world buried here?" A shade of worry darkened her eyes. "The whole getting sacrificed thing doesn't sound so crazy anymore. We need to warn everyone!"

"We need to worry about ourselves!" Vayp's eyes flared as the ground shook. "Don't try to save the world—I'm getting us out of here!"

"We can't leave Han'sael!" S'rae said.

The shaking stopped at once. "Fine! Let's get him, then we're leaving!"

"What about the person in the tower and the sacrifice? We need to stop it."

"That's crazy! We don't need to stop anything. What we need to do is leave."

S'rae wanted to say no, but she didn't want to argue. She held back her tendency to say what was on her mind, which always did more harm than good. "Okay, let's get cleaned off. We can't have them track us down. Han'sael will help us out with that." S'rae glanced at Vayp. "Can you get us back up there?"

"Can I get us up there?" He laughed with a mocking voice. "Can you spell your name?"

S'rae and Vayp met up with Han'sael, who cleaned off their clothes—in a way that made Vayp disgusted—using his own sweat to channel water. They relayed the earlier events: how there was a traitor amongst them, a danger was coming, and a boy about to be sacrificed. They all then agreed to leave the Valley together. But as they turned the corner to exit the Spire, they hit a human wall.

Thud! Raaz'a may have looked frail but he was as solid as a Sol. "Interesting to see the three of you here." Raaz'a smiled creepily. "And where did you come from?"

"We wanted—"

"To get—"

"A drink?"

"Is that so?" he said coldly. His eyes wandered between them suspiciously, but his face was full of suppressed triumph. "Well, be careful what you drink around here. We have some liquids that can wipe your memory clean. A sip and you'd forget that you were here. Anything more and you'd forget that you had lived."

"Thank you, we'll be caref—" S'rae swallowed, apparently unable to finish her sentence. A fear rushed through her like a gust.

"Oh, looky here." Raaz'a wore a crooked smile. "The hour is up. Back to class we go."

S'rae walked with regret, staring down, knowing that their window of opportunity had slammed shut. But like a caged bird, she planned her escape for the next time it opened.

Their lives depended on it.

Professor Ki was right. Every one of S'rae's senses told her that danger awaited them. Her village would have told her to always follow her gut instinct, it was the difference between making it home from a hunt and being the story that shed a thousand tears that night. Something bad was going to happen here. She knew it. She just needed to find a way to stop it.

"HERE LIES THE BODY OF DESTROU," a boy said, standing inside a rubble of ice chunks. ". . . a small kid who caused big problems. How does that sound?" He chuckled at his own joke.

Destrou narrowed his eyes at him as he patted a block of ice protruding from the ground. It was about three feet tall with random marks and scribbles carved into its sides. The boy wore a white, furry one-piece except the hood covered his head, revealing its stubbed ears. The way his sleeves extended beyond his hands, sagging to the ground, made his outfit seem like it once belonged to a beast twice his size. The long sleeves covered his three remaining fingers after frostbite had claimed the other two. He was one of the unlucky ones, though they were all unlucky.

"Shut it, Ascel," Elu replied, walking over to Destrou who sat on a pile of crushed ice with his knees tucked to his chest. "He saved me and you're being mean?"

"Relax." Ascel pointed to the ground. "He's getting buried like the rest of us, anyway."

Destrou didn't expect sympathy from any of the boys, but he anticipated a dampening of their hatred after giving them their best shower. That would be too much to ask for though. His body still felt heavy, waiting to see what happened next.

The boys scurried about, picking up the rubble from the demolition. Normally leftover ice was sent to the Yard to be saved for showers, but now it looked like they'd be used for building.

Some of the boys were working, and some weren't. There wasn't enough for everyone to do. When the space was crowded, the boys that did nothing got in the way and slowed progress down more than helped.

Minutes later, Destrou stood alone in a narrow path between two igloos until he felt someone yank him into the shadows. He assumed it was Ranmau, but he was wrong. Elu offered Destrou her hand, he slid his into hers. Her hand was smooth yet rough around her knuckles. The scarf wrapped completely around her face, dangling over her shoulder. Destrou felt there was something he should say, but he couldn't think. Before he could respond, Elu yanked him again, pulling him out of the mess.

Without a question asked, they sprinted toward the southern end, a side of the Village that Destrou rarely ventured to. Elu guided the way behind one of the igloos at the edge of the Village. He felt his nerves flare with every beat of his racing heart. *Where's she bringing me?*

Elu looked down another narrow path, turning her head from left to right. They then ran across a frozen stream, sliding to the other side. Elu stopped. Four boys had gathered in an open area, blocking their route. Elu ducked quickly, hiding behind a pile of snow, and pulled Destrou down with her.

"What are we doing?" Destrou looked around.

"Shhh." Elu pressed her fingers to her lips. "You're not good at

this sneaking around stuff, huh?"

The boys were digging next to a ledge, overlooking the Valley that was about ninety feet below. They grunted from the effort, putting all their weight into each strike, digging their spades into the ice. A huge shape was pulled out of the hole. Some kind of animal was slammed onto the snow. It was frozen solid with scales and a long tail, one of the many animals that had lived in the ice in the past.

Destrou looked confused so Elu explained that it was their job to dig tirelessly until they extracted food. They couldn't stop until they retrieved something.

"Why don't they keep it for themselves?" Destrou poked his head over the snow.

"They don't want to end up like Boxy, remember?"

"Boxy?"

"Yeah, he tried to hide food for himself. Once the Guardian found out, he threw him in the Box. He lasted the whole seven days, but when he came out, he wasn't the same—didn't last long after. It's a shame, I liked him"

"Wow, I remember him. I just didn't know his name."

"There are *a lot* of things they don't want you to know." Destrou's hands began to shake as he wondered what other horrors may be hidden from him.

Elu noticed that the four boys had their backs turned away from them, facing the Valley. She nudged Destrou's elbow, grabbing his hand, leading the way again.

They sprinted toward the ledge. *We aren't going to jump, are we?* He kept running because Elu's little fingers clamped tightly around his wrist, but if it were up to him, he would have preferred to be doing anything else. He felt like there was a storm in his chest that expanded more by the second, threatening to make him faint right before the jump.

He followed Elu closer the cliff. Too close. They both ran with their clothes flapping in the wind. The only difference was that Elu may have not felt like she was about to die, and from what he could tell, her lips weren't trembling so hard she had to pucker to steady them. Instead, she was smiling through her teeth. *That is not a good smile!* That type of smile meant only one thing: They were in for an experience that only she was looking forward to.

Elu jumped to the edge of the cliff and pulled him with her. Destrou's fear of heights kicked in, feeling like he was going to faint as he saw the Valley below. *I hate you for this!* He wanted to scream.

As he was about to fall to his death, they landed at the tip of the cliff, crashing through a patch of snow, revealing a tunneling slide.

They slipped and slided the entire way down the wall. Elu shrieked excitedly the entire way down, finally touching ground, shoulders first, tumbling around a few times before coming to a complete stop. Destrou realized how different they both were. He feared danger and the consequences it brought, but Elu was obviously an adrenaline-crazed thrill-seeker.

"That jump gets me every time!" Elu leaned over, panting with a huge grin on her face.

Destrou didn't feel the same way as he stumbled, attempting to reorient himself.

"What just happened? How are we alive?" Destrou fumbled to create a coherent thought.

"I'll tell you later." Elu laughed. "But I need to figure out something about you first."

"Me?" Destrou said, excited to hear that she was interested in knowing more about him. "But I'm not as fun as you . . . I'm actually quite boring."

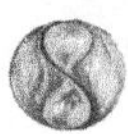

"No, silly, you're actually the most interesting one in the Village now. I'll show you why when we get there."

They walked through the Valley, gliding over a path of pure ice which exuded a salty aroma. It was the clear type of ice where one could see deep inside of it. Destrou identified little shadows that looked like potential food they could catch for dinner if they weren't so far below the ice.

They finally reached the Wall. It was even whiter than he remembered the closer he came to touching it. He was unable to see the top no matter how far back he arched his neck. And it was made with a different kind of ice than what they used to build igloos. Unlike the other types of ice, the Wall shimmered in the light when Destrou stood at a certain angle, and he saw a clear reflection of himself. The past few days had taken a heavy toll on him, but he didn't appreciate seeing the proof in the mirror. His brown eyes looked bloodshot, his forehead etched with fine lines and his face covered with grime and sweat.

Symmetrical carvings covered the Wall and he admired the craftsmanship and wondered what artist had created such intricate work. It made Destrou feel so insignificant. It was evident that the Wall was something that no normal man could have created. Who or what did?

"Fascinating, huh?" Elu blurted out as she brushed up to Destrou's side.

"To be honest, I've never really thought about something that trapped me as fascinating . . . but I can see it now." Destrou paused, wanting to find a way to talk about the events from the night before. "About last night—"

"Have you seen this yet?" Elu interrupted, pointing at a carving in the Wall.

"That looks amazing." Destrou hesitated. "But—"

"How does something like this exist? It makes me believe there has to be a Divine One, you know?" Elu said, raising her eyebrows at him.

Destrou shivered, and felt goosebumps travel up his arms. Something inside him collapsed. Looking up at the Wall, thinking about a Divine One, his chest felt tight, and he couldn't breathe, feeling so small and helpless. He sank to the ground, dragging Elu with him. He pressed both of his palms against the Wall to check if it was real—that this beautiful but terrible barrier to the outside world was real. Sadly, it was.

He cupped his palms over his mouth, feeling his warm breath seep through the cracks of his fingers, calming him down.

"What's that?" said Destrou, breathing heavily as he pointed north at a shadowed area wedged underneath a slab of ice that arched over the Valley. Miles were in between Destrou and the mysterious abyss but the uneasiness that surged through his body made it feel like he was there.

"Oh," Elu said, "that's the Ruins. You don't want to go there. The Guardian would kill you if you even thought about going in. Don't ask how I know. The story hurts too much."

"So many things I don't know. What is this place? Why are we trapped behind this . . . wall?" Destrou said, breathing in slowly. "If there is a Divine One, why would he do this to us?"

Elu failed to answer the barrage of questions; she was more attentive to Destrou's palms resting against the Wall. "This is why I brought you here."

"So I can freak out?"

"No . . . this." Elu touched Destrou's hands. "So you can understand how special you are." Destrou didn't know how to respond. He still wasn't used to this feeling, a calming touch from another person. It felt strange. Despite some coarse skin on her frostbitten

hands, Elu had a comforting touch. "The Village doesn't know this but the Wall is made with unbreakable ice. Only a Crystal Sword can penetrate it."

"What does this have to do with me? How do you know these things, anyway?"

"How are you still surprised at the things I know? Remember, I'm the one with a million secrets, silly." Elu smiled in a way that removed any doubt on her face. "This ice is the same kind that the liquid ice tower was made out of—"

"Prove it," Destrou said, backing away from her.

"I designed it, silly. The ice was supposed to be indestructible to everything but a Crystal Sword, they said. But somehow you were able to destroy the unbreakable."

Destrou quickly pulled his hands off the Wall, analyzing them. "W-what are you saying?"

"That's what I was hoping to find out." Her quiet tone alarmed Destrou. "When something doesn't make sense to me, I have to find the answer. You did the impossible. I don't know how you did it, but something special happened, Destrou. I wanted you to see what I see." Their eyes met, and they mirrored their smiles. "That you are special. I know it more than I know when the sun will set, which will be in exactly six hours right about... now! I may not have an answer yet, but—"

A loud horn, the same exact one from last night, roared throughout the Valley.

Elu's eyes widened with fear.

"Two horns in a row?" Elu stuttered. "This can't be good!"

"That's weird, I've never heard two in a row before. Do you know what this one's about?"

"I hope I'm wrong, because if I were to take another guess . . . this one will definitely be about—" Elu gulped.

BANG! The sky tore open again as a blue light zapped through the air, striking the NoGo.

Destrou knew what she wanted to say for she had already said it once before. "War."

Destrou and Elu had ran back to the Village. Right before they came in the southern entrance, Elu gestured to Destrou, pointing her fingers to the west. She then ran off to the opposite side, toward the Forest. Destrou got the hint—it would be a terrible end to the day if they were caught together.

Destrou ran quietly, Elu's stealthy tactics were growing on him. He was calm as he reached an igloo, standing with his back pressed against it, feeling the cold through his clothes. Through an opening, he saw boys talking, gathering up the remaining scraps of rubble. He understood why Elu was so impatient with the message last night about Eve. This new one was all he could think about now.

Destrou ran to another igloo, then another, getting closer to the center of the Village. At the other end, Ranmau stood at the entrance of the NoGo. His brother held something in his hand but was too far away for Destrou to make out what it was.

Destrou tried to walk as quietly as possible, making his way through the paths. He passed by random conversations and laughter. Some of them mentioned his name.

"Why you sneakin' around?" Destrou heard, so close that the breath from his mouth grazed Destrou's neck. Without looking over his shoulder he recognized the voice and knew who it belonged to. "We've been lookin' everywhere for you. No more hidin'. There's a trial with your name on it." It was Ascel.

A trial was more like public humiliation than anything else. The boy would stand in the middle of the stage in front of NoGo to await his punishment. It was never a good thing. At times, Destrou hid behind igloos to avoid the look on the boys' faces when they heard the verdict. It was a look of dread so vivid in his mind that he remembered their faces better than his own.

Ascel grabbed onto Destrou's clothes, pulling him up. Destrou squinted. The thought of telling him the truth about where he had been all day made him feel weary. Ascel kept his eye on Destrou the whole time, escorting him to the center where everyone awaited. Destrou caught a brief glimpse of Elu amidst the crowd. The gathering parted open like a boulder splitting in half.

Ranmau stood at the NoGo's entrance, this time no longer holding anything in his hand. Was Destrou seeing things again? The platform was made of solid ice, raised about three feet high, and ten feet long and wide. Destrou watched Ranmau's face carefully as he walked on top of it, searching for any sign of disappointment. To his surprise, Ranmau gave Destrou an assured look, like everything was going to be okay. What did he know that Destrou didn't?

The Guardians' slumber was over. The *BANG* definitely woke them up, he could tell by the silence. They were loud snorers and would rest for days at a time, letting the Village run itself. The less work they had to do, the better. They hardly guarded anything.

Destrou tensed up. He had no idea what was going on. Was he going into the Box? Thrown off the Edge? Were the clacking sounds that he heard them preparing a tomb? Destrou thought of every possible outcome that could occur. None were good.

Destrou's heart stopped as a loud scraping sound made his head hurt.

It was happening. The Guardian's door dragged along the ice.

The door was about twelve feet high and eight feet wide. It was solid ice and incredibly dense. Not even the Giant could budge the door—he'd failed more times than his number of missing teeth, which said a lot. Despite its weight the door slid open easily. Destrou watched as the crowd of boys held their ears during the shrieks of grinding ice.

The Guardian and Commander Gronk looked the same but different—the main difference was the way they wore their white-furred faces. The Guardian had a wide beard that extended past his cheeks. The Commander had a wavy beard that extended over his potbelly.

They stood there with food still dangling from their beards, in front of a crowd of boys who hadn't eaten in days. Their bellies were wide enough to fit both Destrou and Ranmau inside of them, yet being full never satisfied them. They ate until they vomited. Then ate some more.

They sleepily marched with their eyes practically sealed shut, and grabbed a piece of paper wedged inside a boy's hand. It was the message from the Kingdom: a glistening, silver paper that sparkled like ice. The boys knew that it must be important; it was urgent enough to revive the Guardian.

The Guardian stared at it with a lot of difficulty. Still caught in a daze, his eyes weren't quite open. He mumbled words while flipping the paper upside down and front to back.

"Mer. This can't be good." He finished reading the letter, muttering the words so that only he and the Commander could hear.

But the Guardian's words created a wildfire of whispers as gossip blazed through the circle of boys surrounding Destrou. Words dispersed from boy to boy, sounding like a hissing snake that circled around him. Destrou was able to piece together a few of the words. One word in particular made his head jerk up the moment it rang in his ears. He looked over, glancing in Ranmau's direction.

"Freedom." Destrou smiled. He knew what that word meant to Ranmau.

The sound of an explosion abruptly ended the chatter, focusing

everyone's attention on the shattered ice in the Guardian's palm. Maybe the paper was made of some kind of ice.

His lip snarled up, revealing disgusting, chipped teeth with food stuck between them. "Hah!" he laughed, belting a mixture of laughter and gas. "Looks like the Supreme General said that one of you will be lucky." He reached down into his pants with his right hand, scratching his crotch, and then wiping his hand on the boy who held the paper. "But first . . . sleep. I'll let you krillens know about it tomorrow. Bright and early! Any lateness will be punished."

The Guardian turned around and headed back into his lair. The Commander began to seal the door shut behind them. It was apparent from their sluggish movements, the way they dragged their feet and slurred their words, that the two of them only had sleep on their minds.

Freedom? Even thinking of the word felt dangerous. He looked at Ranmau. Ranmau's eyes carried his, and as the silent seconds passed, Ranmau looked less and less calm. Destrou swallowed a deep breath, hearing his own heartbeat. They stared at each other for too long as if trying to warn each other of something, although Destrou could've been imagining it. His vivid imagination had fooled him too many times before. It had been too long. The stare. Ranmau's expression was alarming yet comforting at the same time—very misleading. Destrou's heart pounded even harder; Ranmau's eyes penetrated deep into Destrou's soul.

Run?

"Run?" he said to himself, wondering where that thought came from.

Run! he thought as Ranmau's look registered.

Destrou quickly put all of his weight forward, ready to jump off the platform until a loud roar halted his progress. It was deep: raspy and trembling.

"*WAIT!*" the Guardian shouted, turning around furiously before the door slammed shut. "You!" he growled, pointing at Destrou. His eyes bulged.

Destrou froze with one knee in the air and his body arched over it. Fear immobilized him. He didn't know whether he should turn around to look or continue to stand as a petrified statue. Destrou had completely forgotten about his trial and apparently the Guardian had, too. The look that Ranmau had given him was one of hope. That the Guardian would go back to sleep. That he'd forget about all of this. And Destrou would remain unpunished. The plan failed.

"Don't think I forgot about you, krillen!" the Guardian growled, staring at Destrou. "You'll love the announcement tomorrow . . . it's to die for." He laughed as his voice trailed off, the door slammed shut behind him.

Destrou didn't know what hurt more: the public humiliation, the Guardian's torturous way to drag out a punishment sentence, or the disappointment he saw in Ranmau.

So much for this being a day that couldn't go wrong. Eve being alive didn't change the fact that this had been his worst day ever. Destrou had always looked forward to each day. Tomorrow wasn't one of them and he already wanted this one to be over.

THE DOOR TO THE NOGO CLOSED behind Destrou, and he was alone—at least that's what it felt like. It was never good for him to feel alone. He felt his terrible foe, the monster in his head, slowly start to reveal its ugly face. It was the great beast— what his mind considered to be an Archon—with scales of black leather, digging its claws into his brain, trying to end his life in one squeeze. It felt more real than ever.

He shook his head to clear away the thought.

The Villagers left for their igloos and Ranmau soon followed.

He sat around for hours, thinking about the events that had happened since meeting Elu. He thought about the cliff, the Eye, the Tree, Elu being a girl, the Dream Words, the stories, he thought of everything. He even thought of the danger he had been in and how he'd gladly go through it again if that meant having Elu in his life.

He would have escaped into his memories longer if it weren't for the wrenching feeling of hunger. It had been days since he had eaten. His stomach growled in retaliation. Although, he had built up a tolerance to hunger, no one was immune to starvation.

"I'd eat if I could," he whispered to his belly, patting it. "I'm sorry, buddy. I know you're mad."

"Hungry?" Destrou heard a familiar voice behind him. He turned around to see Elu, leaning against an igloo with her palm pressed against it. *Why can't I look cool like her?*

Destrou's legs went weak at the sight of her, and he struggled to stand upright. Then he felt a rush of warmth after seeing her inviting crinkle in her eyes. *I'm so glad that I have you in my life*, he wanted to say aloud. He realized how much he enjoyed seeing her actual smile, when her mouth was free and her hair could flow in the wind. When she could be free from the terrors of being a girl. He looked forward to those nights when they are alone with the stars and laughter filled the air. His eyes watered just thinking about it.

Elu's voice brought him back into the moment. "I can get some for you." She smirked.

"Seriously? How? Are you sure you're not Eve?" Destrou asked.

"I wish." Elu chuckled. "A million secrets, remember? Follow me and I'll show you more!" Elu grabbed his hand and pulled him toward the NoGo. His stomach fluttered when her hand wrapped over his.

They sneaked around one of the igloos, snow crunching at their feet as they tiptoed toward the NoGo, at least Destrou tried to. Despite night settling in, the ground shone a glimmering white that helped lead the way.

They appeared at the rear of the NoGo. It was tough for him to appreciate the beautiful designs carved into its walls when he knew of the horrors that lived inside.

"Let me know if anyone's coming," Elu said, kneeling down, shuffling her hands over the snow.

Destrou turned and saw rows of igloos reflecting a deep white light, and before he could turn back toward Elu, she was gone. Destrou looked around, glancing at the icy wall of the NoGo, the untouched, sparkling snow around it, and the many igloos surrounding him. There was nothing else around.

How does she always do this? He jumped back, startled by a touch, grabbing his ankle. Elu's hand appeared out of a hole covered with snow.

Elu dragged him down into it as the snow molded back into place like the hole was never there. She adjusted the white cloth wrapped around her head before smiling wide, eyes crinkling.

"How'd you do that?" Destrou looked up as if he had seen an Archon.

"Stop looking at me like I'm Eve, I'm not. It's just a different kind of snow." Elu shrugged, pointing down the tunnel. "Look!"

The tunnel glowed a mix between white and blue—probably from the light that seeped through—and was just wide enough to fit them inside, long enough so they could barely see the end and carved in a perfect circle.

When they reached the end of the tunnel, breathless with pounding hearts, they both climbed up through the exit into a large room. Then the ground closed across the gaping hole, as it did when they first entered.

Overhead they heard a deep rumble, around them were dark walls, and behind them a window revealing the sky. It was dark blue and starless. Some light entered through the window, providing them with a glimpse of their surroundings. There seemed to be no way out.

"Where are we?" Destrou touched the walls, searching for some kind of hidden opening.

"Where else would we be, silly? What else can that terrible

snore be? Stupid loud, huh?"

"Are we in the NoGo!?" Destrou screamed. His heart raced faster. "It's called the No . . . Go . . . for a reason. No! Go!"

"Shhh." Elu pressed her fingers to his lips. "Stop being a baby. You trying to wake them up?"

"You trying to get us killed?" He didn't know if he wanted to bite or kiss her finger.

"Well, tomorrow may be your last day, anyway, so what do you have to lose, scaredy pants?" Elu said with a giggle.

Destrou felt like he should've been mad—or at least worried—but for some reason he felt a warm glow inside. He chuckled. "Good point."

"This way." Elu pressed her palm against the wall. She pushed the door open and hurried down a hallway. The shimmering ground reflected enough light so that Destrou could see where Elu's shadow stood. He ran toward it.

The loud snores weren't far. Destrou hoped that Elu would change direction at any moment, but she kept heading toward the noise. The louder the snores became, the faster Destrou's heart pumped.

The hallway spiraled the exact direction Destrou wished to avoid. He couldn't see Elu ahead of him, or anything for that matter. He stumbled, hitting his knee hard on something, and stretched out his hand. It pressed against something—a step of some kind, maybe for a giant. The cold numbed his palm, sending a shock through his arm. He pulled his posture up, so tense that his body trembled. He hoped Elu didn't see his clumsy fear.

"Do you know where we're going?" Destrou whispered.

"What kind of question is that? Of course. Almost there. Look!" As the hallway turned, light flowed into the aisle, until Destrou was able to see the end. He focused on matching Elu's pace to avoid

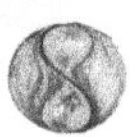

knocking into her. There was some visibility, but more darkness than light. Elu pointed at a door at the very end of the aisle that had a faint beam glowing from underneath it. Before the last room, there were two open doorways to the right and left. Loud snores erupted from both, causing the rolling thunder.

Destrou swallowed a very difficult breath. "Do we have to go? We can turn back around if you want."

"Of course," Elu said. "We've made it this far already. Watch my back. Let me know if any of them wake up. You wouldn't believe me with all of this snoring . . . but they're actually light sleepers."

That was exactly what Destrou didn't want to hear. His palms were already too sweaty.

Elu lowered herself to a crawl, inching her way past the open doors. Just the soft sound of skin scratching against the ice was enough to create a stir in their snoring. "Light sleepers" was an understatement. The Guardians' years with the Crystal Soldiers must have taught them how to sleep cautiously behind enemy lines.

Destrou crawled to the opening of the doorway. His back pressed against the wall. He jerked his head closer to the entrance and peeked through. Darkness obscured most of the items in the room, but he vaguely spotted silhouettes of armor, weapons, and miscellaneous objects. This room must be the Guardian's—too many weapons.

The bed was as wide as the door, about ten feet long and five feet high, and the protruding belly that continuously went up and down was at least an extra two feet higher. Next to the bed there was a painting that had five circles drawn onto it: one large circle in the middle with four smaller ones on each corner. It looked like some kind of map.

The snores ricocheted between the walls before making their

way out. Destrou pressed his palms against his ears, squeezing with all his force, scrunching his eyelids together. He wished he could shove his foot down the Guardian's stinking mouth. When he pulled himself back, he crawled to the other side of the aisle, and looked into the Commander's room.

Gronk slept in a similarly sized room without the luxuries from the Kingdom. His bed wasn't as high as the Guardian's, but Destrou still noticed miscellaneous junk underneath it. Stray bones, ripped fur, shredded pieces of rope, nothing of use to the Guardians, but treasures to any Villagers.

Everything seemed good to go for Elu. She made it to the door at the end of the hall and had already begun to inch it open. The door was about ten feet wide—no easy task to move it. But the way it slid back silently made it seem like she had done it countless times before.

Destrou had too many questions to ask. How did Elu know about the tunnel? The food? Their sleeping patterns? Was there anything that she didn't know? He wanted to know more about this mysterious girl. He wanted to know her real story. What brought her into this life. And what made her into this amazing, crazy adventure-seeker.

It took a while for him to register that the snoring had stopped. It was odd. When one stopped, they both did—as if they were somehow connected.

Destrou heard a shuffle from within the Guardian's room. He was too scared to turn and look. He let his eyes shift to the side. It looked like the Guardian was about to roll off his bed.

He saw Elu crawl into the room, out of sight. Destrou's stomach twisted. He needed to do something. To warn her.

A crash was followed by a large shadow eclipsing the light. The darkness grew as the footsteps became louder. Destrou felt his

chest quake with each step.

He wanted to move, but his feet and hands were frozen in place—welded to the ground like a statue. He was so tense that even his body forgot how to breathe; he feared that the sound would alert the Guardian. The footsteps grew louder; the shadow completely engulfed the entrance. Time was up.

The moment Destrou saw a greasy hand shine in the light, he slid into the Guardian's shadow, clenching his teeth.

The Guardian entered the aisle, opening his drowsy eyes, looking around at an empty hallway. "Mer," he said. "Must have been my dream."

Destrou had slipped into the Commander's room, hiding behind the wall. He slid a few inches to the right, hoping he was far enough from the entrance. The air around him was heavier, breathing was difficult. He wondered what Ranmau and Elu would do right now. They always had an answer.

But it was too late.

The Guardian's face entered Destrou's line of sight, poking into the room.

Destrou looked up as stray hairs fell from his wide beard and almost smacked him in the face. It sent a putrid smell in his direction. His head jerked forward, holding back a cough. He covered his face with his palms. His eyes watered and mouth trembled.

"A little snack never hurt." The Guardian licked his lips. His saliva splashed on the ground next to Destrou. Remnants of it landed on his hand, smelling like vomit. Destrou wanted to cry. But if the Guardian caught him, Destrou wouldn't have to worry about tomorrow's punishment. Because there would be no tomorrow.

The Guardian stood at the entrance for a few moments before turning back. Had there ever been a more disgusting moment, Destrou thought. He used this opportunity to sneak in a few uneasy breaths, chomping for air. His lungs burned; he hadn't breathed in a full minute.

The rolling thunder of the Guardian's footsteps headedtoward Elu. Destrou's entire body was filled with energy. His friend was in danger—it wasn't the time for second-guessing. He saw the Commander's bunioned-filled feet, with long, overarching toenails, extending beyond the bed. He didn't want to look at them, never mind get close, but he crawled near the bed and kept his eyes forward. He didn't know what smelled worse: a rotting meat, the Guardian's beard or the Commander's feet—he was beginning to think that they were all of the same class.

He moved one hand closer, pressing his other hand over his nostrils. *Things you do for a friend.* His finger pressed forward, touching the Commander's slimy foot. Destrou tried his best not to release whatever he had left in his stomach.

Elu sat in a large pantry. There were shelves packed with food— some stacked too high for her to reach—but nothing to hide behind. She saw the Guardian's fingers reach around the door, pulling it open, when the sound of laughter distracted the Guardian. His attention shifted toward the Commander's room. Elu crawled between his feet. When the Guardian looked back, he reached in and grabbed a handful of meat, stuffing it into his mouth and chewing noisily.

Elu slid underneath the bed, crashing into Destrou.

BANG! The Commander shot up wide awake, slamming his heels onto the ground. As dust fell from the grooves in the bed, the Commander's repulsive feet were inches away from Destrou and Elu's faces. The Commander stormed out of the room, glaring at the open food door.

"Yah stealin' a night snack are yah!" the Commander shouted,

running at the Guardian. "I knew yah was the one takin' the food."

"I only did it cause you've been taking extra food." The Guardian shoved more meat into his mouth.

"Yah was caught and now yah blamin' me? I knew yah been doin' this for a while. I finally catched yah." The Commander grabbed a large leg of lamb out of the Guardian's hands.

The two of them fought over it and other things that had gone missing while Elu and Destrou retraced their steps back to the tunnel. It wasn't until the Guardians' shouting settled into a distant hum that Destrou felt they'd actually escaped. By the time they exited the tunnel and the NoGo, and arrived back into the Village, they couldn't contain their laughter.

Destrou and Elu tried to be as quiet as possible to not wake up the boys, but it wasn't working out well. They were giggling while creeping their way toward an empty igloo.

"Able to get any food?" Destrou laughed.

"What do you think, silly?" Elu laughed, pulling out a bag filled with food.

"You stole food from them and got them to fight over it." Destrou laughed. "You win!"

"Anything for a friend." Elu smiled. "See, wasn't that a lot of fun?"

"Your definition of fun is interesting." Destrou laughed. "But why'd you need me?"

"If I got the food for you, then I would've only fed you tonight, but if I taught you how to get your food, then you'll be okay for a lifetime—even if it ends tomorrow." She smiled wickedly.

"Well, I guess that makes sense. But why don't you feed the entire Village then?"

"Because the Guardian and Commander don't notice when I

take little things, but a lot would be pretty noticeable."

Destrou nodded. "I'm just glad that we can finally eat now." He patted his growling belly.

They stared at each other, seeming to have forgotten that they were not alone.

For a moment Destrou thought the area was empty, and he felt a wave of relief. Then he heard a voice and it all changed.

"What are you little boys doing here?" Destrou heard a deep voice behind him that felt like it slid ice down his spine.

There were five boys, much taller than him, crouching on the ground. Their white clothes were the perfect camouflage, blending into the snow between two igloos like wolves waiting to pounce. If not for their eyes blinking, he wouldn't have noticed the others.

The tallest one yanked the bag of food out of Elu's hands. "Thanks for the food, krillen."

"Hey!" Destrou lunged forward for the bag "That's Elu's!"

"Whose hand is it in?" He stepped backwards. "Exactly. It's ours now."

"We don't want any trouble," Elu said softly, cowering on the ground.

"Heh, pathetic." The boy grabbed Elu by the head, tightening his grip around her scarf. "I never got to see what's underneath this stupid thing, anyway." He yanked the scarf with all his force as Elu fell to the ground. "Tighter than I thought."

Destrou could see the damage that was done. She curled into a fetal position as her scarf unraveled.

The boys gasped, as if they had seen an Archon, and knowing the consequences, Destrou lunged forward in panic, kicking the boy across the jaw. A shriek tore itself from the boy's throat as blood sprinkled onto the ground. The boy's grip loosened from the bag and Elu. As the others helped him up, Destrou saw more spawn

from the shadows. He was outnumbered and there was no Ranmau. The boys circled around him and Elu like hyenas. *I need you.*

He helped Elu to her feet, and wrapped the scarf around her head before giving her the bag of food.

Despite everything telling him to run, he pressed forward. *I'll save you.*

"This is going to get ugly." Destrou pushed Elu behind him, as if he was a human shield. "But I won't let anything happen to you." He wanted to say *I promise* but he never wanted to break one. Not with her. *There's only five of them. I think I have a chance.*

"Looks like we may have to tell the Leader about what we just saw, Elu. But come with us into this igloo and it'll be our little secret." The tall boy grinned. "So whose side are you gonna choose. We all know what'll happen to you when you choose wrongly."

"I'll protect you, don't worry." Destrou reached his arm back to comfort her.

"I'm sorry," Elu whispered to him. "Forgive me."

Destrou nearly turned around when he heard something hum through the air. He tried to duck, but it was too late. A block of ice shattered against the back of his skull, and he collapsed into darkness.

"Oh no she didn't!" S'rae screamed. She felt a flash of rage and barely managed to swallow some of her words. "I can't believe I ever liked her!" She hated how invested in the book she got. She wanted to plan their escape, but something about Destrou and his world drew her in.

"You should know better than most—" Aralinda scoffed from afar, "—to not trust a girl like that. You never know what we're capable of."

The Sereni Sisters laughed in unison.

"I wouldn't trust you girls if I was dying of thirst in a desert," S'rae snapped back. "There's something about pretty girls that I've learned to not trust." She smirked at Aura'li. "Thanks for that lesson."

The Sereni Sisters gasped. "What a brat!" For a moment it looked as if they might faint. They clutched their throats and made a coughing noise.

"Why would Elu betray Destrou?" S'rae asked. "I thought they were real friends."

"S'rae," Gabrael said coldly, "throughout life, we sometimes find out, one way or another, that there are times when some decisions made may not be the right thing to do, but they are indeed what is best."

The way his words hit her made her heart skip a beat.

Like sacrifices? she thought.

25

G ASPING FOR AIR, Destrou rolled over and tried to scramble to his feet. He felt weakened from the blow. He winced, as he raked his hands through his hair, smearing them with his own blood.

"You shouldn't move so quickly," said Elu's voice in the distance.

As Destrou lay there shivering and aching, he heard the crunch of Elu's feet in the light snow.

"I'm sorry," she said gently as she tried to pick him up.

"Leave me alone." Destrou shrugged her off.

"You have to understand—"

"Understand what?" Destrou growled. "What it's like to live life in my shoes? The second you even thought about living it, and joining me, you left."

"That's not it, I swear. You—" Elu pressed forward, trying again to help him to his feet.

"I understand. You don't and never will." He put his palm up, halting Elu in her place.

"It's just that—"

"It's just nothing." He muttered as he struggled to pick himself up from the snow-covered ground. A rage boiled within. "It's just that you're a scared little krillen. I protected you even though I knew I could've been killed. And when—"

"Exactly! They would've killed you if I didn't do that. I had to think of something."

Destrou felt the silence that followed shiver straight to his bones.

"I did that to save you." Elu grabbed Destrou's hand. "Please, don't hate me. Everything happened so quickly. I knew what they could do, and I knew that I couldn't picture my life without you, so I—"

"Can't picture your life without me? Why?"

"Because—" She hesitated, her eyes like blue crystals soaked in liquid ice. "You're the only good left in my world. You give me hope. You need to live. So you need to leave tonight before the Guardians kill you."

Destrou heard genuine sorrow in her voice and saw tears in her eyes, but still he felt empty. "I don't trust you. That was the second time you didn't help me when I needed it. How can you be my friend when I can't even trust you when things get bad?"

"I understand why you're mad. I would be, too. It's just very dangerous for me, so I get scared, and then I freeze. I'm sorry. Please believe me! I promise it won't happen again."

"Fine, but don't break it." Destrou sucked air through his teeth before rolling back his shoulders and reaching his hand out.

"I promise," Elu said as they grabbed each other's forearms, binding their words.

The setting finally dawned on Destrou. "Wait, where are we?" Destrou said. Elu brushed her palms through the fur of her pants

and walked around the room, past Destrou, who turned eagerly around to watch Elu bending over an ice pick on the ground. When Elu straightened up, Destrou saw the familiar designs on the icy walls with pictures and clocks carved into them.

Elu paused for a moment, nervously brushing the thin layer of snow with her feet. "The Tree."

Once his eyes regained focus, Destrou noticed the carving of a tree underneath him.

"How'd we get here?" Destrou asked. Elu's face flushed red as she turned away. "Did you bring m—"

"I was afraid of what they'd do to us when you were out. I couldn't take the chance."

Tears welled up in Destrou's eyes. "That's way too much work for one person."

"It took only about an hour—maybe three. No one's counting—*cough*—maybe four."

"But how'd you get out? And won't they tell your secret now?"

"Don't worry about me or them, we took care of it."

"What do you mean?" Destrou heard the worry in his voice.

"I said don't worry about it. I have my ways." Elu smirked.

"I guess . . . but you did all of that for me? Why?"

"Because you're special. You should know that by now."

"I'm not the special one here! I don't see what you see."

"I wish you could," she said softly. Their eyes met, her lip curled. "But, no offense, that's because your eyes are kind of swollen. No worries, they'll be back to normal in no time!"

Destrou burst into a laugh that quickly formed into a wheeze. "Now I feel like the biggest jerk ever. You did all of that for me."

"I really want to make it up to you. I want to show you that I'm here for you."

"We keep talking about what's good for me, but what do you

want in life?"

She didn't have to think too hard about it. "I only want three things," Elu said. She ticked each one off on her fingers. "I want to see an aurora—"

"What's that?"

"Only the most beautiful thing ever!"

"Does it look anything like you?"

"No, it's a bunch of amazing lights in the sky."

"Then it's not the most beautiful thing ever."

Her face went red. "Oh, you're being a silly butt! The other thing is the Eye of Eve."

"I'll get it for you then!"

Elu gave him an appraising look. The one he had hoped and waited to get from Ranmau but never came. It was the type of look that said, *I know you can, but it's not safe.*

"And the last thing is . . ." She paused.

"What?"

"It's embarrassing."

"You can tell me anything!"

"Okay, well . . . I really want to leave with you. Like right now. Tonight. We can explore the Forest!"

"Leave with me?" The words tumbled out in a rush, and Destrou stood up, his forehead crinkling. "To the Forest? That's crazy! Why? Your life is good here, better than mine."

"Things are changing. They'll know I'm a girl sooner than later, and I need to leave before everyone finds out. The Village is too curious now."

"What's changing? Do you have"—Destrou pointed in between his legs—"I don't know what girls have, but if it's starting to grow hair, then I guess it's normal."

"Oh my Divine, you're sooo gross!" Elu shrieked. "We are *not* talking about this!"

"Well, what do you wanna talk about?"

"I don't know . . . dreams, goals, the meaning of life. Literally anything else!"

"Well, what's the meaning of life to you then?"

She paused for a moment. "Stories. I love them, and I think lives are just a bunch of stories; life should be about making it worth reading. When the day comes and we're in the ground, how do you want your story to be told?"

"Well, there'll never be a story about me, so I don't have to worry about that."

"I would read your story!"

"So it could put you to sleep?"

"No, silly krilly." Elu laughed. "So I can read the story about the amazing boy who saved a girl and changed the world. It'd be called 'A Warrior's Past.'"

Destrou burst into laughter. "Hey, you're the one who saved me! And I'm not even a warrior!"

"Not yet." Elu raised her chin in the air. "But that's the point—it'd be about the adventures you went through before you became one of the greatest warriors *ever*!"

"You sure you're not talking about Ranmau's story? Mine will be boring."

"It doesn't have to be. You have the power to make every day matter." Elu shot up with excitement. "Let's shake to that!"

"To what?"

"To making sure our lives are the greatest stories ever told. And that we make every day worth reading about." Elu stood up proudly. "This is your life, Destrou, make your one chance count! To making sure that we don't live and die in the Village and that we explore the world!"

As crazy as Destrou thought it was, a warmth in his heart made him go with it.

They shook, grabbing each other's wrist, binding their words.

Destrou thought about how he had never once envisioned traveling beyond the Village. The idea scared him. But something within him sparked like a fire. Elu changed the way he viewed the world. Around her there was no Archon prowling through his mind—only hope.

Destrou saw light twinkle in her eyes. They were glowing with an unknowable certainty of their future. And if they could speak, he would have been able to hear the three words they had been dying to say.

"Destrou," Elu said softly. "I—"

Then, in the most beautiful way, the room resonated with bright colors—pinks, greens, and blues—flowing like streams across the ice.

"Oh! My! Divine!" Elu shrieked, stomping her feet as if he she was running in place. She scrunched up her face and pressed her palms against her cheeks.

"What's going on?" Destrou peeled one eye open.

"This is the aurora!" Elu screamed. "It's said that people can live their lives without ever seeing one. It's actually happening!" Elu grabbed Destrou's wrist and yanked him through the color-changing tunnels of the Tree. The lights glowed for long moments, ranging between every color in the rainbow. Once they arrived outside, at the edge of the cliff, clouds formed.

"Eek!" Elu squealed. "This is a dream come true!" She looked over at Destrou with widened eyes. "I'm so glad that I get to experience this with you!" Her happiness spilled out in waves of tears. It was clear this night meant everything to her. And to him.

He smiled, unable to imagine how there could ever be a more

perfect moment.

Then, as if the Divine One wished to prove him wrong, flakes of every different color descended from the colorful night's sky, looking like flower petals drifting through the air. The Wall normally being an object that caused dread, instead brought life into Elu's eyes. It looked like an animated canvas, splashed with bright watercolors, moving to the rhythms of the wind.

"This is more beautiful than I could've ever imagined," she said softly.

Painted with green and blue and pink and purple lights, Elu and Destrou sat over the cliff, shoulder to shoulder, with their feet dangling. The colors flowed in the sky like rivers. The snow looked like colorful glitter floating down. It was a magical moment, perfect.

Destrou felt a tingling sensation in his stomach that was soothing. He never wanted this night to end.

"There's something in me . . ." Elu gazed into Destrou's eyes. Destrou saw pink and green streaks reflect off her sapphire eyes. "I don't know what it is, but everything in me is telling me that you're going to be special. I want you to live your life. Not Ranmau's. Not mine. This is why you should leave tonight. Just live your life and let your story shock the world."

"I can't tonight. But it's not going to be my story—it's going to be ours." Destrou's mouth widened to a smile as he pointed ahead at the Forest. "We're going to live in the trees!"

"And you're going to teach me how to fight like a boy."

"And you're gonna teach me how to—" Destrou hesitated. "What's different about us?"

"Nothing!" Elu laughed. "We do everything the same, we're just more awesome."

"Teach me how to be awesome and smart and read like a girl."

"I'll definitely teach you how to read. But, let's be honest, I don't know if you'll ever be this smart and awesome." Elu chuckled, resting her head on his shoulders.

When Destrou closed his eyes, he could feel her soft heartbeat pulse against his arm.

"I'll protect you from the cold." Destrou smiled.

"And I'll protect you from the Archons."

They went on for hours, talking about their dreams and all of the adventures they would have in the Forest of Ness.

Everything felt surreal. That was until the beautiful aurora borealis had faded away. And the night along with it, revealing a bright blue, clear sky.

"Oh no . . . we need to get back." Elu grabbed her scarf from the ground.

"Wow, that went by too fast." Destrou focused on the yellow light spilling over the Wall. It was the brightest sunrise he had ever seen and felt. He was warm, not just inside.

"Let's meet here. You can say your good-bye to Ranmau, then we start *our* story!"

Elu leaned in, kissing him on the cheek. "There!" She smiled, as if kissing him was something that she had always wanted to do. Destrou looked at her glowing smile and again saw what the night meant to her. She wanted to feel like herself—a girl—for a moment removing the mask that kept her safe. It was a brief kiss, a quick touch of her lips on his cheek. But as she pulled away, Destrou saw that her cheeks flushed. He wondered if he'd embarrassed her.

Destrou didn't know what he was feeling. He thought of Ranmau. This sensation reminded him of the way Ranmau used to make him feel. The way his stomach felt weightless each time their eyes met. The way Ranmau wrapped his arms around him to keep him warm. During the coldest nights, when sleeping seemed impossible, he was there. Destrou missed this feeling. Suddenly, he was scared. Afraid that someone else was the reason for his happiness. Like Ranmau was being replaced. Forgotten. As if a world with Elu meant one without Ranmau. He wished for a world where he could have both. *He* was the reason he couldn't leave tonight.

Elu asked for help wrapping the scarf over her face. Destrou felt her soft skin and hair graze along his fingers. A chill shot through him. When she turned around, their eyes met and connected. Destrou saw his eyes in hers—they suddenly seemed to unlock the meaning of life.

He thought about how out of everyone who had ever lived, he was happy that she existed during his gash in the circle of time. "I'm glad that you're in my story." Destrou smiled.

He reached in, softly grabbing her neck. She closed her eyes, puckering her lips.

"There you go." He pulled the scarf, wrapping it around her mouth. "Now you're ready!"

"Thank you," she sighed, her eyes rolling.

"Elu," Destrou said. He reached for her face and brushed the strands of hair back from her eyes. Their gaze met again. "Thank you for saving me."

This day began on one of those perfect mornings that only existed in dreams and never in reality. The sun was warm. The sky was bright and heavenly. Even the muted grey of the Forest appeared to give in to its light. On both sides of the Village the Wall shimmered a bright yellow.

All said, Destrou couldn't hope for a nicer day to find out how he will die. Today was unknown, but one thing was certain: Their lives would never be the same after that night.

26

*S*MACK!

Destrou woke up to a sting on his face. His cheeks burned even though he knew it was one of Ranmau's weak slaps. He'd seen how powerful his slap could be, having the ability to wake someone up or put them to sleep.

"Get up," Ranmau said. "We don't have much time. They may start without us."

Ranmau carried himself like a statue, with his wide shoulders thrown back and his chin pointed to the air. His silvery hair was slicked back, accentuating his flawless, pale skin. Contrary to Destrou's constant weary look, Ranmau always appeared immaculate and clean. As he headed out, his eyes seemed to sear the ground, maintaining his aura of an unblinking fierceness at all times.

Destrou lunged out of bed and darted for the entrance.

He crashed into what might as well have been a solid block of ice. It surely felt like one. From the ground, he saw the Commander's rock-hard belly, his grizzly beard curling above it.

Gronk leaned into the igloo with a snarling face and a curled lip.

This was the closest Destrou had ever been to him. He was taller than their igloo and almost as wide. His stomach was large enough to stop him from entering and he chewed with his mouth open.

"Yah two bettah had a good reason why yah aren't at the 'sembly." He poked his head into the igloo as food spilled out of his mouth, falling onto Destrou.

"I—I—" Destrou stammered, wiping his face clean. He didn't know if he was even allowed to speak back to him.

"It was my fault." Ranmau glared at the Commander with narrowed eyes. "Some of us need extra time to sleep."

"I happened tah fell asleep good these last nights." He had a belittling laugh. "Well, there be problems if yah two are late again. I'm sure yah don't want any problems, do yah?"

With unwavering eyes, Ranmau nodded.

"What was tha—" Destrou stopped, remembering that he shouldn't ask questions.

Ranmau hobbled toward the entrance.

Before Ranmau exited the igloo, Destrou pressed his hand on his shoulder, one of his fingers touching the bare skin in between his shoulder pad and neck. His body was cold, almost too cold. He forgot what it felt like to have a physical connection with his brother. The thought of it made his eyes well up. He fought the tears back and mustered up the courage to say what was on his mind. "You know that I always wanted to be here for you . . . right? If I did something wrong, you can tell me now. I . . . I . . . just want my brother back." Something was holding Ranmau back, making him stay here, making him suffer. And Destrou knew that the something was not a thing at all, it was a someone. It was him. "I don't feel like I'm losing you, I feel like I already lost you. I don't want this to be how you remember me. I'm sorry for ruining your dreams."

Ranmau looked back, acknowledging his brother with saddened eyes. "It's not you." His voice was colder than the ice that surrounded them. "I know you made a friend. I am happy for you." He left the room and it felt like he took the air with him.

Destrou remained speechless for a few moments, digesting the meaning behind his words. They were the most he had spoken in years.

He knows about Elu?

Moments later, he heard a muffled voice shout: "Where's the other one?"

Not wanting to anger his tormentors even more, he raced out of the igloo.

The Villagers sat in a circle, surrounding the platform in the center. The brothers made their way to the front, passing through hisses and brooding glares. The Guardian stood on top, wearing a grin on his face that looked as unpleasant as his stain-covered pants. The Commander was to his left. And there they stood, giants in front of an emaciated crowd.

Where is she? Destrou's eyes darted around the crowd.

"Before I was rudely interrupted by the krillen twins"—the Guardian tapped his lips carefully—"where was I?"

"Yah is talkin' bout the Supreme General's request," Gronk said.

The Supreme General was the Master of the Kingdom whose identity was as mysterious as his legend. What little they did know of him was that he wore a full crystallized armor, covering his body from head to toe. The suit was said to be made out of the same material as the Crystal Sword. He wasn't the King but might as well had been.

The Supreme General was the best of the best. A true time-tested warrior. It was said that the greatest warrior was needed to lead the Crystal Soldiers. The elites. The protectors of the Kingdom and the reason the Archons were defeated during the First Great War, history claimed.

Joining the Crystal Soldiers was what every boy dreamed of—but none more than Ranmau. It had been his dream since the first time the Guardians mentioned their name.

"Ah yes, the tournament! Well, for those of you who were smart enough to not choose death by the Forest or the Wall, there's another chance for freedom." He held back laughter then continued, "The Supreme General told every Guardian that he's looking for the strongest fighter from each village to join the Crystal Soldiers. He apparently thinks one of you worthless krillens would be good enough to join the force. In my day, we had people like you scrubbing our feet, not fighting."

"*Hah!* They'd do much more than that for us." The Commander glanced at Ranmau.

Destrou saw Ranmau's fists clench so tightly that his veins bulged. Destrou leaned closer and whispered into Ranmau's ear, "You can finally get your freedom. I knew this day would happen; I'm so happy for you."

Ranmau's eyes lit up at the sound of the word. *Freedom.*

"Per his request," the Guardian continued, "we'll begin the tournament in two months. This will give you enough time to prepare yourselves and not embarrass me."

Destrou felt a block of ice slide down his throat as he noticed that all eyes were on Ranmau. There was an uneasiness in the air that felt life-threatening.

But Ranmau's eyes focused only on the Guardian's. He seemed unfazed.

Staring back at Ranmau, the Guardian continued, "Although

the order will be set at random for those interested in freedom, the first match has already been decided." Destrou noticed how Ranmau's nostrils flared and how his breathing became heavy, as if he knew something that Destrou didn't. "You, the Great Ranmau. The unbeatable krillen of the Village. You will face off against—"

Anticipation was in the air. The entire Village looked on with widened eyes, as if hoping their name wouldn't be called. Destrou felt heartbeats escalate, or was that his own? Even the Leader trembled. Fighting Ranmau was in no one's best interest. Those who tried their luck became unrecognizable.

After what seemed like an the eternity, the Guardian continued, "—Destrou."

The silence that followed was the worst type of silence. It was in the heart of Destrou's worst fear, greater than the fear of death: life without Ranmau.

There was a muffled roar, as if his ears were plugged. He tried to stand upright, but his knees shook so hard they were ready to buckle at any moment. He saw the curled lips of the boys, but he couldn't hear any words. He saw their eyes dilate as they leaned forward like scavengers awaiting the kill. A pungent smell hit his nostrils. Destrou shook his head, wondering if the fear he felt showed on his face. The roars that filled the area were audible now; he felt horror strike through his chest like The Giant with a knife.

Desrou looked around desperately. His eyes came to rest on the ground.

Ranmau glared at the Guardian with a rage that screamed as loud as silence could. He remained focused on the Guardian, as if he knew that there was still something left unsaid. How did he know? His ability to read body language apparently wasn't used just for combat.

With a belittling tone, the Guardian recited one last heart-wrenching notice. "And don't think that I forgot about your punishment, krillen." He turned to Destrou. "To ensure that only true warriors join, all matches will be a fight . . . to the death."

Destrou felt like an Archon was ripping apart his insides. He felt nauseous. Devastated. He turned slowly, his sad eyes finding Elu's. Hers appeared just as gloomy. He didn't expect Ranmau to reassure him, and he made no effort to, but, during that moment, he just needed to be held. To know that he wasn't alone. That his life mattered. That the thought of him being gone meant something to Ranmau, not just his way out.

Destrou didn't know how he should feel. He wanted to be happy. For Ranmau. But it felt impossible. Two months at least gave him the chance to leave with Elu—the only thing that he looked forward to now. He tried to believe that the delayed sentence was a kind gesture by the Guardians, but he knew how much satisfaction they'd receive watching brothers fight to the death.

"And Destrou," the Guardian growled, as if he heard Destrou's thoughts, "if you even try to think about leaving, then I'll kill Ranmau myself in the most painful way imaginable. We've learned many things while being Crystal Soldiers—that's our specialty." He laughed. "I can't wait to see what he does to you to get the freedom he always wanted." The Guardian smiled as he walked back into the NoGo, slamming the door shut.

Destrou looked at Ranmau, unable to tell what he was thinking. His eyes were cold, but his lips trembled. *Does he care?* Destrou whispered into his ear. "I'm still happy for you. You deserve this. This is what we always wanted for yo—"

Destrou choked up before finishing his sentence.

His heart pumped faster. The reality began to settle in. His sentence was worse than he had ever imagined. He would rather jump off the Edge than be killed by his brother. His stomach wrenched.

She was right. Neither of the brothers knew how to take the sentencing. They stared into each other's eyes as if they were already set to say their last good-bye.

You should leave tonight, he remembered Elu's words. *We should have. And I should have listened.*

When Destrou blinked he could see the top of her head as she pushed her way through the crowd. Her eyes appeared glazed and teary. She whispered an inaudible "I'm sorry," while being shoved around.

The crowd became uneasy. There was a tense breeze that felt like a lit fuse—something horrible was about to erupt at any moment.

He had two months left to live. That was what his life was worth. *Two months . . .* After that, no more Ranmau and Destrou. No more brothers, challenges, life, laughter or Elu—just darkness. Two months until his story ended.

"We have to go," Ranmau said, observing the crowd ready to prey on their targets like wolves. "Now." It was as if he had sensed their envy and knew their rage.

Before they could react, something hit Destrou's collarbone. He slammed into Ranmau, his head hitting his spine, before falling to the ground. His palm braced for contact, pressing against the ground, and his other hand grabbed Ranmau's leg for support.

Destrou stood up, turning slowly, every limb heavy with tension. He looked at the crowd around him. They were in an uproar. Before Destrou could get far, he felt another push, a hand on each of his shoulders, forcing him to the ground.

He felt a sharp object slam into his back. He clenched his teeth to keep from crying out. Pain immediately flooded his body. Ranmau grabbed Destrou's cloak and pulled him back up.

Destrou was frightened more by Ranmau's eyes than he was of

the bloodthirsty crowd.

"You okay?" Ranmau asked.

"Yes," Destrou said. That was the only response to prevent Ranmau from going berserk.

Ranmau's brows arched with hatred. Destrou had to look away. Anyone with eyes could see that Ranmau's blackened eyes looked like a ravaged, wild animal's—he was one wrong move away from striking for the kill.

If only . . . the boys knew what Destrou knew.

Elu observed the chaos from afar. Destrou's words rang through her head. She couldn't stand back and watch her friend be treated like this. Not again. He was her friend—maybe something more— and she was going to prove it. She had to. Their secrecy no longer mattered to her. She promised him. And that was more important than anything else. More important than the village's opinion, the punishment, or her secret—was her heart. And right now it raced. She knew Destrou needed someone there for him, and she wasn't going to let him down. Not again.

She took a deep breath, tightened her scarf, then pushed forward, squeezing her way through the crowd.

The roars became louder the closer she got to Destrou. She didn't know what she was going to do but she couldn't do nothing. She shoved her way to the front, passed boys twice her size. She felt a spasm in her heart that told her danger was nearby. She fought off that feeling and pushed ahead.

In that exact moment was when it happened.

One of the boys didn't like her push. He turned around with force, throwing her back, slamming her into another. Then someone grabbed her from behind. She started to scream, but a fist connected into her jaw. She thrashed about, wriggling to get free, but the arms that held her were too tight. She kicked and punched in random directions, trying to free herself.

"Let go!" she screamed.

"So you can help your friends?" a boy shouted. "You think we didn't know about you and them? They're going down now and anyone who helps is going down, too."

"Get him!"

"Grab him!"

"I got his legs!"

A rough pair of hands covered her eyes, and a new pair of hands grabbed the scarf at the back of her head. She struggled to breathe. There were too many hands pulling her in different directions, pushing her forward, pinning her down, dragging her backwards. Her limbs hurt. They shoved her to the ground, trampling her.

Her heart raced as their feet and fists pummeled her, and she tried to focus on the location of the boys. Guiding her feet in between one of their legs, she lunged her foot upwards, kicking into the groin of one of them.

She heard one crash to the ground. She thrashed around, feeling their rough hands scrape her skin. She screamed, hoping that Destrou would hear her, but the roars were too loud.

Her scarf began to unravel. Her heart pumped so fast her chest began to hurt. She couldn't breathe with them on top of her.

She tried to stand up but her head slammed forward and struck the icy ground nose first. The air stank of moldy feet. She barely had time to curl into a protective ball. She held her arms together as close as possible and prayed that her head wouldn't be crushed when they stomped the ground.

She was hit hard again, pain screaming up her arm. Something splashed up in her face; there was a coppery taste in her mouth that she had never experienced: her own blood. She tried to scream again but the wind had been knocked out of her. She wheezed, gasping in the odor.

She wanted to defend her exposed body, but she gripped her scarf, making sure it wouldn't unravel. That was her priority. But it continued to loosen despite her efforts.

Her options ran out. Her eyes watered as her body was unable to handle all the pain. But worse, her blond hair was almost fully exposed.

In that a moment, she heard a loud thud then a boy's face smashed to the ground directly next to her. She could see his eyes roll backwards. There were a few teeth dangling from his bloodied mouth. Something must have hit him hard.

Another body crashed to the ground. Hands grabbed her. Her feet left the ground with ease. She pushed her scarf to the side to see whose hands they were. Strands of her long blonde hair fell through, blurring her vision.

"What you doin'? Dangerous—for you," the Giant said, hoisting her up onto her feet. His body had recovered since that knockout by Ranmau. His shirt was ripped, revealing his shredded muscles. His face, under the white shroud over his head, was scarred but mostly healed. He smiled, showing gaps where teeth had once been. She wondered why he looked so happy.

"Thank you so much," she said, wiggling her body free.

"Lijah want you back," he said, pulling her away.

"Let me go. I need to go." She tried wrenching his fingers from her clothes, but the Giant's grip was too strong. "Listen, I'll get you some of the best food you'll ever have, okay? It's called Sensu . . . it's amazing," she said weakly. But if she'd expected a response, she didn't get one. Instead he threw her over his shoulders, holding her tightly to him. His clothes smelled of sweat, and his fingers were long and coarse, pressing on her bruises. Still, it was a relief nevertheless to be free. From the savages. From pain. From—

Elu gasped as she saw Destrou. She needed to react quickly. And without thinking, the taste of decay caused her eyes to glaze as she realized that her teeth had chomped deep into the Giant's fingers.

"Ow!" the Giant cried.

She shifted her body weight just enough to release his grip. Once her feet made contact with the ground, she limped after Destrou. "Thank you! I'm sorry! Forgive me later," she yelled over her shoulder, thinking forward to Destrou: *I'm here for you.*

The brothers hadn't covered much ground, seeming trapped by the chaos surrounding them. She saw boys running back into the crowd with sharp objects in their hands. This was not good. She needed to warn them. Those weapons meant only one thing: that someone was going to die. *I can't let this happen.*

She pushed forward, getting shoved in every direction. She was unable to look over the shoulders of the taller boys in front of her, but she saw in between the cracks. The heat of the many bodies around her made it difficult to breathe.

A break in the crowd revealed a small opening. She saw Destrou straight ahead. He was fine—for now.

Their eyes met. He had a glowing smile on his face. She knew what he was thinking. For the first time, someone from the Village decided to fight for them. She knew what this moment meant to him. That was exactly why she did it. To return the favor. To repay him for her best night ever. A night she would never forget. A night she'd write about in their story.

They gazed at each other, smiling with a radiance that made everyone else disappear. For those short moments, it felt like the world had frozen during a time of peace. A glimpse of what life could have been like if things were different. If there were no walls, hunger, or anger. No worries or problems—just a moment that she wished could have lasted forever.

A cold breeze tossed her blonde hair across her face. It was in that moment, being surrounded by everyone in the Village, when she smiled wide. She smiled because she no longer hid who she was. She was bold. Brave. A brilliant girl glowing as bright as any star could.

She thought how there couldn't have been a more precious moment in time. No matter how messy her hair looked, she felt radiant and powerful beyond words. Destrou's mouth moved in a way that Elu understood as a silent *thank you*, though she imagined him saying something entirely different. Twelve years of living and for the first time, Destrou had finally made a best friend.

Elu never took her eyes off Destrou.

As the brothers moved forward, Destrou lifted his head, catching Elu's eyes once more. He smiled at her. Elu smiled back. Her gaze changed in a way that alarmed Destrou, widening into a horrified glare. A cold feeling jolted through her body, revealing her thoughts.

"*NO!*" she screamed with the force of a last good-bye.

The first sharp projectile was thrown, ricocheting off Destrou's head, carrying blood. Elu collapsed inside; she saw Destrou fall.

Blood splattered onto Ranmau's cloak, but he hadn't seen what happened yet. Elu ran toward Destrou, screaming. Her chest was on fire; her heart couldn't handle the messages that were sent to her brain.

This couldn't be the end of his story! There was too much she had wanted them to do.

Destrou hit Ranmau on his way down.

Turning around to spot his bloodied brother lying face down, Ranmau lost his calm. The wrong move had finally been made. A

rage erupted in his eyes, as if the moment that Destrou feared had occurred.

With one crazed reaction, Ranmau turned around with a clenched fist that held the power of a thousand men, blindly releasing all of it into the first person in his sight—Elu.

She only had an instant to react. Her eyes grew as Ranmau's fist cracked into her chest cavity. She barely had enough time to say Destrou's name before the slam was heard around the Village. Air escaped from her lungs. Her blue eyes rolled back. Her vision faded to black.

Her breath performed its last dance in the wind.

"IT'S OKAY." VAYP WRAPPED HIS ARMS AROUND S'RAE as she soaked his chest with tears. He felt a warm glow as he comforted her again. He felt like the brother she never had. The one he had always wanted to be for her. But he couldn't tell her that. Expressing feelings was something that boys were ridiculed for doing. Not by their elders, they encouraged it, but by peers. But right now it didn't matter. He held her. As tight as anyone could. He wanted to tell her what she really meant to him. That losing Ah'nyx hurt. A lot. But losing S'rae only added to the pain. He wanted to tell her that she wasn't alone. That he did not want to let go. Or lose her. *You're all I have.*

"I take back what I said," S'rae said in between sobs. "I did like you, Elu. Why'd you have to die. You and Destrou could've lived such a great life, together."

"That poses the timeless question, S'rae," Gabrael said omnisciently. "What's worse, a love that ended or one that never began?"

"I don't know," S'rae sobbed. "I'm sorry but I need a break." She stood upright and ran toward the door, flailing her arms.

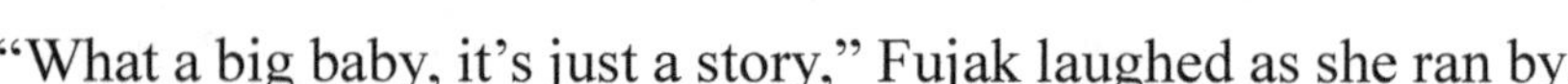

"What a big baby, it's just a story," Fujak laughed as she ran by.

"I'm going to go check on her." Vayp followed closely.

"And I'm gonna be there for him while he's there for her." Han'sael shrugged, trailing behind. "She gets a little crazies." He twirled his finger around his head, rolling his eyes.

"Wow!" Vayp lifted S'rae in the air, shaking her. "That was amazing! That had to be the best acting I've ever seen."

"Thank you, thank you." She bowed, rubbing her eyes.

"I'm a profreshenal crier and I don't think I coulda done that better." With his tongue between his teeth, Han'sael inched closer to S'rae, his lashes almost touching her eyes. "Unless . . . those were real ones!"

"N-no," she sniffed. "I was acting."

Vayp knew that she really had been crying, but he wanted to make her feel better. Either way, whether the tears were real or forced, their plan had worked. They only had a few minutes to save the person who was trapped in the tower, and when S'rae went over the plan again just to make sure that everyone knew their roles, Vayp saw her grab something from underneath a cobblestone. It looked like a white ball of some kind.

Like cats scattering from a loud noise, the three of them ran the moment they heard a door open.

While they ran through the golden hallways, Han'sael kept on talking. He liked to talk, a lot: about how he couldn't afford any books so he learned by watching the rich kids cast spells, food, how the people in his head used to be his only friends, food, Destrou and Elu, and food were pretty much his favorite topics.

There was nothing above them but the high-rise ceiling, charred and black in places as if it had been burned in a fire. A hall to the right led to a bridge that connected into the floating tower they planned to break into. The pillars on either side were engraved with a collection of flames and weapons. A steel door guarded the bridge, the only way in. As S'rae glanced out the window at the tower, Vayp noticed the thing in her pocket took the shape of an orb. He wondered how she'd gotten it. She was too secretive to ask, though. He knew her too well.

"This door would be locked," S'rae said, hearing resistance when she pushed.

Vayp nodded. "Time for Plan B."

"What's Plan B?" Han'sael scratched his head. "I didn't sign up for no Plan B. What's the B stand for? Bad? What if we die? What if we end up gettin' sacrificed or what if—"

"There may be food up there," Vayp said.

"Great! I like it! So, how many plans are there?" Han'sael said alertly. "Let's try 'em all!"

"Well, we can try—" S'rae started.

Her words were cut short by a piercing scream that sent a cold shiver through Vayp.

"Was that the scream you heard?" Vayp whimpered.

S'rae nodded. "We don't have much time."

Vayp noticed from the way that her pupils dilated that she was scared, though she refused to admit it.

"Looks like we have to skip Plan B and go straight to Z," she said.

"Z?" Han'sael gulped. "Why does that sound scaredy? What does the Z stand for? Zeadly? Zerrible? What the? Hmm . . . what word even starts with a Z? Zam. Zom. Zim—"

"Plan Z?" Vayp said, not paying attention to Han'sael mumbling a list of incorrect words.

"You see that up there?" S'rae pointed at the octagon-shaped window on the tower. It was about thirty stories above them with

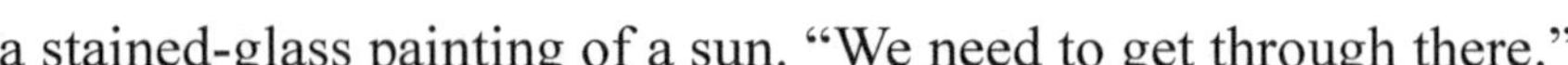

a stained-glass painting of a sun. "We need to get through there."

"Zuper! That's it. I knew there musta been one word!" Han'sael shouted. "Wait . . . *zuper*! Hmm . . . why does that sound weird when I say it out loud? I swear it made sense in my head."

"Do I even want to know how you plan to make that happen?" Vayp said to S'rae, ignoring Han'sael. He felt his stomach sink.

"Nope!" She chuckled.

Vayp watched as S'rae stood in the center of the courtyard, her arms at her sides, looking up at the tower. The night had settled in, covering the area in darkness. He was becoming fond of his time here, the Valley felt oddly welcoming with its worn stone walls, deep craters, and richly carved statues that stood the test of time. Even the fat kid waddling toward the floating tower felt like an old friend.

Mostly he couldn't help but stare at S'rae and memorize every line on her face. Somehow she changed, yet remained the same. He wished he could tell her—

"Okay, so here's the plan," S'rae said.

"I have no idea how you 'spect us to get up there." Han'sael stuck his tongue out of the corner of his mouth as he jumped an inch off the ground. "Why'd he have to be all the way up there? Why couldn't he just be on the first floor?"

"Yeah, keep trying for it," Vayp suggested sarcastically. "You're getting closer."

As Han'sael's grunts and thuds went on, Vayp asked S'rae what the plan really was.

"Remember that time you dragged me through the wall?" S'rae said.

"Yes."

"You turned stone into water," S'rae said. "And since both carbon and oxygen are in water and air, I—" S'rae's eyes went white, muttering words and twirling her fingers. A breeze blew by them, sending a cloud of dust into the air.

Han'sael could be heard in the background as wind picked up. "The scariest part about all of this is that . . . if they find out what we're doin', they're gonna take away all my food! My food!"

"*Mi'zu ku'ki . . .*" S'rae said as gusts of wind spiraled around her feet, tossing her hair.

"And?" Vayp asked.

"*Shui.*" S'rae let out a whisper.

The roars and wind stopped, leaving behind an eerie silence.

"No maw bubblin' fruits," Han'sael gasped. "Banawamas, crispy crescents, chewy bottoms, frisky fries, fried feet. And—"

Vayp felt a cold sweat breaking across his forehead as his stomach felt weightless.

"No more Songlings! And my — Hey, what the . . ." Han'sael shouted as his voice trailed off. "Look!"

Vayp turned, eyes widening inquisitively, and saw Han'sael suspended in air.

"S'rae," Vayp said, shock pounding him. "You remember how much I hate heights, right? So, the plan has nothing to do with us flying, right?"

As he turned to S'rae, he realized that he was looking down at her.

Han'sael squealed like a pig. "Yay! I'm flyin'! Who said fat kids can't fly? Look at me now, krillens!"

Instantly, Vayp felt his stomach sink as he soared through the air next to Han'sael. His heart pounded faster as S'rae started to shrink.

"How did you do this?" Han'sael shouted. "I know this feelin', I'm a Sereni, after all, and this feels like swimmin'."

"You're right." S'rae flew toward them, breaststroking through the air. "I tampered with the air molecules to give them the same compression as water—so, in a sense, you're swimming through air."

"Yahooo!" Han'sael blazed by Vayp and S'rae as fast as a falcon. It was clear that he was an expert swimmer, showing off his flawless backstroke as he twisted and twirled through the courtyard.

"There's one problem." Vayp gulped.

"I know," S'rae reassured him. "I'm not the best swimmer either. Just hold on tight. And try to keep your eyes squinted." S'rae placed her goggles over her eyes as Vayp heard a hum that sounded like the buildup of a large turbine. "I'm not joking when I said hold on tight," S'rae screamed as the hum turned into a roar of an airship before liftoff.

And just like that, Vayp felt pressure build up at his toes like he was standing on solid ground.

A force catapulted him through the air like a missile, and he just had time to wrap his arms around S'rae's torso. It was nothing like swimming—to him at least. Wind pushed uncomfortably on either side of him, pulling his fingers apart and making him feel he was about to fall to his death. He whirled around, deafened by the hum of the wind. Air rushed through his hair, and his robe whipped out behind him. It was tough for him to see, the wind smacked his face like a tornado. He understood why the Fujitas wore goggles.

They swooped in and out of the bridges, circling around the Spire and towers multiple times, rippling through the clouds as they ascended higher. Vayp looked back at the shrinking roofs, and tried his hardest not to scream. Wind whistled in his ears, mixed in with the excited screams from S'rae and Han'sael. The moment he opened his mouth, the weightless feeling subsided. Blood rushed to his head as they floated thousands of feet in the air. They saw the entire Valley and it truly looked like a wasteland. Everything was dark and dreary, with no signs of life anywhere. At least the Spire looked beautiful with its intricate details and the towers floating around it, looking like the bridges held them from drifting away. But it surprised him to see that the sky had cleared up for the first time since being there.

Then it happened . . .

No matter how dark the Valley looked, a smile sprawled across Vayp's face—the widest it had been in years. Yes, a real smile. He didn't need to force it, it just happened. If only S'rae could see it. He couldn't remember the last time this happened. He briefly thought about Ah'nyx. But this memory was instantly stored in his bank as one of his favorites—the ones with Ah'nyx that he'd resort back to whenever he wanted to force a smile.

It felt wrong to be this happy. As if being miserable was the only way he was supposed to live. As if being happy meant he had moved on from his past: His home; His family; Ah'nyx   . . . But that was far from the truth.

He knew this feeling wouldn't last long, so he tried to enjoy his new found contentment. Unlike Destrou, he hoped this was a dream. One that would last forever. If he had more dreams like these he wouldn't be so afraid to sleep. Anything to avoid the monsters lurking in his head.

He understood what Destrou was going through. The feeling of an evil presence within him that he had no control over. It gave him some comfort knowing someone else could relate.

Vayp was snapped back into the moment as he felt S'rae lean forward. He wrapped his fingers tighter around her robe.

"The sky looks beautiful," S'rae said, observing the hundreds of flickering stars. "We're going in! Hold on tight, and make a wish!"

"Actually, from what I learned," Han'sael said, "when you wish

upon a star you're actually a few million years late. The star is dead, just like your dreams, Vayp."

Vayp wanted to laugh, but the next moment they were gathering speed in a steep dive, heading straight to the window. Vayp screamed as S'rae stretched out her hand. Right before they made contact, a burst of wind shot from her palms, shattering the glass. They toppled gently onto the stone floor, as if landing on an invisible pillow.

"That was fun!" Han'sael screamed. "Let's do it again."

Vayp felt dizzy and nauseous. "Let's not." His head shot forward, and he cuffed his hands over his mouth to stop himself from vomiting. "Let's just save this person and get out already."

In no time they were looking straight at a metal door with no handles.

"This is the one," S'rae said. "I can't explain it, but someone's in there. I feel it."

"How ax-axectly do we get in?" Han'sael said. "Hmm, is that right? Axect—"

"It's exactly." Vayp pressed his shoulder against the door. "And it won't even budge."

"Retro'ku?" S'rae whispered to the door. "You in there?"

Immediately the door glowed red as if it was a charcoal on fire.

"Get back." Vayp pulled S'rae away as it sizzled, emitting the scent of burned flesh.

"We're here to save you." S'rae leaned in closer. "He won't hurt you anymore."

"We bringed you food, too!" Han'sael squirmed, pulling a bag out of his robe.

"Really?" Vayp shook his head. He leaned forward and breathed in the bag's sweet scent. Ah'nyx would've loved whatever was inside.

"What?" Han'sael said, wiping his mouth on the back of his hand. "He must be hungry in there. I know I would be."

"You're always hungry, fatty! Didn't you just eat?"

"I haven't ate since the last time I ate! I'd rather be hungry than stupid."

"Who is you callin' stupid?" Vayp mocked Han'sael, shoving him into the wall. The bag of food fell from his hands, rolling to the door.

"Take that back, big head." Han'sael pushed Vayp.

"Rather have a big head than a big belly."

"You wish you looked this good." Han'sael jiggled his belly. "Take notes, krillen!"

The door cracked open slightly—just enough for a hand, as black as a shadow, to wrap around it. Its steamy fingers grabbed the food, then slammed the door shut.

The slam shook the room.

"Oh no he didn't!" Han'sael's chin tucked into his chest as he glanced around in disbelief. "Did the food thief guy really take all of my food and not even say thank you? Let's keep the jerk locked up . . . after we get my food back, of course. I was *this* close to gettin' it back!" Han'sael placed his fingertips an inch apart. "Hey, you two aren't lookin' at my fingers! Look, I was this close!"

"I don't get it." S'rae appeared puzzled, ignoring Han'sael. "If he's locked from the inside, then he's not a prisoner?"

"Fatty lost his food." Vayp poked Han'sael's belly. Vayp and Han'sael promptly had a fight over who would put their eye into a tiny hole in the door. Surprisingly, Han'sael won. Vayp imagined that Han'sael's hidden strength had something to do with him really wanting to get his food back. Vayp, catching his breath, lay flat on his back; the warm brick massaged his body. Though he would never admit it, he enjoyed the bantering and play-fighting with

Han'sael. "Maybe if you stopped eating and actually read a book you could have reacted quicker. Feed your brain, not your belly."

"That's it! You talkin' about my food?" Han'sael smiled, rolling up his sleeves before diving onto Vayp. "Now you crossed the line!"

"What are you going to do with those flabby things?" Vayp grabbed Han'sael's biceps. "It looks like your belly is having a party that your muscles weren't invited to!"

The two of them play-wrestled, bumping into S'rae. Vayp noticed the orb shoot out of her pocket, ricocheting off the ground. The orb rolled into a crack just before S'rae slid to grab it.

Vayp was about to shove Han'sael but then his body went numb with shock.

The ground shook him with such force that he felt paralyzed. It was the protective spell. A scent reached his nose that made his pupils dilate and nostrils flare. His heart pounded faster and his breathing became quick and heavy. The air stank of toxic fumes and machinery.

"No . . ." Vayp quivered. "Not again."

"What's wrongiong with this guy?" Han'sael shook Vayp. "Hey, S'rae, something's up!"

"This . . . smell—" Vayp's voice trembled. Flashes of screams and explosions accompanied random images of bloodied bodies sprawled across a war-torn village. It no longer felt like he was in the tower with S'rae and Han'sael, but he had been transported to a place where bombs fell on top of children playing in an open field. He heard their cries, and the sounds of bones crunching, and blood splattering. He smelled burned flesh, fumes, and machinery. A screeching whistle from a missile falling overhead.

BANG! Vayp's eyes shot wide open, waking up to Han'sael shaking him.

Han'sael's mouth was moving but Vayp couldn't hear any words. After a few moments, they became audible.

"What's goin' on with you?" Tears poured down Han'sael's eyes. "You goin' crazies and S'rae is holdin' some shakin', glowedy thingy."

Vayp looked over at S'rae who had the same fear in her eyes. In her palms she held the orb that fell out of her pocket, which was now the size of her head and resonated a white glow, striping through her fingers.

The way her hands trembled, it seemed like it took all of her strength to hold it.

"Danger . . . when it glows?" S'rae said in a quivering voice, trying to put the orb in her robe, but it was too big, and her hands were shaking. "This isn't good!"

"Can someone explain what the heck is goin' on?" Han'sael belted. "But more importanter, how we gettin' my food back?"

A humming sound drifted by them as if a massive airship was coming to take them away.

The sound vanished around the corner.

"Snap outta it!" Han'sael shook Vayp.

Vayp's eyes then turned white. The ground shook. "We gotta leave. *NOW!*"

28

VAYP SPRINTED FASTER than he thought was possible to run, the wind wrapped around his body as he circled down the spiral staircases. His heart pounded against his chest. And as he approached the door to the bridge, he jumped, tucked his knees, and flipped. The stairs liquified, spiraling around him like water whirling down the drain. His body turned into a boulder, rolling down the smooth slide that formed. His momentum increased as he rolled up the twisting walls.

BANG! He burst through the door, tumbling over the bridge before smashing his way into the Spire. He slid as the stone dissolved into a streak of dirt, then ran through the hallways until he reached the classroom.

The door flew open, crashing into the wall. S'rae and Han'sael ran in shortly after.

"*Unacceptable!*" Gabrael roared. A few candles changed to blue, and Vayp felt the warmth wash over him as if he'd sunk into a hot bath. The entire room turned their attention toward Vayp. He stood there, resting his palms on his knees, his chest heaving up and down.

The moment Gabrael met Vayp's eyes, his nostrils flared, as if a scent piqued his interest.

Gabrael whispered.

The candles extinguished immediately.

The room became dark with twirls of smoke dancing around. Gabrael's whisper pierced through the room, hushing the students.

The silence was broken by a hovering, mechanical sound just outside. It started as a hum, gradually advancing into a roar as it got closer.

The ground shook, feeling like an earthquake was directly underfoot; books flew off the shelves.

Vayp's body trembled. Sweat soaked through his clothes. His fists clenched so tightly blood trickled down his fingers.

A red light peered in through the window, shining on the ceiling, slowly making its way down the wall.

Gabrael snapped his finger.

A spark fizzled away as quickly as it appeared.

In that instant, the students understood the warning and transported themselves behind the wall, pressing their backs against it—just under the window—clamping their hands over their mouths and ears.

Vayp remained in the open. Petrified into a statue.

The ray expanded into a wide spectrum, filling the room with a red mist. The light scanned the stone slabs used as seats, the walls filled with books messily scattered across the shelves, and the floor, showing intricate designs that Vayp hadn't noticed before.

The red beam inched closer to his feet.

For a moment he couldn't breathe. He didn't think anyone could. Fear paralyzed every inch of their beings.

He had to move.

No, he needed to move; but the messages weren't being delivered. His senses slowly came back to him. Now he could hear the students' whimpers, not to mention the droning hum and the sizzle from the light that was about to touch—

Quickly and silently, he felt a breeze whip by him as hands grabbed his body and yanked him to the wall. The sheer speed left him feeling dizzy from the whiplash.

His first thought was S'rae, but the hands were too rough. When his eyes focused, he was shocked to see they belonged to Fujak.

Slowly, his senses came back. The wall was warm with a grainy texture that prickled Vayp's skin. The window carried in a heavy scent of rust, metal, and some type of fuel.

The red light traveled from top to bottom and left to right before thinning into a cylinder, and retracting back through the window.

It left the room in complete darkness.

Vayp looked outside as a massive, ivory hundred-foot-tall machine with a solid red eye in the middle of its face roared by. It hovered toward the top of the Spire, scanning every room on its way up.

How did it know which room to target first?

"Was that—" Han'sael whimpered.

"Shhh." Vayp pressed his finger on his lips. "Yes . . . a Mecha, a PriMecha—"

Before he finished his sentence, the hovering stopped, the wire-infested joint that would be considered a knee visible through the window.

The temperature rose in the room.

Whimpers escaped through the cracks of fingers.

They waited.

The students stiffened; grips tightened on their clothes. No one moved . . . no one breathed. Somewhere a creak could be heard.

The air became thicker.

Another creak, this one louder.

From his angle, Vayp noticed Gabrael's eyelids squeeze tightly, as if praying for the PriMecha to pass. As if praying to a Divine One somehow above himself. Apparently even Gods can experience fear.

And he had reason to fear. This was no ordinary Mecha. Pri-Mechas were more sophisticated and deadlier than regular ones. They had been auto-created in their factory—hidden somewhere deep in the mountains—after data from previous Mechas were collected. When one Mecha died, its information was used to create a PriMecha to prevent the same demise from occurring. They were dangerous machines designed to be the perfect soldier, the perfect killer. Sad, things that were once designed to protect Gaia were now slaughtering it.

This one came specifically for Gabrael. He must have known.

A fourth creak turned into a hum that magnified into a sudden shriek.

"GET BACK!" Gabrael yelled.

BANG! A massive fist punched through the ceiling, then scraped through until it ripped out the wall.

Quickly, Vayp dodged to the side and held S'rae. Looking back at the fist pulling away, he saw exposed wires and large chunks of stone topple overhead.

The wall was pulverized, revealing the crimson red night's sky. Thick, dark clouds covered the atmosphere. Even if the sun was out, its light wouldn't penetrate. What had happened to cause that? Where did the clear sky go?

Vayp didn't know what was more horrific: standing on a stone plank a few inches from a thousand-foot drop, the Mecha ready to kill them, or the boulders from the rubble overhead ready to crush

them.

"Help—"

"We're dead—"

Boulders tumbled down, moments away from crushing them.

Vayp felt a wave of panic.

He said nothing, biting the inside of his lip. He hated the idea of death—especially by this monster. Again . . . It touched upon memories buried so deeply that he couldn't reach them.

Some boulders were twice his size, more than enough mass to flatten him.

Death was moments away.

No . . . not again!

BANG! Vayp punched the air. His feet cratered into the floor as the boulders—an inch overhead—froze in place.

Blood floated up through the cracks of his fingers.

His eyes flashed a bright green for a split second before fading to white.

"NOT — AGAIN!" Vayp screamed, pushing his palms forward. At once, the boulders crashed into the PriMecha, throwing it out of sight.

Gabrael moved toward Vayp with a presence that sent chills up his spine.

He said nothing, but his hand came up to touch Vayp's shoulder.

Vayp could feel the power in it, draining all heat from his body.

Vayp closed his eyes.

He heard himself gasp and suddenly went cold all over, cold as Ah'nyx. So frigid it hit his skin like hornets. He pulled his cloak close, gritting his teeth at the freezing wind. And when his eyes sprang open, he watched his breath dance in the air.

His jaw dropped.

It was happening—

Gabrael's once dark eyes now blazed with fire. His palms ignited with a crimson glow. Crackling sounds of embers emitted from his feet. Flames ignited around him. His cloak flowed like water before disintegrating into ash.

He was going . . . Elemential—

Gabrael's clothes vanished as his head, eyes, and body went ablaze.

Vayp felt the flames' scorching heat sear his skin.

Gabrael dove off the ledge, leaving a fiery trail.

The thick smell of ash and smoke felt like a wall blocking air from entering Vayp's lungs. He coughed uncontrollably, grabbing his neck before falling to the ground.

When he peeked over the edge, his eyes widened. He felt a lump in his throat.

Gabrael flew circles around the PriMecha, shooting waves of fire from his palms that unfazed it.

The way flames dispersed around its body, Vayp knew this PriMecha had Gabrael as its target. This ivory one must had been a planned attack years in the making. Maybe centuries.

Vayp became more aware of his surroundings—the gaping hole and the weakened structure, the anxious faces of S'rae, Han'sael, and Fujak. The GroundStone trio stood unmoving. Vayp winced at the sharp pains in his hands, and looked down to see red lines scraped across his skin where his nails had dug in. It then occurred to him . . . no matter how gifted these students were at learning, none of them were prepared for the horrors of battle. Of war.

None of that scared him as much as the creak he heard. He closed his eyes and became one with the stone structure. It spoke to him. The Spire felt weakened beyond repair.

CREAK!

The ceiling—and the dozen or so stories above them—swayed

side to side.

Oh no!

Very slowly, he concentrated on molding the areas that needed the most support. If he didn't, he was sure the Spire would collapse.

He pushed his hands into a puddle of mud. Now he heard more sounds, and the falling and shattering of rocks.

Wondering what he should do, he suddenly heard a *boom* much closer; the entire top section was about to crumble down.

"What's wrong?" S'rae touched Vayp's back.

"This isn't good," Vayp said. He dropped his voice so that none of the students could hear him and told S'rae about the Spire collapsing.

"We need to do something!" S'rae squealed.

"Do what?"

"Why?"

"Yeah, what's she talking about?"

"Tell us!"

"What do you see?"

"I'm hungry."

"Shut up!"

"WHAT'S GOING ON?"

When Vayp was ready to tell them, it happened. Too quickly.

The ceiling overhead rumbled, then collapsed.

There was no chance for survival. There was too much stone for normal students to control.

But Vayp was not normal. He was far from it.

Vayp's body tingled. His mind went blank, a swirling green mist was filling Vayp's brain. He no longer had control over his body. The ground spiraled underfoot like water draining down a funnel. A bright flash made him temporarily blind, his vision obscured by dozens of white and green spots. Green mist appeared underfoot, circling around his toes, then instantly surged through his entire body, feeling like the coldest shower ever.

Colors swirled behind his eyes, tinting everything in green. He felt a pressure, unexplainable energy in his hands and feet. He felt like he had the weight of the world in his hands, being slowly crushed.

What was happening? He needed to save everyone. Why was he just standing there? They needed him . . .

"How did you do that?" Vayp heard through the ringing in his ears, trying to make sense of what was happening.

"Vayp your . . . eyes . . . they turned . . . green. I saw them. I swear I did."

"I've never seen such power before . . . even from GroundStone professors."

"You sure you saw that? Green? That only happens when—"

"—Yeah, that only happens when—wait, did he go . . . Eleme—"

"No way! He hasn't gone through any training, that'd be impossible! And he's no God."

Vayp could hear the voices, but they made no sense. He didn't have a clue what they were talking about or where he was. All he knew was that his arms and legs were aching as if he was—

He looked up and noticed the entire top section of the Spire rested in his hands. The same hands that trembled uncontrollably.

He couldn't move.

He could barely move his lips.

"Shh . . . he's trying to say something."

"He—"

"Hi?"

"Hel—"

"Hello, do you remember us?"

"HELP!" Vayp screamed. The weight was too much for him. The ceiling inched closer and closer to his head. He felt helpless. Impossible to fight, like a bug ready to be squashed.

"HELP HIM!" Adalia screamed.

The GroundStone trio snapped out of their daze and slid to his aid, pressing their arms up. They muttered words simultaneously, helping to lift the weight. At least they tried to.

"Umm . . . this is way too heavy."

The ceiling slowly inched lower.

"We need a lot more help than this!"

"We got this," Fujak said, waving down the other Fujita students.

Vayp felt his muscles tearing open, feeling like a knife was slicing through its fibers.

With Fujita and GroundStone's assistance, they managed to tip the mass forward enough for it to crash along the side of the Spire.

It took almost all of their energy, but Vayp could tell by S'rae's sweat-soaked brows that none worked as hard as she did. She looked exhausted.

She crashed into Vayp's chest, her arms wrapped around his torso. He felt his clothes drench where her face was, and knew that wasn't because of sweat.

She pulled away awkwardly, as if she had forgotten how to walk. She hobbled for a second before straightening up.

Vayp met S'rae's gaze. He knew that they were both thinking the same thing: how glad they were to see each other alive.

A smile appeared on his face. And as quickly as it appeared, it vanished. S'rae's eyes rolled up. She stumbled briefly before fainting.

Vayp's heart pounded faster.

He reached out for her limp body, but it was too late. She collapsed over the edge, falling toward the shattered rocks a thousand feet below.

"NO!" Vayp screamed.

Fear surged through his body, immobilizing him.

"Someone help her!" Fujak shouted.

"Vayp, do something!" Han'sael shouted.

Vayp's eyes blackened. His heart pounded and he had a strong impulse to do something, but dread froze him in place.

"Vayp, snap outta it!" Han'sael grabbed him by the shoulders and shook him. "S'rae's gonna die!"

Moments passed. A distant explosion occurred—one that could only be described as a volcano erupting.

A missile came screeching toward the students. Before it made contact, it shot straight up like a rocket.

BANG! The explosion overhead rattled their eardrums.

Most of the students covered their ears.

Vayp wanted to cover them, too, but he needed his hands to save S'rae. He looked over and noticed the Fujita trio crouched in an aggressive stance, punching the air. They must have deflected the missile. Speaking of Fujita, S'rae didn't have much time. It might already be too late.

Squinting, he pressed his palms onto the warm floor, muttering words. The ringing pain made his fingers curl and head sink.

A large stone hand then appeared on the side of the Spire, traveling down like an elevator chasing S'rae.

Vayp squeezed his eyes shut and pushed his hands through the floor. It rippled like quicksand.

S'rae was only a few seconds from impact.

Vayp's gut twisted at the thought of her splatting across the ground.

His worst fear was about to happen. He was going to lose her.

Forever.

I'm not losing you!

Before S'rae hit the jagged rocks, a second stone hand reached out from the Spire, stretching open. Vayp clenched his fists, tightening his grip around the squishy stone. His palms tingled. A foot from the ground the two hands wrapped around S'rae just in time.

"*Hijr-ma'an!*" Vayp screamed. The stone hands—holding S'rae—were pulled into the Spire, splashing like water upon impact. Moments later, Vayp lifted his hands out of the puddle, revealing a mud-soaked head.

Realizing he held S'rae, the students helped pull her out. Hoots and hollers were followed by clapping sounds. She was dirty, wet and sticky as if she had swum in mud. Her clothes, once silver, were brown and drenched.

Vayp smiled, wiping mud off her face. Tears poured from his eyes.

"Is she okay?" Adalia asked, shoving her way through the huddle of students surrounding S'rae.

"I don't know." Vayp pressed his face onto her shoulder, sobbing. He couldn't even think of the possibility of losing her. Not like this.

"Han'sael," Adalia said. "You're a Curadai."

"Curadai?" Vayp asked, lifting his head up.

"A healer," Adalia said. "Much better than me. The best one I know."

Though Vayp tried his hardest not to lose focus, he couldn't help but analyze Adalia's high cheekbones and blueish eyes that almost looked green. Her blonde hair was brown at the roots, unlike her sisters who were fully blonde. She smelled like roses and something else he recognized from his home—the fresh scent of a fruit garden.

Why didn't he recognize how flawless Adalia looked until now? Maybe because he hated everyone? But she seemed pleasant compared to her sisters. Maybe she was adopted.

Han'sael's smile wavered, probably because he figured it was the first and last time a beautiful girl would be that friendly to him. "You really think so?"

"Of course." Adalia smiled. ". . . you're the reason I dropped out of the program. I knew there was no way I was going to beat you so I became a Soturi."

"Soturi?" Vayp asked.

"A warrior." Han'sael walked closer to S'rae with a confidence Vayp had never seen from him. He paused. "The best one I know." He placed his palm over S'rae's mouth. *"Giji'mas."*

S'rae's head jerked forward, coughing dirt onto Vayp's face. "You're welcome." She smiled.

The students clapped and cheered. But the excitement didn't last long.

A missile screeched before exploding underfoot, blasting Adalia off the ledge.

But before anyone could blink, Han'sael'e eyes went white as he pressed his palm outward. In that instant, he was thin again, and a channel of mist froze Adalia in place. Her eyes widened looking at the ground below. As if she was fully submerged in water, Adalia floated into Han'sael's arms.

Adalia gazed into his eyes. Probably because he looked handsome when he became thin.

Then suddenly he went plump again, but still the glow in her eyes didn't fade. It was as if she saw through the extra weight, and noticed the character inside.

"You smell good," Han'sael said.

"Thanks, I use both nostrils." Adalia smirked.

Vayp couldn't help but chuckle. Then the weirdest thing happened. As he watched Adalia and Han'sael gaze into one another's eyes, he felt . . . jealous? Of Han'sael? Impossible!

"Is that your hand on my hip?" Adalia asked, a subtle smile playing at her lips.

"Yes, sorry, it was an accident," Han'sael said, not breaking eye contact.

"It's . . . still there." Adalia blushed.

"It's still—" Han'sael said softly, leaning closer toward Adalia's face. "—an accident."

Her smile grew wider.

Now how in the what-the-heck-this-can't-be-real-life did Mr. Fatty-Can't-Fit-In-My-Pants become Mr. Smooth-With-The-Pretty-Girl? What else has he been hiding in his bell—

Vayp's train of thought was shattered by the volcanic eruptions from all around the Valley. The dark sky became darker; black ashes and thick smoke filled the sky.

Vayp saw Gabrael swoop around the Spire and throughout the Valley like a comet.

When Vayp leaned over the edge, a sizzle rose to a roar. He looked up and saw a dozen or so missiles heading straight at them.

"Look out!" S'rae pulled him back.

BANG! Geysers of lava spouted upward, engulfing the students within a fiery cylinder. Sweat drenched from Vayp's pores, darkening his robe. Vayp felt his insides evaporate—dying of dehydration could kill him before the burning did.

Vayp felt a wave of relief when the Sereni sisters waved their arms around before touching palms. They formed a triangle, and at once, the air cooled as a soft breeze of steam swirled about. There were sizzles and hisses and pops, like the sounds of water coming to a boil.

Then explosions boomed overhead as if the fire consumed the missiles.

"Get down!" Kaul lifted his hands. The other GroundStone students joined in, saying: *"Hijr-di're!"* The floor spiraled around them, morphing into a shield.

All Vayp could think about was making sure S'rae survived.

It couldn't end like this.

And after what felt like years of waiting, a blaze roared outside, resembling a flamethrower. It dwindled to a crackle, then fizzled out with a spark.

"We must leave," came a deep voice.

Vayp snapped his finger.

The shield absorbed into the ground.

Vayp was kneeling next to Gabrael, blinking as if he couldn't believe it. Gabrael's clothes were crumpled and burned, and his cloak no longer neatly rested over his shoulders, but he seemed otherwise unharmed.

"More will come, we need to go." Gabrael reached into the podium—which to Vayp's surprise, looked untouched—and grabbed the Book of Eve.

"You kidding me?" Vayp shouted. "You still want to read this stupid story to us? Our lives are in danger and that's all you want to do? I'm getting out of here!"

"You are all free to leave," Gabrael said softly. "I will not force anyone to stay . . . just remember what I said about your great destinies. You must trust me."

Vayp glanced around, noticing that he stood alone in his opinion. His heart stopped when he saw S'rae look away.

They all had a perplexed expression, gazing at their hands like it was the first time they'd seen them.

"S'rae, let's go!" Vayp screamed. He felt blood rush to his head,

making him purple. "You're all gonna die when more Mechas come, trust me! And they will. Who's coming?"

Nothing was said.

A mound of dirt protruded from the stone, lifting him a few inches off of the ground.

Vayp's eyes narrowed. "Don't say that I didn't try to help you, S'rae."

S'rae gazed at her hands, confused. "I have a feeling that all of this has happened before. I can't explain it, but it's telling me I need to stay."

The other students looked around with the same glassy eyes as if they too had experienced a moment of déjà vu.

"Déjà vu isn't real! Don't be fooled. Han'sael, you coming?" Sand slowly morphed around Vayp's feet.

Every eye in the Spire turned to Han'sael. Before Vayp could speak again, Han'sael cupped his hands around his face; a familiar sting hit Vayp's chest. The bite of being deceived.

Just as he thought, no one would come with him. Why would they?

Vayp felt foolish, hurt, and betrayed beyond words. Mad that he even hoped for someone to join him. His stomach churned, but he didn't want to show his frustration. He was too proud.

"Fine. Don't expect me at your funeral, then," Vayp said.

"Wait!" Han'sael screeched. "You can't go alone."

"Han'sael, remember, once gone, you will be unable to return. The Valley will be invisible to you. Don't let your great destiny end here," Gabrael said in a hurry. "As for those who are staying, can the Fujitas bring us down to the courtyard?"

Fujak walked forward, placing his hand on S'rae's shoulder. "I thought we lost you." He looked away, rubbing his eyes, then spoke with his head down. "I know I'm the last person you'd expect to hear this from—" He looked up, his eyes were watering. "—but Fujita was too close to losing one of its best."

S'rae smirked. Her eyes narrowed. "Really?"

"Really," Fujak said. "I . . . There was too much I'd regret if anything bad happened to you."

S'rae fell silent. And for a split second, her eyebrows rose.

"Now let's bring everyone down," Fujak said as he clapped his hands. "*Feng'yun!*"

Wind howled through the Spire, lifting them into the air.

"I can't believe you're choosing them over me again!" Vayp shouted. He felt pressure build up behind his eyes. "You always choose them over me! I hate you for that!"

He waited for a response, and when she gave none, he growled.

S'rae looked away, covering her eyes.

The wind roared, carrying them down on top of a cloud of mist.

"So, it's just me and you, Han'sael," Vayp said. "We don't need them, anyway!"

Han'sael put his head down, mumbling some words.

"It takes a lot to want to come with me, so I appreciate it. Especially since I seen the way that water girl looked at you."

"Water girl?" Han'sael lifted his head, his eyes were glazed.

"Yeah, that one you saved, the way she looked at you was like the way you look at food, that says a lot!" Vayp tried to chuckle but it felt too forced.

"You're just sayin' that!" Han'sael replied with a half-chuckle of his own.

Vayp felt Han'sael's uneasiness, he tried to lighten the mood. "I don't know, I feel like I'd be the last one to say this, but I think you may have had a chance with her. Maybe one in a million, but there's still a chance!" *Please don't stay with them. I don't want to be alone again.*

Han'sael said nothing. He looked away and put his head down again as if he had too much to say.

"Do you ever think you'll fall in love?" Vayp asked. Doubt started to wrench his chest. Anytime something felt too good to be true . . . it was because it was. They were always lies.

"I don't know . . . I think if the girl likes to share her food, then probably."

Vayp laughed, cuffing his stomach. "Well, this will be a fun trip! People always choose others over me, but that's how I know you're my real friend, right?" His eyes met Han'sael's.

Yes, Vayp didn't have a plan for them, but that didn't matter. An earth and water user together, they'd be able to survive in any desert. They'd escape the laws and the danger. And experience actual freedom, not the type that bound them by the invisible shackles his father had warned him about. He started to feel optimistic about their adventures. They could even—

"Actually, I'm stayin'," Han'sael said softly. "I said I'd stay to try and convinced you."

He knew it. Of course it wasn't just in his head. "Are you stupid?" Vayp felt a rage boil inside. "You must be, because I'm *convinced* that you're gonna die, you know that, right?"

"I dunno. I felt somethin'. Somethin' told me we need to stick together. Somethin' made me feel like the book and us are important. Like this is our destiny."

The stone floor beneath Vayp's feet slowly sucked him into the ground. "Once this starts, I can't reverse it. You're either coming or not!"

"I'm sorriorry, Vayp. I can't."

"You should be *sorry*. If we met at a different time or life, maybe we could have been friends."

"No! We are friends!" Han'sael's eyes watered. "I don't want to go back to the dark place anymore. You helped take me out of it! We are friends! Say it, please!"

"We were friends." Vayp fought back the tears. "It's best you forget that I ever existed."

"Don't say that!" Han'sael cried. "You are my friend! You are. You are! It's just that—"

"Not anymore. Just when you were growing on me." He couldn't stop the tears that fell from his eyes. A few seconds later, the sand had covered his entire body, reaching his chin.

In that moment, two shadowy figures materialized out of thin air.

They jumped out at Han'sael suddenly, blocking all light like an eclipse. A black cloud like a dense fog filled the air.

Vayp's heart pounded faster. "Han'sael!" he screamed. He blinked, and they vanished.

All that remained was a spiraling section of dirt and gravel, slowing down to a complete stop, and a wisp of dark air that drifted away like black sand.

There was no more Vayp nor Han'sael.

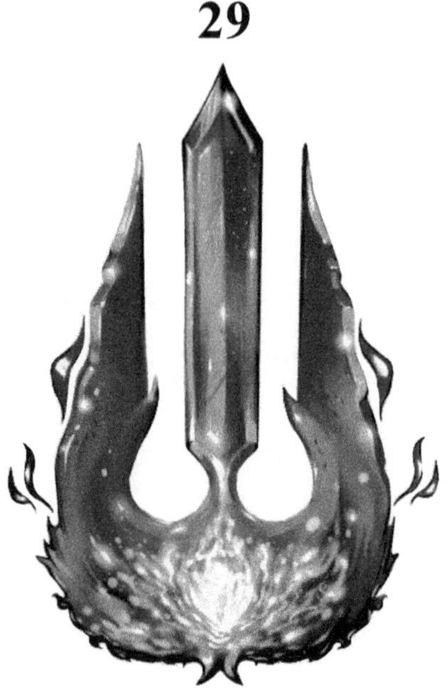# 29

GABRAEL, RAAZ'A, AND THE STUDENTS stood in the center of the courtyard. The rubble from the Spire gleamed dully in the red torchlight. Between the cracks of the grey stones underfoot, magma glowed hot and wild, as if it was ready to erupt at any moment. The only sounds were the occasional pops and sizzles from the lava that funneled into holes on the sides of the Spire. It was now clear that the students were in over their heads. That this trip was bigger than any of them could have imagined.

"Again, our destinies are the greatest of them all," Gabrael said to S'rae who sobbed intensely into her shirt. "This quest is not for everyone. I would be lying if I said this path is safe. In fact, the greatest dangers still await us. This was nothing compared to what lies ahead."

No one said a thing. The students glanced at one another, not knowing what to do. Everything was unknown to them except that their lives would never be the same.

They were just kids. Being sent to the Valley was thrust upon them. Forced. But they were given the option to leave. Yet somehow it seemed as if there was only one choice.

Gabrael turned his attention to a glowing moon that suddenly appeared in the sky, and fell into a trance. He heard the sound of running water, he felt the soft breeze wrapping around his body, and he saw the blossoming of a beautiful, sun-touched flower amidst a sea of green. Seconds went by before he could see definite objects in his surroundings: the contours of the students and the Spire and sky. The Valley was no longer what it once was. It was now a graveyard void of life. A blackened memorial of the damages of war. As he walked toward the students, he considered closing his eyes and pretending that everything was okay, but then his eyes connected with theirs and it was too late. *It is not the same without you, Eve.*

He turned his attention again to the blazing object in the sky, except now it looked more like a sun. Its light cast long shadows of naked trees across the Valley.

It had the qualities of a sun except for its size. As it descended closer to the courtyard, it resembled a medallion shining a honeycomb-yellow. A blast of hot air from the roaring flame hit him as it plowed into the ground like a foot through sand. Ignoring the heat, the wide-eyed students circled around it as it molded into different shapes. Smoke billowed from it and once settled, a handsome, black boy was revealed. Black smoke radiated off his body. His bald head glistened, and he wore charred clothing, a black cloth wrapped around his waist and over his shoulder—revealing his muscular body. He appeared to be around the same age as the rest of the students.

Judging by the gasps and dropped jaws from the girls, they liked what they saw. S'rae blushed and slowly, yet awkwardly, crouched behind a rock, as if not wanting to be seen.

"I am glad that you are okay, Retro'ku," Gabrael said, sticking his hand out for the young man to grab. Heat bounced off them in waves, blurring their dark skin and clothes.

S'rae peeked over the rubble before quickly hiding again once the boy spoke.

"Thank you, Father," Retro'ku said in a silky voice, his accent rolling off of his tongue.

Aura'li, the Sereni Sisters, and even S'rae suddenly giggled.

Gabrael noticed how the other girls tucked strands of hair behind their ears, and smoothed out their eyebrows and the folds in their robes, barely able to meet his eyes.

Gabrael stood upright. "Vayp was right, more will come. And they will not stop coming. Not until the Valley is no more." Gabrael pulled a golden, bladeless hilt from his torn robe. He ran his fingers over it. "It has been too long since I have used you. A great battle awaits, and I have never run from a challenge. If it is death they seek, it is death I will deliver." He turned to Retro'ku and Raaz'a. "Time is fading. Raaz'a, bring the Sols underground and shadow Retro'ku while he completes his training."

Gabrael ran his fingers over his hilt again. He examined its detailed engravings more closely. There were a dragon and phoenix spiraling around it.

He closed his eyes tightly and tried to think of what Eve would do at this very moment.

It came to him in a sudden flash.

"S'rae!" Gabrael shouted.

S'rae came forward from her terrible hiding spot behind a rock. Her eyes widened.

"Raaz'a will teach you our secret."

"Secret?" S'rae asked. Her head remained facing the ground as if something troubled her.

"You asked how it was possible to create an element from nothing, no?"

"I did? When?" S'rae tilted her head as if sifting through the questions she had wanted to ask him but never found the opportunity. "Well, I had one question, but I didn't—wait, were you in my head? How did you know?"

"That is part of our secret."

"Why me?"

"I see it. You have fire in your eyes," Gabrael said. He leaned toward Raaz'a to speak into his ear, but then noticed S'rae circling her fingers around in awkward ways. His eyes narrowed suspiciously before turning his back from the students and whispering: "That one Mecha was only a test. I fear I will not be able to stop their army. We do not have much time."

"What does the girl have to do with this?"

"If anything happens to me. If the Valley falls, I need—"

"Do not speak like that, Gabrael."

"I sense something special in her. I need the secrets to live on. And I need to be ready for all possible outcomes."

"Then what shall we do if we are not ready when they arrive?"

"I do not know. We must be quick so we do not have to find out."

"How much time do we have?"

"I would only be guessing. But if they are coming from the Forgotten Continent, then we have at most a full day."

"Oh, splendid! That should be enough time."

"I hope. One Mecha is enough to clear out a village in seconds. I do not want to see what hundreds can do."

"Oh my, this is *not* desirable. What do you assume their plan is?"

"If they are here for Eve . . . then their plan is to bring him back. He will return."

"*Him?*"

"That is a problem. Retro'ku is the last disciple of Fire. He alone is not enough to win."

"Who is him?"

"If we make it out alive, we will need to find others who also have the fire that burns within. They were forced into schools they were not destined for. We may have time to train them."

"Gabrael . . . who is him?"

"Raaz'a . . . the only him that I fear."

Raaz'a turned around with a hand over his mouth, trembling, muttering sounds to himself. His gaze met S'rae's who looked pale, drained of all color, as if she had seen—

"Geddon."

30

I KNOW MY BROTHER. *I know his yells only mask his pain. But I miss him so much. Why'd I stay?*

S'rae had a feeling that Gabrael meant well, but that didn't stop her from being angry at him. Or at life. Suddenly, she felt too many emotions, uncertain of the culprit for her sudden misery. Sad that she lost her brother and her only friend. Angry that Gabrael kept everyone in the Valley while an army of slaughtering Mechas was on their way. Annoyed that Retro'ku saw her at her absolute worst: her hair was a mess from the thousand-foot drop, and she was still covered in mud. Yuck! And helpless that she had zero control over her life. They were sent here because of some stupid doctrine made thousands of years ago. And worse, it was signed by the blood of Gods. They were in over their heads. She knew that. She just didn't understand why.

She wanted a bath. She wanted Vayp and Han'sael back. She wanted Retro'ku to take his shirt off again. And she wished for Elu to be alive, for her and Destrou to live happily ever after. They deserved it. But, most importantly, she wanted to direct her hatred at the one person who she felt was at fault for all of this: the traitor. The one Elu tried to warn her about.

Whoever the traitor was, she hated him for doing this to them. To her.

Him. Vayp's voice was in her head. His rants about Fujak being the traitor no longer pointless, no longer to be ignored. She needed to find out to be sure. For her safety. And sanity.

The traitor made her more furious than she had ever thought possible.

She had never harmed anything with the intent to injure. Sure it happened once or twice—maybe ten times—but they were accidents. However, the cold wave that surged through her body, making her shake with rage, was a level of hatred far beyond inflicting injuries.

The traitor endangered everyone. Harm wasn't enough. She aimed to kill.

The air felt different. Cold and crisp like the morning of Ah'nyx's funeral. It was then when she felt it. Not the temperature. A shiver. A scary vision that someone was about to die.

"Follow me," Raaz'a said, escorting the students into an opening in a rift. It was dark. Exactly the place he had warned them about. But she felt safe. His lack of concern comforted her. "Sit tight right here. I will bring the Sols to a safer location." When he snapped his fingers, candles flickered on, revealing an open room with statues of dragons, phoenixes, swords, and flames engraved into the walls. He then cheerfully walked away, humming a terrible tune.

S'rae wanted to be that happy. Instead she observed the students with fiercely squinted eyes. Which made her a target. She was alone, but not helpless. And was ready to make an example out of anyone who tested her. Someone needed to pay for what happened. The brief sense of home she had with Vayp and Han'sael had vanished. If Gabrael and Raaz'a didn't care to find out who the traitor was, then she would.

"Hey." Suddenly Fujak was right in front of her. "You okay?"

S'rae blinked, wondering what he meant. *How the hell can I be okay?* Then she realized he was asking whether she was going to cry. "Doesn't matter." She had an attitude in her tone.

"Um . . . I just wanted to ask you what you think is really going on here."

"I don't know." S'rae's eyes narrowed. "You tell me."

"Um . . ." Fujak rose an eyebrow. "You know, you don't always have to be so . . ."

"—so what?"

He cleared his throat and continued. "You."

"And what's that supposed to mean?"

"I don't know, you have an attitude problem. Y-you get defensive for no reason."

"I do have a reason. I don't have an attitude problem, you have a perception problem."

"Really? Well, what is it this time? I just wanted to have a simple talk."

"Everything is simple about you. Funny how that works. Well, why don't you tell me where you've been sneaking around to? You always were the one with a trick up your sleeve."

"What are you talking about?" Fujak shook his head. "Whatever. I thought everything was fine now. But nope, S'rae is being the classic, loner, too-good-for-everyone S'rae."

"You thought everything was fine now? *Honestly?* My brother, who you have been an absolute jerk to, just left. He is the only person I have been wanting to see for the past five years. And he's gone. My only friend left with him. Like I was nothing. Like my opinion on what's going on DIDN'T EVEN MATTER!" S'rae screamed so loud her head hurt. Pressure built up behind her eyes. It seemed as if she finally awakened the real reason for her fury. "They didn't even care! And now I'm left with insecure jerks who take their anger out on people who are better than they will ever be. For years I've been perfectly fine by myself. Taught myself how to fight. I learned tricks on my own. Studied by myself. Excelled by myself. I did everything just fine on my own. I don't need family, friends, or anyone! I didn't need them then, and I definitely don't need them now!"

"S'rae, but—" Fujak said.

"No!" S'rae felt a mass in her throat. Her eyes teared up. "I never had a family or friends. And you know what? Who needs them! Because I'm going to get through life, alone. I'm going to graduate by myself. Raise children by myself and make sure each one knows what it feels like to love and be loved. I will become an Elemential, save the world, and be a great person. I don't need support, and I'm going to prove it to every single one of you! Because there's not one thing any of you can teach me about how to live and love!" She turned away from Fujak, rubbing her eyes. She did not want to cry. For a few moments she tried her hardest not to. But it was too much. Tears ran down her face. Then poured. "Why doesn't anyone love me—"

She felt a sudden *SNAP* on her spine.

In that instant, she regretted giving her back to an enemy. Her dad had taught her better.

To her surprise, it didn't hurt.

It was . . . warm, enfolding her in the smell of roses.

She felt muscles tighten around her arms and chest. There was just enough pressure to feel like it was an ambush, but gentle enough to feel like . . . a hug.

Fujak's forehead caressed her ear in waves. She didn't fight it. She couldn't if she tried. His deep breathing felt like silk against her skin. He whispered. Or at least tried to. All that came out was a gasp, as if he couldn't say what was on his mind.

"S'rae!" Raaz'a shouted from across the room. "It is time!"

S'rae felt paralyzed. If Fujak hadn't let go, she may have remained where she was.

A sense of peace rushed through her body. Was it the hug or the person? Whatever happened, it calmed her rage as if he wrapped around her heart and soothed it.

She was calm as she walked toward Raaz'a, but hesitated for a moment, wanting to turn around—an explanation. Her eyes darted side to side as she rubbed her palm with her fingers.

She was about to whip her head back to Fujak when black smoke appeared in front of her. A hand pulled her into it as her body transformed into a fiery blaze.

And she was gone.

"Where are we?" S'rae observed her surroundings. There were no doors or windows, just pitch-black domed walls and floor with hundreds of glowing lights all around. Maybe thousands. It felt like she was drifting through space. This looked oddly familiar. She recognized some of the designs as constellations from her Usurpers of the Universe class.

The position of the stars, moons, and galaxies looked exactly as they did when she had stargazed with Vayp and Ah'nyx. Sadly, at times there was too much light at Fujita to see the stars there. Space—the Deep Abyss—was quite possibly her favorite subject to learn about. The enormity of the universe made her feel so small, yet important at the same time. Like she had a purpose. Like her life

was a small piece that was part of a bigger puzzle. A greater plan.

"This room is the room." Raaz'a giggled. "Silly, I know. Some things are better left unnamed. No word can do this room any justice. No sense in diminishing its value with a title."

"It looks amazing."

"That is because it is amazing. But we are not here to appreciate its beauty. We are here to open your eyes to the truth."

"That Time is a circle?"

"No, that truth is quite obvious, dear. I am talking about the way the universe works."

S'rae remained silent. Raaz'a piqued her curiosity. Intelligence was her favorite quality in others. She loved the way bright minds could stimulate her own. She was a perfect fit for Fujak, after all. *Ew!* Not Fujak, she meant Fujita, the school. Why was he still on her mind? She quickly removed that disgusting thought. Instead, she fixated on something almost equally disturbing: though she hated to admit it, Raaz'a was growing on her.

"Do you know what atoms are?" Raaz'a asked.

"Of course!" She hesitated for a second, knowing this must have either been a trick question or a really, really offensive one. *Obviously!* The progress Raaz'a had made earlier had vanished. Yup. She went back to not liking him. "They are the smallest units of a chemical element." She continued, wanting to prove a point to not underestimate her. "They consist of a nucleus, which has a positive charge, and a set of electrons that move around the nucleus."

"Oh, well aren't you quite the know-it-all." Raaz'a smiled. "Well, you are correct . . . somewhat."

S'rae was taken aback. She had the highest grade in her Elements of Elements class, surely he was mistaken. *Heh!* He didn't actually mean to say 'somewhat.' Right?

"And?" Raaz'a squealed like an annoying dog begging for attention.

"Um . . . and?" S'rae's eyebrow rose.

"Well, aren't you going to ask me why I said somewhat?"

Yup. She really didn't like him anymore. He was officially placed on the top of her imaginary unlikeable list, kicking Fujak out of the spot he held for years. That said a lot.

Fujak . . .

She felt something wiggle in her stomach.

Why did it feel like Fujak no longer belonged on the list? Impossible. He was the enemy. The traitor. She knew it. She wasn't going to fall for his deception. Not again.

"*Well,*" Raaz'a's eyes bulged like a parent who lost his patience.

"Well, why did you say 'somewhat'?"

His eyes grew as he leaned in. The starlight deepened the grooves in his cheeks and jaw.

"Why did you say 'somewhat,' Raaz'a?" S'rae said with a grunt.

Raaz'a smiled. "Thank you!" He cupped her head with his thumbs resting on her face. Her head swayed side to side as he hummed. Yup, he was crazy. And if she could somehow place him higher on the list, she would. "You see, we are created from the very same matter that created stars. They are in us, the air, in fire, water, and ground and trees."

"And?" she said, feeling nauseous from the dizzying head movements.

"And once you understand they are everywhere, you realize the truth: You do not live in the universe . . . the universe lives within you. Only then is when you can connect with them."

"Connect?"

"Yes. Before Gabrael showed me the secret, I was like you, I didn't know anything. But once he opened my eyes to the secret, the universe made sense. It showed me all its glory." He snapped

his finger and a flame combusted above S'rae's nose. "How do you think I did that?"

"I honestly have no idea."

"Atoms."

S'rae looked around awkwardly, scrunching her nose. "Umm, yes . . . atoms." She puffed her cheeks, suppressing a chuckle.

"You see, atoms are life. They are everything and everywhere. And once you develop a connection with them . . . you can turn them into anything you wish. Feel them. Visualize them. Transform them."

"So you are going to teach me how to create fire?"

He cackled. "Oh my divine, blessed no! You are not *that* gifted. You are restricted to the element that you know."

One more backhanded diss from him and she was already considering the consequences for punching his ugly nose. She wasn't in the mood. Not today. Yes, fire wasn't the element that she studied, but if what he was saying was true, she didn't need to go to Harahm'be to understand how to create it. She was smart enough to know that fire consisted primarily of carbon dioxide, water vapor, oxygen and nitrogen; so all she needed to do was to find a way to transform the atoms into them. Which made her very interested. "So what's the secret?"

"When you master how to control an atom, you can make an element out of nothing."

A smile flooded her face. "Are you saying I can create wind in the airless chamber?"

"No, much more. I am saying when you master it, you will be able to create air in space."

"I want to learn," S'rae said, trying her best to maintain her composure. Though she wouldn't show it, inside she was ecstatic. "What do I do?"

"First, you must let go of your pride and embrace fear. Accept that fear exists, and hold onto the single thought that you fear the most."

"What does fear have to do with atoms?"

"Oh my, dear S'rae, fear is the most powerful of emotions. Har-ahm'be was known to have countless debates with Sereni, saying that fear is even more powerful than love. Fear, and overcoming it, is the one key way to unlock your true potential. Conquer it and bring forth your greatest power." Raaz'a slowly vanished into the shadows. "And that is why we are here." His voice deepened wickedly. It felt life-threatening. "Most students fear death."

S'rae's heart raced.

It happened too quickly.

This was a set up. She should have known better. The reason the room resembled the universe. Why he spoke about creating wind in space. How most students feared . . . death.

At once, S'rae's feet floated off the ground. Gravity wasn't the only thing that disappeared. She couldn't breathe. It was as if the room teleported her into outer space.

She concentrated—at least tried her hardest to—but was suffocating. She thought of atoms. Tried to feel them. Understand them. But all she could think about was the vise grip squeezing her windpipe shut.

This was it. This was how her story ended.

The stars around her faded to black. The thought she had earlier about death was her own. She was sure of it. Darkness engulfed her.

S'rae jerked back to life. She was lying flat on her back. The faces of students were looking down at her.

She felt ashamed. And now everyone saw that she was a loser who failed to the point of passing out. A rage crept in. Like Ran-mau, she felt one wrong move away from something. Something bad. She didn't know what exactly. And that was the problem.

To make it worse, Raaz'a entered the circle, smiling. SMIL-ING! *Really?* She had almost died, and he saw something worth smiling about? That was enough for her. She knew she should respect her elders, but at some point one had to give respect to expect it in return.

Raaz'a bent over and gave her his hand.

She smacked it away.

Raaz'a pulled his chin back, alarmed. Disgusted.

S'rae then turned her frustration to the whispers she heard coming from the Fujitas.

Her fingers circled, making sure to hear what they were too chicken to say aloud.

"Maybe we should bring her loser brother back."

"Yeah, she's coo-coo crazy now. Isn't it scary the things a smile can hide?"

"Heh, Vayp and Han'sael are probably dead already. Serves them right."

"PUT! IT! DOWN!" Raaz'a's voice erupted. "DON'T DO IT!"

Everyone's attention was diverted to Raaz'a. His hand trembled, pointing at S'rae.

In S'rae's hand was a large silver bow. A sparking arrow slung back. She knew what she was doing. Many animals had lost their lives by the tips of her arrow. It was the same thing. A bow pulled, an arrow shot. But this one was made of wind and infinitely more deadly.

It was angled straight at Fujak's heart.

When it came to animals, she'd shake or cry before the kill. And it would hurt as if it physically went through her as well. But now there was rage and no signs of tremors in her hands. Someone had to pay for what happened. The traitor. *You,* she wanted to growl.

Her gut told her it was Fujak. She knew someone was going to die. It was him.

"Please . . . don't." Fujak placed his hands to his side.

It was a defensive tactic. Just like in the wild. To expose the most vulnerable parts as a sign of trust. Peace. She remembered everything Vayp had taught her. But there was nothing trustworthy about him. And there couldn't be peace without war, right?

In his eyes was fear. Complete fear. She had his life in her hands. *Let go. Do it!*

She didn't have time to question the source of her dark thoughts. All she knew was that this was for Vayp. For Han'sael. For revenge.

A *whoosh* interrupted the silence. A gust blew. The arrow was launched.

31

"*YOU WERE RIGHT. It wasn't all in your head. The look in your eyes told me that you always knew. Just know it was never you. You did no wrong. Don't ever think you weren't good enough, you were the best brother I could have ever asked for. I—I am not leaving you . . . I am finding me.*"

Destrou woke up, trying to remember the words in his vivid dream. It felt all too real, but details escaped him whenever he thought too hard. Rubbing his throbbing forehead, Destrou slowly opened his eyes. A spot on his forehead felt moist, as if it had just been kissed.

"What happened?" he asked aloud, brushing his eyes. He sat there for several moments, too overwhelmed to move. He didn't know how long he had slept—it could have been a few hours or a few days. He'd stayed tucked into the corner of his bed all that night and woken late the next day to find his body had stiffened into a tight knot of pain.

What happened?

The back of his head throbbed. At a slow pace, he reached up with his arm and touched his scalp, trying to find the source of his headache. Beneath his dreads, he found hard bulges of dried blood.

Where are my gloves?

He closed his eyes, trying to remember the events.

Nothing.

Think.

Only darkness and a faint scream that sounded oddly familiar.

Elu?

Destrou turned his head, but the movement sent a spike of pain radiating through his skull. He took deep breaths to lessen the pain. Then, very gently, he surveyed his surroundings.

There was Ranmau's bed. Empty. No furs. No clothes. No cloak. Nothing. It was as if he never had a brother. Destrou saw his own clothes on the far corner of his bed. They were covered with blood.

He slowly turned his head toward the window beside his bed. It was dark outside. He then looked at the patch of ice that reflected his image—an emaciated boy, drained of color, with sunken eyes, wearing a loose white sweater too large for his tiny body.

"S'rae," Gabrael said, placing his finger on the page.

"Yes?" S'rae lifted her head with difficulty as if a great sorrow weighed it down.

"You seem troubled."

"Me? No. I'm okay. I am," she replied, fluffing her hair as if to wake herself up.

The truth was that she wasn't troubled. She was much worse. She felt terrible for nearly killing Fujak before Gabrael had arrived. She made sure the arrow dispersed into wind the moment before it pierced through his chest. It was a warning shot. But was it really? Everything in her didn't want it to be. She wasn't troubled, she felt gone. No longer herself.

"Would you mind doing the honors?" Gabrael said.

"Excuse me?"

"Would you like to read for us?"

"Huh? Are you sure?"

"Yes, it appears that your mind has traveled off elsewhere. You seem worn and torn and broken. And that is okay, because I have never, in the countless battles I have been a part of, heard of a clean and immaculate sword that won a war. And that is what we are in: war. We do not have much time, the book is too important. We must all pay attention to its words." Gabrael walked over to S'rae. He opened it back up to where his finger rested. "You can start from here."

She took a long, deep breath, causing the pages to flutter for a moment, and saw the words move and change before her eyes. Her anxiety caused her deep breathing to continue as she read.

Destrou thought that he heard voices outside, but that could have been the whistles from the wind that never seemed to stop. Snow gusted inside, twirling under the cloth that served as a door. The blankets were warm, but it wasn't enough to shield him from the wind chills that froze his bones.

Despite his injuries, he pushed down his blanket and rolled away from the too-cold window. He felt strange and dizzy. He tried to press his toes onto the cold floor, but he failed, crashing to the ground.

From the ground, he realized there was absolutely nothing left on Ranmau's side.

"Ranmau?" he croaked. His voice felt strained.

There was no response.

"*Ranmau!*" he shouted, attempting to stand up. His malnourished body hadn't fully recovered. He stumbled, making his way to the entrance. His palm pressed against the cold floor, using it for support. He reached his other hand onto his bed, balancing himself. His body felt heavy. The thought of his brother missing weighed him down even more.

"*Ranmau!* Where are you? What'd they do? Where are you?"

Destrou had no memory of how he made it to the front of the NoGo, delirious and nearly crippled. He walked most of the distance with his hands shielding his face from the fierce winds. That was until he stopped in his tracks. A white cloth draped over an object with the contour of a human body lay dead center, as if on display for every igloo to see.

He froze. It felt like his heart and lungs stopped working. He knew what this meant. He had witnessed too many deaths. Much more than any twelve-year-old should. But the sight of this had sent his body into shock. Something told him this was the worst one yet.

He shambled toward the object. His widened eyes began to freeze up, his tears turning into crystals. "No . . . no! It can't be." He tripped over his feet and fell to the ground. "Ranm—"

To his surprise, the body was too small to be Ranmau's.

He crawled closer, confused. If not him, then who? The last he remembered, only he and Ranmau were in trouble. What else happened?

The right hand hung off the side of the platform. The fingers were frostbitten, slender and small. His eyes welled up even more. He had seen that hand before.

He grazed his fingers across it with a gentle touch—he had felt it before.

He couldn't bring himself to speak, his mouth trembled. One glimpse of the hand and it was like his throat had been filled with ice.

It couldn't be who he thought it was. He was sure with everything he had ever loved that it wasn't—it couldn't be. But he needed to know.

He grabbed the cloth and squeezed his eyelids together. Ice crystals dropped from his lashes. If ever there was a time he wished he was wrong, it was now. Please be wrong. Please!

In one motion, he pulled the cloth off and opened his eyes. They widened. At once he felt everything. Fear. Anger. Regret. Sorrow. Then nothing. Just an immobilizing sadness so strong his eyes glazed over, unblinking for minutes. He couldn't. As if he was challenging her to one last staring contest. One that he was sure to lose. For Elu's blue eyes appeared as frozen crystals barely visible through half-closed eyelids. She lay there cold; pale and lifeless.

The snow rustled in the wind, but then it went still and the whistles hushed, as if they wanted to hear what Destrou would say.

He gave a near-hysterical laugh that quickly became a sob. "H-hey, Elu . . . is this a joke? One of your pranks? Elu . . . hey!" Destrou wiggled her body, then pressed his ear onto her chest. His breathing came in spurts.

Pain racked his body with sobs.

This can't be real! No, no, no! Please no! Please, Divine One this can't be real!

"Please be a dream! Please, if I can have any wish at all, please let this be a dream!"

He cried with the force of a person choking for their last breath. It was not a dream.

"You were right! You were right about everything! This was all my fault. You shouldn't have tried to protect me—I shouldn't have put you in danger. You didn't need to prove that you were my friend!" Destrou grabbed his dreads. Then he pulled. With all his force. He pulled even after it felt like his scalp was about to peel. He pulled to punish himself. Because he felt he deserved it. But though his head hurt, his heart ached. And that was a far greater pain than he could have ever imagined. "You were the best friend ever. It's my fault! We should've left that night. Then none of this would've happened if I had listened to you! Don't leave me, not now   . . . not ever. Please don't! I don't have anyone anymore. I'm nothing without you. I need you. I need you in my story." He knelt, watching his tears drop down onto her face.

"Life isn't fair," S'rae said. And as her tears dropped onto the page, words appeared and shifted.

Sorrow weighed down Destrou's chest, breathing became difficult. The dark gray sky shifted, releasing droplets of snowflakes, appearing to cry with him.

She's gone. Realization hit him harder than the Giant ever could.

Everything was still and quiet. Then, he leaned forward and pressed his lips against her forehead. It hurt knowing that was something he had wanted to do while she was . . . alive.

"Whoever did this to you will pay . . . They won't get away with it. I promise!" he growled through clenched teeth. "They won't!"

Destrou sobbed on Elu's belly for long moments while many footsteps gathered around him. He then buried his ear against her chest, closing his eyes, hoping to hear something. Anything. But the silence wrenched his gut so hard that he curled up in pain.

When he opened his eyes, he couldn't stop looking at Elu, more peaceful than ever, like the angel she was. Destrou questioned if angels were even real. Because if there was a Divine One, he wondered why he'd be this cruel. But then he was reminded of a time when he and Ranmau would search for crystals. They had always chosen one over all others: the most beautiful one. Maybe that was why Elu was taken from the Village. From life. From him. She was

too good, beautiful, and pure. The Divine One chose her—to be in a better place. He wanted to believe it.

Destrou would have never stopped looking at Elu if it weren't for the mob of boys that now surrounded him and the sharp shards of ice in their palms.

The way they pointed the shards at Destrou was unsettling. But their eyes, and the way they narrowed, let him know that trouble awaited him.

It then hit him. A Divine One didn't kill Elu. Someone did. Somewhere here. And he thought, for a moment, of stabbing the shard into the murderer's chest. "How. Did. This. Happen?" Destrou said in between sobs. There was anger in his voice.

He wanted to do something, right there, right now, to make them go through the pain he felt. That Elu wasn't one of them. She was much more—someone worth dying for. And he would prove it. He was no longer afraid of the consequences of their friendship.

The Leader pounded the side of a stone club against his palm. "I spent my whole life protecting her . . . making sure she'd be safe from everyone . . . from these krillens . . . from the Bruisers . . . the Guardians . . . and the Kingdom." The pain in his glazed eyes, the way his voice choked up, it almost made Destrou feel like the Leader was human. As if right now he was Eli'jah, mourning the death of a close friend. "I did things I never wanted to do, but it was my word, my promise to keep her safe. And I did. But it was Ranmau I needed to protect her from."

"Ranmau?" Destrou's eyes narrowed.

He's lying!

"If you find the murderer, he'll be able to tell you how this happened to my sister."

Destrou's eyes shot wide open. As if the Leader's words were delayed, it finally hit him that Elu's identity was no longer a secret.

He spent his whole life protecting her . . .

Everything began to make sense. Why the Leader saved them from the accident: He wasn't helping Destrou, he was saving Elu.

There was something else different about the Leader. Destrou's gaze wandered up and down and noticed that he wore new white furry gloves and boots.

Those are mine! Since Ranmau was gone, he knew better than to accuse the Leader of stealing.

"W-where . . . d-did . . . Ranmau g-go?"

"Oh . . . you won't be seeing him anytime soon . . . not where you're going," he replied coldly. "You have a better chance seeing Elu than him."

"Why . . . are you doing this?" Destrou said. "What'd I do to you? I lo—liked Elu . . . she was my friend."

"DON'T YOU *EVER* CALL ELU YOUR FRIEND, YOU KRILLEN!" he shouted with crazed eyes, surprising Destrou when tears leaked from them. "Ranmau will go through what I just went through . . . it's only fair." He walked toward Destrou, holding his club forward. "He isn't here to save you anymore. He took the easy way out—most likely killing himself, anyway."

The Leader, accompanied by the Giant and two other boys, reached in and pulled Destrou off the corpse. Destrou shoved them off of him.

The Leader's eyebrows rose, observing Destrou's power.

"Hmm . . . being protected by Ranmau for your entire life, I didn't think you had that in you," he mocked.

"Leave . . . me . . . alone." Destrou raised his fists out of frustration. He wished for nothing more than to mourn for Elu. He didn't want to fight—not now—not even for own his life. Now, he wanted to be alone.

"Oh, you don't really want to do that, do you?" the Leader

laughed. "This little guy thinks he's even half the boy that Ranmau is, right?" He looked around at the boys. "Right?"

Laughter trickled throughout the crowd.

The Leader glanced at three boys who were closest to Destrou and barked a command.

They charged in.

After three agile moves, Destrou looked down at the boys squirming, holding their injured faces.

"Hmph . . . looks like I should never send boys to do a leader's job." The Leader took off his fur armor, unscathed by the cold wind wrapping around his shoulders. The Giant went to move toward Destrou, but the Leader placed his hand on his shoulder. "No, you had your fun last time. It's my turn now."

The crowd gasped. Besides Ranmau, the Leader was known as the best fighter. But he had always let the Giant do his dirty work. He glared at Destrou with dark, abused eyes ready to inflict the damage that they had endured.

Destrou attempted to remain confident. He remembered Ranmau's words. *Do not show them weakness.* He brushed off the uncertainty and entered into a ready fighting stance.

The Leader was untroubled; with a slow pace, he prowled toward Destrou, smirking.

The two were face to face; although it was more like face to chest. The Leader gave his club to a nearby boy then pounded his fists.

Be ready. He's gonna make the first move—he always does.

As expected, the Leader lunged in, throwing all his weight into his fist. As he leaned forward, Destrou bobbed his head, diving sideways, evading the attack. Before the Leader could turn to grab Destrou, he slid past him, his fists up, ready for the next attack.

The Leader roared like a savage animal, jumping at Destrou

with his fists pressed forward.

They engaged in an exciting battle. The Leader threw vicious strikes and Destrou eluded each one. That was until the circle of boys surrounding the two closed in.

Destrou glanced from side to side, looking for an opening to escape.

There was no place for him to go. The Leader charged at Destrou, ready to tackle him, but Destrou ducked out of the way, driving his fist into the Leader's jaw.

Destrou heard Ranmau's voice in his head, telling him that agility was his best weapon against bigger opponents, but it didn't seem to help too much against the Leader.

Despite every disadvantage against him, Destrou kept fighting. *I have nothing . . . to lose.*

Destrou pressed his palms together to stop them from shaking.

The Leader glared at Destrou, rubbing his jaw with his knuckles. "That was a big mistake."

Destrou blocked a punch with his elbow. A stinging sensation that felt like a swarm of hornets pricked him; but he had no time to think about the pain surging through his body.

The Leader followed quickly with a kick, connecting into Destrou's ribs, causing him to lose balance and crash into the crowd. He gasped in pain, unable to breathe for what felt like hours.

Destrou saw an opportunity to strike back, but he had accepted his fate. *It's already over.* Destrou's chest burned and his hands felt like they weighed a hundred pounds. He could no longer fight gravity. His hands dropped. Face exposed. Even keeping his eyelids open took too much energy.

Their eyes connected only for a moment. Then the Leader threw all the strength he had. There was a loud CRACK as his fist collided into Destrou's jaw.

Destrou had a feeling of being asleep then awake then asleep all at the same time. The world was spinning, with angry faces spiraling around him. While standing he had the feeling of falling; while falling he had the feeling of standing.

The Leader gripped Destrou at the chest, lifting him off the ground. Destrou attempted to free himself, but the messages from his brain weren't being delivered.

The Leader spun Destrou around and threw him across the snow. His elbow struck the ground and his arm went numb. The Leader gestured to a boy, grazing his finger slowly across his neck. Destrou swallowed a very difficult breath. He knew what that meant. The boy left his field of vision for a moment before coming back with the Leader's club. The Leader grabbed it, placing it over his shoulder. The air hummed before the club cracked against Destrou's back.

"You'll pay for what he did!" The club struck him again, this time across the chest. Destrou thought he felt one of his ribs crack as he squirmed in pain. His eyes rolled to the back of his head as if his body was shutting down to turn off the pain.

"No, no, no, you're not gonna die on me this easily. I need to have some fun with you, first." The Leader laughed again while Destrou tried to blink the tears out of his eyes. The Leader kicked Destrou across his face, and Destrou tasted blood as his head bounced off the ice.

Destrou curled into a ball, but his body went limp the moment the Leader struck his foot deep into his stomach. He lifted Destrou up again, smiling at the bruises forming on his face, then threw him to the ground next to Elu's corpse.

Snowflakes gently landed onto their faces as they lay together in peace.

It looked as if their stories had ended together.

32

"LIFE ISN'T FAIR," S'RAE SAID. "Destrou's alone. In one day he went from having his best day ever to his worst." S'rae knew that her frustration wasn't just because of the book, but she saw herself in Destrou. She finally had her brother back, and made a great friend in Han'sael, but, like Destrou, it all changed. And now they were gone.

A flame scorched in the background. It was the only source of light and heat. S'rae fumbled to sit upright—her stone seat was uncomfortable. Her mind had been preoccupied because she was now observing the details of her surroundings. She saw a large room that seemed to be underground, somewhere in the basement of the Spire. There were stone slabs for the students to sit on, textured stone walls, and a massive statue of a dragoenix, bearing a bronze emblem that read: "Here lies Harahm'be. May he protect your lives in spirit as he protected ours in flesh."

In the darkness, S'rae saw Gabrael's eyes twinkle like a flame.

"Do you think Destrou will hate Ranmau when he finds out

what really happened?" S'rae asked, looking up at Gabrael through glazed eyes. He appeared blurred and distorted.

"Hate is too strong of a word. The wrong word, I must say."

"Why?"

"Being one of the brightest pupils I ever had the privilege of being around, I am sure you know how cold is created, no?"

There was something about the way Gabrael asked that question that made her feel alive. A fire burned within her chest. He didn't question if she knew, he assumed she did. And he was right. "Yes, you can never gain cold, you can only have an absence of heat."

"You are correct," Gabrael said, snapping his finger. A fire appeared at its tip. "Cold is the absence of heat. And much like cold, hatred doesn't exist, there is only an absence of love. So for hate to exist, there must be no love. But I see fire in his eyes."

S'rae said nothing. She had studied the science of the elements and knew that only a God of Ice could create cold, but never had she thought of hatred in the same way. Her eyes welled up, absorbing his words.

"You may continue reading," he said. "This is just the beginning of his story. While I do not know the depths of his story, I assure you that although it was his first loss, it will not be the last. This is the story of the boy who never lived and how he became the greatest warrior—the one to finally survive the darkness and defeat the unkillable beast within. Warriors were defined not by what they had done but what they had been through. Just as he has yet to experience his greatest victory, I suspect he has yet to experience his worst loss—the type of loss that even Gods cannot recover from."

Destrou felt snowflakes press against his face. It was a cold reminder that he was somehow still alive. He was too numb and tired to be afraid. In his weakened state, he imagined death in the form of an Archon. Its dark shadow hovered above, watching, waiting to consume him.

The Archon wrapped its sharp fangs around him. He imagined death being a warm feeling, its teeth ripping into him, opening his body from the inside.

But in reality, the pain was just starvation and crushed ribs as he felt two hands roll him onto his side.

He peeled one eye open and saw a blurry boy wrapped in white. *Elu?*

The sight of Elu startled him. His good eye shot open; his swollen one remained sealed shut. The warmth that he'd felt a moment ago vanished, leaving his body cold and sluggish.

Fighting a whirling sensation, he heard words that came in pieces like patterned snowflakes on ice.

"Get . . . up! Get . . . out . . . now!" the vision of Elu said in a muffled voice. After a few moments, the words became clearer. "They're coming back with stones. They're going to kill you."

Destrou noticed the white headwrap around her face, but the eyes didn't have the same blue sparkle. They appeared brown and wide.

"Go! Can't you hear me! This is for Elu!" The person who wasn't Elu set Destrou unsteadily onto his feet and brushed away the snow that covered him.

Through his good eye Destrou saw the white cloth hanging over Elu's body on the raised platform to his side.

She's still gone.

"Who are you?" Destrou said, shaking to stand upright.

"That doesn't matter. You need to run!"

"Run? Where?"

"Anywhere but here. If they find you, you're dead. Don't ever come back!"

Destrou couldn't think of a response, so he concentrated on maintaining his balance. He heard the sound of distant footsteps.

The boy looked nervously down the path. "They're coming!"

He leaned in closer to look at Destrou's face. His white shroud looked like a foggy snowstorm in his blurry vision.

"Your eyes are swollen shut. If you can't see much, just follow this path. This way." He turned Destrou's body. "Go north. Toward the Hanging Star. Go! You'll be safe in the Tree."

"Thanks," Destrou muttered. He tasted blood in his mouth.

"Anything for Elu," he said, quickly looking over his shoulder.

The footsteps became louder. They were mixed with the sounds of yelling boys.

It took a moment for Destrou to understand what he needed to do.

The boy held out his hand. But how did he know about the Tree?

Destrou became more focused on what he held. It looked like a slab of meat. Enough food for him to make it a few more a days, but not enough to satiate his hunger.

He took the food, but his hand was so numb he couldn't feel it. He looked down to make sure it was in his fingers.

Suddenly there were voices of dozens of boys as they rushed toward him.

He needed to run, but he couldn't feel his legs. Without knowing, he was already running though he didn't remember telling his legs to move. He moved away behind an igloo and felt his back press up against the ice, then he rolled until he fell through the entrance that faced Elu.

It was cold and empty and made his igloo look like the Guardian's room. There was nothing in there except two blocks of ice nearly on top of each other. It was windowless and much too small for two boys to live. Seeing this igloo made him realize how fortunate he was.

He felt terrible, then sad. As if he had forgotten what his life was like before Ranmau had won the challenges. Before the prizes, fur, and food, they too once had nothing but one another to keep warm throughout the night. How could any boy survive in these conditions?

A rumble of footsteps appeared outside.

Destrou lay on the ground and watched the boys from underneath the cloth draped over the entrance. Their screams went silent. The Leader stood tall with a large club in his hand.

"Where'd he go?" he shouted, slamming his club into an igloo. Its wall shattered into a million pieces. "Find him and bring him to me. *Now!*"

All eyes were on the Leader. No one saw Destrou slip out of that igloo and into the shadows of another.

Nearly a second later, two boys stormed into that igloo. Destrou couldn't feel his fingers, but he could somehow feel his heart trying to burst out of his chest. It took a few minutes for all of them to pass. Only then did he emerge from the shadows and begin to make his way toward the light in the sky. It seemed a million miles away. He knew that he wasn't in his right mind, but he didn't remember the walk taking this long. Even the path felt different; he trudged through knee-high snow. He checked his feet every few seconds to make sure they were still moving.

He didn't know how long it took to get there. The walking warmed him slightly, though his feet still felt heavy and numb. He thought about how desperately he needed his gloves and boots. When he looked back, he saw that he'd left a trail of blood, staining the pure white snow. He was happy to see that it was only his blood that followed him.

His eyes widened suddenly when the reality hit him.

They can track me!

He looked around and saw a boy talking with another one and gesturing in Destrou's direction. They weren't normal, emaciated boys, they were tall and upright. They wore furry white animal skins with the animal's head as a type of hood, and each carried a stone club as long as their arms. The Bruisers liked to prowl at night anonymously when causing trouble. Destrou froze in place.

"There he is!" a Bruiser shouted from a hundred feet away.

"Hey, everyone! He found him! Get here now!" the second one shouted.

"You're dead!"

Destrou tried to run, but it quickly turned into a limp. The boys were catching up to him. He limped ahead, clutching his chest in pain. It wasn't until he held his shirt that he realized he was using the hand that had been carrying the meat.

He looked back and saw it resting in the trail. He wanted to head back for it but there wasn't enough time. Behind him there were bloodthirsty boys. But worse, in front there was a dip that led into darkness. The entrance to the Maze.

Not just any maze. The Maze of No Return. The last place he wanted to see.

He looked up and noticed that the light he traveled toward was the reflection of the Hanging Star. His vision was too groggy—he had traveled south instead of north. There was a saying in the Village: If traveling south was a death wish, then entering the Maze of No Return was that wish being granted.

He didn't have much of an option. As the boys came within arm's reach, he darted for the first opening he saw, his feet slipping on the light layer of snow that covered the ground. He heard their heavy stomps pounding behind him as he turned down into a new opening.

His breath was burning his chest as he looked for another path to take, somewhere to hide. But he had never entered the Maze before. There was nothing but an endless trail with dead end after dead end that kept forming out of nowhere. No holes to worm into, no cracks to climb through.

He ran into another dead end. Then he heard laughter.

"You actually ran in! We don't have to kill you, you did the work yourself."

Destrou's heart pounded faster. Part of him wished that they had chased him into the Maze, hoping that its title was something to scare everyone away.

He was about to run back toward the entrance when he felt a cold grip close around his ankle and pull him to the ground.

His head hit the ice and the world spun dizzily as the ground absorbed around him like a puddle of quicksand. It smelled like dirt and rotten corpses. He cried out until the floor sealed above him, drowning out his screams. The Maze was once again empty.

"WHERE AM I?" Destrou said, hearing his echo. What faint light there was spilled down through an ice-like ceiling smeared with dirt. He saw his footprints from the Maze directly above him. Piles of bones, like the ones that his meat had been attached to, along with broken shards of ice and bundles of mud littered the floor. The smell of decay hung in the air.

"What is this place?" He limped toward a distant light at the end of the tunnel, stepping carefully amongst the bones and ice in case any of them were sharp. Each step became heavier, harder. In the faint light he looked half transparent, bleached of color, wrapped in white like a dying spirit. He certainly felt like one as he gripped his ankle, wincing in pain.

I think it's broken. Though the cold had numbed it, it was not enough to mask the feeling of knives jabbing through his bone.

He pushed his way forward, dragging his swollen ankle along the ground. For a moment he thought the tunnel was empty. He then heard faint noises up ahead, what sounded like laughter. After a few minutes, he reached an open room that smelled like expired fish, and a heavy layer of mud covered the floor. He walked for an hour more. Until the sounds finally became clear.

"So, did you watch him suffer?" he heard from a voice overhead.

"Yeah, we went in there and clobbered him until he begged for his life, then we let the Maze finish him off."

"Good work," another deep voice chimed in. "That's the last we have to worry about them. I'll win the tournament, then you can take my place as the Leader. When you win the challenges, there'll be plenty of food to share—unlike those greedy savages."

"Thank you, Leader."

"The first is always the worst. After that you get used to it, don't worry," the Leader said. "The Guardians . . . you have to remind yourself that you're doing this to help feed everyone. Always remember that the cause is greater than the pain."

"Right. I understand . . . I think. I won't let you down."

"Speaking of pain, do you know what happens in the Maze?" another voice said.

"I don't. I just know that you never see them again."

"What if he's hiding?"

"Well, if he's alive and hiding, he needs to come out for food. And when he does, we can finish him off the fun way."

"Oh! I want to throw the first stone!"

"Why do you get—"

"Stop fighting, we don't even know if he's alive," the Leader interrupted. "But first, let's find whoever helped him. Make an example out of anyone who helps the enemy. Anyway, I want privacy. Leave."

Destrou felt sick to his stomach. He wasn't sure if it was because of what he heard or smelled.

Wait . . . is this . . . He looked around in bewilderment. It was cold in the room, despite the slight heat radiating from the mud. He took a step forward, crushing his feet on stray bones. He bent down to free his ankle, and heard a distinct, unpleasant sound.

There was a hissing that reminded him of the release of gas. When he straightened up, he saw a large clump of mud land onto his face.

It smelled like fish and feces. He wiped his face with his sweater and noticed that's what it was.

The realization hit him as his head lunged forward to vomit. His body jolted uncontrollably for a few moments

I'm going to pretend that the Leader didn't just poop on my face. Yeah, this never happened.

He fell to his knees. His palms pressed into the feces surrounding him.

Negative thoughts once again formed in his mind, appearing as an Archon ready to consume him.

When things got really bad, Destrou's imagination would take over and remember a happy memory. The last hug with Ranmau. Sprinting toward the Edge while holding hands. But tonight he thought of Elu, laughing with those beautiful crinkles at the corner of her eyes. He saw her as a girl loving life, the way she would want to be remembered. He heard her voice sing the sweetest songs to him—like poetry. When he closed his eyes, it felt like she was there, so he refused to open them—refused to accept that she had gone. That she was dead. Her voice began to fade away. Destrou heard the last few notes of her song, and he tried his hardest to capture them. To save them.

He tried to hold on to that moment of peace, but it slipped away, leaving him sadder and lonelier than ever.

And what followed was the worst silence ever, as if he were at his own funeral.

Maybe he was . . .

Sorrow was drowning him. It was suffocating. He lost his will to do anything, to breathe . . . to live . . . to survive.

I'm a nobody with nothing. No more Ranmau . . . or Elu. My story—He felt around through the pile of bones and found one with a pointed top, pressing his finger on its edge.

Destrou closed his eyes.

He gripped it with both hands and straightened his arms ahead of him. The point faced his heart. He saw the Archon grab ahold of the bone as well, as if to make sure that he pushed with enough force.

He took a deep breath—*Ends here.* Then he plunged it toward himself.

"Nooooo!" A cry of fear escaped S'rae as she stood up, slamming her palms on the book.

Everyone in the room directed their attention toward her. Gabrael looked away as a strong gust fluttered the pages madly. The students shielded themselves from the wind.

"I'm sorry," she apologized. That moment struck her sharply. She had been there in that dark space, and was close to getting there again. She wanted Destrou to push through. No. She needed him to. She needed to know that it was possible to persevere pass the pain. That they shouldn't give up.

She sat back down pressing her fingers through her hair, looking at her feet. "I'm sorry," she sniffled. And with the corner of her eye, she saw more movement on the pages.

Destrou stopped after hearing a faint, echoing cry for help. His eyes moved from left to right, to see if someone else was there. A few

moments later, a roar came from the tunnel as a gust of wind forced him into the air. The ground trembled and the bone flew away, landing without even a thud as he hit the ground.

Destrou was still too numb with shock from the events of the day to make sense of what happened. He tried again to think of happy moments to bring him back to a good place. Since none came, he forced it by humming the last tune that he'd heard Elu sing. Her voice appeared drowsily, but was still so beautiful in his mind. Sadness swelled inside him as he closed his eyes and pictured her face. Just a brief glimpse of her sapphire eyes and the smiling crinkle around them was almost enough to take him away from this hell. If she were here, she'd be exploring, laughing at Destrou getting pooped on. She'd make the most of this situation. She always found the beauty in everything.

Destrou then briefly thought of the last time he saw Ranmau, so strong and protective. They were gone. Elu was dead and Ranmau was somewhere. He had no doubt that if anyone was able to climb the Wall, it would be Rammau. He no longer had to feel he was holding Ranmau back. He always had a feeling that he wasn't meant for this life. That if he wasn't around, Ranmau would have already left. That he was the only thing keeping Ranmau around . . . forcing him to go through this pain. That idea hurt even more than him leaving.

But he hoped that Ranmau had finally got his freedom, and that Elu was sleeping peacefully in the heavens with Eve. He missed her, so much that it hurt. He missed everything about her. Her smile and the little gestures that made her unique. The way she would throw her head back when she was amused, as if to taste her laugh before she let it out, and a trick of sinking her lips slowly when anything charmed or moved her. He loved noticing the details about her that others would easily overlook. But to him, it was the little things that helped sculpt her into the masterpiece she was. It hurt knowing he'd never see them anymore.

Destrou hummed all night to numb the pain, trying not to remember anything, until he fell asleep. His tears made it difficult for him to sleep fully throughout the night. At least the pain and sorrow made him forget how hungry he was. After a few hours of hanging at the breaking point of exhaustion, his mind finally shut down.

"Students," Gabrael said. "How many of you can relate to the pain Destrou is experiencing?"

S'rae wanted to say something, but she didn't want to be embarrassed. She knew she'd be the only one who related to his emptiness. Weakness was something she never wanted to show.

"No one?" Gabrael said. "Not a single one of you has felt so low that you wished there was an easier way to end the pain? I find that hard to believe."

S'rae looked around as the students placed their heads down, as if feeling the same way she did. Defeated. Alone. So, she gave in, clutching her robe before raising her hand slowly.

Maybe others would join in . . . but she was wrong. They didn't relate to the grief that she felt. How could they? Their lives were perfect compared to hers. They didn't know real pain.

Then something unexpected happened. First it was Adalia. Then Fujak. Then Aura'li hesitated a little before raising her hand. One hand after the next, arms lifted until S'rae noticed that each student had joined. She choked up, rubbing her eyes. She was not alone.

"You see, children," Gabrael said. "The schools have not failed you because you do not know how the Quizzes came to be, the Story of Time, or the Last Great War. They failed to teach you that we are all the same. We all share struggles. And we can get through them, together."

34

D ESTROU AWOKE SLOWLY.

A sound traveled in the darkness—a deep, unpleasantly familiar voice. He staggered to his feet, using one hand for support and the other for balance. He felt his hand squish into the ground. It was sticky like dough and the scent of manure caught his nostrils.

Normally he'd squirm with disgust, but now it barely got a reaction. Slowly, his head began to clear. He hoped that sleep would have been enough of a retreat from the world and its pain. It wasn't. He had experienced bruises, gashes, and fractured bones before, but this wound—the feeling of loss—seemed too deep to heal. Time was said to heal all wounds, but this was different, like putting a bandage over a tumor; there was no healing to be done.

He stood upright, limping through the dark tunnels toward the voice. By the time he found its source—a hole in the ceiling—he saw the sun's white light streaming through the ice. The ceiling was about ten feet high, and the voice was muffled. He looked around for anything to stand on to get higher. There was a huge rectangular stone lying on its side against a grimy wall. A few days earlier he might have been able to move it.

A loud thud overhead, like a stone falling to the ground, caught his attention. At once, the voice became clear—then was joined by another just as deep. He closed his eyes and pointed his ear to the sky.

"But . . . since the Eye of Eve is still shining . . . that means one of two things: Either Eve is really back . . . or we're in big trouble."

"Probly both."

"If they're back, will they be able to climb the Wall?"

"If they is back, then we is already dead."

"Unless we get Eve first."

"Too bad that dead girl ain't her. We were so close to gettin' outta here."

"Yeah, it's unfortunate, I woulda loved to get to know her."

"Me too."

Their laughter made Destrou's stomach twist.

"We're doing a lot of good for the Kingdom, it's a sort of reward for our good work. But how do you know that girl wasn't Eve?"

"If Eve dead, we'd saw it. Ice Age, remember?"

"Ah, the Ice Age myth. I miss the Crystal days and Prophet Va'han's crazy stories. You still actually believe the ones he wrote?"

"Course! He was weird, not crazy."

"More like weird and crazy! All the nut would say is 'I am Va'han' and you think I'm the dumb one?"

"Well, we woulda still been soldiers if ya weren't dumb and bad."

"It wasn't just me. But . . . to be safe, let's not tell the Kingdom about this girl dying."

"Ya thinkin' what I'm thinkin'?"

"There's nothing wrong with seeing how she looked, right? We haven't seen a girl in years, it's our right to peek."

Destrou covered his mouth as a whimper escaped—his fingers had calluses hard as stones that scraped against his face. A rage boiled inside of him. *I won't let them do anything to you!*

"We'll do it tonight before they bury her."

Destrou stopped at nothing to find a way out. *I need to save her.*

He knew he could do it now. Escape. It wasn't about him anymore. Not his bruises, his ankle that felt like it landed on needles, or his stomach, so empty it felt as if something was eating him from the inside. He didn't care about his pain. It was about her. Her cold eyes. Her face that was no longer smiling. He was determined to never let anyone disrespect Elu. They would not ruin his image of her. Not any more than they already had.

By the time Destrou noticed twilight's purple sky cast its glow into the room, his muscles felt weak after the hours upon hours of lifting whatever he could find. He stacked bones on top of one another, pushed rocks to form a foundation, and used the sticky substances on the walls and ground as glue to hold them all together.

Eventually he made a ten-foot-tall tower and called it the Tower of Eve. Elu had told him that he had to name his creations—they were his, it made them personal. It was far from majestic and looked more like stray bones thrown in the garbage than anything else, but it was his work. He took pride in his only way out.

Soon after that he climbed to the top of it, pressing his hands against the icy ceiling. The hole was smaller than his fist.

The purple light faded to a dark blue—night was on the horizon. His time dwindled away like the daylight.

His heart pumped faster. He had anywhere from a few minutes to an hour before the Guardians woke up. After realizing that he could chisel his way out, he reached into his tower, grabbing the sharpest bone and rock he could find.

He hammered away but barely made a scratch. The ice appeared too solid or his muscles were too weak—either way, he needed a new plan.

"My story can't end like this!" He slammed his fist against the ceiling, splitting the skin on his knuckles. Blood dripped down his fingers as he curled into a ball of regret.

Destrou saw the ceiling shake and heard distant thunder as if the Guardians had just rolled out of bed.

Oh no! Time had run out.

Destrou didn't hesitate; he thought about Elu and how she always had an answer. Her words flashed through his mind like scattered puzzle pieces tossed across the floor, desperately trying to find the right one to solve his problem.

Your hands, he heard a soft voice say. *There's something special about you . . . liquid ice. Indestructible.*

Rub your hands together, a thought whispered to him. The chill swept him, and his eyes rolled up for a moment. Elu's words rang through his head like an alarm, remembering her shock when he melted the liquid ice tower. *That's it!*

Panic swelled up in him as he heard footsteps rumble overhead.

Destrou closed his eyes, bringing his palms together. His anxiety calmed as he took deep breaths, moving his palms in a circular motion. Something took over him. His lungs burned; his next breath roared on the way in as he prepared himself. *I can do this.*

When he stared up at the hole, his body felt different. There was a warm sensation that pulsed through him, traveling from his head to toes then back up through his body. His heart pumped faster. *I will do this.*

Liquid ice poured onto his face as he pressed his palms into the ceiling. His dreads and clothes were drenched within seconds.

The moment his head poked through he knew that he was in the NoGo—the room was too big for anything else. There was ice all

around and the little light that did spill through was from a window too high for him to reach. It was pulverized, as if a giant hammer had smashed the wall. Ice shavings lay everywhere. He was midway through lifting himself out of the hole when he heard the Guardian's voice and his deep breathing just outside. Destrou fell to a crawl, dragging his body against the ice, inching closer to the door. The smell of mold caught his attention.

As the voice grew louder, he felt a hot anger inside. He tensed. He couldn't fight them, but maybe he could outrun them. *Not with this ankle, don't be dumb, Destrou.* If he managed to make it out, he could lose them and be safe—but then what about Elu?

He heard two clicks like locks being undone. Then came the distinct shriek of ice scraping against ice. The door slid open.

By the time he managed to blink his eyes, he could see the Guardian's bare bottom squatting down onto him. It looked like two crater-filled moons that crashed into each other.

Suddenly both of Destrou's arms pushed against the floor, propelling him into the air. He pressed his foot forward, wincing at the pain that shocked through him. He kicked off the naked bottom, then glided through the window, like a perfect dive.

He leapt with such force that he overextended his flip and with a deafening crash landed flat on his back.

A shock jolted through his spine as the world spun around him. He barely made out the roars that erupted from inside of the NoGo.

"What the—I'm stuck in the damn pooper!"

Destrou stumbled to the path that went around the NoGo to where Elu's body lay. Several snowflakes fell before him, but his vision was too blurry, and he could barely see. With a shaking hand, he touched his forehead and found it freshly wet.

The snowstorm would cover his tracks, but it would also wake up the Village.

A shadow fell over him as he heard the thundering stomps of the Guardians rush through the NoGo.

He focused on the mound of snow in the center. The faint contours of a human body underneath it.

He grabbed Elu by the arms—they numbed his fingers as if they were blocks of ice—and pulled with all of his strength.

The voices grew louder as he pulled her body into the shadows. They turned the corner just as her feet slid behind an igloo.

"Where'd she go?" the Guardian screamed.

"Follow the tracks," Gronk said.

Destrou felt the ground shake as the Guardians scurried toward him.

This is where my story ends. Seconds stretched into what might as well have been years.

Destrou saw a large hand smash onto the igloo.

"Nooo!" S'rae screamed. A current of wind flushed through the room, fanning the pages. "I'm sorry." She wished she could be there for him. That she could tell him he wasn't alone. That she was on his side, rooting for him every step of the way. Even though this was just a story . . . it somehow felt like more. Being involved made her feel less alone. Alive. Like she had a purpose.

"Do not worry," Gabrael said. "You left off . . . here. Continue."

"What's that?" the Guardian said. A faint roar made them jump and turn. The wind howled, stronger than Destrou had ever felt. It was so strong that it lifted the Guardians into the air, twirling them like leaves in the wind.

Destrou threw his cloak to the ground and placed Elu on top of it. He scrambled into the darkness. The wind pushed Destrou from behind, giving him the momentum he needed to pull the weight.

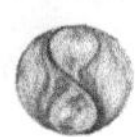

After an hour or two, something rattled behind him. He spun around quickly, ready for an attack.

A beautiful glow shone down upon his sunken, bruised face. It was the Eye of Eve.

"The aurora. The Eye of Eve. Leaving with me." Destrou recalled Elu's three wants. He looked up, searching for hope. *I promised that I'll get it for you. I have nothing to lose.*

He leapt to his feet and wrapped Elu's scarf around his hands after slinging it around the pole. He used his feet for leverage and the cloth for balance and support—just as Elu suggested. He gritted his teeth, squeezing his eyes shut. His feet had gone numb as soon as they touched the pole—the vibrations made it worse. "Come on," he whispered as he stared above at the Eye. "I can do this. Close your eyes. Don't think. Just do."

He had whispered those words before.

A few years ago, he remembered the first and last time he had ever beaten Ranmau at anything. Ranmau had always pushed a boulder twice his size for miles. Destrou thought it was impossible; but Ranmau challenged him to do it with a cloth wrapped around his eyes. Ranmau said how if Destrou knew how far he had to go, his mind would stop him before his body did. Ranmau assured Destrou that he was just as capable, as long as he believed. Destrou laughed at Ranmau's foolishness, but decided to give it his all. He pushed and pushed until his muscles tore open. Though his body burned, begging to stop, Ranmau didn't let him. He yelled "Keep going!" over and over again. "Don't stop! You can do this!" was all Destrou heard over his own screams from the pain that surged through his body. And after what felt like hours of torture, when he had finally given up and collapsed, tears ran down his face. He was mad at himself for pushing his body to its absolute limit but it still wasn't enough. He let Ranmau down. His muscles were so drained that he couldn't untie the cloth around his eyes or stand for longer than a second before his knees buckled. But when the blindfold fell from his eyes, Destrou's eyes widened. He was shocked to see that boulder was a hair ahead of Ranmau's. He actually did it! Ranmau had taught him important lessons that day: That the impossible was possible as long as he believed, and that the only thing that stopped one from achieving their goal was their own fear.

Despite his fear of heights, he kept climbing. He felt weightless as his body spiraled around and around. His eyes were closed. His breaths were slow. And his heart was calm despite the pain surging through his body. Ranmau's voice was in his head, urging him to keep going.

Without him realizing it, something impossible happened. His hand pressed against a warm sensation that gave life to his limbs. When he opened his eyes, the Eye of Eve was in his hand. It was beautiful beyond words. That thought alone reminded him of Elu. Her eyes and her smile. The pole then stopped moving as if the orb was its source of power. He found himself sitting on top of the pole, overlooking the Village and Forest. Everything seemed so small and peaceful.

He appeared as a beacon of light. Of fight. And of hope. For he had done the impossible.

Something not even Ranmau was able to accomplish. But it wasn't about gloating or proving people wrong. This was personal. It was about keeping a promise for a friend. For love.

Not only was he able to open both eyes, but life entered his body in waves, eliminating all pain. His body felt brand new. But his mind still carried the weight of a dozen emotions.

"This is for you, Elu!" Tears poured down his face as he punched the air with the Eye.

Destrou dragged Elu's body out of the storm and eased her into the Tree. It was almost unrecognizable. Every surface was now dull, as if her death had drained the light from it. Nothing in the room was more different than Elu who lay next to the Tree of Eve. Dismayed, he touched her gently. Her skin was blue, lifeless, and cold. Her lip was split, and there was a long gash on her jaw, but that wasn't the worst. Her mouth wasn't smiling. It was chalky white and frowning. He couldn't stand to see her like that. He pressed his fingers to her face, widening her lips to a smile. *That's how I'll always remember you.* His breath came in short bursts, each one sounding like a gasp.

Elu was gone. He knew that. There was nothing he could do to change what happened. But Ranmau. He was somewhere. Destrou felt it in his chest. If only there was a way to find out where he was.

He flinched, hearing a whisper. It was so soft that it sounded like a thought.

The odd noise became more clear. *Where are we . . . where are we . . . where are weee.*

"Where are we?" Destrou said to himself. His eyes widened. "Where are we!" He shouted. "Thank you, Elu!" His lips pressed against her cold forehead. "You're still there for me."

At once, he devised a plan to somehow find the location of the Chamber of Echoes. It wouldn't let him know exactly where Ranmau was, but it'd give him the assurance he needed. To know that he was alive. Since Elu was . . . gone, Ranmau needed to—

Elu . . . It was tough to think about anyone else. She was the main source of his agony.

When Destrou placed the Eye of Eve on her chest, the entire room pulsated in a white glow. The glow traveled throughout the Tree, illuminating every crevice. She would have loved to have seen this. "I miss you so much." He struggled to say each word. He cuddled beside her, his body becoming desensitized to the cold as his eyelids closed peacefully.

A loud *whoosh* hit Destrou's ears, waking him up almost instantly. It was an eerie, ghostly sound, like a screaming whisper. It came from overhead, outside. Suddenly his body went into shock, noticing that Elu's corpse was nowhere to be seen. There were many dark shadows on the ground, like puddles of ink, leading up the spiral steps to the entrance of the Tree. He stood there mute and frozen. Then he followed the tracks.

As he exited the Tree and looked out toward the Forest of Ness, he saw a large shadow that stood upright and felt a fear pound through his body. A wisp of black smoke broke his line of vision. Destrou stood and looked about aimlessly, realizing that the smoke resonated off the shadowy body like a black flame. The person was wrapped in shadow atop the cliff. Though the Forest behind it was dark, its presence omitted an emptiness darker than the night.

"Elu?" Destrou choked out. He felt a tenseness, a change in the texture of the air. "Is that you? Are you"—his heart stopped—"an Archon?"

The shadow spread its arms—or were they wings—and darkness billowed from underneath like an inky fog. Destrou staggered backward, falling on his hands. The shadow leapt into the air, dozens of feet high, before soaring deep into the Forest of Ness.

Destrou was speechless. Motionless. Was he the first person to see an Archon and live?

"Does the Eye of Eve turn the dead into Archons?" S'rae asked, gripping her robes to stop her body from shaking.

"Indeed," Gabrael said. "That is one of the reasons the Village placed it out of reach. It has great powers, at times terrible, but still

great. It is important that it does not fall into the wrong hands. Unspeakable danger can occur."

S'rae gulped, her palms and feet sweating profusely. She took deep breaths to calm herself down. "I have a question."

"I may have an answer."

"Do you think Destrou will ever forgive Ranmau if he finds out what happened?"

He looked at her with saddened eyes as if he knew her question came from her torn heart, not her curious mind. "Forgiveness is to love as a shadow is to light. As long as there is light, there will always be room for a shadow, no matter how dark the world may seem. And I see light—enough to illuminate the stars."

S'rae hoped he was right. But she knew a secret was like death's touch, it always found a way to reveal itself to a person at the worst times.

35

A BRUISED AND BEATEN DESTROU WOKE UP, looking down at a horde of at least sixty angry boys. He winced at their glaring hatred at the sight of him, their fists clenched. They grabbed his arms and legs and he was suspended a few feet in the air, tied to a large ice spike near the pole that used to hold the Eye. It seemed as if every boy in the Village had surrounded him. Chunks of ice were clenched in their hands.

He tried to recall what happened. How did he end up here?

He remembered running to the Village, screaming for his life. He remembered Elu . . . shadows . . . an Archon? Then darkness.

His head hurt as if he had been knocked out unconscious. It wasn't the first time he felt like this. That was probably what happened.

Destrou wiggled around sluggishly, attempting to make his way out of the ropes. They were tied so tight that the fibers burned into his skin.

"Why are you doing this? I have nothing left . . ." Destrou tried to scream. His voice cracked.

"Then there should be no problems with putting you out of your misery." The Leader bounced a ball of ice in his hand. "I'm doing you a favor, you ungrateful waste of life. You're lucky that we're even thinking of you as food after."

Destrou cried in disbelief. His heart pumped faster, knowing that even if his voice reached the Guardian, help wouldn't arrive. He hoped that maybe his scream would reach the one person who could save him: Ranmau. After moments of silence, his hope faded.

"Help! Help me! Oh no . . . poor Destrou doesn't have his brother helping him anymore." The Leader imitated crying. "You can't eat anymore while the rest of us starve. You can't be warm anymore while the rest of us freeze. Stop crying! You don't know what suffering is. But I will show you."

"I didn't do anything wrong." Destrou squirmed around to get comfortable. A throbbing sensation burned his back as if he lay on top of acid.

"You did nothing, which is worse than doing wrong. And now you'll become nothing." He threw the ice at Destrou, hitting him in the face.

Destrou let out a cry of pain that had a shrieking undertone of fear. Blood formed underneath his lip.

With a swollen eye, he squinted to focus on a blurred dot disrupting the purity of the Wall. The Wall was too tall to notice anything on top, but he hoped his imagination wasn't playing a trick on him again.

The dot faded away.

Wherever you are, I'm happy for you, Ranmau. I hope you finally got the freedom you deserve.

"Whoever gets the final blow, gets first dibs," laughed the Leader, picking up more ice.

The boys followed suit, readying for the command to begin. The thought of a full meal made their mouths salivate. They had hunger in their eyes as they arched their arms back, preparing to attack.

Then a roar rumbled through the sky as clouds twisted into one large mass before tearing open.

BANG! A light zapped through the sky and struck the NoGo.

Another message? Destrou lifted his head. It was normal to get three a year. But a week? Unheard of. Something was brewing beyond these walls. He wished he would live long enough to find out. Or maybe it was better that he didn't.

"What are we waiting for?" yelled the Leader. "We don't have much time now. Get him!"

A piercing scraping sound rang Destrou's eardrums.

"What's that?" A boy looked around.

The longer the boys searched for the source, the louder it became. The shriek grew so loud that the boys held their ears in pain. Destrou wished he could.

Glancing at the Wall with a pain-filled squint, one of the boys directed everyone's attention to a white, misty streak plunging down the Wall.

"What's that?" a boy screamed, pointing at a traveling cloud of mist.

"I dunno . . ." the Giant's voice trailed off as he tilted his head up.

The shrieking ended with a crashing *BANG!* A wave of snow obscured the entire area with a white fog.

Moments later, sounds of coughing masked various thuds, grunts and moans. When the snow settled, the Leader saw bodies squirming on the ground.

There was an individual wearing a white fur cloak, untying Destrou from the spike.

The Leader looked in with shock, as if his heart jumped un-

steadily in his chest.

The mysterious individual, with his face covered by a shroud, whispered into Destrou's ears: "I can't leave you . . . not like this."

"And neither can I."

S'rae heard a familiar voice ring through the darkness as the ground shook.

As she peered into the shadows, she gripped her robe and rolled her shoulders.

The stone tiles rumbled against each other before molding into a human. The speaker appeared directly in back of the statue of Harahm'be, so that it was difficult, at first, to make out more than his silhouette. As the ground stopped trembling, and his head rose, his face shone through the gloom.

"Vayp?" S'rae said softly. A stiff wind rattled her clothes. She stood upright to get a better look. Her heart pounded with excitement. "Is that really you? Did you really come back?"

"I'm sorry I ever left," Vayp said. S'rae heard his voice soften as if sorrow weighed it down.

"What happened?" S'rae said. The way her stomach twisted, she knew something felt wrong.

"Nothing," he said icily.

"How'd you make it here? Wasn't it said to be impossible to find?" S'rae asked.

"My tracking spell," he said in almost a whisper.

S'rae should have known the answer. He was a master at tracking and finding locations. His spell would always guide villagers to the perfect hunting grounds.

"Impressive. A tracking spell to find your way back," Gabrael said. "Where's Han'sael?"

Silence hung in the air.

"Vayp, where is he?" S'rae asked.

Nothing.

"Vayp . . ." Something definitely felt wrong.

There was a brief silence in which the distant echo of Vayp's stuttered breaths reverberated through S'rae's chest. It was contagious. S'rae gave a little gasp and began to cry in earnest. She sobbed intensely as if she had seen it for herself.

Gabrael lifted from his seat and glided toward Vayp. "You must tell me all that you know."

"I will," Vayp said softly.

"No." Gabrael gazed deeply into his eyes. "I mean everything. I need to know what happened to you. Your history with the Mechas. And—"

Vayp dove into Gabrael's arms, crying. "I'm not ready."

"I understand." Gabrael caressed Vayp's head. "Some stories are too painful to relive. But believe me when I say this, I understand all the pain you have been through. I too know what it feels like. The memories will never go away. You are not alone. Not anymore." Gabrael paused and took a deep breath as if what he had to say next took everything he had. "I am not just talking about losing your Sol."

Vayp's eyes widened. Tears poured, trailing down his neck. He nodded and within the blink of an eye, he and Gabrael erupted into a flame. Smoke filled the room, and once it cleared, they were gone.

S'rae jolted upright and ran toward the stairs.

"Where are you going?" Fujak grabbed her arm. "It's dangerous out there."

"I need to know." Her eyes were glazed. "I need to know what happened to him."

Fujak's fingers loosened. "I forgive you for that stunt you pulled earlier. I can't imagine what you're going through. Can we put our hate aside for once?"

S'rae remained silent. Opella taught her that if she had nothing nice to say, then say nothing at all.

"Be safe." Fujak released her arm.

S'rae didn't care to think about Fujak. Nor about him being nice or the traitor. So she didn't. This was much more important. Anxiety rushed through her, feeling like Elu in the Chamber of Echoes. She needed to know what Vayp was going say. This was driving her crazy.

She ran through the dark tunnels and up the spiraling staircases. They were smooth stone steps; they looked new as if this passageway was never used. Though night fell, the tower glowed with light; copper lanterns hung from the wall and lit up as she passed and the earthen floor was coated with a glaze that reflected the orange flames. As she sprinted, her shadow rippled, expanding into dozens of shadowy shapes across the walls. Finally, she exited the tunnel, emerging out of one of the towers. She jumped into the courtyard, sliding as a gust of wind sent her robe behind her. She squinted, circling her fingers, searching for any sounds.

The wind reached her again as she crouched and placed her goggles over her eyes. It lifted her through the air. She floated across the sky weightlessly as if gravity was weakened. Her toes landed gracefully; a gust of wind channeled around her soles before lunging into the air again. Wind hummed through her ears as her hair flurried across her face. Her heart nearly ricocheted off her rib cage with worry. What if they had already started?

Without warning, she had drained most of her energy and now fell like a bird without wings. She broke her fall with a roll, then jumped up, shaking her head with disappointment. *Where can they be? Think!*

Her head shot up as if a fire sparked in her mind. Darkness! She immediately thought of the restricted caves, and traveled to each one until she finally heard a sound.

She found herself sitting at the base of a stone that curved out of the ground like a hill. She didn't want to get too close so she kept her distance. A pulsating lump surged to her throat as she listened.

"Very sorry to hear, Vayp. Tell me more about the Mechas."

"There isn't much else to it. They killed us. All of us—without warning. In seconds, we were wiped from the map like we never existed. That's all. I'll spare the details of what happened. I won't talk about the bombs I heard. About the screams or the cries. The pleas for help as the walls crumbled. How my father refused to give up his only son, or how he waved the white flag and surrendered. I won't talk about my entire village walking peacefully unarmed, being arrested for battling against the system. Or the hundreds of Mechas that fired away at them even though it was over. Not about the sounds and smells of bodies being burned alive, or when they splattered into a million pieces. How they massacred and wiped out an entire village, history, and culture in just a few seconds. But what I will talk about is the aftermath—after the Mechas left and the vultures started to pick at the corpses. None of that is the reason why I'm scared to fall asleep at night. Two men came, and that's when the nightmare begins . . ."

VAYP LAY IN THE GROUND, perfectly camouflaged by a protective spell his father cast on him right before the bombs dropped. While he was safe from danger, his body remained paralyzed until the spell wore off. He could barely move his fingers, and his vision was murky as if watching life through mud-smeared goggles. A cry tore from his lips when he saw his dead companions.

Behind him, where his home had been, smoldered a circle of

burnt grass and splintered wood. The grass beyond the charring was flattened. A wisp of smoke curled in the air, carrying a burned smell. In the center of one of the blast radii was his father. Mist slithered across the scorched area and swirled around his body.

Vayp's heart pounded as he saw the mist darken into a black fog. And as he heard the chomping sounds of vultures picking at the bodies, two figures emerged from the darkness with a sizzle. They were as black as the night with no definite features, just like shadows.

Vayp's stomach twisted as the larger one stabbed a sword straight into his father's body, as if to make sure he was dead. Droplets of blood splattered in the air and froze in place, looking like rubies against a black canvas, as if there was no gravity.

"Are there no survivors?" a chillingly cold voice said.

"Do you not feel that?" the tall shadow said, pulling his sword out of the body.

"Feel what?"

"The fear."

Silence.

"We are not alone."

Vayp's heart pounded faster.

"The fear . . . is increasing . . ."

Vayp felt footsteps get closer. There was a thundering rumble with each one, as if an earthquake followed shortly after. A veil of darkness hovered nearer like a fog. He felt a tightness in his chest that he tried to control with still breaths.

Slash! A cold blade grazed his cheek, and his blood absorbed into the ground. His eyelids squeezed shut as he tried not to scream.

"*You* cannot hide," the shadow said, pulling the sword out of the ground. Vayp felt it rip through his cheek.

"Should we kill him?"

"Why?"

"Because . . ."

"So, there is no purpose for his death . . . yet you'd want to . . . kill him?"

"I suppose . . ."

Vayp felt a thud above him followed by gagging sounds.

"Do you think of death as purposeless?" The voice rose. "Just as there is purpose in life, there is purpose in death. I hope you don't think this massacre was without purpose."

The other voice coughed.

"I can't hear you."

The cough sounded more forced. The other shadow managed to squeeze out a "no" between gasps.

"These deaths have a purpose, his does not. However, his life may have one."

Vayp felt another thud.

A great shadow crept closer to Vayp, accompanied by thundering footsteps that rattled his insides. His stomach swirled with emptiness. The rattling stopped and he was completely eclipsed in darkness. In that moment Vayp felt the life drain out of him. He couldn't describe the feeling—it was like all of his organs shut down at once. All senses were eliminated and the only thing left working was his brain, trying to make sense of the nothingness. He was suffocating but couldn't hear his gasps for air. Couldn't feel the warmth of the ground or his hands as he clenched them. For that moment, it felt like he was hovering in space, watching a starless galaxy drift by. Empty seemed full compared to this.

Am I dead? Is this what death is . . . darkness?

A cold whisper came through, appearing as a thought in his mind.

The beauty about death is that if you think you are dead, then

you are not. You won't know when your time is up, but I will. It is not now, but will be soon. By then you will wish that I had killed you quickly. But I'll be waiting for you . . . in your nightmares.

Vayp wanted to cry, but he couldn't.

"In one flash, the darkness faded away completely, and I could finally breathe . . ." S'rae heard the last whisper trail off as if Vayp had lost his breath. "I'll never forget my dad's last words: 'Always remember us. They'll say we're the enemy, or eliminate us from history like we never existed. But always remember that all we wanted was freedom.'"

S'rae rubbed her stinging eyes, and heard the sounds of a door opening and the thud of it slamming shut. She could picture Vayp vividly in her head as he walked out of the cave.

Silence.

Moments later, S'rae saw Vayp and Gabrael emerge from the shadows. Vayp appeared confused, seeming surprised that it was a warm night rather than the cold day of his story.

S'rae's watery eyes met Vayp's. Tears had been pouring down her face for the past five minutes. "I had no idea." She heard the sorrow in her own voice. She felt the pain in it as well. Pain was her body's way of telling her something was wrong, but this was different. This was the type of pain that let her know life was wrong. And that it was cruel. Her body wasn't in pain, her heart was. It ached for her past. Her home. Her family. She knew that what she was experiencing must have been nothing compared to the emotional weight Vayp had been harboring for years. Now, more than ever before, she wished she could hold him and tell him that things would be better. But she knew that was a lie. Things now seemed worse than ever.

"This is worse than I thought," Gabrael said, confirming her fears. "My darkest fears have come to light."

"What do we do?" S'rae said, wiping her tears.

"We? *We* do not have much time. We must finish reading. But *I* will make a stand. The last battle for the Valley is about to begin."

36

DESTROU OBSERVED THE BLURRY FIGURE as he turned around and took off his cloak. "R-ran . . . Ranmau . . . y-you . . . came . . . back," Destrou wept, feeling like he'd swallowed his heartbeat.

"Ranmau?" the Leader said alertly, grabbing a staff with sharp bones tied to its ends.

He looked around at the remaining boys who were searching for answers on what the next action should be.

"Let's get our revenge!" he roared.

Ranmau placed the cloak over Destrou's body, shielding him from the onslaught of ice hurled at them. Destrou lifted the cloak just enough to watch Ranmau duck from every projectile, as he then charged at the group with full force.

Once he was in close range, Ranmau attacked swiftly, his fists, knees, and elbows dropping one boy after the next. Despite being surrounded by dozens, he felled them as quickly as they charged. His precision was uncanny; every attack landed exactly where he wanted it to. He aimed his uppercuts low and his kicks high then his uppercuts high and his kicks low. If there was an opening, he found it.

There was no way to defend against his strikes. This exchange occurred for a few minutes until there were only three boys left standing: Ranmau, The Giant, and the Leader. The rest of the Village had fallen.

Ranmau had never officially engaged in a fight with either one of them before. The challenges were games designed around agility, speed, intelligence, and, at one point, fun, but never combat.

The Giant stepped forward. There was about a seven year age difference between the two. Ranmau was well built for his age, but The Giant was in the transition from a teenager into a man; his bigger, muscular physique made that apparent.

"We will win this," the Leader said. "Look at him. He's weak now."

"Weak . . . now?" Ranmau glared. "Don't be confused . . . I still have five different ways to knock both of you out. Twenty if I use both hands . . . Fifty if I open my eyes."

Ranmau's breaths were heavy; his eyes drowsy with exhaustion. The Leader and The Giant both lunged in for the attack. With fists, legs, and elbows, they exchanged rapid attacks, counterattacks, and parries. The injured boys looked on with dropped jaws.

The Giant was much slower than the Leader. Ranmau dodged one of his attacks, countering with an attack just below his belly-button. His fist sank into the Giant's stomach, forcing a loud gasp that breezed past Ranmau's ear. As the Giant attempted to regain his breath, Ranmau swept around with a vicious roundhouse kick, knocking more teeth out of his mouth. The Giant's massive body fell hard on the ground, creating a tremor followed by a whirlwind of snow. Ranmau pulled his foot back and directed his attention to the Leader.

Their eyes met for what felt like an eternity. The Leader pressed his palms on top of his head, gasping for air. Normally the Leader was known to strike first, but this time was different. Ranmau lunged in for the attack.

Both Ranmau and the Leader fought for more than pride; they had their younger siblings on their minds with every strike. Destrou saw it in their faces. The Leader had revenge in his eyes.

Although Ranmau was more sluggish than usual, he still outclassed the Leader. For every one punch the Leader landed, Ranmau landed three. Three turned to four, then five, six; it wasn't long before Ranmau's fists became too familiar with the Leader's face.

The Leader may have been fast, but Ranmau was faster.

Knowing he was at a disadvantage, the Leader picked up the staff he had dropped in the fight, the sharpened bones on both ends gleaming wickedly in the light as he lifted it from the ground.

The two stared each other down, waiting for the next move to be made.

The Leader whipped around with the speed of a shooting star. His staff swung over Ranmau's head one moment and at his leg the next. Though the crowd gasped, Ranmau didn't miss a beat.

When the Leader lunged again, Ranmau arched his back, bending it farther than Destrou thought was possible, and dodged his attack. Ranmau was still arched when the Leader struck again, this time slamming the weapon with the force of a Crystal Soldier.

Ranmau threw himself to the side, sliding across the ice as the Leader's staff embedded deep into the ground.

The Leader tugged and tugged on his staff, but it was stuck. He grunted and moaned and even cried as he pulled with all his power. Destrou almost felt sorry for how defeated he looked. He lost his sister . . . He suddenly seemed vulnerable. Human, even.

Ranmau stepped toward the Leader with a confidence that was

horrifying. "If you are to lose, lose with pride, Eli'jah."

The Leader roared as he pulled the staff out of the ground. In one swift motion, he twisted his body and thrust his staff toward Ranmau.

Ranmau remained still. He didn't even flinch.

The staff collided with a loud crack. Destrou put his head down, afraid to see what had just happened. The sound of a bone breaking echoed throughout.

When he looked up, his eyes widened.

Ranma stood there with his forearm above his head and the Leader's shattered staff still reverberating from that blow. *H-how did he do that?*

"Too easy," Ranmau said.

In that instant, when the Leader thrust the staff toward Ranmau's heart, Ranmau pushed off his right leg and swung his arms for momentum, cartwheeling in midair. As he flipped over the outstretched staff, Destrou saw that the fight was now over. The Leader's face was completely exposed as Ranmau's heel cracked into his jaw.

The Leader crashed to the ground, panting deeply.

Ranmau stood above him with bloodied fists and fiery eyes. "You are no leader of mine."

"Please . . . don't—" The Leader's hand gripped Ranmau's wrist.

In an instant, Ranmau's hands were around the Leader's throat.

He mounted on top of him, tightening the grip. The Leader struggled to speak, as if air was unable to enter through his throat. His eyes bulged with fear as they twitched around before rolling up. His tears looked white like ice in the sunlight.

Ranmau had no intentions of stopping, until he heard the soft, familiar voice whimper: "Don't do it . . . brother."

Despite the terror the Leader imposed on Destrou, he felt empathetic. He understood that the problem was bigger than the issues between them; he understood that food was scarce, warmth was forbidden, and competition was how they were bred. Elu's message had begun to settle in: *We aren't the problem. We live in it.*

"He was . . . angry because he wasn't able . . . to . . . feed . . . his family . . . how would you feel?" Destrou forced each word out of his mouth. "He was angry . . . because he lost his sister . . . how would you . . . feel?" This was for Elu. Destrou owed her for saving his life.

Destrou spoke directly to the innocence inside Ranmau's heart. He knew him for who he was—not what he had become.

Ranmau's grip remained tight. After a few seconds, his hold slowly loosened. He exhaled a calming sigh, releasing the Leader. The other boys of the Village stumbled to the Leader, attending to him. Ranmau looked at Destrou with saddened eyes that told a story of regret. He took a step toward Destrou. Then another. And when he grabbed Destrou by the arm, tears filled his grey eyes. But he said nothing, as if there was too much to say. Instead, he placed Destou's arm over his shoulder, partly carrying him back to the Village.

Once they entered the Village, they passed through the narrow aisles, heading toward their igloo. They bore smiles from ear to ear. Destrou's greatest fear was quenched—Ranmau had left but came back for him. He felt his life was partially restored. The void in his heart that missed Ranmau was filled, but now another void took its place. He had many questions that he wanted to ask, but was afraid to ruin the moment.

Finally, he had his brother back. It felt like a dream.

"You know . . ." Destrou coughed. "I was just about to win right before you came."

Ranmau smiled, and it softened up every hard line in his face. "I know." He pulled Destrou in closer, kissing his forehead. "But I can't have you stealing all the fun."

Destrou's laugh quickly turned into a wheeze. And then it happened. A sound resonated in his ears. One that he had waited years to hear. Ranmau broke out in a long winded laugh, and tears of relief filled Destrou's eyes as smile lines appeared on Ranmau's eyes. Now they both were laughing. And despite Ranmau's best efforts, Destrou could see more tears starting to pool up in his eyes. Destrou had never seen him cry before. Not like this.

Destrou didn't want to put too much thought into it, but why the sudden change?

"Family forgives one another, right?" Ranmau said out of the blue, wiping his eyes.

Why would he say that? What did he mean? For leaving me? For saving me? Destrou didn't know, but he was too overwhelmed and tired to ask. He closed his eyes and dug his nails into his palms, letting out a deep, shuddering breath. He never wanted this moment to end.

Destrou smiled to himself, hearing Ranmau's laugh echo through his mind. He forgot how deep his voice had gotten comparing it to the last time he heard it. A blessing he could witness every day.

Unfortunately, the celebration was short lived.

Immediately after entering their igloo, something collided into them, slamming Destrou to the ground and pulling Ranmau, lifting him high into the air.

The Guardian had Ranmau dangling by his arm. Destrou screamed to let Ranmau go but the Guardian pulled him away, throwing him in the air like a rag doll.

Destrou screamed, watching Ranmau get dragged across the ice and snow.

The Guardians brought Ranmau into the center of the Village. They showed no regard for his comfort as the Commander pressed his elbow onto Ranmau's back against a block of ice.

The Village gathered around.

"Did Ranmau kill the girl?" the Guardian asked.

They nodded in approval.

Lies! Destrou clenched his jaw.

Muffled whispers broke out among the boys, quickly silenced by a sharp wave of the Guardian's hand. Destrou shot them a glare before focusing on the Guardian.

"Who's going to invent everything now?" the Guardian growled. "We lost our best Villager. The penalty must be paid."

Destrou's stomach twisted in pain. *Ranmau didn't do it! He wouldn't! This isn't right!*

The Guardian pulled Ranmau's arm, practically dislocating it from its socket as he screamed in pain. "Was this the arm he used?"

Destrou glanced around as the Village nodded.

He didn't do it!

"Well, this won't be enough fun." The Guardian lifted a large club of ice, extending Ranmau's right arm. He examined it for a moment before throwing it to his side.

The Commander appeared puzzled.

"Ranmau's bones are too tough, that wouldn't be enough. If he wants to become a Crystal Soldier, he's going to be treated like one."

"But . . . the Kingdom said we aren't supposed to show them—"

"The Kingdom isn't here, are they? Plus, I've been waiting to use this for too long."

The Guardian lifted his hand and waves of blues and whites circled around his palms. A burst of gasps hit Destrou's ears as he watched a solid block of ice form in the Guardian's palm. It molded into many different shapes: a staff, a sword, and an axe before finally taking the shape of a club that sparkled so white it seemed as if the sun was trapped inside. Destrou couldn't explain what he was seeing, but he knew that Elu would have an answer.

The Guardian grinned. "Oh, it has been too long!" His sneer disappeared as his eyes narrowed; his killer instincts emerged.

A chill traveled down Destrou's spine. He had seen that look before. "Don't do it!" he screamed.

But there was nothing anyone could say or do to stop him. It was in that moment when Destrou realized just how powerless he was. How powerless they all were. And then how right Elu had been. Not just about how they all were living in a problem, but how she said that by the end, after finding out the Village's secrets, he'd want to explore the world too. He was no longer scared of the mysteries and dangers that existed beyond the Wall, he was curious. *I miss you so much.*

Destrou was snapped back into the moment by a thundering BANG! The Guardian smashed the club down on Ranmau's arm.

Ranmau's shriek of pain was as traumatizing to hear as his punishment was to view. The boys looked away to avoid nightmares.

Unfortunately, Destrou witnessed it, unmoving since hearing Ranmau's cry for help.

Ranmau has saved me more times than I can think of. . . and when he needed me most, I just watched. The one time he needed me, I didn't save him . . . I couldn't. I'm useless.

The Guardian pointed at the Commander.

Ranmau curled into a ball, trying his best to contain the pain, breathing heavily, rolling from side to side.

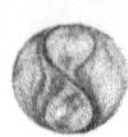

The Commander dragged a large cube made of the most dense type of ice and about four feet wide and tall with a removable slab on top. It was what they all dreaded: the Box.

A few boys had been victim to the Box. But they were no longer around to show the full effect of the punishment, only their stories. The Box was more than a confinement; it was a torturous punishment that tormented their minds. Physical torture wasn't as gratifying to the Guardians as a mental breakdown. Watching boys crumble from the inside made them excited.

Those who were placed in the Box came out as corpses, dead or alive. By the end of the week long suffering, one would freeze, starve, or wish for death.

The Commander pushed the slab off the top. It crashed to the ground.

They grabbed Ranmau's broken arm, his bone bulging out like a ball under his skin, and hoisted him up. Ranmau's shriek made some of the boys cringe. He glanced at Destrou and tilted his head away with a frown. He didn't want any Villager to see him like this, especially Destrou. The quiet in the Village was uneasy, like they were awaiting a burial.

Destrou buried his face in his palms, knowing that was what Ranmau would've wanted. He did know his brother the most, after all; Ranmau was much too proud.

Destrou heard a scuffle from across the space and lifted his face from his palms. His eyes adjusted to the light, staring through his teary glaze. He heard dragging and the squeak of ice scraping ice.

Destrou felt a chill stretch across his body that froze his blood and made his hairs stand on end. His brother, Ranmau, was about to be sealed shut inside the Box. The same Box that had ended many lives.

After all this, this is how your story ends?

After you saved my life, I now watch you die?

Do something, Destrou ordered himself. *Run. Help. Something. Ranmau wouldn't just watch. But the Box means death. Don't do anything Ranmau wouldn't want you to do.*

But the despair in Ranmau's eyes pulled him in. Because despite every ounce of his body telling him not to, Destrou threw his head back and jumped toward the Guardian. He didn't know what his plan was, but he knew that he couldn't just watch. He ran toward the Box, slowing down so he didn't trip over anything. What was the plan? What could he do?

Destrou fell to his knees in front of the Guardian, clutching his face. Thoughts spiraled through his mind in waves; he finally caught the one that grabbed his attention.

"I'm going in with him," he shouted, blankly staring at the ground.

"You must be crazy, krillen. This isn't a game." The Guardian laughed.

Destrou lifted his face. It was cold and serious. He didn't even blink when the Guardian mentioned the grim tales of soldiers choosing death over the Box. No amount of fear could change his mind; he chose to be there for his brother during his lowest point.

"You krillens are crazy and stupid." The Guardian threw Ranmau into the Box.

Destrou heard Ranmau crash onto the floor.

There was a moan inside the ice. Cold crept up Destrou's spine. He reached up and grabbed the top of the Box, pressing his hip to its side, hoisting himself up. He was unaware of what might happen next, but regret was the last thing on his mind. A weight settled on his chest, like each breath carried a boulder along with it. Tension built up inside of him until he couldn't stand it anymore. *It's time.*

He climbed in. A harrowing cold overwhelmed his body into

shuddering, a level of freezing that he had never experienced or imagined.

Destou sat beside Ranmau and placed his hand on his arm. Holding it there, he gazed at Ranmau with such empathy. Their eyes met. It was as if Ranmau understood the depth of Destrou's love for him, and that, if it were possible, Destrou would willingly switch places to relieve his suffering.

The ice slab slid over the opening, trapping them inside.

Amidst the darkness and trembling, a soft, quivering whisper resonated inside the Box. "I will not leave . . . *you.* Not like . . . *this.*"

Destrou tried to absorb the gravity of the situation he put himself in. But he only felt the cold chill of death creeping its hand closer, ready to greet them. And though he tried his hardest to concentrate on the faint voices overhead, all he could hear was the *clack clack clack* from his chattering teeth.

"But do you wanna know the real reason I'm punishing the krillen?"

"Why?"

"That message—"

"Yeah, wot about it?"

"It's . . ." There was a long pause. ". . . about Eve."

"Wot about her?"

"Prophet Va'han had said that something terrible happened."

"Terrible? Please tell me she did not die."

"She's not dead. But—"

"Oh praise the Divine One! That would have been our heads!"

"She's no longer alive either."

"N-not dead or alive? W-wot does that mean?"

"The worst thing that could possibly happen. She's... one of *them. She's a*

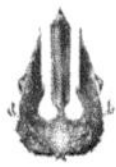

When the words vanished from the pages, so too did the candle-light. At once, a chilling darkness swept the room. Only the students' voices and chattered teeth were heard.

"One of what? What's *them*?"

"Wait, what happened?"

"Does that mean Elu was really Eve? What happens when Eve is an Archon?"

"No, it can't end like this! I have way too many questions!"

"Yeah, this would be the worst book ever if they ended it like that. It can't do that to my emotions!"

"Oh stop being a baby."

"Stop with the insults."

"I'm not insulting you. I'm describing you."

"That's it? What happens after the darkness?"

"It appears that the first part has ended."

"Ended?"

"The words have disappeared. Retro'ku must now be ready. It is time."

37

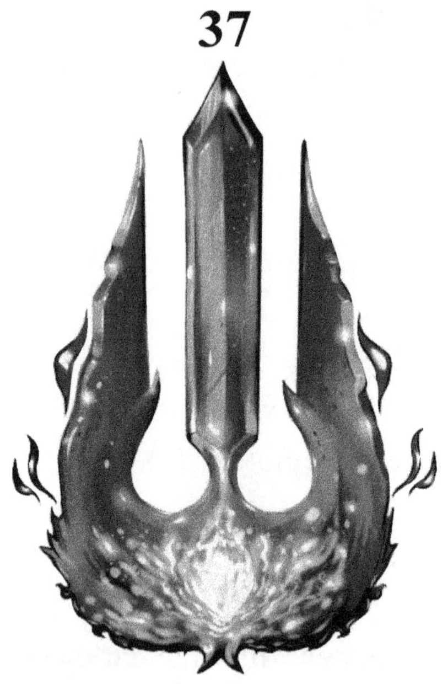

FOR A LONG MOMENT AFTER GABRAEL FINISHED READING, there was silence in the room. The only sound was the faint crackle from the fire in the center.

Finally Gabrael spoke: "Students, it is said that the two most important days of your life are the day you are born, and the day you find out why. Today is the latter." Gabrael lifted the Book. As he stared at it with pursed lips, the seconds stretched into minutes, and the students began to shift restlessly. The sound snapped his attention back to them, and he spoke again. "The Book of Eve is special. It dates back to a time before written language was even created. Its words were created by the elements and its secret locked away within its pages."

"Locked away?" S'rae's voice heightened with curiosity.

"Yes," he sighed. "Each school has a Chamber of Eve. It is not a room but instead a challenge designed for only the most gift-ed pupils. The reward is an Elemential Orb which when placed here"—Gabrael twisted the book in his hands to show its cover, then pointed at one of the five empty sockets—"the words will ap-pear, unlocking the next chapter. The rest of *his* story. Unfortunate-ly, there comes a great risk."

"Risk?" Fujak asked. His eyes narrowed and his voice wavered with worry.

"If you do not complete the challenge, you do not come back."

"Do we get to retake it or do we—" S'rae paused.

Gabrael said nothing, letting S'rae finish the sentence for her-self.

"Die?" S'rae's voice shook. "That's why we're here—that's the sacrifice? Get the orb so the book continues or we . . . die?"

After moments passed, Gabrael nodded and his fists clenched. Flames ignited around them. When he opened his palms, sparks shot out like shooting stars, lighting up the tunnel that led outside. "Follow me."

"But how do you know?" Gabrael heard the worry in S'rae's voice. Though he said nothing, the pain in his eyes seemed as if he had seen the horror for himself. The breathless sigh that followed shortly after must have confirmed S'rae's suspicions. Her eyes nar-rowed, as though she knew there was a dark story hidden inside, one that would never be retold.

The walls of the path were darkened, and the candlelight flick-ered from red to blue as Gabrael walked by. Their footsteps echoed around the spiraling staircases until they made it outside. When they walked up to an open area west of the Spire, there were metal statues of warriors all around, and a heavy, tight feeling in Gabra-el's chest.

"Retro'ku," his voice boomed. "Are you ready?"

There was nothing but the sound of clothes flapping in the wind.

The students looked around, wondering if Gabrael saw something that they didn't.

Then, they heard distant sounds of struggle: kicks, punches, and the clangs of metal.

A boy covered in flames dashed across the horizon, leaping into the air, creating a smoky trail. A shadow followed suit, jumping through the air, lunging in for a kick. The boy on fire blocked it and exchanged attacks of his own.

"Watch out!" Vayp shouted. He would have charge forward if not for Gabrael's tight grip on his robe. "What are you doing? Help him! It's one of them!" Vayp's eyes bulged.

The fighters attacked with blazing speeds. They moved so quickly they appeared as poofs of black smoke and sparks of fire bursting throughout the sky. Clacks and clangs and grunts and moans accompanied the rumbles of explosions.

Vayp looked around cluelessly, as if unable to track where they were.

Gabrael followed each strike, his eyes scanning the scene. *He's fast. Very fast. He may be ready.*

Gabrael shouted, "Enough!"

At once, the flame dispersed and the shadow faded into the ground.

Vayp's brows creased, as if he was angry and confused.

"He has no one else to train with," Gabrael said, releasing his grip. "The path of Fire, is the loneliest of the elements. He is the last of us; so, he trains with his shadow everyday. There is nothing wrong with being alone, if anything, that is when Fire feels most alive. As a student here, you learn that you are *never* alone . . . if you have yourself."

"I think that explains the screams that I heard," S'rae said to

Vayp. "He was training."

"How's that possible?" Vayp asked aloud.

Gabrael ignored the question and directed his focus toward Retro'ku. "Ready?"

Retro'ku ran toward Gabrael with a cheerful bounce and a wide smile, seeming like the type of boy who wouldn't even harm an insect. A thick, black fabric wrapped around his waist and over his left shoulder. Sweat glistened like glass against his dark skin, contouring his chiseled frame. "I don't know, Father." He smiled. His gaze met S'rae's. He stared at her like she was the only flower in a vast desert.

S'rae blushed, then dove behind a rock.

"You either are or you are not." Gabrael shook his head. "And you are not."

Retro'ku's shoulders drooped as he crouched down. He nodded, looking down at his big hands, open on his knees. "I'm sorry. Will you not look at me the same now that I am not?"

Vayp knew the look he spoke of. It was the gaze a proud father gave to his son. The one that said 'you are special' without a word being spoken. The one that faded away whenever he messed up during training.

"Of course," Gabrael said, sounding almost apologetic. "It is okay. You only get one chance, I want to make sure you are ready. Though we do not have much time left, I am not ready to say goodbye. Unfortunately, the brightest flames cast the darkest shadows."

Despite the disappointment, Gabrael's mouth curled into a smile. In a moment, it vanished like the time he thought they had. The color drained from his face, the fire in his eyes extinguished.

A loud, droning hum caught everyone's attention. Danger had arrived all too soon.

The students looked down at dozens of large shadows eclipsing over them.

A *boom* reverberated around the area, sounding like a wreck of mechanical noises all at once.

"Get to me," Gabrael shouted. "*NOW!*"

Dozens of red beams shone down on them from all angles, consolidating into one ray of light.

The students pressed their hands to their ears as the Valley roared like thunder.

When Gabrael looked up, he saw a sky filled with rockets. Their propulsion carried fumes that stank of oil and machinery.

"Protect it with your life!" Gabrael threw the book to Raaz'a. He caught it then dematerialized into ash as a swirl of smoke remained.

Gabrael lifted his hands and screamed with all of the force that his lungs allowed.

The ground tore open. Lava spewed out of the earth and filled the cracks like rivers.

The students' section broke away and separated. They were on an island amidst a moat of molten magma.

"*Su'rah-mo'to!*" Gabrael shouted, pressing his palms together. He thrust at the ground with his fist. It penetrated an inch at most; below that the solid earth melted around his fingers. He had his eyes closed only for a moment before opening them and freeing his hand into the air. "*Su'rah-mo'to!*"

His eyes burst into flames; fire spiraled around his body. The ground rumbled as flaming orbs mortared into the air. The sky exploded like a fireworks finale. It would've been a majestic moment if not for the toxic fumes in the air.

Gabrael clapped his hands together when lava spouted over the children, forming a barrier before engulfing them.

The strands of Gabrael's hair waved a fiery red, flowing in every direction as if they had a mind of their own. Sparks crackled from his fists. A flaming aura surrounded him, glowing almost as tall as a Mecha.

BANG! He rocketed through the sky, dodging missiles while shooting fire from his palms.

Around him soared dozens of Mechas with silvery metallic bodies and single red eyes painted with black symbols. They resembled robotic men with giant, dense feet and fists made for crushing. A pair of swords as long as their arms were strapped to their backs, crisscrossed.

But they were no match for the God of Fire. One by one, the Mechas fell lifelessly into the lava.

A hissing sound, like steam boiling out of a pot, reverberated through the sky.

BANG! A missile slammed into Gabrael's side, exploding at once. He fell like a comet, splashing into the lava. His body disintegrated instantly.

Moments passed and bubbles reached the surface before popping into a sizzle. A massive one formed out of the ripples, floating into the sky, dripping magma, like blood from a wound.

Dozens of red lasers scanned it as the orb soared higher. They unleashed rockets in response, which exploded around the orb.

It appeared unfazed. Then Gabrael's muffled scream was heard inside, growing in intensity until the orb burst open. In that instant, magma shot skyward, covering the entire area. What happened next was nothing short of horrifying. Gabrael had truly lost his mind. For miles and miles, volcanoes spawned from the ground and erupted, forming dark clouds and scattered lightning storms.

If there ever was a visual for what the end of the world looked like, this was it.

Gabrael's fingers twisted like arthritic hands. All of his training had led to this moment. He grabbed his hilt from his robe, grazing his fingers along the carving of a dragon. He extended his arms then forced his hands deep into his chest as if he grabbed his heart, slamming the base of the hilt into his breastbone.

Another explosion shattered the night. With an ear splitting scream, he slowly pulled a sword out of his chest. The lava broke into waves, splashing chaotically. Dark clouds swirled around him as he held the blazing sword in his hands. Its blade moved sporadically like a flame, but would erratically harden into a solid metal.

With bated breath, Gabrael looked at the Mechas. They suddenly seemed larger. "You dare come to the Valley and challenge the King?" he yelled. "Tell me something: Do machines like you fear death?" His blade combusted into a flame that sliced through a dozen Mechas.

With the burning blade in one hand and a glowing orb in the other, he soared by the Mechas, slashing and blasting his way through. The blade extended for a sweeping strike then would contract to the size of a dagger, over and over. His fingers twisted, manipulating the routes of his fireballs as they punctured the Mechas, melting them from the inside.

The more Mechas that fell, the more they were replaced. They poured in endlessly like water from a broken dam. Gabrael scrunched his eyebrows. *Is there no limit to this madness?*

He refused to admit it, but this was not good. His energy was finite, unlike Mechas.

He was supposed to somehow kill every single one? It was a mandman's task. But Gabrael was considered the crazy God for a reason. His only encouragement was that he saw no PriMechas.

Not yet, at least.

S'rae was surrounded by darkness and heavy breathing. She felt the hot breaths combine together, creating an uncomfortable sauna-like environment.

She felt weightless as if tossed into the air.

The momentum shifted immediately, toppling the students over one another.

"Get us out of here, Retro'whateverku," Vayp said.

"Me?" Retro'ku said.

"You're the only fire one!"

"Right. *Wuta-uwa.*"

Their barrier disappeared into ashes. S'rae's eyes widened, stunned to see what looked like the end of the world: lava, dark clouds, and lightning storms as far as she could see. Judging by the others' shocked faces, they had never seen such chaos, either.

Suddenly Gabrael's words flashed in her mind, *the valley, for what it really is.* For what it really is? She understood the moment she noticed the gray swirls that made up the ground? This was not a valley at all . . . This was an active volcano—the perfect fortress for a God of Fire. But it was S'rae's worst nightmare. *Fire consumes air.*

S'rae observed Retro'ku, standing like a statue of a god: muscular and in a battle-ready pose. His palms sizzled with fire. His black cloak was now red and moved like flames in the wind. He was handsome, and S'rae felt intimidated by his beauty, fiddling with her hair, looking for a rock to hide behind. But there was nothing. So she hid behind Vayp.

"It's not safe here," Retro'ku said. "This lava is too much. I cannot control it all."

"We need to help Gabrael!" S'rae poked her head out, then looked away nervously.

"Stop being so weird, S'rae." Vayp looked over his shoulder at her, then looked to the sky. "Look! More are coming! Can he win?"

She saw Gabrael slash through lines of Mechas, but they continued to stream into the Valley at a ferocious rate.

"He is a God, but he is only one." Retro'ku stared up at Gabrael. "She's right—we need to help."

"We can't do anything," the Sereni Sisters shrugged. "No water, and too much fire!"

"Me neither," Vayp replied.

"He's right," Kaul chimed in. "I don't think there is enough Earth." He and the other GroundStone students formed a triangle, touching one another's palms and chanting ancient scriptures. Their shoulders slouched after nothing happened.

This truly was the last battle for the Valley of Gaia because there was already nothing left, just an ocean of lava.

"What about you?" Retro'ku asked S'rae.

Her eyes widened in shock. His presence made her nervous.

"Fire consumes air," S'rae said, not making eye contact. "There's barely any left. It's impossible to control wind like this . . . I've tried. Too many times." She put her head down.

"You were chosen, right? You are one of the special ones. Anything is possible."

She felt giddy as her face went red.

"Okay, we got this!" Fujak said, blowing into his palms, rubbing his hands together. Aura'li and Chung joined in, exhaling in unison. They hardly created more than a breeze.

"That's not enough," Retro'ku said. "Help them out, *S'rae.*" Their eyes met with a piercing gaze.

While her heart raced when he said her name, her mind froze, thinking about the meaning behind S'rae. *A gift from the Divine.* That was her name. It was given to her. By her family. Though it wasn't her real family, it was as real as one could get. She never truly appreciated the home they had given her—the love they had shown. She felt terrible. They did everything a family should: sheltered her, clothed her, raised her as their own.

BANG! The ground trembled as if an asteroid crashed into the planet. Fear shot through S'rae as the rumble faded and the sound of electricity crackled behind her.

When she turned around, she saw exactly what she had dreaded: a Mecha.

She was too shocked to move. Her eyes widened as it lifted its giant hand, and a red orb glowed inside its palm.

"Get away!" Vayp roared, diving to S'rae. He clapped his hands before squatting as a stone wall formed around them.

BANG! The barrier deflected a red laser that burned into the base of the Spire.

At once, the GroundStone trio stomped their feet and pushed their arms forward. Boulders erupted from the ground and launched at the Mecha. They were hardly effective, like pebbles thrown at a rhino.

"Help us," Kaul shouted. A stream of mud traveled from the

ground to his forearm before hardening into a shield.

"We got this," said Fujak as wind burst from his clenched fist, transforming into a solid spear, and he dashed toward the robot. A gust of wind shot him through the air. Chung and Aura'li mimicked his action, digging their spears into the leg of the Mecha.

The Fujita trio then ran up the side of its body with blazing speeds.

"We need to help them," Adalia said, turning to her sisters.

"What do want us to do?" the twins asked.

Adalia thought for a second before lifting her head up with excitement. "Han'sael used his water weight to save me, we can do the same. I know it sounds disgusting, but there isn't enough water to do anything else." She pressed her palms together. "*Voda'cuerpo.*" Her face became sunken. Skin tightened around her high cheekbones as beads of water spiraled around.

Alaricea and Aralinda joined her. Within moments they amassed a large bubble of water that floated overhead. It then swirled into a pillar that crystallized into a giant trident.

S'rae watched the GroundStone students launch rocks and boulders, the Fujitas soaring around, evading each of the Mecha's strikes, and the Sereni Sisters channeling a powerful spell. She needed to help them, but when she looked at Retro'ku, his narrowed eyes were focused on the sky. On his father, Gabrael, who blazed through the air like a comet. But she understood the concern in Retro'ku's eyes; she saw that Gabrael was fighting a battle he would never win.

Her mind then went blank as she examined more of her surroundings, watching the Mechas fly above. Everything finally came to her. Her focus had been on Eve, Elu, the scream, the story, and the traitor. The present, not the past. She was reminded of Vayp and his story. Of the massacre. Of the bodies sprawled across the floor.

A family that wasn't her own, but took her in with open arms, giving her light in a dark world.

The Mechas ruined all of that.

S'rae fell to her knees, the sorrow weighing her down. Her heart vibrated as the reality of her loss finally dawned on her. *They destroyed the only home that I had.* It was a fear she always had buried within her: losing the only family she had known. A breeze drifted across her face, her hair danced to its rhythm. *They destroyed my village.* A gust of wind slowly swirled around her feet. *They destroyed my brother.* Her palms crackled with lightning as she pushed her clenched fists forward. A staff made of wind appeared in her outstretched hands. They made one mistake. She rose to twirl the staff. It cut through the air like a knife, more powerful than any staff she had ever created. A howling flurry rushed around her, flapping her clothes. "They messed with the wrong family!" she yelled as a flash of white waved behind her eyes, seeing particles in the sky appear as foreign colors. Atoms.

And when she slammed the staff into the ground, a tornado as tall as the Spire and as wide as her village channeled down from the sky.

Fujak, Aura'li, and Chung froze. Their clothes and hair flurried about. With jaws dropped, they gazed at the descending storm, as if it was the largest they'd ever seen.

Tears floated from S'rae's face. "I. WILL. AVENGE. THEM!" Her eyes turned white as she levitated into the air.

"Impossible!" Fujak screamed over the whirling noises. "How . . ."

"Amazing!" Retro'ku said.

Overhead, Gabrael fought tirelessly until a black and red PriMecha spawned out of the clouds.

The PriMecha showed its mechanical heart as its chest opened up, a deep growl pouring from the hole. It lowered its shoulders, a move that somehow seemed both defensive and offensive at the same time.

BANG! A brilliant light beam shot out, destroying Mechas in the blast radius and swallowing up Gabrael.

Like water through the cracks of fingers, it seemed like Gabrael's life ebbed away.

The students watched Gabrael fall toward the ground as rapidly as a blazing comet.

"Father needs help!" Retro'ku screamed. "It's now or never!"

The whirling gust grew massive, making its way deep into the lava, turning into a flaming tornado.

Retro'ku placed his palms together, muttering words. "*Babban'hadari.*" His eyes emitted a red glow that formed into steam. He placed his hands at his sides. "*Mo . . . toh . . . kaaa!*"

BANG! Flames shot out from the tornado. Before Gabrael crashed to the ground, the twister launched a slew of meteors, spiraling by him as they rocketed toward the Mechas.

Retro'ku floated around S'rae, chanting louder. In a matter of seconds, the storm drained the lava, leaving empty craters, and filling the air with stars of fire shooting through space.

Gabrael cratered into the ground. The crimson glow that engulfed him faded away. The fire in his eyes vanished. His flaming hair was doused, drooping over his face as solid dark strands.

As S'rae and Retro'ku channeled their spells and Gabrael lay on the floor, the Mecha targeted the weakened King of Gods and opened its palms. Its body hummed as its canon charged up for another blast.

This was the end of Gabrael's story.

The hum magnified into a roar as a massive ball of nuclear energy formed at the Mecha's hands.

"Now is our chance!" Adalia screamed. "We only have one shot!" A blue aura formed around the Sereni Sisters. The twins stood on either side of the trident, their eyes closed and hands pressed forward. The trident was angled upward, straight at the Mecha. At its rear, Adalia pulled it back, loading it up like a crossbow.

Then the ground swirled around the Mecha's legs.

"We won't be able to hold it here for long," Vayp screamed. "Shoot it now!"

The Sereni Sisters screamed as the trident blasted forward, rippling the air like a torpedo through water. Two of its points shot into the opening of the Mecha's palms, and the middle point burst straight through its eye. The red lights on the Mecha faded to black. Its body crashed down, cracking the terrain open.

The students cautiously stepped toward the Mecha, as if to see if it was really dead, then quickly turned their attention to Retro'ku's ear-splitting scream. It erupted like the lava that surrounded him in waves. He screamed until the sky was filled with fire. Then he kept screaming until it was empty. Until every last Mecha melted away. His narrowed, red eyes looked like they belonged to a devil, not the angel S'rae considered him to be. But they faded back to brown as he collapsed to the ground.

S'rae fell in a similar way.

"We did it!" Fujak and Vayp said, hugging each other. After a moment, reality settled in, and they shoved each other away, brushing off their clothes.

The lava drained out through the cracks, revealing a torn terrain and mountains that had never previously existed.

With swift gestures, Vayp helped the other GroundStone students seal up some of the cracks. "That was. . . *awesome!*" he screamed.

The voices hit S'rae in distorted waves. Her eyes were closed

and she remained in a dreamlike state. The warmth that surrounded her was too comfortable to leave. The voices sounded again. "You were amazing, S'rae! We won! We actually did it!"

S'rae nodded, but she couldn't bring herself to speak. There were no words. Only the prickling sensation left behind.

"Are you okay?" A fuzzy voice was heard. She blinked her eyes to find Fujak hunching over her, appearing upside-down.

She reluctantly forced her eyes open and found herself cuddled next to Retro'ku. Was it him that she felt? It was more than his body heat that kept her warm. That was physical. The sensation she felt was as if he warmed her up from the inside.

Disoriented and confused, she let her eyes roam across the Valley. The entire world felt like it was spinning, fast. "We won?" S'rae gasped.

"Yes." Vayp came to her side. "You don't remember what just happened?"

"I . . . don't know."

"Well, you missed out, because you were awesome!"

"You uncovered the secret," Gabrael said. "You overcame your fear. Now you must learn how to control it."

Pride and honor and pain swirled in her chest when Gabrael placed his hand on her shoulder. Not trusting herself to speak, she remained silent. This way nothing could ruin her moment. She placed her hands on top of her head and inhaled the familiar scent of burned charcoal and ash.

"Impressive." Gabrael stumbled to his feet. "Great things happen when elements come together. You all were exceptional. I am proud of you, son." He approached Retro'ku with a smile though his body seemed drained of energy.

"Thank you," Retro'ku said, rubbing his neck and smiling sheepishly. "I couldn't have done it without S'rae. She deserves the credit." He peeled off charred clothing and S'rae lowered her eyes—she was used to seeing Fujak and Chung show off their bodies when training in the wind tunnels, but there were muscles on Retro'ku's body that she didn't even know existed.

A warm flush rose to her cheeks as she realized that her eyes and jaw were locked open for too long. She wiped the drool from her lips, then squealed, diving behind Vayp.

Retro'ku turned and surveyed the area, unable to find her.

Vayp turned to her. Though he stiffened at first, he held her tight, squeezing away the pain. He pulled back to say more, but stopped as his nostrils flinched and eyes blackened.

She had seen that look from him before . . .

Vroommm! A rumble roared overhead, infinitely louder than the previous ones.

And the peace that had begun to descend over the students separated, just as their hugs did. Their smiles turned to frowns, and creaks and roars of exhaust filled the sky.

They lifted their heads as hundreds, maybe thousands, of Mechas appeared in formation.

One could wipe out a village. An army . . . the world. She remembered Fujita's teachings of how dangerous the Mechas were. How their technology was so beyond our understanding, there was a myth about them being an advanced race from another planet. Then she remembered what Gabrael taught her: *You'd be surprised at how many truths rests in myths.* But this group of Mechas didn't seem like an army . . . it looked like every last one of them. This was the end of their stories. She was sure of it.

38

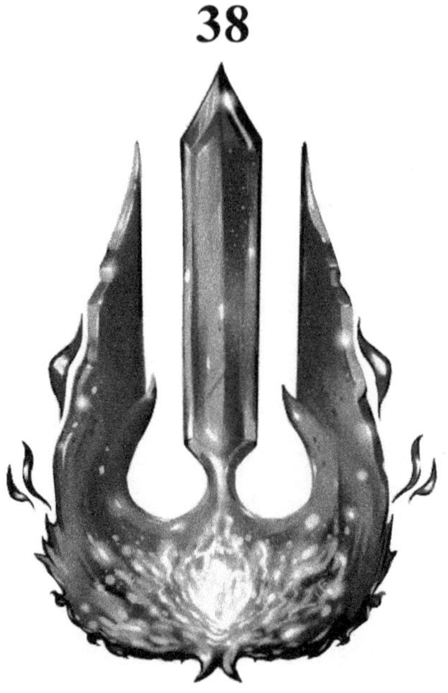

GABRAEL DID NOT WANT TO SHOW ON HIS FACE exactly what his mind knew. The students needed faith, not fear. But there were too many Mechas for one God to handle.

The shimmer of the slaughtering machines spanned as far as their eyes could see. There was more metal in the sky than clouds.

Gabrael knew that he did not have enough energy left to fight. And even if he was at full health, he was unsure if it'd be enough.

He struggled to form words. "Students . . . the time has come." He knelt down on the ground, waving off the flickering flames attached to his clothes. "I am sorry."

S'rae jumped to her feet as a staff of wind shot out from her palms, ready to fight at a moment's notice.

Thousands of red beams targeted Gabrael. He waved off S'rae and knelt inside of the red ray of light.

This cannot be the end to our story.

The thunderstorms overhead ravaged louder.

Lightning struck and thunder boomed. Rain fell, though just a drizzle.

The storm crackled again, sending dozens of spiderwebs of lightning overlapping through the clouds.

"It cannot be . . ." Gabrael gasped.

Lightning *boomed* again numerous times, followed immediately by thunder. The storm was nearly over him. The rain turned into a downpour.

Sweat and water rained down from his hair onto his forehead. His eyes caught a flash of lightning and a sharp pressure clamped his heart.

Immediately, another white light boomed overhead, fissures of lightning crackling across the red sky. The rain poured down harder, and then another clap of thunder erupted.

The students shared the same awestruck expression, widened eyes and dropped jaws.

BANG! A burst of lightning struck within a foot of Gabrael. Debris blasted into the air, but rather than falling, the pieces remained frozen in place. The looks on the students' faces were locked. Their drifting hair and clothes were unmoving. Raindrops appeared as scattered crystals floating in the sky.

Slowly, the line of lightning, stretching from the ground to sky, molded itself into a malleable orb, contouring into different shapes. The sparks began to pull something from the ruptured soil. An amorphous head emerged. Then shoulders. Then chest. Then legs and feet. It continued moving until definite features revealed themselves. Long white hair. Piercing, angular eyes: one was sky blue and the other pearl white. The pearly eye was coated over by a scar covering a quarter of his face. His clothes appeared from the sparks. He wore a similar cloak to Gabrael's except his was white that moved with a metallic shimmer.

"It has been a while," came a booming, deep voice but his mouth didn't move.

"I thought you were gone," Gabrael replied, his mouth unmoving still.

"I would have been if not for Yosh'i."

"Does he know the truth about—"

"He does not."

"I thought I lost you . . ." Gabrael said. Everything around him remained still. And in one flash, the scene distorted, ripping away earth and sky, until all that remained was blackness, a void of ether, where they were the last two beings left in an empty galaxy painted with lightning.

"You haven't yet, but you will. You will lose me just as we have lost hundreds of thousands of lives if you continue to stay here. We need you, brother. The world needs you! The Mechas have started a war, massacring villages while you stay here."

"I know now, but I cannot leave, Vy'ken."

"Why? Because of that book? That's absurd! The innocent are being eradicated and all you care about are senseless words on a page?"

"The shadows are trying to stop it from being read for a reason. You were once a believer in its words, too. You were the one who convinced me to find it, remember?"

"That was my fault. I should have convinced you to leave with me. Do not let the world suffer for my mistake. It is a book written by man and man has flaws."

"Its words are bound by the elements, Vy'ken! The elements! Men are incapable of such a thing! There is no greater sign. The truth lies in its words. And with time I will be able to find its secret to save time."

"Save time? You don't care about saving our world but you care about saving time? The truth is that for every second you spend here with that foolish doctrine, thousands are dying a horrible death. We need you! They need us: the Elementials, the protectors! We swore by it. The elements need to stick together to overcome this, or we need to run to survive."

"Who are we to run to, brother? The ones designed to protect the world are the ones slaughtering it."

"They are my mistake and I have lived in its shadows of regret for many years. I should have let them die off instead of study them."

"I am not just talking about the Mechas, Vy'ken."

"I am sorry that I made you obsessed with this false prophecy. I am sorry that I forced it upon you, but, brother, please, the world is dying. Why must you allow your pride to let the world crumble along with it? At least let me take the children. Let me save them. There is time."

"You know that I need them for this. They are our most gifted pupils; their destinies are of the utmost importance."

"Utmost importance? What is more important than the present?"

"The future. Eve. Nature. She's dying. *They* are killing her with each species that fades to oblivion. She feels their pain. If we fail, darkness will consume her. And the universe. We cannot let it happen again."

"It is already too late, then."

"If it is too late, then at least the book has the answer. Eve swears by it. We need to find out how to defeat the darkness. And the monster inside—it has been done once. This anomaly child, Destrou, found a way, and we need to find out how!"

"Oh, brother, you and this fascination with the boy who never lived! What if time does reset? What is the harm in being given another chance at life? What is so wrong in being brothers again?"

"That is the problem, brother! You think only of yourself! What of the ones less fortunate? What of the slaves forced to watch their children killed before their very eyes, their wives touched by another man. What of centuries of tortures and pillages that occurred? Why must they relive such terrible trauma, billions of times? For what? So you can enjoy an eternity?"

Vy'ken said nothing.

"It is not the way the Divine One intended life to be lived," Gabrael said.

"*WE* are the divine ones! WE are the Gods! And *YOU* are supposed to be our King!"

"*We* are Gods yet we are troubled by our creation? *We* are Gods but we are not perfect. Where did *we* come from? What created us? *We* are Gods but who governs the galaxy? Surely not us! How are we the Gods of planets we have never set foot on! There is something much greater. I know it and you once believed it. We have lived billions of times. Too many times. Who are we to control who should be given the right to live? Let others be given that chance!"

"Why? So they can have the same pain and misery that humanity is experiencing now?"

"*Let them have their pain!* Let them have their misery, too. But like all humans, they will also experience love—the first moment that took their breath away as well as the last. They will have their joys with their sorrows. They will have their cries as well as laughter. This world was ruined long before the Mechas were recreated. I am a King yet I did not want to rule over us. That was never my intention. I wanted happiness for us all: the elements and our people. But life was destroyed when we focused on hate and fear as a means to bring people together instead of love and peace. We live in a world where they are divided without realizing that we all came from the same place. We were not designed to hate one another, we were meant to love."

Gabrael observed his surroundings, the darkness and the lightning strikes scattered around, then into Vy'ken's eyes, as if hoping he was going to tell him something. But he didn't, so he went on. "But greed damaged the world and corrupted their minds. They desired to make the world better with advancements but then needed to find the cures for the problems that they created. There was this desire to do more without realizing it took away more than it gave. By giving them great technology, it took away their freedoms. By giving them the ability to travel anywhere, it took away the concept of home. More than vanity they needed acceptance. More than searching endlessly for love they needed to love themselves. Focusing on machinery, they lost sight of humanity. Focusing on humanity, they lost sight of nature. Instead of living freely with nature, they chose to destroy it without realizing that is the one Divine God they should protect. They became the machines and the machines the people."

Gabrael threw a sharp glance at Vy'ken, seeing the pain and regret in his watering eyes. "And now the 'people' who protected the world are the ones slaughtering it. For what? For a life of comfort yet sacrificing health? Of ease yet lacking human interaction? They aimed for intelligence yet lost their knowledge—knowledge of a better life that existed once before. The world was over long before the Mechas came. I do not wish for the end, I wish for a beginning. A new beginning that never existed."

It seemed that Gabrael had reached the point he was most anxious to discuss, the real reason he had been so passionate about his prophecy. His voice had never cracked with as much emotion as it did now. He hoped for a response, but Vy'ken did not answer.

"A beginning beyond the Last Great War," Gabrael pressed on, "where prosperity triumphs over despair and the word 'enemy' no longer describes family. Where we live life the way the Divine One designed it. The enemy is all around us and it shouldn't be. Family is. Why should they die by their own hands and not the hands of time? We cannot fix the problems using the same minds that we used to create them. Each time this moment has happened we failed. But inside these creased pages of time there is an answer. I promise you . . . there is an answer! A way that we have never seen before. So when I say that there is something more important than the present it is because the present is already the past. We need to stop taking steps back for each step that we think we are moving forward. Instead, we must step back and see how this Evil was finally destroyed in the past, so we can prevent *time* from being destroyed in the future. This book has that answer! This is bigger than any one of us . . . even Gods. Something special happened. We could either pretend that it never happened and let this book and its secret perish with all life . . . or we can use it to save the future."

Silence.

"I forgive you, brother," Gabrael said.

Nothing.

"I forgive you, Vy'ken. And I am glad that I was given the chance to tell you."

After a few more moments of silence, Vy'ken's voice was slow and deep. "I will take care of the Mechas, brother, but don't make me regret saving you. By coming here another village was lost. Don't let their deaths be in vain."

"I will not. Thank you," Gabrael said. "By you saving us, we may finally be able to win the Last Great War."

BANG! The lightning strike vanished as if it was never there.

The students watched in awe as the streaks of light filled the sky.

"Our time here is done. GroundStone, shield us," Gabrael said with such conviction that no questions were asked. The burned remains of the Spire and his land reminded Gabrael of a graveyard. It was eerie to walk toward the students. This place that flourished long ago with vibrant nature and animals of all walks of life and families of all races now sat dead as a grim reminder. It became a blackened memorial of a time that once was considered peace.

Vayp waved his arms around then pressed his palms together. A hole opened underfoot and as if on cue, everyone met in its center, disappearing as the earth closed above them.

BANG! Crack! BANG! The Mechas fell as lightning surged into an army of pillars, sweeping through the entire area. Some Mechas tried to flee but they never stood a chance. Thunder reverberated throughout the Valley as the hole sealed shut.

"This isn't good-bye," Gabrael whispered in darkness. "This is only the beginning . . ."

39

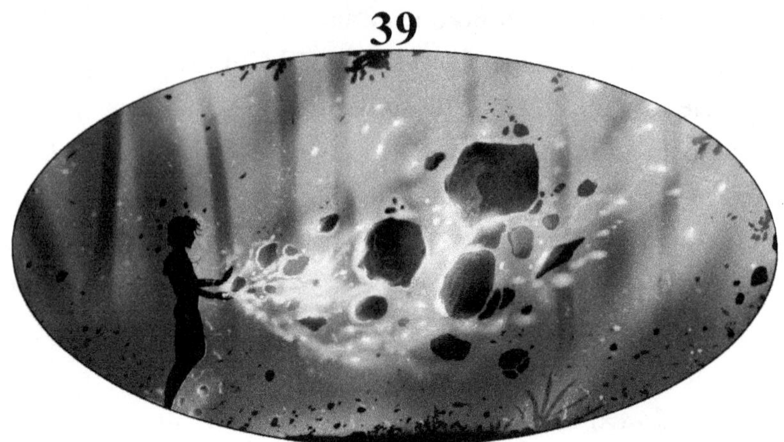

THE EARTH SHOOK AND TORE OPEN, like a spear piercing through a shield. Vayp's arms lifted as the platform rose to ground level. The courtyard was abandoned now, and the slanting light from the moon cast strange shadows throughout the metallic graveyard. The Valley was filled with Mechas, some melted into pieces, others still intact as if unharmed, but their normally red eyes now blackened graphite. Vayp felt a weight lift from his chest. Partly because he felt like he had proven himself during his time at the Valley. It wasn't a mistake why he was selected. He did belong. And then he smiled because he never thought that seeing such death would bring him joy. But did these monsters have a soul to be considered dead, or were they just broken?

He looked down at a Mecha. There was a ticking sound from within that reminded him of a dying heart; it kept beating slower and slower until it stopped. He visualized the air and fuel moving through its tubes before being burned, then dispelling into the atmosphere, like carbon dioxide from his lungs. He realized it mirrored his own body. They were not so dissimilar, this machine and him. He could almost feel how alive they really were. And that was why it brought him so much joy to see it no longer functioning. No longer alive. But why did he suddenly feel different? His stomach tightened. If he did not feel joy, then what?

Vayp stared at this *thing* created by man and almost felt sympathy for it. It did not choose this life, it was a pawn forced into it, just like he was forced to leave his family. This machine had a heart like him. A voice like him. And now Vayp realized it could die . . . like him.

He felt connected to it in an unexplainable way. Its life, its victimhood, and its . . . metal?

The Mechas weren't evil. The ones controlling them were. They didn't deserve this.

And though he witnessed the aftermath of the battle, Vayp knew the war had only begun.

"It is important for you students to know the truth," Gabrael said, grabbing the book from Raaz'a who had emerged from a poof of smoke. "Our time here at the Valley of Gaia is done. Our quest will move on to a new area—one that even I am unsure of." His eyes focused on a pair of metallic legs, which poked out upside down from the earth and flinched. "Retro'ku, my son, you have proven to be ready. Are you?"

There was silence all around except for the few sparks that crackled from the Mechas' exposed wires. There was a whole sea of them, toppling over one another like metallic mountains. The smell of fuel hung everywhere.

Retro'ku stepped forward, solemn, his face hidden by a shroud. He pulled his hood off. In his hand he gripped a black cloth, which he raised and wrapped around his shaved head.

Gabrael walked over to Retro'ku and placed his hand on his shoulder. "It is time."

Retro'ku's expression remained neutral but there was a glow of confidence in his eyes. His eyebrows were flat, his eyes unmoving yet focused.

Gabrael directed the students to a chamber underneath what was left of the Spire. The spiraling staircase was dark and dry and hot. Steam seeped out of the cracks between the cobblestones. Vayp asked Raaz'a where they were going, but he was ignored.

They climbed down the final stairs and arrived at the bottom, staggering into the scorching dry air. Beads of sweat dripped down Vayp's face.

Gabrael walked to the gigantic double doors that reflected the flickering golden lights all around. In the center was a hole no bigger than a fist, which Gabrael placed his hand into. His palm sizzled and crackled, and the smell of burned flesh filled the air. White smoke poured out from underneath, filling up the hallway. The smells of tar and ash joined the burned flesh.

The door hissed reluctantly, as if this was its first time ever opening. Beyond it, rather than a room, there was a wall of pure darkness. No light entered or exited. Vayp felt an uneasy skip to his heart as he looked into it. Surprisingly, the void didn't remind him of his nightmares; instead, his heart wept for Han'sael. The void reminded him of something that had been taken away from him. An emptiness. He saw his friendship with Han'sael as a seed taken out of the ground before being given the chance to bloom. And now it was gone. He wiped the sweat and tears with his palm and watched Retro'ku step toward the wall. There was an awkward silence in the air, the type that one experienced at a wake; everyone had questions, but no one wanted to talk.

Retro'ku clenched his fists, though a smile broke onto his face. "Do you think I'm ready?"

"You are more ready than I would be," Gabrael said with saddened eyes that told a story of worry. Vayp had seen those eyes before—they were the ones that his father had when he refused to give him away to the schooling system. They were the ones that said how Gabrael had always enjoyed the safety that the Valley provided him; he never had to worry about Retro'ku, and as much as he'd always wanted to escape its walls, he preferred the familiar comfort that his son was safe. "Be careful in there. Remember to use everything that I've taught you—even the abilities you cannot use in our world." The confidence in his voice started to crack. Though his voice was quiet, it pierced through Vayp with such emotion that his eyes started to water without him knowing. "Remember . . . the brightest flames cast the darkest shadows. I cannot witness this happen to you, too. There is no second chance, but this isn't goodbye."

"He wasn't ready though." Retro'ku nodded and walked toward the darkness, holding out his slender hands, as if bracing himself for a fall. "I am." The wall rippled like a rock through a puddle of ink. And with a shadowy flash, void of light, he was gone.

Immediately, the hall shook furiously.

Vayp held on to S'rae to brace himself, and in that moment, when their eyes met, he felt normal. The comfort of home that had long abandoned him. She was there, bearing the same markings under her eyes, the mark of their village. The last of the Opella, of Earthies who specialized in tracking and hunting—its memory and heritage lived on through them. And, like Gabrael, he never wanted to say good-bye.

Vayp snapped back to reality when a fireball flew out of the darkness. The pupils dove out of the way as it cratered into the stone floor, like an asteroid. The fire was at least ten feet high with no sign of stopping. Slowly, it molded into large wings that expanded off of a crouching body amidst the blaze. Black smoke erupted from its body. Deep gashes revealed themselves across its arms, legs, and torso, glowing like hot iron. The smell of blood and burning flesh filled the air. In between the roars of the flames, there were sizzles, as if the blood was coming to a boil before evaporating. The body shook and dug its fingers into the soil. Molten lava formed at its fingertips.

The room went silent and the only thing Vayp heard was the blood pounding in his ears.

After a few moments, the figure arched up, revealing a muscular physique. His chest expanded as if his lungs were trying to escape. The flames extinguished, revealing a naked body that pulsated like hot embers. Vayp noticed how red the girls' faces had become. He knew it wasn't because of the heat.

Vayp even noticed the GroundStone trio blush as Kaul bit the corner of his lip. Surprisingly, the one who didn't stare was the girl—her brown eyes seemed fixed on S'rae.

"Yup! I will take two of him to go, please, and thank you," the one who looked like a boy said. "Three thousand years would *not* be long enough with this fine specimen."

Vayp shook his head. When the thick smoke and the crackles and sizzles faded, Retro'ku stood panting and shaking.

"What happened?" Vayp said. "You were only gone for a second!" His eyes landed on a small red orb resting in Retro'ku's hand. Beautifully crafted.

"Really?" Retro'ku might've said more, but his breath was short as he struggled to regain it. He limped over to Gabrael, handing him the orb that flickered like a fire burned inside of it. Vayp's jaw dropped. More bright than anything he had ever seen. The size of his fist, it shone with yellows, reds, and oranges blazing within its smooth exterior.

"You okay?" S'rae said, stepping closer to Retro'ku.

"Interesting," Fujak said curiously. "And can you put some clothes on?" He frowned.

Vayp chuckled at the irony of Fujak, the show-off, as if he was mad that Retro'ku made his ripped abdomen look like a deflated balloon.

"It felt like I was in there for hours," Retro'ku said. For a moment it seemed like he was relatively pain-free. Then, straining, he lifted his arm to crack his neck, and blood dripped down, splashing on the warm floor.

"Oh Divine!" S'rae said, pulling her cloak off, wrapping it around him.

"Thank you." Retroku's eyes met hers and silence hung in the air. Vayp noticed the redness in S'rae's cheeks evolve to cover her whole face. "Even though I thought I was going to die . . . that was the most fun I've ever had."

"That's it! I'm in." Fujak stepped forward.

"In what?" Chung and Aura'li said.

"I want in on this adventure."

"You crazy? Your dad won't let you," Chung replied with wide eyes.

"I don't see my dad anywhere. If I want to, no one is stopping me. Especially not you."

"But—"

"I thought I was like Elu the whole time, trapped, unable to be myself. But I'm not." He pounded his fists together, appearing frustrated. "I didn't want to admit it, but I realized I'm really more like the person I hated the most: the Leader. And then—" He looked away, rubbing his eyes. "I realized I'm actually worse than him. I saw myself as a random villager. A follower. Like I've been my whole damn life. But for the first time, I don't feel the pressure to live up to my name. I can escape, find myself." He paused, then turned to look at S'rae. "I guess no one ever thinks they're the bad guy in someone else's story. But now I see it. And I'm sorry."

A smile widened on Gabrael's face, as if Fujak was the last person he'd expect to join. "That takes a lot of courage to admit. Your father would be proud." He nodded at Fujak. "Anyone else? This is a dangerous quest, but it is also a great destiny. You will have the chance to have your story be told as the warriors who saved Time."

Vayp wanted to say something. His muscles were strained so tightly, they felt like they'd snap at any moment. The idea of Fujak having more courage than him made his teeth clench to the breaking point.

Gabrael scanned the students for a few moments before speaking again. "Fair enough." His voice became soft. He placed the orb into a socket on the book, and it caught fire; words burned themselves onto the cover and throughout its pages. "*His* story will be told."

S'rae stepped forward. "You're not going to have all the fun," she said to Fujak, smirking. "Plus, I realized the same thing. I always thought you and Chung and Aura'li . . . and pretty much everyone else at Fujita were the most evil things ever created—"

"Hey!" Aura'li pouted.

"I'm sorry." S'rae brushed the ground with her foot. "I never realized how mean I was to you at first. I was in a terrible place. I left my home on bad terms . . . and I took it out on everyone else. You all were so nice to me at first. It's easy to forget the good times when you only focus on the bad."

Fujak stepped forward, his eyes glancing at something cupped in his palm. "Here," he said, reaching his hand out. "Not that it matters anymore, but I think it's right for you to know."

S'rae hesitated, her trembling hands clutched her robe before Fujak gently grabbed her wrist. He peeled back her clenched fingers and placed a metallic orb on her palm.

When she squeezed her hand, it dissolved into an ivory bird that said in a cheerful voice, "Congratulations, S'rae, you have been accepted into our prestigious Elemental Program."

She burst into tears, wrapping her arms around Fujak. His arms opened wide and he froze momentarily as if he did not know where to place them. "I did it! I really did it!"

"You did." Fujak slowly placed his arms around her. "You deserved it more than anyone."

When Vayp managed to pull himself away from the memories he had with S'rae and Ah'nyx, he was shocked to see that S'rae had joined, but more surprised to see that they were hugging. He thought only for a few seconds of what life would be like without her again, and he stepped forward.

Their eyes met. "Friends stick together." S'rae smiled, twisting her body toward Vayp. "Let's start a new adventure, together. Just like the good ol' days!"

"You're not my friend, S'rae," Vayp said. Pressure swelled up behind his eyes.

"What?" S'rae choked. Her body went stiff like a board. Vayp noticed her smile tremble.

"Han'sael is my friend . . ."

S'rae looked down at the floor, appearing devastated.

"But," he said, pushing her chin up, "you're . . . my sister."

He was shaking harder than she was.

Her head rose slowly, her eyes twinkling.

"Family sticks together," Vayp said.

There was a collective gasp.

S'rae smiled as a shriek tore from her lips. "I've never heard you say that before."

"Family sticks together?"

"I'm your sister." She burst into tears, wrapping her arms around Vayp.

"I love you," Vayp said, tears pouring down his face. *You're all I have*, he longed to say.

"I love you, too." S'rae dug her face into his shoulder, soaking his clothes. "I'm so glad you came back!" Her smile was so wide that she winced, holding her jaw for a moment. She understood how Destrou felt getting his brother back into his life. It was surreal, she couldn't contain her excitement. "Umm, I really don't want to ruin the moment but—"

"You already did." Vayp smirked.

"No, but listen, just hear me out, okay! It sounded *really* cool, soooo . . . can you call me your sister again? Just one more time!" She danced around before placing her hands on her hips.

She smiled awkwardly for what felt like an eternity.

"Nope." Vayp laughed. "It felt weird. Don't get used to it."

"Okay, *brother*." S'rae giggled and pushed her hands together, covering up her reddish cheeks. "Okay, this is officially the best day ever, mark it on your calendars! Let's do this! Let's do this! Let's save Time!"

Vayp smiled and his stomach twisted. "That's what family does, right? They forgive one another." He felt his voice trail off. He held his breath to stop more tears from forming.

"Yes." S'rae shot him a look, trying to see if it was genuine or if there was another meaning behind it. It was genuine, but very unlike him to say something like that. She did know Vayp well, after all. She pressed her lips together and then smiled. "That's what we do."

"Touching," Gabrael said impatiently. "But we must move along. Anyone else?"

The Sereni Sisters glanced at one another. "Sorry, we cannot.

Family sticks together," they said almost in unison. There was a slight mumble that came from one of them.

"That's understandable. I'd expect nothing less from a Sereni."

"What happens if we choose to not go?" Ada said. Ala and Ara, the twins, stepped back with a gasp.

"You go back to your school and—" Gabrael replied.

"And?"

"You drink this." He pulled out a vial the size of his finger. It contained a dark, thick substance, like blood.

A salty scent reached Vayp's nostrils that was so familiar it sent chills up his spine. Where had he smelled that before? The vial. What was inside it? He had to ask. "I feel like I've had that before, what is it?"

"This?" Raaz'a giggled, pulling out a vial of his own. "Oh my, I assure you, it's impossible that you have come across this. This is the only place you will find it. Plus, you wouldn't remember even if you did." He waved the vial in front of Vayp's face.

In that instant, flashes of blurred images burned through his skull. He shook his head to clear his thoughts. "You sure? Why's that?"

"Because." Raaz'a's voice deepened. "No one has access to this. It is the most powerful brew Time has ever created. It comes from the blood of an Archon." He waved the vial across Vayp's face once more before putting it back into the pocket of his robe.

"I'm sorry." Ada looked back at her sisters. "If all of this is true, then they'll need at least one of us. Besides, I do not want to forget about Han'sael. Not what he did for me. And if what Vayp said is also true, then I'm sticking with them to help bring him back. I want in!"

"But family sticks together," Ala said.

"Well," Ada said and smiled. "At least you'll be the prettiest

now."

Both Ala and Ara were taken aback with joy.

"Wait, she was definitely talking to me," Ala said.

"Ew, you wish. We all know I'm the prettiest," Ara said. They then kissed each other twice on the cheeks before focusing on Ada. "We'll miss you so much."

"I'll miss you more."

The twins puffed their chests, crossed their arms, then turned away from her. "Hmmph."

"Interesting, Adalia," Gabrael said, placing his hand on her shoulders. "I see fire in your eyes."

"Please—" Adalia said, looking back at her sisters as if expecting approval. They nodded at her. "Call me Lynn."

"You're brave, Vayp," Kaul said, stepping forward, "but I can't go." He rested his hand on Vayp's shoulder. This was the first time they had ever touched each other without it being a fight. It felt weird. Nice, but weird. "I'm glad I finally got to see how great you are."

Vayp crossed his arms, not wanting Kaul to think he wanted a hug.

But Kaul didn't hug him. He did something more. His head jerked up and lifted his fist to his shoulder. Unable to explain how, Vayp responded in the same way. One fist to Kaul's shoulder and the other to his own shoulder. *My first musafa*, he wanted to say.

"You're a very special Earthie," another GroundStone student said, walking up to Vayp, giving him a hug. It was awkward for Vayp, not because of how embarrassing it was to be called a very special Earthie, but because he had absolutely no idea if the student was a boy or a girl. And had no idea what *his* name was. Vayp had never introduced himself to anyone. It made sense not to. It was easier to not care about what happened to someone if he didn't know their names. The same day Vayp had accepted that everyone dies, that it was inevitable, was when he realized a stranger's death was bearable, but a friend's would crush him.

But he then reflected on what S'rae told Fujak and realized that he himself may have been the bad guy in others' stories. Much like S'rae, the students at GroundStone had approached him with open arms, excited to learn about the unique types of spells that people from Opella mastered—each Village had their own specialty. They were friendly and curious. Maybe too curious. They had no idea how sensitive it was to bring up his past, his Sol, or his village. He always met curiosity with fury and rage. They weren't the jerks, he was. He was even terrible to Han'sael at first, for no reason.

He didn't deserve it. No one deserves to be treated like that.

But that was why Ranmau was Vayp's favorite. Like himself, Ranmau was misunderstood. But he was also willing to die for the ones he loved, even if he never showed that he loved them. He'd like to believe that through all the bad, the trauma, and the rage, he was a broken spirit with a good heart. He wanted to believe it for himself, even though no one else would.

"T-thank you." Vayp said to the boy, struggling to not say something sarcastic. "You'll all do great things at GroundStone. And in an odd way, I'll miss all of you." Vayp had something that he had been dying to get off his chest. "By the way, what are you? Are you a boy or a girl?"

"I'll be whatever you want me to be, honey." The student winked. "Oh, and by the way." *She* leaned in close to Vayp's ear. "I thought you were ridiculously hot when you were a bad boy. But now that you're kinda normal . . . you're more like lukewarm. Still cute, though. But I'm going to miss the old you. If you ever want a fun time, find me." *He* winked.

"I'm normal now?" Vayp may have said more if it weren't for

the fresh memories that still troubled him. He shook his head, pushing the thoughts away.

"So, it is settled, then," Gabrael said. "Vayp, S'rae, Fujak, Ada—I mean Lynn—, and Retro'ku. We have assembled the team that will save Time. I shall call you the Time Savers!"

Vayp's cringe was mimicked by everyone else. They shook their heads in unison.

"Okay, I admit I am not the greatest at naming things. Forget I ever said that," Gabrael said, rubbing his neck. "But Raaz'a and I will be sure to protect you all with our lives. Thank you for believing in me, this story, and your destiny."

"You will be in the greatest of hands." Raaz'a's voice heightened as he clapped excitedly.

"So where are we off to?" Fujak said. There was a new energy to his voice.

"Good question." Gabrael paused. "I wish I knew the answer." An awkward silence hung in the air. "Odd. Eve should have left us a clue. It could be anything out of the ordinary, big or small."

S'rae walked forward, reaching into her pocket. She had her head down, as if she felt guilty. When she approached Gabrael, a white orb rested in her hands.

"Is that"—Gabrael gasped—"the . . . Eye of Eve?"

A bright white light radiated from her palms.

"How . . . when—how did you find this?" Gabrael's eyes widened as he shook his head in bewilderment.

"I found it outside."

"Where?" he said with haste.

"Near a cave. It was in a stone surrounded by dirt."

"A stone inside of the ground." Gabrael paused for a moment. "Clever Eve. A *stone* in the *ground. GroundStone!*" He smiled. "Well, children, it looks like our first stop is the wondrous Ground-

Stone, the School of Earth and Rock. GroundStone students, can you do the honors and bring us there?"

"Is Eve going to be there?" S'rae asked, looking away.

"I do not know where Eve is," Gabrael said, following her gaze. "But this is all a part of her plan to find her and this secret. She may very well be. I trust that she will steer us in the right direction." Gabrael took the Eye of Eve.

Vayp could tell by S'rae's fidgety movements that she still had more questions to ask.

"What else is on your mind," Vayp asked S'rae. He knew that she was too nervous to blurt out another question.

S'rae smiled at Vayp. "Well, I've been very bothered about a burial garden I saw here."

"Ah yes," Gabrael replied. "The Burial Garden is my way of paying respects to those who lost their lives defending our freedoms. The Last Battle of Gaia took place in the Valley of Gaia, where many lives were lost. And since our walls were sealed up, we had no way of sending their bodies off to receive their proper farewell."

"Oh," S'rae said. "That's very amazing of you."

"We must treat the dead with the same respect as the living," Gabrael said.

"Why?" Aura'li asked.

"As the living becomes the dead, the dead becomes the living. It is good karma. For this life and the next." Gabrael then placed the Eye of Eve back into S'rae's hands. "This is a very special orb, unlike any other in existence. If it was in Eve's destiny for you to find it, then it is in your destiny to keep it. Be careful. Hold it close. Though it can heal, terrible things can happen when it is in the wrong hands. We cannot let that happen."

Vayp's stomach tightened, thinking about the Eye of Eve's abil-

ity to heal. He briefly thought of his village, his father, and his Sol, Ah'nyx. Then another thought appeared in his mind, darker than his nightmares. He shook his head, clearing his thoughts. *This isn't good at all.*

S'rae's eyes sparkled. "I can't wait to finally meet her!"

"She will be just as honored to meet you, S'rae," Gabrael smiled.

"Oh my divine, the time! Okay, okay, gather up," Raaz'a said, waving his hands around, directing the students and Sols. "For those of you who will not be joining us, you must take a sip of this." He walked around, tipping the vial into each student's mouth. Even the Sols needed a sip. Earthies would have the ability to remember what happened through their connection with Sols. Judging by their faces of disgust afterwards, Vayp was happy that he didn't have to drink it.

It was then when a streamline of memories flashed by again. This time they were clearer. He saw Opella, his Village, the Mechas. Then there were the shadows, Ah'nyx . . . and even S'rae. These images were much different than the ones he had of the dragoenix in the arena. He knew that must have been déjà vu. He became a believer in its mystery. But these flashes were entirely different. They felt real. Fresh. And more important than what he saw, it was what he smelled. The same bitter, salty scent that had reached his nose.

But how?

He then felt a tremendous amount of guilt as if the weight of the world crushed him. His eyes widened, as all of his hidden memories finally surfaced. He suddenly knew why he was sent here. To the Valley. A part of him felt like he knew it all along, he just refused to believe it, as if he was at war with his two selves. His eyebrows soaked with sweat and his heart raced. He glanced woefully at S'rae. There was so much he wanted to tell her. But he couldn't. Not right now. She wouldn't understand.

"It'll take all we have," Vayp said as his pupils whitened. Kaul and the others joined in, holding one another's hands, "but we'll get us there." The ground shook as rocks lifted off before splitting in half. "We're going through the ground, it'll get a little bumpy. Try not to throw up."

A dirt elevator materialized, slowly descending them deeper until gravel spiraled over the gaping hole, covering it up as if untouched.

"Family forgives one another, right?" Vayp whispered.

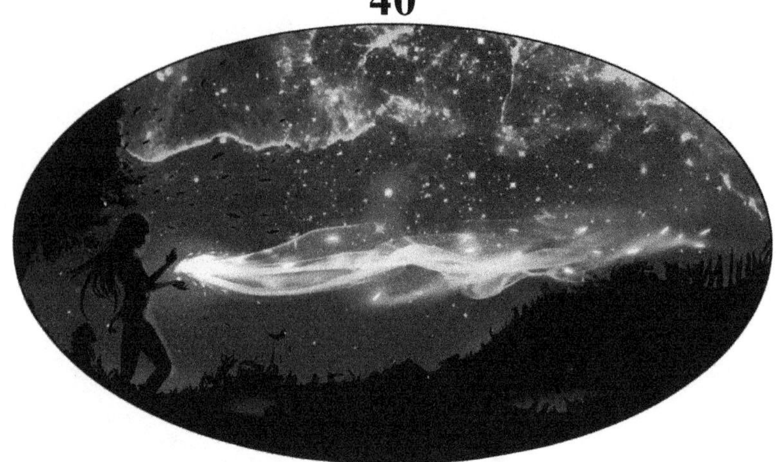

40

"OF COURSE," S'RAE WHISPERED as her insides twisted and turned. She felt like she was thrown into a ball that tumbled down a mountain. The weightlessness made her nauseous, and she felt helpless since there was nothing to cling to.

Suddenly her brain bounced off her skull, disorienting her as the feeling of falling instantly turned into the feeling of jumping. The shift in gravity made her head spin trying to understand what happened. She fell through the ground and was thrown into the air before falling back down.

Splat! The pond of mud that formed under the students softened the fall. Her face was completely covered in it, smearing her vision. She tasted the dirt as she spat, trying to clean her tongue. The smell of mold had vanished and now a familiar scent of wildlife reached her. She smiled wide, instantly knowing she was back at her home territory. *GroundStone.*

"Wow, that was one awesome ride," Fujak said, taking off his goggles, revealing silvery eyes. "Oh yeah, I forgot to tell you to put your goggles on." He laughed.

Why didn't I think of that? S'rae clawed chunks of mud off of her face. After countless attempts to unknot her hair, she gave up, accepting her fate of looking like an absolute mess. She had to avoid Retro'ku at all costs.

Her head shot up. *Oh my Divine! I need to tell Vayp about all of the cool whispers that I heard. They think I'm soooo awesome. They think I'm soooo cooooool. They think I'm soooo greaaaat. They think I'm . . . okay, I get the point, S'rae. Relax.*

She was especially excited about finally going to the School of Earth and Rock. The S'rae and Vayp duo could live up to the hype of their childhood. Maybe now she'd be able to learn how to connect with a Sol. But, possibly even more important, maybe she'd be able to enroll into Herbology classes and find cures for poisons. Since Sols were GroundStone's specialty, there should be some information about how a Sol could die before its human. Her countless sleepless nights in Fujita's library got her nowhere. She really needed the answer to the one question that plagued her nightmares: was there actually a fruit capable of killing a Sol?

Though her vision was still blurry, she noticed the sky clear up, revealing a beautiful sunrise. A family of large felines cast its silhouette against the sun as they moved across the horizon. She then glanced around at the Sols and students, smiling at Retro'ku who she thought could do no wrong even when covered in mud. She looked up with widened eyes, seeing endless golden stone walls with statues of Sols that were dozens of feet tall. The animals looked beautiful and powerful with their manes, wings, and tails frozen in motion. Beyond the walls, she could barely see the tops of trees that must have been equally as tall. The leaves were stringy and had earthy tones, of course. Behind her was the Jabal Range, known for their sandy grand pyramids seen far in the distance.

A horn blared in her ears, and then she heard the large gates grind open. Sand spilled down in waves.

Some of the students gasped as the ground shook, others wandered around aimlessly, wondering where they were. Sir Raaz'a was found separating the groups of children and Sols, but it looked impossibly difficult, like herding blind sheep. S'rae had many questions to be unraveled, but she couldn't ask them now aloud. *How are the ones who drank the blood going to get back to their schools? And how do they adjust back to their normal lives?*

As S'rae went through her mental log of questions, it occurred to her that she still hadn't seen Vayp. She wanted to desperately tell him the great news about how awesome everyone thought she was, but the excitement started to fade away. As she looked around for him, her attention got misdirected.

Blinding lights appeared from the school. A deafening roar rattled the ground under her feet. As the gates opened, a row of bright green grass with colorful flowers appeared, like a carpet being rolled out onto the sand. Quite the entrance. Then there were Gabrael and Raaz'a in the distance. Except . . . Gabrael looked worried. And Raaz'a was waving his arms around frantically.

Are we in danger right now? She felt her stomach twist at that possibility.

After a few moments, she saw Gabrael pat around his robes as if he was looking for something. Her palms became sweaty. Curiosity overwhelmed her; she needed to know what they were talking about. Her fingers created a funnel for their soundwaves.

"I don't know where it could be."

"Where could it have gone?"

"We *need* the Book of Eve. The only reason we are here is to get the orb to unlock the pages. Without the book, our destiny, our purpose is destroyed."

He lost the book?

"Oh divine! It must be somewhere. But do you know what else troubles me?"

"*What?*" The voice was loud and heavy with impatience. S'rae's body tingled hearing its anger.

"We never did find out which student was the one who gave away our location."

S'rae saw Gabrael's face drain of color. She could see by the way his eyes shuffled from side to side that he was deep in thought.

As she muddled through her own thoughts, thinking about everything that had happened in the Valley of Gaia, Fujak interrupted her, giving her a light shove on the back.

"Isn't this great?" he said.

S'rae blocked him out instantly as her memories made her eyes widen. *If Fujak isn't the traitor . . . who is?*

Fujak wasn't the traitor . . . It was in that moment when she had a painful realization that stabbed at her stomach. She was definitely the villain in this story. It made her feel even more awful about her friendship with the Fujitas. Fujak was innocent. He had only wanted to be a friend. And maybe something more. She was the one who pushed him away . . . them away. The rest of the students had also approached her with open arms. She was still too torn about what happened with Ah'nyx to be friendly toward others. That was how she tried to justify it . . . to make her feel better about herself; but there should had been no excuse to being a jerk to people. The first time they invited her to a party, she left without a word, as if she was too cool for them. When others asked for help on their assignments, she'd ignore them. When boys would compliment her, she appeared disgusted. She was no better than the Sereni Sisters, who she thought were demons. She was even terrible to Han'sael at first, just like them.

And worse, she had almost killed Fujak because she thought he was the traitor. *I'm evil.*

The traitor, she thought, searching her mind for the answer. Who was the one who knew how to track and lead people to a location? The one who had a troubled past? The one who had dealt with the shadows before? The one who could pickpocket people through the ground? The one who had nothing to lose? Who would want to resurrect lost ones with the . . . Eye of Eve?

Her heart pounded faster as she searched her pockets for it. They were all empty. She felt her stomach sink to the ground. *It's gone . . .*

She then realized there was a much smaller object in one of the pockets she never used. Her heart stopped as she pulled out her bronze amulet with a lotus engraved into it. V.A.S. was etched into it. How did it get there?

"Family forgives one another, right?" she whispered to herself, hearing the fear in her own voice.

She growled through her teeth as an earthquake shook the area. She felt rage in her heart just thinking about the traitor. And when she clenched her fists, the ground cracked and shattered like the amulet in her hands.

She quickly turned to Gabrael who turned to Raaz'a who turned to Gabrael and they all said the one word that came to mind: "Vayp."

The traitor . . .

No one ever truly knows when they are the villain in someone else's story. She now knew her role in others' lives. She was the reason why she had no friends. *I was the jerk.* At GroundStone, she would start anew. She would become the person she thought she was. This was her chance to start a new life. One without Vayp.

The traitor. The enemy.

Family forgives one another? You're no family of mine.

41

FRAGMENTS OF VAYP'S MEMORIES continued to flash through him. A storm of dark moments and emotions overwhelmed him, making it impossible to think. He was in the eye of the storm, he knew neither who nor where he was. He saw violent images of disfigured bodies sprawled across a war-torn field. There were piles and piles of bodies. Innocent ones slaughtered by machines with no emotions. No fear of death or the consequences for killing. There was no escape from the horror that surrounded him. He screamed and screamed, wishing for a way to escape this nightmare. And as he prayed for help he saw Ah'nyx's eyes, then his father's—dark and distant—and then S'rae's. He was lost and needed guidance. To be heard. To be understood. He was confused and needed someone to show him the way. He had that person. Once. But he was murdered. Just like his Sol. Suddenly shadows exploded behind his eyes until he cried out as loud as silence could to numb the anguish.

Wait, why was it silent? How did he get here? Wait, where was he? He opened his eyes. At least he thought he did. All he saw was darkness. He felt nothing, stuck in a void absent of light and senses. But somehow he knew his heart must have been beating so fast it might burst.

Just as he remembered the last time he had felt this way, he realized that he was in a valley void of light. And that was when two shadows emerged, darker than the night.

It is nice of you to come back, said a cold voice that appeared as a thought.

Where am I? Is this my time? The time you were talking about? My time to die?

Time to die? Oh no, no, no. You will know when it is your time. I will make sure of it.

Why am I here?

Surely you must remember why you're here, no?

What are you talking about? Why'd you bring me here?

Bring you here? You came here on your own accord.

Lies!

If you dare call me a liar one more time, your time will end before you finish the sentence.

Vayp was too afraid to speak or think. So he did nothing.

Much better, Vayp. Now you're learning how to talk to someone who can and will kill anyone you've ever known without thinking twice. So, back to why you are here. You should know, all of this was your plan.

My plan? He knew better than to accuse him of being a liar again.

Yes, I told you that I will be seeing you in your nightmares. What exactly were your nightmares about? The ones that you so desperately tried to avoid, but eventually a body shuts down. And yours always did.

Vayp's head hurt as if something was inside clawing at his brain.

Let me help you remember all that you forgot.

Suddenly a shock surged through him, traveling from his brain, through his spine, as if claws dragged their way through his veins and organs. It wasn't pain that he felt, this was much more. This was a torturous sensation that made him want to die rather than to go through another second of it.

A cluster of memories burst through. All the events since he had been born came to him in the light of revelation. His struggles and joys. His losses and his gains. How he made it into the top four at GroundStone, remembering the blackened eyes of the professors who told him the great news. They looked . . . possessed.

Oh did they? What could possess masters to grant a worthless, failed student access into such a prestigious spot? Surely you didn't actually believe you belonged among the best. Surely you are not that pathetic to blindly think of yourself as worthy.

Vayp remained silent, his dormant feelings of not being good enough once again resurfaced. It was true . . .

Yes, it is very true. You were never good enough to be in the top four. Now, why you? Why would you be chosen . . . selected . . . to visit the Valley of Gaia?

This was your plan! Vayp felt rage boil within him. He had too much pride to be used as a puppet.

My plan? Oh no, you're mistaken. I want you to think back to the first day we met. Oh, how lovely your father's blood was. Such a rich red. Why were we there? Why was your home massacred? Why would Opella, the last village of gifted hunters, be targeted? Why would the son of the King, the next greatest tracker . . . why would his Sol die? Surely you don't believe all of this was just a coincidence.

You killed Ah'nyx, too! Vayp regained his senses. He felt anger surge through his veins. His heart raced. Blood poured through his clenched fingers. Decay was in the air, as if they were on a battlefield filled with rotting corpses. More than the feeling of claws digging into his brain, the thought of them killing Ah'nyx sent a sword straight through his heart. The entire valley shook with an unexplainable force, as if the world was splitting in two.

Such power!

You will pay for what you did to him!

Oh no, you are mistaken again. I am not that evil. I would never kill a Sol. But I understand destiny and war. And I understand that a weakened soul, one who has nothing left, would do anything.

You would kill a Sol! You killed my family!

Why yes, I will always take credit for that mastery, but I cannot take credit for Ah'nyx.

You're evil!

Am I truly the evil one? What is evil to you? Let me ask you a question. Is a shark considered evil because it feasts on the innocent fish to survive? Is that evil or is that natural? Is it evil when something needs to kill to survive or is it evil for someone to create a world where that exists? It is natural to want to survive. I see it in your eyes. You feel for people like me . . . like Mechas . . . like you. The ones who are forced into a life with no control over the decision. Who is truly evil? The one who was born evil, or the Divine One who created the evil?

You killed Ah'nyx! Vayp cried. *He was just a pup! He was innocent. He didn't deserve it!*

My condolences, Vayp. For I did not kill Ah'nyx . . . but I did witness who did.

Vayp felt his stomach tighten, wanting to throw up. He wasn't sure if it was his memories of Ah'nyx that made him sick or not. He felt sweat rain down his hair down onto his forehead. Something was wrong, very wrong.

You see this? The shadow shot his arm out as a large blade materialized in his hand. It appeared in waves of black smoke before hardening. A substance oozed from it, dripping like tar. *The poison that runs through this blade is strong enough to kill a God. And apparently a Sol. It also happens to be the same poison that is coursing through your veins, right now. You only have a few minutes left until your blood hardens and your heart fails, so if you would allow me, I'd like to tell you what really happened. It's important for you to know. Do I have your permission?*

It was the poison that made him nauseas. Even now, he felt needles scrape through his veins and organs. He only had a few minutes left to live. *Tell me . . .* he coughed a substance from his mouth that felt thick like blood.

This exact type of poison is found in a very special fruit from a magical tree. It so happens that a very curious girl found it. Quite the selfish girl, if you ask me. Because she had a growing suspicion of the fruit as if she knew something was wrong with it. I truthfully don't know how she could have known. I will give her credit and say that her intuition is impeccable. But, though she had a feeling it may not have been safe to eat, she decided to have someone test it out first. It so happens . . . that day her only companion was a Sol that she was left to watch over.

No . . .

The terrible girl had the audacity to let an innocent pup take the first bite, to see if it was edible. It was horrible to see the pain the poor little pup went through before his body froze over. I believe you know in your heart exactly who that girl is.

No . . . no! She wouldn't do that!

Oh but she would. And she did. And a part of you knew this all along, didn't you? Do you remember what you said to me in your dreams when I asked you what you were willing to do to bring back

your family? To bring back Ah'nyx?

Vayp's heart stopped—was it the poison? No, it was the realization. He thought back to the word that the school accused him of shouting in his sleep. Anything . . .

Ah, yes, you'd do anything! *So your memory is clear now. You see, this was your plan from the very beginning. To bring them back. All of them. It was the best plan you had ever created. We just needed you to drink Archon blood so Gabrael wouldn't be able to read your thoughts. You needed to forget what happened to carry out the plan. If he found out, your plan would have failed. Your plan. And a shadow lived within you to make sure you did. That was why it felt like there were two people living inside of you. Because there were. There were times when your shadow would take over your actions and do things you were too afraid to do. Too weak to. But now that you are here, I imagine your plan was a success. Hand me the Book of Eve . . . and the Eye.*

An earthquake ripped through the land again, sounding like mountains toppled over one another, bursting into rubble. He heard ripping sounds as if the ground cracked open. Vayp felt hurt. Betrayed. Lost. He didn't know what or who to believe anymore.

You can believe me. And trust me. I will bring them back. Hand me the Book and Eye.

Vayp was reluctant. He remained still, battling the storm in his mind and thickened blood that was suffocating his heart, pumping thorns through his veins. *How could she . . .*

I see what the issue is. You still think I killed Ah'nyx. Want me to tell you who did? Am I the evil one—or are you—or is she?

It then hit him. He was the villain in this story. He was the Leader. The reason why the Valley was destroyed and the students' lives were in danger . . . and why Han'sael—

The shaking and trembling stopped. "No!" he growled. "I know who did it." His eyes blackened. He felt no emotion. Not anger. Nor love. But his voice was cold in his reply. "It was S'rae." *She is no family of mine. And there will be no forgiveness. Not anymore.*

You see, we are not sharks, we are much more than that. And the truth is that we don't know what kind of people we truly are until the moment before our deaths. Your time is coming soon, I can feel the poison tearing you apart from the inside. As death comes to embrace you, you realize what you really are. Do you see yourself as the villain or the hero?

Vayp said nothing. Not because he didn't want to, but because when he tried to speak he felt pins scrape against his throat. It was like his arteries and windpipe had already begun to seal shut. He pressed his fists to his forehead as if he wanted to smash his own skull to end his life before the poison did. *This is the end. What am I going to die as—a hero or a villain?*

But, it doesn't have to end here, Vayp. Give me the Book and the Eye, and I will save your life. I can remove the poison, the decision is yours.

I am not afraid of death. I have nothing, remember?

If it is not death that you fear, what is it?

Vayp thought of the rage that burned within him.

Oh my, is that love I see? Ah . . . I get it! You fear being hurt again. You fear the idea of losing something you care so much about . . . again. So you refuse to love. To open up. You and I are more alike than we thought. We will make a great team. The shadow lifted his hand as a channel of black mist steamed out of Vayp's body. In that moment, the pain was gone. *Fear is the most powerful emotion . . . use it, overcome it, and you will be more powerful than you could have ever dreamed. You will be able to protect all who you love. And never have to watch them die again. I will be able to bring them back to you. Give them to me. I need you to do so willingly. Please.*

Vayp reached into his robe and pulled out the items. The Eye was the only source of light in this dark valley. Vayp was able to see the damage he caused. The terrain looked devastated, like an army of Mechas had its target practice.

Poof! The shadow instantly emerged in front of Vayp. And without a second thought Vayp placed the Book and Eye into the shadow's hands.

At once the Eye of Eve glowed then turned black. So black it made the shadows appear light. Vayp was able to see them for a brief moment. They didn't look so scary. Not anymore. He saw their blurred features, they looked like real people. Human.

It was then when he saw *him*. His anger faded. He felt compassion, horror, sympathy, and fear.

Drifting in a cylinder filled with water, a body floated with dozens of tubes attached. He knew who was inside. And since all of what the shadow said was true, it was his fault Han'sael was captured. And probably tortured. Vayp was in over his head, and much too deep to escape now. It was then that he realized how much he could relate to Destrou. They were both stuck in a life destined to get worse by the day. He had dealt with death after death. More death than any fifteen-year-old should have experienced. No teenager should know what this unhealable pain feels like. But he did.

When he glanced at Han'sael once more something else dawned on him. Worse than feeling like he had no control over his life was knowing that he played a role in destroying other people's lives. And now his friend was suffering because of it. Han'sael would become another pawn in their plan.

The pain from this sudden realization was so intense he doubled over, clutching his stomach.

"Please don't do anything bad to him," Vayp cried into his arm.

"He's my only friend."

"I will do as I please with him." The shadow chuckled. "You really don't know much about your friend, do you?"

"What are you talking about?" Vayp swallowed a difficult breath.

"The blurred line between good and evil. I should be considered a hero. I saved the Valley by taking him away. Do you know that every second that went by, your *friend* was considering casting a forbidden self-destruction spell, one that would have eradicated the Valley ten times over? Every single one of you would have died a terrible death, much darker than what I have planned. So, who is the evil one?"

Vayp knew better than to accuse him of lying again. "I think he'd only do that because everyone was mean to him."

"Why yes, you and your sister may have saved everyone by befriending him, but neither of you are innocent. Both of you have unclean hands. So, who is evil, the one who wanted to kill, or the ones who pushed him to that point? It seems like you are justifying his thoughts because a few people didn't like him? Then tell me"—the Eye radiated in the shadow's hand, fading from white to black—"what happens when the entire world wishes you were dead? You watch the world burn and become King of the ashes." The shadow punched the air with the Eye in his hand.

There was a humming sound that reverberated through the valley, but Vayp paid it no attention. Instead, his mind was fixed on one goal: find a way to save Han'sael. He knew that it was a death wish, but he had nothing to lose. *I don't want you to go through what I went through. We were all mean to you, myself included. You don't deserve my pain. No one does. Except you, S'rae. Family forgives one another, but you are no family of mine!*

BANG! A pillar of light shot up through the sky, fading from

white to black, rippling through the clouds, and shaking the planet.

Vayp saw a Divine-sized figure forming in the cloud. The planet shook harder as if it had broken orbit and shifted on its axis. He felt a powerful pounding underfoot, like something was trying to escape. *BANG! BANG! BANG!*

Then the loudest *BANG* occurred. The soil tore open as a hand as large as a mountain and as dark as the night emerged in front of Vayp.

It was in that moment when Vayp had realized the damage he had imparted on this world. And now he needed to do something about it. He knew that Gabrael, the other students, and Ground-Stone would soon know what had happened. Maybe one of them could understand, but they wouldn't, because he was the traitor. His absence would not be missed, and he would be a story told to others about the student they knew to watch out for. He would be considered the bad fruit that they should have taken out of the bunch so the others could flourish; so his rotten existence wouldn't ruin the happy, healthy students who wanted perfect lives. *I always ruin everything.*

No one truly knows when they're the villain in someone else's story. I know that every story has a hero and a villain . . . and I know that I am not the hero. But I will change that.

A screeching voice boomed through the valley. "THE END . . . WILL COME!"

Although this book has ended . . .
the journey has just begun.

Thank you for being a part of it.

CPSIA information can be obtained
at www.ICGtesting.com
Printed in the USA
BVHW030840140219
540287BV00001B/93/P